HIMBA POND DANCE

Dave Gioia

ISBN: 1480173282
ISBN 13: 9781480173286
Library of Congress Control Number: 2012920329
CreateSpace Independent Publishing Platform
North Charleston, South Carolina

Dedication

For Adrian and Forbes.

CHAPTER 1

Trey pushes the chunks of pot roast and potatoes from around the outside of his plate toward the center, forming them into a circle the way pioneers did their wagons on the prairie when they were attacked by Indians. His going to cotillion was his mom's idea but to listen to Walt you'd think it was his. Walt's going on and on about the importance of learning proper etiquette and how to conduct oneself in polite society and Trey knows by the way his mom's keeping her eyes on her plate that she wishes Walt would shut up as much as he does. The guy loves to talk just to hear himself and the only person who enjoys listening to him is his brat daughter Julie.

Trey glances at her sitting across the table from him and sure enough there she is, just waiting for him with a smirk on her face. Lately she's been driving him crazy by accidentally on purpose giving him glimpses of that seventeen-year-old body of hers, which he has to admit is hot and if it weren't for that he'd really hate her. She's a jerk just like her father.

He glances at his sister and sees Kim's focused on cleaning her plate. If she's listening to Walt or even aware that he's speaking you'd never know it. Kim's smart. She knows how to make herself invisible. She never makes eye contact with Walt and keeps to herself and rarely says anything and it's easy to forget she's even there sometimes. He wishes he could tune Walt out the way she does, but he can't. With his dad not around he considers himself the man of the family, the one who has to stick up for them. Walt gets to him. Never mind the bullshit that comes out of his mouth, just the sound of his voice grates on him and if the guy weren't three times his size he'd shut him up.

He glances at his mom. What happened to her? She used to stand up for herself. She sure did with his dad. His dad couldn't find work for the longest time and was drinking too much and all they did was argue about money, which his mom put up with, but then they had that big argument and his mom said some really awful things to his dad that he and Kim couldn't help hearing from their bedrooms and she threw him out. Where's that person now?

He feels sorry for his dad. For as long as he can remember his dad worked on one construction job after another and then that big development beside the 405 in Irvine was put on hold and to this day there's an enormous hole in the ground where buildings were supposed to be and his dad couldn't find work anywhere and that's when the arguments about money and his dad's drinking began. His dad always used to have a few beers with his buddies after work, but without work he just drank with his buddies or in their house in Fountain Valley, watching TV and sometimes he and Kim would find him passed out on the couch when they arrived home from school and would try to get him into some kind of reasonable shape before their mom arrived home from work.

His grandfather helped them out with the mortgage payments for a while, but something happened between his dad and his grandfather. He doesn't know what, but something must have because his grandfather's help ended and his mom and dad had that big argument and his dad went to live with one of his buddies and they fell behind on mortgage payments and the bank finally foreclosed and they spent a few months at the shelter. The people there were nice and he didn't mind being there and Kim didn't, either. It was kind of an adventure to them, but he could tell his mom was ashamed that they were there and he figures that's probably why she agreed to move in with Walt, just to get them out of the shelter. So, here they are, like prisoners in Walt's house, with Walt the warden and Julie the snitch.

He watches Walt out of the corners of his eyes bring another heaping forkful of roast beef and potatoes to his mouth and chew slowly, like a cow. Good. At least Walt doesn't talk with his mouth full. What is it about the guy that creeps him out? It's not that Walt's a mortician. A job's a job and somebody has to do it. He imagines Walt talks to the bodies while he's making them look presentable. They're the perfect audience for him. No, it isn't that. There's just something about him.

Maybe it's that Walt always has that smug smile on his face, like he thinks he's better than they are. He tries to ignore him and stay out of his way, but there was that one time he challenged him, when Walt told his mom that Julie had complained about him and Kim supposedly hogging the hall bathroom and reminded his mom whose house they were living in and said if her kids' behavior didn't change, she could take them back to the shelter. Trey saw how upset that made his mom and told Walt never to talk to her like that again and Walt turned on him and he'll never forget how red Walt's face got and the look in his eyes and he was sure Walt was going to hit him and would have if his mom hadn't stepped between them.

As much as he hates to admit it, when his dad comes to pick him and Kim up for their day together he can't help feeling embarrassed and a little ashamed of him and knows his mom does too. His dad's face is always stubbly and his eyes are always bloodshot and his clothes wrinkled. He looks like he's just waiting to be hit over the head and put out of his misery. Still, Trey loves his dad, unconditionally, the way you love a dog or a dog does its owner. He's learned that you can love someone that way when you don't expect anything from him anymore. You just love him and that's all there is to it. He likes to think of his dad the way he was when they'd go on fishing trips to that lake in the Sierras. Those were fun times.

"He's going to need clothes," Trey hears Walt say and glances at his mom to see her reaction. Implied in Walt's tone of voice was that she's on her own where paying for them is concerned and Trey knows she doesn't have any extra money to spend on anything, let alone new clothes for him to wear to cotillion. She didn't escape money worries when she moved in with Walt, that's for sure.

"I'll take care of it," June says softly without looking up from her plate.

Trey can count almost to the second how long he's been in the bathroom before Julie raps sharply on the door and says, "Hey, lunch tray! Other people need to use the bathroom!" He doesn't say anything. He stopped doing that long ago. He just finishes and flushes the toilet and brushes his teeth and rinses off his tooth brush and wipes his mouth and opens the door to leave and sure enough, there's Julie standing in the hallway in her tee shirt and underpants with no bra on and her tits are big and he can see her nipples poking against the inside of her shirt. He can tell by her smirk that she's enjoying him staring at them and knows that as much as he dislikes her he wants to touch them but isn't going to let him. He takes one last look and says, "S'cuse me," and walks past her down the hall and hears her say, "There isn't any," as usual.

He climbs into bed and picks up the book he's reading and glances over at Kim. This having to share a bedroom with his sister business is a real drag, not that Kim bothers him. She always has her nose in a book and seldom even looks up at him. It's just the lack of privacy. There's really nowhere in the house, other than the bathroom with the door closed, where he can be by himself and, well, take care of things when he needs to, which he does more frequently lately. The bathroom is risky though because of Walt's "no locked doors in my house" policy. That's all he needs, to be sitting on the toilet with his dick in his hand and have Julie come barging in. She'd love that and he'd never hear the end of it. Instead he has to wait until Kim falls asleep and he's sure she's really sleeping and not just faking it.

For the longest time all that stroking himself did was produce an erection and a sustained thrill and he'll never forget the day he was sitting on the toilet masturbating as he gazed at a picture of a scantily clad big-breasted model in a magazine ad and felt something deep inside him begin to stir and want to come out and did, in spurts, all over the picture. He was hooked on the feeling and for awhile his entire purpose in life seemed to be to masturbate as often as he could, but now his encounters with himself are reserved for when he's in bed in the dark and is sure Kim is asleep. He sometimes wonders what her reaction would be if she did catch him jerking off. She's thirteen and he remembers how much he knew about sex when he was her age, but he's not sure about Kim. If she knows as much as he did she doesn't let on. She's hard to read. "G'night," he hears her say as she turns off her light and snuggles under the covers with her back to him. "I'm going to read awhile," he says and hears her say, "Sure."

He feels badly for Kim that she's somtimes mistaken for a boy. It's her short hair and the fact that her body hasn't developed and could easily be that of a thirteen-year-old boy and she's not into looking or acting girly that makes it hard to tell and he knows kids at school tease her about it and he tries to look out for her but, really, there's nothing he can do and she just has to deal with it. He knows it hurts her, but she'll be okay. She'll probably end up looking beautiful. She just has to figure out how to get from here to there with her self-esteem in tact. She'll get there. Kim's tough.

He reads until he begins to forget what he just read and can't keep his eyes open and bookmarks the page and puts the book on the nightstand and takes a tissue slowly from the box, trying not to make noise, and turns off the light. He stretches out on his back under the covers and closes his eyes and goes to that place in his mind where all the exciting images of women are stored, images from porn he's watched with his friends at their houses. Some of the women are naked, others are wearing only panties, others lingerie and garters and stockings and high heels. Some are alone, playing with themselves, masturbating or fucking themselves with dildos. Some are with men, although the men are a blur in his mind's eye. Some are being fucked in the pussy, others in the ass and others in both. Some have their bright red lips wrapped around a cock and suck hungrily. All the women, no matter what they're doing or is being done to them, gaze at him adoringly and he feels the tingling begin and slides his hand down his stomach to the waistband of his boxer shorts and beneath it and wraps his hand around himself and begins gently stroking as he browses through the images, trying to decide which he wants to dwell on, which would be the best, but it's difficult because they're all equally exciting.

He used to be able to single one out and hold it in his mind's eye and gaze at it until he came, but lately he's discovered that when every image is equally exciting it's really difficult and he conjures up the one image he has no trouble holding in his mind's eye and never fails to do the trick. It's the image of Julie, naked and kneeling in front of him as he sits on the toilet. She's playing with her tits with one hand and stroking herself between her legs with the other and she's wearing bright red lipstick especially for him, because she knows that's the way he likes her mouth to look when she sucks him and she'd do anything and everything to please him, there's nothing she wouldn't do and she's looking up at him adoringly and begging for his cock and he puts it in her mouth and watches her head move back and forth, keeping her eyes on his as she sucks and when he's on the verge of coming she slowly pulls her head back and asks sweetly, "Where would you like to come, Trey? In my mouth? On my face? On my tits? Come wherever you like. Just come on me," and he does into the tissue, gasping, and it feels so good in so many ways and for so many reasons. "Are you playing with yourself?" he hears Kim ask. He wipes himself and wads up the tissue and tucks it under the mattress and rolls onto his side. "Go to sleep," he says.

Keith glances over his shoulder at the group of young women seated at a corner table in the bar area of the restaurant at South Coast Plaza. "She's definitely checking you out," he says and Michael looks at the woman's reflection in the mirror behind the bar. She's an attractive brunette with glistening shoulder-length hair and bright eyes and a big smile displaying unnaturally white teeth. She and her friends are typical of a certain type that frequents the plaza: perfect makeup and nails and hair, dressed chicly and showing a lot of tan skin, toned bodies, glittering jewelry. Judging from the array of shopping bags bearing the logos of upscale stores, they have money and are accustomed to spending it and this is probably one of their regular get-togethers to shop and have drinks afterward and discuss the goings on in their lives. They strike Michael and Keith as trophy wives, for all they know the wives of some of the partners in their law firm. You never know. There are a lot of partners.

Michael eyes the brunette in the mirror and sees her looking at him and then away and then back again and now they have this looking-at-each-other-in-the-mirror thing going on and he smiles and shakes his head slightly and complains to Keith about the pro bono work that's been dumped on him. On top of everything else on his plate, already overflowing, now he has to defend some undocumented Salvadoran and he doesn't know shit about immigration law and he's sure he'll lose and the guy will be deported and it just seems like a complete waste of time.

They order another round and talk about the Dodgers, not that they're Dodgers fans — Keith, being from Minneapolis, is a Twins fan and Michael, from Boston, a Red Sox fan — about how lousy the team is doing ever since the McCourts took over and the precarious financial situation of the organization and how Walter O'Malley must be spinning in his grave and what a bozo that lawyer in Boston is to have drafted two versions of the pre-nuptial agreement, one naming Jamie and Frank as co-owners of the team and the other giving Jamie ownership of their properties and Frank ownership of the team.

And how about the Heat? Talk about a bunch of bozos. Well, it serves Lebron James right for having shafted the Cleveland fans that so desperately wanted him to stay with the Cavaliers and then his boastful prediction that with him and Dwayne Wade and Chris Bosch on the team the Heat would win seven — count them, seven! — NBA championships and then they lose to the Mavericks and Michael and Keith couldn't be happier for the good people of Cleveland. Justice has been served.

Michael asks Keith how things are going with Beth and Keith says she's still learning the ropes in her new job as a pharmaceutical sales rep and likes it okay, but that it can be a pain getting face time with the docs and the job is going to get tougher because the states are beginning to scrutinize the practice of giving gifts to doctors and bills are being proposed to prohibit it and Keith's fed up with government, in general, and the Obama administration, in particular, which seems to believe it knows what's best for everyone and is poking its nose in every aspect of public and private life in America with the intention of turning the country into a nanny state and what a joke that guy turned out to be.

Keith asks Michael how's he holding up with Kaitlin traveling so much and Michael says he's okay with it, that they knew it was going to be tough going for a while, not being able to see each other all that often but, hey, that's the price you have to pay if you want to get ahead in this world and given the long hours he puts in at the firm, they probably wouldn't see any more of each other even if she didn't have to travel.

Michael glances at the mirror and sees the brunette looking at him and she smiles and looks away and Keith asks if they're still planning on getting married in Hawaii in the fall and Michael nods and says they're thinking of the Royal Hawaiian and having the reception on the beach and it should be fun. He needs to buy a suit but doesn't know what type yet because Kaitlin hasn't decided on her dress and Keith mentions that he bought a couple of suits recently at Brooks Brothers during a suit sale and got a pretty good deal and the guy who helped him, Henry, knows his stuff and Michael should definitely see him when the time comes. Michael says he will and glances at the mirror and there she is, looking at him and smiling, only this time she doesn't look away and he sees her companions begin to stand and gather their bags and she stands and gathers hers and he watches her in the mirror as the women make their way slowly toward the exit and he glances over his shoulder and sees her looking at him over hers and then they're gone and he turns back and sees Keith grinning at him.

They stroll down the corridor and outside and head toward the pedestrian bridge leading from South Coast Plaza over

Bristol Street to their office complex and Michael notices the glowing tip of a cigarette out of the corners of his eyes and glances back and sees the brunette sitting alone in the dark at an outside table and maybe she's waiting for someone to arrive and pick her up, but probably she's been waiting for him and he doesn't think Keith noticed her and they walk on and reach the bridge and Keith stops. "Did the bartender give you back your card?" he asks. "Mine was in the folder. I don't remember seeing yours."

Michael puts his hand on his back pocket. "You know, I don't think he did. See you in the morning, buddy."

Keith grins. "Don't do anything I wouldn't do," he says and walks on and waves without looking back.

Michael sees the brunette looking at him with slightly raised eyebrows as he approaches. He also sees that having reeled in her catch, she's dropped the smile. She's posed with her legs crossed and one arm hugging her waist and the other propped up and he notices the way she's holding her cigarette between her extended index finger and second finger while slowly rubbing her ring finger and thumb together, sensuously, suggestively. He smiles down at her. "Hey."

She cocks her head and looks up at him and wiggles her foot impatiently. "Hey," she says and taps her cigarette to knock off the ash.

"Waiting for a ride?"

"Yeah. It just arrived."

They walk over Bristol Street, Michael carrying her shopping bags, to the Westin Hotel and an hour and a half later they're standing out of the light in the parking garage by her black Mercedes S-Class sedan with their arms wrapped around each other and their tongues in each other's mouth and they finally untangle themselves and she steps back and points her key at the car and unlocks the doors. "Nice meeting you," she says. "Maybe we'll do it again sometime."

"Yeah, see you around." He walks to his car and drives to the apartment at Promontory Point in Newport Beach with the nice view of Balboa Island that sold Kaitlin on the place. It's good that he knows absolutely nothing about this woman he's just had sex with. He doesn't even know her name. He didn't bother to ask and neither did she. It was just a good fuck and, hey, she even paid for the hotel. He glances at the time and wonders what his fiancée's up to.

Kaitlin's trying her best to avoid contact with Manfred but it's difficult with him sitting directly across the table from her. She watched him choose that seat as she and her colleagues seated themselves around the table and knows he did so deliberately. She'll feel a whole lot better with nine time zones and six thousand miles between them and if she can just get through this last evening she'll be on the plane tomorrow headed home. Of course, she'll be back in two weeks but she'll deal with that when the time comes and maybe by then she'll have worked out her feelings for him. Should she tell Michael about it? She probably should. After all, one of the things they promised each other when they got engaged was that they'd always share whatever was going on with each other, both the good and especially the bad. It's being able to confide in each other about the difficult stuff that's really important they told each other. They know it's inevitable that sooner or later they'll encounter difficulties of some sort in their relationship and they know that most marriages fail because people keep whatever it is that's bothering them to themselves and they want their marriage to work, unlike their parents' marriages, so, yeah, she should definitely tell him about it. Feelings are feelings, right? They just happen and you can't help how you feel about people. It's what you do about the feelings that matters and so far she hasn't done anything other than try hard not to act on them and if she can just get through this dinner and the rest of the evening and make it back to her hotel room alone and get on that plane home tomorrow she'll be okay.

She takes a last bite of her pork roast and puts her fork on her plate and picks up her glass and takes a sip of Riesling and glances at the faces of her colleagues seated around the table in Hans the project director's favorite restaurant just off Marienplatz and her eyes meet Manfred's. He's looking at her and she sees him smile and pick up his glass and tip it toward her, as if to say, "Here's to you," or, "us," and he takes a sip and puts his glass down and looks away and rejoins the conversation at the table, which she should probably do too to avoid drawing attention to herself, although when she last tuned in it was about soccer — okay, "football" — which she knows nothing about and isn't at all uninterested in and now she's aware of her colleagues looking at her expectantly and she looks questioningly at them. "Sorry?"

"This Weiner guy?" Hans asks. "Is he through politically?"

Oh, my God! Not Anthony Weiner! Who cares about some jerk politician stupid enough to send a 21-year-old female college student a Twitter link to pictures of himself in his underpants with a hard on? Are these guys that clueless? Do they never learn? "Probably," Kaitlin says, "but you never know. Politicians have a way of resurrecting themselves." She sees her colleagues nod in agreement and listens as they discuss the foibles of Bill Clinton and Silvio Berlusconi and Dominic Strauss-Kahn and how Europeans used to be much more tolerant of the sexual escapades of their political leaders but how that's changing now and probably because of the poor economy and on and on it goes. She has to get through this and on that plane tomorrow.

Why did this have to happen? She and Michael have everything going for them. They both have well-paying jobs in their chosen professions, she an engineer at a multi-national corporation and he a lawyer at one of Southern California's largest and most prestigious firms. They knew it would be hard, both of them working long hours and she constantly traveling, but this is what they wanted, to have their careers and be successful and make good money and, when the time comes and they can afford it, have children, at least two. Years of scrimping and saving, they agreed, would be well worth it to put themselves on solid financial footing and have the money to buy a house in a good neighborhood and send their kids to private school and take nice vacations. It's the same dream all their friends have, the "American Dream", although they both know that for many people in their generation and many more in the next and probably the one following that it's a dream that's no longer attainable. No, despite the hardship, they feel fortunate to have received the education they have and the opportunity to put it to good use and make a living doing what they enjoy doing, although at this early stage in their careers the work can be pure drudgery. Michael's description of the long hours he and Keith and the others at the firm put in doing case discovery work as being a matter of "who wants another plate of shit?" is pretty accurate and only mildly amusing and in her case it's a matter of scrutinizing project plans to root out even the hint of a potential cost overrun. Still, they tell themselves it's worth it. It will all pay off someday.

She reaches for her glass and glances at her engagement ring, which she's been trying to use over the last two days to send a signal to Manfred that she's spoken for and that while his interest in her is flattering, any advance on his part would be unwanted and unwelcome. Even the slightest gesture with her left hand seems to her to be like flashing her high beams at an oncoming car, but Manfred seems undeterred and determined to crash head on into her.

Unwanted and unwelcome? That's what she tells herself anyway, but she's not really sure. The truth of the matter is that she's as attracted to him as he seems to be to her, to his handsomeness and languid eyes and self-assured smile and expressive hands, which she tries not to stare at when he gestures with them as he speaks but follows with her eyes like a hypnotist's subject watching a swinging pocket watch and she can't help imagining what they would look and feel like touching her.

It occurs to her as she sips her wine that in thinking about life's unforeseen and unexpected twists and turns and the challenges she and Michael will face, they've spent all their time and energy preparing themselves to confront the enemy without, and now she realizes it's the enemy within that poses the greatest danger and feels woefully unprepared to defend herself against it. Well, not entirely. All she has to do is make it to her hotel room alone and get on that plane tomorrow. Just keep your knees together, she tells herself, and you'll be all right.

She steps into the plane and slowly makes her way to her seat in Business Class halfway back and settles in next to an attractive woman who looks to be in her mid-fifties. She has shoulder-length auburn hair and is wearing a white blouse and navy blue business suit and is reading a thick, triple-spaced legal-looking document with pen in hand and her reading glasses on the tip of her nose. She assumes the woman's a lawyer and strikes her as being a careful and thorough one. She notices that just before the woman makes a notation she frowns slightly and makes a "tsk" sound. She shoves her briefcase under the seat in front of hers, thinking to herself that she wouldn't want to be the object of the woman's scrutiny, and settles into her seat and fastens her seat belt. The woman looks at her and removes her glasses and smiles.

"Beatrice."

"Kaitlin. Nice to meet you."

Beatrice glances at Kaitlin's briefcase. "Here on business?"

"Yeah."

"What do you do?"

"I'm an engineer."

"With?"

"Albrecht Industries."

"A client of mine. I'm a lawyer. Travel a lot?"

"Yeah."

"I live on airplanes," Beatrice says. "You get used to it. She notices Kaitlin's ring. "I like your ring. It's antique, isn't it?"

Kaitlin holds out her hand so Beatrice can inspect the ring. "Yeah. It was my fiancée's mother's."

"How nice. When's the wedding?"

"Late October, in Hawaii."

"Big affair?"

Kaitlin shakes her head. "Twenty or thirty people, maybe. There's still a lot of planning to do. I'm trying not to feel overwhelmed."

Beatrice smiles sympathetically. "Just remember to have fun. That's the important thing. What does your fiancée do?"

"He's a lawyer."

"With?"

"Harriman DiGiorno."

"Friends of mine." Beatrice looks around the plane's interior with an expression of resigned familiarity. "Well, if your marriage can survive this, it can survive anything. My first couldn't."

"What does your husband do?" Kaitlin asks.

"Physician. Cardiac surgeon. Great guy. Very patient and understanding."

"So's my fiancée. I know my traveling so much is hard on him, but he doesn't complain." Kaitlin sees Beatrice frown slightly and half-expects to hear her make that "tsk" sound.

"That's good," Beatrice says. "It's important to have a supportive partner." She studies Kaitlin's eyes for a moment and puts on her reading glasses. "You look tired."

"I am."

"I'll let you rest," Beatrice says and looks down at the document, her pen poised.

Kaitlin sits back and closes her eyes. Beatrice is nice, but she senses she has a harder side and is probably a penetrating questioner at depositions. Maybe it's just her guilty conscious and anxiety that she makes her wonder what it would be like to be grilled by Beatrice about her feelings for Manfred. She tries to collect her thoughts about the trip.

From a professional point of view things went well enough, but this business with Manfred took her completely by surprise. In fact, it scared the hell out of her. She's always been able to keep her emotions in check, probably as the result of being the youngest of four who were forced to live through the bitter dissolution of their parents' marriage. Her mom and dad were at each other's throats for as long as she can remember and it wasn't until shortly before they divorced, when she was eleven, that her oldest sister told her their dad was seeing another woman. This news confused her because she wanted to blame her dad for ruining the marriage and making life at home miserable but couldn't bring herself to do it. She loves him. He's a sweet and thoughtful man and a loving father and devoted husband to his second wife Debby, the woman he'd been seeing.

She thought her mom was emotionally cool and prickly because of her dad's infidelity, but her mom didn't change after her dad left and is just as uncomfortable letting her feelings show and with others showing theirs now as she was then. She often wonders what her mom was like when she and her dad first met. She must have had something going for her, a sense of humor, maybe her smile or laugh. She must have been good in bed otherwise she can't imagine her dad would have married her. She thinks the reason her dad sought companionship elsewhere is because her mom wasn't much of one. Did having children change her? She wouldn't be surprised. It happens all the time. She's been meaning to ask her dad about it.

As understanding as she is about her dad's infidelity, it's a sensitive issue for her. It's the reason she ended her relationship with Josh when she learned from a girlfriend that he was fooling around on the side with another girlfriend who's no longer a girlfriend. Despite his apology and promise that it would never happen again she ended the relationship.

Then her friend Erica at work invited her to go on a camping trip to Big Sur. One of Erica's boyfriend's friends named Michael was running in the Big Sur Marathon and there would be eight or so people going, not all of them couples, and why didn't she join them? It would be fun. She decided to go and wasn't too impressed at first by Michael. He was handsome and in great shape, but he struck her as self-absorbed and she wasn't really attracted to him. They saw him off at the start of the race and went to have breakfast and were back in time to watch him cross the finish line, which he did in good time, beating his personal best.

With the race behind him he began to relax and loosen up and she realized that what had seemed self-absorption was really intense inward focus and part of his pre-race preparation and he actually was very outgoing and friendly and they talked at dinner at that nice restaurant, Dametra Café, in Carmel that evening and talked some more around the campfire when they returned and decided because the moonlight was so bright to take a long walk to the hilltop high above the shimmering Pacific.

They found a spot and sat and talked about this and that, trivial stuff, but his questions gradually became more personal and probing and he seemed genuinely interested in what she had to say and she opened up and they talked well into the night and ended up making love under the full moon and she remembers thinking the Man in the Moon looked more astonished than usual, as he should have, since it was her upturned ass he was looking down at. It was the first time she'd ever made love on top, although she'd only had a few sexual encounters with men before then, and to this day she doesn't know what possessed her to want to. It was a spontaneous decision and a bold stroke for her. It was fun and exciting and a great way to begin her relationship with Michael.

As far as she knows, Michael's been faithful to her ever since, although now that she thinks about it she has no way of knowing for sure and would it really make a difference if he hasn't? What if he were screwing around with someone and still treated her the way he does, lovingly and respectfully? What would be wrong with that? It's the trust thing, that's what. If you say you're going to be faithful to someone and aren't and don't tell her about it, that's sneaky and wrong. What type of person would that make you? Not the type of person she'd want to be with, that's for sure, and certainly not the type of person she'd want to marry.

What is it with her and airplanes? No sooner does she get in her seat than she's sleepy and begins dozing off and she opens her eyes a slit and glances at Beatrice and sees she's diligently reading and annotating her document. There's a real pro for you, working away non-stop while she can't even keep her eyes open.

Strictly speaking, she wasn't unfaithful with Manfred. Okay, she did accept his offer when they left the restaurant to drive her to her hotel. It was on his way home anyway and it would have been rude not to. Yes, she thought his suggestion to take a walk in the park across the street from her hotel was a fine idea and they did stop and she did let him put his arms around her, which is what she wanted him to do, and she did put hers around him and they did kiss and, no, it wasn't just a friendly peck, it was a pretty steamy kiss and, no, she didn't want to let go of him and, yes, she did want to take him back to her room. Instead she settled for a drink in the hotel bar and enjoyed listening to him talk about growing up in Bavaria, about how much he enjoys hiking and camping and hunting wild game in the fall with his father and how he learned from his father when he was a boy to dress and cook the various meats, wild boar and venison and pheasant, and that it's the most delicious meal and especially so when enjoyed with one of the many tasty locally brewed Oktoberfest beers. He said that every fall his family spends a long weekend at their cottage in Berchtesgaden and this is the meal they enjoy and they look forward to it all year long and she's welcome to join them and bring whomever she likes.

It's that "whomever she likes" part, as if he wouldn't care in the least if she showed up with another man that's driving her crazy about Manfred and what's been worrying her. She wanted to take him to her room and have sex the way those wild animals he hunts in the fall do, rutting, panting, slobbering bellowing sex and while she was sure he knew that's what she wanted and was just waiting for him to give her some indication that he did too, he didn't and she has the feeling it wasn't because he was being respectful and gentlemanly, but because he was toying with her and enjoying doing so.

Should she tell Michael about it? Isn't that the deal? Isn't that what they promised each other they'd do? Share whatever's going on in their lives, both the good and the bad and especially the bad? So what is there to tell him? That she made a complete fool of herself with a man who doesn't seem to be as interested in her as she is in him?

Beatrice's movement in her seat rouses Kaitlin and she opens her eyes a slit and sees her stuffing the document into her briefcase and lowering her seatback tray. The flight attendant places a napkin and cellophane bag of peanuts on it and asks Beatrice what she'd like to drink and Beatrice says a scotch and soda, which strikes Kaitlin as the type of drink Beatrice would order. She straightens up in her seat and the flight attendant asks her what she'd like to drink. "White wine, thanks," she says and lowers her seatback tray and the flight attendant places a napkin and cellophane bag of peanuts on it. Kaitlin waits until she and Beatrice have both taken a sip of their drinks. "Can I ask you something?"

"Sure," Beatrice says.

"Do you and your husband share everything with each other?"

"About?"

"What's going on in your lives?"

Beatrice studies Kaitlin's eyes and narrows hers a bit. "Meet someone?"

Kaitlin nods.

"And?"

"I dunno." Kaitlin can tell by the way Beatrice is searching her eyes that she's had the same experience at some point.

"You can't help the way you feel about people," Beatrice says. "It's really a matter of accepting your feelings and not letting them come between you and your partner, unless you want them to."

"Did you?" Kaitlin asks.

Beatrice nods.

"Do you regret it?"

Beatrice purses her lips and frowns slightly as she considers her answer. "No," she finally says. "I ended up with the right man."

Kaitlin unpacks and puts her things away in the bedroom and settles on the couch in the living room across from Michael and picks up the glass of white wine he has waiting for her on the coffee table. Neither of them seems to want to talk, which is fine with her. She sips her wine and thinks about the brief conversation Michael and Beatrice had when she introduced them in Baggage Claim. Beatrice studied him the same way she had her on the plane. Michael said he could tell Beatrice was a tough attorney. He asked in the car how the trip went and she said well, pretty much the same as usual. She made no mention of Manfred and spent the rest of the ride home listening to him talk about what's been going on at work, in particular, this pro bono immigration work he's been saddled with.

She sips her wine and looks around the living room at the furniture and bric-a-brac they've bought and the framed pictures of the two of them made from snapshots taken on vacations. Everything looks and feels different to her now, familiar but unfamiliar, oddly strange, as if she's sitting in the home of some other Kaitlin in a parallel universe.

She knows her lovemaking must have felt half-hearted. She's exhausted and that's probably why Michael didn't seem to mind. They kiss and say good night and snuggle under the covers with their backs to each other and the thought crosses her mind to caress the soles of his feet with her toes, which she likes to do, sometimes with surprising results, but decides not to and soon enough she's lying in the dark listening to the sound of his breathing and then gentle snoring and she thinks of her conversation with Beatrice. Beatrice is right. You can't help the way you feel about people and it doesn't serve any good purpose to share with your partner that you're attracted to someone else. What if she did? Then what?

She closes her eyes and remembers those hot, humid summer nights, hanging with her friends in the backyard of her best friend Jill's house in Schuylkill Haven, getting high and sipping beer and watching the moths attracted by the porch light swirl dizzily around it and crash into it time and again. That's what it's like to be driven by desire. It's senseless and self-destructive. Is that the price to be paid for maintaining a stable relationship over the long-term, a passionless existence? That doesn't seem very appealing, either. No wonder most marriages end in divorce. Does she really want to get married? She thought she did, but now she's not sure. What she's sure of is that she's tired of thinking and tries not to as she waits for sleep to overtake her.

CHAPTER 2

Henry stands in his bathrobe and sips his coffee and gazes thoughtfully at the suits and ties and shoes and accessories neatly arranged in the closet in his bedroom and considers which outfit to wear to work. The June day dawned overcast and cool so, yes, the light gray Prince of Wales suit with a white spread collar shirt and light blue pattern tie and matching pocket square would reflect the mood of the day nicely.

He's reminded of Leo Cullum's cartoon, in which a man stands in front of an open closet staring pensively at the only items in it, two stripe ties, mirror images and each on its own hanger, considering which to wear. It's funny on the face of it but also captures a man's deep connection to his clothing. No man ever simply "throws something on", just as no woman does. There's the favorite shirt, the most flattering trousers, the most comfortable shoes and so on. His job is to help men look their best while, at the same time, instructing them in the art of doing it for themselves.

He ties a full-Windsor knot and glances at the rows of stripe and pattern Brooks Brothers ties hanging in the closet. The look is iconic and the brand venerable and he thinks of John William Cooke's *Generations of Style,* a good account of the company's storied past since its founding in 1818.

The Golden Fleece has been used as a logo by Brooks Brothers since the middle of the Nineteenth century and the most likely explanation is the company's close association with European finery and the woolen trade, which adopted its use from Philip the Good, Duke of Burgundy and of the Netherlands. Philip founded the Order of the Golden Fleece in 1430, "whose Knights were sworn to the glory of the saints and the protection of the Church and who wore the Lamb of God suspended at the heart to symbolize at once both gentle humility and the woolen fabrics to which so much of Burgundian wealth was owed."

They were dandies, those Knights, as was Fred Astaire, who liked to wear Brooks Brothers ties as a belt. Not quite as flamboyant as Astaire, but every bit as conscious of and careful about his appearance, Clark Gable wore only Brooks Brothers custom suits because no ready-to-wear suit could fit his physique. The company's ready-made Oxford shirts fit him perfectly, though, and he was devoted to them. Rudolph Valentino, John O'Hara, F. Scott Fitzgerald, Franklin D. Roosevelt, John F. Kennedy, Gerald Ford, Hilary Clinton shopping for her husband, all loyal Brooks Brothers customers. Surprising to some but not to Henry, Andy Warhol, whose roots were in advertising, preferred the company's white button-down Oxford shirt.

Then there's Abraham Lincoln who wore a black Brooks Brothers overcoat specially made by the company to his second inauguration and only five weeks later to see *Our American*

Cousin at Ford's Theater. Lore has it that as a result of Lincoln's assassination the company didn't offer anything in black for many years afterwards and to this day there's relatively little black to be found at Brooks Brothers. Navy blue verging on black abounds, but not black.

He merges onto the 405 North for the short drive to South Coast Plaza. It isn't about the clothes, really. The clothes are only a means to an end. It's about people, about meeting them, getting to know them and slowly but surely gaining their confidence and trust and establishing a rapport and lasting relationship with them. He's always found people fascinating and enjoys the process of delicately peeling back the layers of their personalities to discover what makes them tick. He sometimes thinks he should have been a shrink and perhaps that's why he began writing in the first place. Each of us is the main character in our own story and a supporting character in the stories of others and learning about people and hearing about the ways in which their lives intersect and interconnect is every bit as fascinating to him as creating characters on the page and breathing life into them, which he's lately begun doing again after a forty-year hiatus. To his thinking, selling Brooks Brothers clothes is an entirely literary affair.

He rounds the corner at the end of the corridor and sees the mannequins in the long display windows of the store, those on the left in dressier fare and those on the right in sportier and the pictures in *Generations of Style* come to mind of the Brooks Brothers store at One Liberty Plaza at the World Trade Center on that fateful September day in 2001. The store's windows were blown out but it miraculously withstood the collapse of the twin towers, an event every bit as cataclysmic in

American history as the assassination of Lincoln, if not more so. In the days following the catastrophe the store served as a place where first responders could rest and change into new underwear, which they gratefully paid for after the fact, and temporarily as a morgue. Few thought the store would reopen for business but as the company said, "We had to return. It was a matter of principle."

He spends the half-hour before store open reviewing his appointments for the day and taking care of customers' orders from the previous day and no sooner do the doors open than a middle-aged man in casual dress strides up to him.

"I need a black suit," the man says.

"Certainly." Henry knows by the look on the man's face and tone of voice that it's for a funeral. He notes the man's height and glances at his shoulders and waist and takes a 44 Regular black suit off the rack and helps the man into the coat, which he knows will fit well, although the trousers will need to be let out a couple of inches, a minor alteration. He invites the man to look at the fit in the mirror and studies his face as the man stares mournfully at his reflection.

"This'll work," the man says.

"When do you need to wear it?"

"This afternoon. My dad's funeral."

"My condolences."

"Thanks. Can I pick it up around one?"

"Certainly. Let's get you into the trousers and I'll call a tailor."

He takes down the man's information in the fitting room and completes the alteration ticket as the tailor marks up the suit. "How old was your dad, Bill?"

"Eighty-eight. His kidneys shut down and I tried to get him to go on dialysis, but he said he didn't want to live like that, that he'd rather be dead and yesterday we found him lying on his bed with a plastic bag over his head."

Henry looks at him in the mirror. "That took courage."

"You bet it did. I couldn't do it."

"Nor I."

"That's the type of man he was. I've spent my whole life trying be like him and I still don't feel I measure up."

"I think all sons feel that way," Henry says, "to a certain extent. I certainly do."

"Yeah," Bill says, "you're probably right. Anyway, thanks for turning this around so fast."

"We always accommodate the bereaved."

"Yeah, I figured you would. That's why I came here. I've been in a few times with my wife. She's the shopper. She's always after me to buy new clothes. My wardrobe is pretty tired. I'll have to come back. Henry, right?

He nods.

"Give me one of your cards."

He takes a business card from his coat pocket and hands it to Bill and escorts him to the front of the store. As he watches him walk away, Didier Beaumont comes to mind. Didier was a customer of his who killed himself the same way Bill's father did. He was in his early sixties and a successful interior designer and one day he came in shopping for clothes for a trip to Las Vegas. Didier told him he'd just learned he had terminal cancer and about three months to live and he was going to Vegas to have the time of his life and max out every one of his credit cards and then kill himself, which he did, apparently swallowing a bottle of sleeping pills and downing a magnum of excellent champagne before putting the plastic bag over his head. There is nothing more fascinating than people and their stories.

The corridor in South Coast Plaza is filled this early Saturday afternoon with slow-moving people. Most carry shopping bags and some are talking on their phones and the ones staring down like zombies at their screens look pathetic to Trey. He eyes the teenage girls traveling in groups, all, it seems to him, dressed like Julie, wearing tops that show off their breasts and shorts that just cover their crotches and asses and the women look to him like older versions of the teenage girls, except the girls aren't trying to look young, they are young. They should enjoy it while they can because it's only a matter of time before they'll begin to look like their moms and get married and have kids and their daughters will look pretty much the way they do now.

He looks at the window displays as they walk toward Brooks Brothers. The mannequins in the windows are all perfectly shaped, unlike a lot of the teenage girls and most of the older women, a lot of whom, he sees, have big butts and are overweight. Not so much the Asians, but most everybody else but it doesn't stop them from cramming themselves into skin-tight clothes. It's laughable to him that the window displays promote a physical ideal that most people will never achieve. He hears all the time that America is becoming a nation of fat people and here's the proof.

He sees the sales people in the stores are all wearing black clothes, as his mom does at work. He's always wondered why. He understands why Walt wears a black suit to work every day. Part of his job is to look somber, but why wear black when you're selling clothes or perfume or makeup or anything else for that matter? So you're easy to spot? Maybe.

That's not all that strikes him as curious as he looks around. The white teenage girls and women seem to prefer flip-flops and sandals while the Asians, especially the skinny ones, seem to prefer clunky high heel shoes and the higher the better. And then there are the Arab families, the men and kids dressed comfortably in casual clothes and the women wearing head scarves and long flowing layered dresses that cover them entirely. He knows this custom of women covering themselves is supposed to be about modesty, but some of the Arab girls and younger women, while they're wearing head scarves, are dressed provocatively below the neck and carrying Victoria's Secret and La Perla shopping bags. What's up with that? He doesn't see a lot of blacks in the crowd, a few, but not many, which is pretty much the way it is here in Orange County. There are a lot of whites and Hispanics and Asians and Iranians and Arabs, but not a lot of blacks, why he doesn't know.

He sees that many of the couples hold hands as they walk along, which his mom and Walt aren't. In fact, he's never seen them hold hands. He knows his mom doesn't love Walt and can't imagine her having sex with him. Just thinking about the two of them in the same bed grosses him out. He can tell just by watching Walt from behind that he's impatient with all these slow-moving smaller people blocking his path. But, then, Walt's impatient with everyone except Julie and he even loses it with her sometimes when she really fucks up, which she did last night, coming home late and drunk and then puking her guts out in the bathroom. Walt went ballistic, but by this morning all was forgiven and Julie had regained her princess status with her father. It's enough to make Trey puke.

He sees Kim eyeing a boy's outfit on a mannequin in WestWave's window display. She's dressed pretty much like the mannequin, although she's not wearing WestWave clothes but his hand-me-downs, clothes his mom buys with her employee discount at Macy's. "Ugh," he hears Julie say as they approach the entrance to Brooks Brothers. He sees her looking with an expression of disgust at the brightly colored sportswear on the mannequins in the store's window display.

"Who wears this stuff?" Julie asks.

He wants to say, "Better people than you." He looks at Kim and sees her staring up curiously at the dangling sheep above the entrance.

The store is busy because of the sale and they make their way to Men's Suits and his mom spots Henry, who smiles and waves and comes to greet them. Walt steps forward and Trey knows he's going to try to take charge of the situation, but Henry shakes his hand and introduces himself and steps past Walt to his mom. Henry says it's nice seeing her again and thanks her for coming and Trey knows the reason they're here today is because Henry told her now's the time she'll get the best price for the outfit. Henry introduces himself to Kim and Julie and then he's standing in front of him, smiling and looking him in the eyes as he shakes his hand and Trey feels like Henry's attention is focused solely on him now, that he's the customer here and he likes the feeling and can see his mom over Henry's shoulder, smiling in a way he hasn't seen in a long time. Henry tells him that a navy blue suit and a white shirt and stripe tie and burgundy loafers with navy blue socks would be the perfect outfit and, as Henry suggested to his mom, he should also get a pair of khaki dress trousers to wear with the suit coat and that way he'll have two outfits for just a little more money. Trey glances at his mom and sees her nod and he looks at Henry, who hasn't taken his eyes off him and is looking at him like he's waiting to hear the most important decision that's ever been made. "Yeah, great idea," Trey says. Henry smiles and nods and looks at Trey's shoulders and waist and collects everything in his size and puts him in a dressing room.

Trey likes the fact that when he opens the dressing room door, there's Henry waiting for him and he escorts him to the three-way mirror and explains what fits well and what will require alteration and then calls a tailor. Trey's admiration grows when Henry asks him, not at his mom, for his personal information for the alteration ticket.

He watches Henry in the mirror as the tailor marks up the clothes and sees Henry watching the tailor carefully, ready to let the him know if he thinks something should be marked differently. Trey can tell that Henry and this tailor have worked together a lot and are on the same page. He marvels at how all along Henry's made him feel like he's his only customer while he's been assisting two other customers with suits at the same time. Henry makes it look easy but Trey knows it isn't.

He gets changed and Henry gathers up his items and places a hand on his back and guides him out of the fitting room and they walk side by side toward the front of the store to ring them up with the others following behind. "It's all about flirting," Trey hears Henry say and looks at him. "What?"

"Cotillion. It's French. The word means 'petticoat.' The practice began in the Eighteenth century. The idea was to give young people in polite society a way to meet and flirt with each other in a socially acceptable way."

Trey's been wondering about this and it's like Henry's read his mind. "What's 'polite society'?"

"People who never raise their voices when they're angry and never stop smiling no matter how badly they treat each other."

They gather at the counter and his mom pays for the outfit with cash – her credit cards were cancelled long ago – and Henry gives her the change and the receipt and walks around the counter and hands Trey the shopping bag with the shirt and tie and shoes and socks in it and escorts him to the entrance. Henry shakes everyone's hand and tells them it was nice meeting them and Trey that he'll be in touch when the alterations are done. Trey can see Walt's peeved about having been kept in a box by Henry and they head off down the corridor toward the parking garage. "You look dorky in that outfit" Trey hears Julie say. He glances at her and sees her smirking at him, as usual.

He sees the same smirk that evening when he's done in the bathroom and opens the door and find's Julie standing there waiting, only this time she's not wearing her usual tee shirt and underpants but a sheer floral print robe, loosely tied, leaving more of her breasts exposed than ever before and her nipples are harder than he's ever seen them. He glances down and sees her robe's open enough to give him a glimpse of her mound, which is probably what she wanted to do. He's wondered how bushy she is and sees now not very, just a small tuft of wispy strawberry blonde hair. What's she up to? He sees her glance down at his crotch and hates himself for the fact that looking at her body has given him an erection, which she can plainly see despite the bagginess of his boxer shorts. It seems to him they're standing there staring at each other a long time, like hockey players in a face off waiting for the puck to drop and he makes the first move to get past. "S'cuse me," he mutters, expecting her to step aside, but she doesn't and he bumps straight into her and steps back, startled. He knows she did it on purpose. She wanted him to feel those nice big tits of hers the same way she wanted him to get a look at her down there, to torment him. He sees her smirky grin widen as she slowly steps aside and lets him pass. "There isn't any," he hears her say as he walks down the hall to the bedroom.

Kim's propped up in bed with her nose in a book and Trey climbs into bed and picks up his book and begins reading and it isn't long before she turns off her light and snuggles under the covers with her back to him. He reads until he forgets what he just read and can't keep his eyes open and bookmarks the page and puts the book on the nightstand and turns off the light. He stretches out under the covers on his back and he wants to go to that place in his mind to relieve himself more than ever right now but he's reluctant to and has been ever since Kim asked him if he were playing with himself. He no longer trusts that she's sleeping and hasn't masturbated in bed since that night. Instead he's taken care of himself in the bathroom, which is not at all the same experience as being in bed. Being in the bathroom sitting on the toilet works in his fantasy, but in reality it's a stark place and an unnerving experience and it's hard to conjure up and concentrate on images of women when he's expecting to be interrupted at any moment by Julie's knock on the door. This erection of his isn't going to just go away, though, and until it does he's not going to be able to fall asleep. He decides to risk it and reaches up and takes a tissue from the box as quietly as possible and settles back and reaches into his boxer shorts and takes himself in hand and begins slowly stroking himself. He hurries through the collection of images in his mind's eye to get to the scene with Julie and just when it begins to take shape he hears Kim whisper, "What's it like?" and freezes. "What?" he whispers. He hears her turn over and looks at her and sees she's looking at him.

"When you play with yourself," she whispers, "what's it feel like?"

"I dunno."

"It must feel good otherwise you wouldn't do it so much."

"Duh."

"Do all boys do it?"

"I dunno, I guess so."

"What do you think about when you do?"

"I dunno, stuff."

"Like what?"

"Girls, women."

"Dirty stuff?" she asks and props herself up on an elbow.

He can hear her growing curiosity. "I dunno…I guess… yeah."

"What does it look like?"

"What?"

"You're thing, when you play with yourself. It gets hard, right?"

He can see where her questioning is headed and he's not sure he's comfortable with it but, then, he's not sure he isn't. It's perfectly natural for her to want to know and ask and it's perfectly natural that she would ask him, her brother, but still.... "Yeah."

"Can I see it?"

"No."

"Come on. Just a peek?"

"No." He watches her pull back the covers and get out of bed and tiptoe over to his bed and crouch down beside it. He can see her looking pleadingly at him in the dark.

"Please?"

"I dunno. It feels strange."

"What's the big deal? I'm your sister."

"That's why."

"Pretend I'm not then. Pretend I'm someone else, one of the girls you think about."

"That's weird."

"Please?"

He knows she's not going to give up until she's satisfied her curiosity. What the hell, she's going to see one sometime or another and it might as well be his now and he pulls back the covers and she leans closer and looks at it, wide-eyed.

"Wow! Does it hurt when it gets like that?"

"No. Well, sort of."

"So what do you do to make it get small again?"

"Stroke it."

"How? Show me."

"I dunno. I don't think I should."

"C'mon. I bet you want to. You were before. What's the big deal if I watch?"

She has a point. He does want to get on with it and relieve himself and it really doesn't matter to him if she watches. In fact, it's kind of exciting that she is watching. He's never masturbated with anyone present and he takes himself in hand again and closes his eyes and begins slowly stroking and it's surprising how easily the images come to mind and he wonders what's going through Kim's mind, crouched there in the darkness beside the bed, watching him masturbate. She seems fine with it and what's the harm in helping satisfy her curiosity about sex? It's the brotherly thing to do.

He works his way through the images and finally arrives at the beginning of the scene with Julie in the bathroom and hears her whisper, "Lemme do it," and feels her hand on his gently pulling it away and thinks what difference does it make whose hand is doing the job? But as she wraps her hand around him and begins gently stroking him he discovers it makes a big difference. It's an entirely new and thrilling experience having someone else doing it and it doesn't matter that it's Kim. No, that's not quite right. It does matter that it's Kim because she's so eager to do it and he can feel she's enjoying doing it and he works her into the scene with Julie. Kim's kneeling beside him, stroking him, and they're both watching Julie beg for it and it's Kim who aims him at Julie's face and they watch as he squirts all over it.

"Wow!" he hears her whisper and feels his ejaculation on his stomach. He sees the insides of his eyelids brighten and opens them and sees Julie standing in the doorway with her hand on the light switch and she he isn't smirking, she's staring at them with a shocked expression. Kim turns to look at her and runs back to her bed and dives under the covers and turns toward the wall. He covers himself and he and Julie stare at each other and finally she turns off the light and pulls the door closed behind her and he listens to her footsteps as she returns to her bedroom. He knows life with her is going to change somehow now and he suspects for the worse.

He's surprised not to see Julie's usual smirk at the breakfast table. Her expression is a new one and he can't quite make it out. The way she used to look at him always made him feel she considered him pathetic. She's not looking at him that way now. For sure her look of superiority is still there, but he thinks he's sees a hint of envy mixed in with it, desire too, even grudging admiration. Maybe she liked what she saw last night and wouldn't mind playing with him herself. He knows she thinks she has controlling power over him now and is busily thinking of ways to use it. He's pretty sure she'll keep her mouth shut about what she saw, though. She had no business coming into their bedroom like that, even if it is her father's house. No, she won't tell, but she will do something. He's certain of it and he can only imagine what and when.

He glances at Kim and sees her attention is focused on finishing the last bits of cereal in her bowl. Surprisingly or maybe not, she hasn't said a word about what happened. She woke and quietly went about the business of getting herself ready for school, as usual. Well, whatever happens, Kim can handle it. She's one tough kid his little sister. "Henry's nice, isn't he, Trey?" he hears his mom ask and sees her smiling at him the way she was at Brooks Brothers. "Yeah," he says and glances at Walt, who's scooping egg and potato and bacon onto his fork with a piece of toast and who, he knows, will undoubtedly have something to say.

"Bit of a dandy," Walt says.

Trey glances at his mom and sees her smile disappear as she looks down at her plate.

"There's a difference between being a 'dandy' and 'well dressed'," June says. "Dressing well is his business."

Trey glances at Walt, his black tie tossed back over his shoulder and a paper napkin tucked in the collar of his white shirt to keep it clean.

Walt chews thoughtfully and picks up his mug and takes a sip of coffee to wash down the food and screws up his face. "Purple?"

"He looked nice," Trey hears Kim say and glances at her and sees she's keeping her head down and poking with her spoon at the last bit of cereal at the bottom of the bowl. This is pretty amazing. Kim's never voiced an opinion about anything at the table and she's certainly never contradicted Walt.

Trey glances at Julie and sees she's studying him and he has the feeling she has been while he's been looking at the others.

"I have some interesting news," Julie says, keeping her eyes on Trey's.

He feels his skin tingling from the rush of adrenaline and stares at her intently, trying to will his thoughts across the table and into her head. Don't do it! Don't say anything! Just keep your big fucking mouth shut! "What's that, honey," he hears Walt ask.

"Brad asked me to the senior prom."

Julie's expression looks playfully menacing. She's clearly having fun toying with him, the way some kids enjoy pulling the wings off flies. He doesn't know why he feels the way he does about this change in her but he welcomes it. It feels exciting, like anything could happen.

Kaitlin and Michael stroll past the carousel inside South Coast Plaza and she looks at the line of young moms and dads waiting with their kids to ride the horses and then at the moms and dads standing beside their kids on the carousel, all going round and round. There seem to be strollers everywhere. There are more young parents with their kids gathered around the balloon vendor, staring up at the canopy of balloons, trying to decide which to choose. Is that what she really wants, to be like them? She not sure how she feels about it. She's still conflicted about the idea of marrying Michael and having children, which not so long ago she was certain she wanted to do. Maybe this is just a phase all brides-to-be go through, but maybe she's having second thoughts for a reason. Well, she'd better sort things out soon because here they are on their way to see Henry at Brooks Brothers about Michael's wedding suit. They ride the escalator up to the second level and there's Brooks Brothers on the corner and she notices the sheep dangling above the entrance. That's how she feels, suspended and wondering what happens next.

They tell one of the associates they have an appointment with Henry and are directed to Men's Suits at the rear of the store. Henry greets them and tells them he's just finishing up with a customer and will only be a few minutes and asks them to please make themselves comfortable at the desk and he'll be right with them. They sit and look around at the racks of suits and the well-dressed mannequins. Like most men, Michael hates to shop and she can see that his eyes are already beginning to glaze over. Keith said Henry's good. She hopes so.

They watch Henry and a middle-aged, heavy-set white-haired man emerge from the fitting room, Henry carrying a brown plaid sport coat on a hanger, and walk toward the front of the store. A few minutes later Henry returns and sits at the desk across from them and shakes their hands and tells them it's a pleasure to meet them and nods toward the front of the store. That's what he loves about his job, Henry says, and they listen as he tells them about the customer he was just assisting. The man came in to buy a sport coat and said he'd been out of the picture for a while and didn't have much fashion sense. Henry helped him select one and while they were waiting for the tailor in the fitting room asked the customer where he'd been and the man said serving twenty-five years to life for first degree murder. He said he'd been wrongfully convicted and finally managed to get his conviction overturned. He sued the city for seven million dollars and won and now he devotes his time to working with groups of lawyers and family members of others who've been wrongly convicted and that's just one of many fascinating stories Henry's heard. Kaitlin sees Henry has Michael's undivided attention. He's good, all right.

Henry asks them to tell him about themselves, what they do and what companies they're with. He knows the managing director in Kaitlin's office and several of the partners in Michael's law firm, all clients of his. Henry asks them to describe their wedding plans and Kaitlin tells him that she hasn't decided on a wedding dress, so they're not sure yet what Michael and his best man should wear. Henry tells them not to worry, they've got plenty of time and when the time comes he'll take care of everything and make sure Michael and his best man look their best and while they're here, he'll just put a suit coat on Michael to make sure of the fit. Henry stands and walks to one of the racks and returns with a solid black suit coat and Michael stands and Henry helps him into it and it fits perfectly. If he made Michael a suit, Henry says, it wouldn't fit him any better. They're impressed and feel they're in good hands and Henry gives Kaitlin his business card and tells her to call him in a couple of months and not to worry about a thing, that everything will be just as she wants it to be, which is as it should be. After all, Henry says, it's her day and they smile and nod and say it was nice meeting him and thank him for his time.

They ride down the escalator and Kaitlin looks at the balloons and the carousel and all the young moms and dads with their kids and strollers and thinks about Henry's comment. It really is all about the bride. For most women, their wedding day is the most important day of their life, the one day they can look and feel and be treated like a princess. She's never felt that way about it. She's always viewed her wedding day as just a ceremony to make things official followed by a party. Still, she was looking forward to it until she met Manfred and began having second thoughts about getting married. She really does need to stop going round and round in her head like those horses on the carousel and sort herself out soon.

Henry puts his customer's sport coat on the rack outside the tailor shop. A nice young couple, a bit quieter and more reserved than most of the soon-to-be-marrieds he's met and he's sure there's an interesting story there. Each couple has a distinct personality but they're all the same, in that they're young and a bit uncertain about what comes next, yet hopeful that things will go off as planned and turn out well, and not just the wedding. He enjoys working with them and as different as they are, they all have that same look in their eyes, a mixture of hope and fear. He feels responsible for them, like they're his children, and gives his all in helping them realize their vision of that perfect day, looking just so in front of their family and friends and the cameras. The choice of the groom's tie, the shade of his pocket square, the break of his trousers, the amount of shirt cuff he's showing are every bit as important to him as the bride's dress. Of course, it's really her vision he's helping to realize. It's her day and the groom is just along for the ride, as he was on his wedding day many years ago. He looked pretty good, as it happened in a Brooks Brothers suit, his first, purchased for the occasion. He takes his work with these young people seriously because of what comes afterward. They think they know what marriage is all about, but really have no idea what lays ahead. It could be happiness or heartbreak and usually it's both and whether the marriage will last is anyone's guess. His job is to help make that day as perfect as possible so they'll always have that to look back on as they journey through life. If things don't work out, it won't be because he didn't make the groom look his best.

CHAPTER 3

Art and Pedro stand together with their elbows up on the back of Art's white Silverado pickup truck parked by the curb in front of a single family home on a nice street in a nice neighborhood in Tustin, sipping their coffee and shooting the shit while they wait for Bud, the contractor who hired them, to finish going over the final details of the solarium the owner wants added on the back of the house and Art's still feeling woozy from a late night of drinking with the usual crowd at the XXXotic on Beach Boulevard. The new stripper, a cute young Vietnamese named Chi, is still gyrating around the pole in his mind's eye with twice as many bills stuck in her G-string as any of the other girls and it isn't just because she's new. She's hot in a way the other girls aren't and weren't even when they were new. It isn't because she's Asian, either. He's partial to Asians and some of the other girls are. She's just got "it", whatever "it" is and it turns him on.

Pedro looks up at the surfboard secured next to the ladder on the rack overhead and slowly shakes his head. "I don't get surfing, man. Seems like a waste of time."

Art glances at Pedro's frog-shaped body and pictures him on a surfboard and it's so improbable that he wants to laugh and has everything he can do to keep from doing so and spewing his mouthful of coffee into the bed of his truck. He manages to get himself under control and swallow the coffee. "You should give it a try. You might like it." He isn't surprised to see Pedro make a face like he's just stepped in dog shit.

"Surfing's a white thing, man. I wouldn't be caught dead surfing." Pedro nods toward his cherry red '62 Chevy Impala lowrider parked behind the pickup. "I get my kicks cruisin' the hood, man."

That sounds about right Art: one man's waste of time is another man's passion. Surfing became his when he took it up as a teenager after his family moved to Southern California and as the years have gone by it's become an act of spiritual rejuvenation, which reminds him that it's been a while since he last took the kids out. "Whatever turns you on," he says and sees the homeowner, a young professional named Joanne, come walking with Bud around the side of the house. She's attractive, about five-eight or -nine with shoulder-length brunette hair and wearing a white blouse and black and white pinstripe business suit. She and Bud stop and have a few words and Art sees her glance at him as she gets in her black Mercedes CLK convertible and he watches her drive off. Whatever it is she does, she's doing all right for herself. Bud walks over to them and takes his cell phone out of the holder on his belt.

"Where the fuck is Ramon?" Bud asks.

Art and Pedro glance at each and look at Bud and shrug.

"You guys get started," Bud says and calls Ramon and walks away with the phone to his ear.

Another day of drudgery, hauling all the lumber and dry wall delivered from Home Depot into the back yard. It's the type of shit job Art never would have considered taking just a few years ago and didn't need to, but he's lucky to have the work. Bud could just as easily have hired undocumented day laborers and is doing him and Pedro and Ramon a favor by tossing them a bone and paying them under the table. Art'll make enough to pay his share of the rent for a few months and keep up his nightly visits to the XXXotic, that and cover expenses when he has Trey and Kim for the day.

He can't blame anyone but himself for being in this situation. He was an excellent student and excelled in math and probably could have gotten into any college he wanted to on his own merits and it was when he saw how eager his father was to use his influence in the academic community to assist him that he decided, to spite him, not to attend college at all, but instead to begin working in construction, which he knew would piss off his father royally. In retrospect, it was foolish and a bad move, but construction jobs were plentiful then and the money was good and he could afford to thumb his nose at his father. But now here he is, trudging along, his life a shambles.

He takes a little comfort in the fact that as foolish as his idea to work in construction was, it was no more so than his father's to marry Landis. His father certainly wasn't the first college professor to become involved with a student and he understands why he was attracted to Landis. She's a piece of ass and a great fuck, which he knows from personal experience, but his father's an extremely intelligent and perceptive man and not the type to be blinded by lust. He must have seen that Landis was nothing but trouble. Her personality when she gets a few drinks in her is like the tornadoes that tear through Decatur, Alabama, where she was born and raised.

The first time Art met her was when he was doing some interior work in his father's condo, another bone tossed his way to assist him during difficult financial times. He saw the long blonde hair, the limpid blue eyes, the big bright welcoming smile, the great body and the languid way she draped it on and over anything handy, the way he imagined she did suffering through those long hot humid summers back home, probably always with a cold bottle of Dr. Pepper in her hand. More than anything, though, he saw trouble written all over her and he knew it was only a matter of time before she'd begin cheating on her gray-haired husband and he wasn't really surprised when she came on to him. No one is off limits with Landis. His father called not long after and told him he was "henceforth persona non grata" and that he could go fuck himself for all he cared and the financial assistance ended. It's only fitting that the work he was doing for his father was left unfinished. They have a lot of unfinished business.

Ramon arrives with some lame excuse and the day wears on and they wrap up at 4:30. Joanne hasn't arrived home yet and probably won't for several hours. She must put in long hours at work because she's gone when they arrive to begin work and isn't back when they wrap up and it occurs to Art that he might never see her again.

Trey stands with nine other boys in a row facing an equal number of girls standing in a row a dozen or so feet away. Missus Sarah Pantages, a white-haired grandmotherly-looking woman, stands between them, welcoming them to cotillion and explaining that this first meeting will be devoted to learning the proper way to introduce oneself to someone and the proper way to shake someone's hand and the very first thing she stresses is the importance of always maintaining eye contact and keeping a smile on one's face, no matter what and Henry's description of polite society comes to Trey's mind. One of the boys, a tall lanky kid named Douglas who's studying French, quickly dubbed Missus Pantages Missus "Tight Panties", the word for "tight" being *serrés* in French, he explained. Trey thought it a stretch but it stuck. The boys are all wearing either a navy blue suit or blazer and khaki dress trousers and he's noticed that his outfit – he decided to wear his suit – is the best fitting of all, not too much shoulder in the coat, trousers not too short or long, a perfect full break, and that his tie, which he tied in a full-Windsor and cinched just so to produce a nice dimple, the way Henry showed him, is the most neatly tied.

The girls are all wearing solid color short-sleeve dresses and flesh-colored stockings and black pumps and white gloves and he has to admit that it's a welcome change from tee shirts, shorts and flip-flops. The girls look older, more mature, more refined. He doesn't know any of the other kids, but he does recognize a few of them from school, in particular, the green-eyed redhead standing opposite him wearing an emerald green dress. He learned her name is Emily Sweeny when she introduced herself to the group and he sees her in the hall on his way to science lab. They've made eye contact in the hall and she strikes him as shy and self-conscious and uneasy about meeting people. She has a pretty face and a nice body and he finds her red hair striking and her freckles cute and her green eyes captivating, even at this distance, and when they happen to make eye contact now, he sees it embarrasses her and she looks away. Well, she's the perfect candidate for cotillion. Missus "Tight Panties" will soon enough teach her how to overcome her shyness and maintain eye contact and smile, damn it, smile!

"Now," Missus Pantages says turning slowly to address everyone, "let's begin with a demonstration of the proper way to introduce oneself and shake someone's hand."

Sure enough, she looks at Trey and then Emily and asks them to join her in the middle of the room and face each other. He can see the terror in Emily's eyes as they do. He tries to encourage her and whispers, "Smile," and she does slightly, but with difficulty and he can see that she's still terrified and stands with her arms held stiffly at her sides and her palms pressed against the sides of her legs.

"Your handshake is a sign of friendship," Missus Pantages explains. "Your handshake speaks volumes about who you are as a person. A handshake is more than a greeting. It's a message about your personality and your level of confidence."

Trey studies Emily's face as she watches Missus Pantages out of the corners of her eyes. He discovers that a few of the freckles in the loose cluster of them on her right cheek resemble the Big Dipper and that he likes the way the end of her nose curves upward and that there's a tiny ball of mucous stuck to the tip of a hair in her left nostril. It makes him feel close to her and protective of her. If he can figure out how, he'll let her know about the booger so she can take care of it before others notice it.

"A soft handshake can indicate insecurity," Missus Pantages explains. "A quick-to-let-go handshake can indicate arrogance." She motions to Emily to step aside so that she can position herself in front of Trey. Emily does and Missus Pantages extends her hand and Trey takes it. "So, web meets web, one or two shakes, then release hold. That's all. Don't use a forced grip, avoid offering a 'fish hand', don't offer 'lady fingers' and avoid 'pumping' the hand. Understood?" She looks around at the nodding heads and nods herself. "Good. Now, girls, when introducing yourself, make eye contact and smile and say, 'Pleased to meet you', with a slight curtsey and then state your first and last name, like this." She looks at Trey. "Pleased to meet you, Trey. My name is Sarah Pantages." She looks at the girls. "Understood?" She sees them nod. "Good." She motions to Emily to take her place in front of Trey. "Let's give it a try."

Trey notices there are now glistening beads of sweat on the downy red hair on Emily's temples and her eyes tell him that what she really wants to do is run screaming from the room. He's heard the expression "painfully shy" and this must be what it looks like. He sees her gloved hand shaking as she extends it to take his and he wraps his hand around hers gently and holds it a moment, trying to reassure her and encourage her. He knows he's imaging it, but he swears he can feel the sweat on her palm right through her glove. He isn't imagining the quaver in her voice, though. Everyone can hear it.

"Pleased to meet you, Trey. My name is Emily Sweeny."

They shake twice and Emily curtseys and nearly looses her balance, but Trey holds on and she steadies herself. "The pleasure is entirely mine, Emily," he says and bows slightly and lets go of her hand. Where did that come from? He remembers hearing someone say it once, probably in a movie. He hears several of the girls giggle and turns to see Missus Pantages looking at him with an expression of delightful surprise.

"My, my! How gallant!"

Trey looks back at Emily and sees she's looking at him differently now, directly into his eyes, like she's searching for something.

They spend the rest of the meeting practicing their introductions and then the proper way to go through a receiving line with the several chaperones present and now the boys and girls are supposed to mingle and chat and get to know one another in the last fifteen or so minutes before parents begin arriving to pick them up, which Missus Pantages has designated "polite conversation time", but after a few minutes spent with the opposite sex the boys gravitate toward each other, as do the girls, and now it's mostly the boys chatting together and the girls doing the same, but Trey and Emily are standing apart from the two groups, as is one other couple. He asks Emily who her friends are at school and she seems to be mentioning everyone's name she can think of to make it seem like she has a lot of them, but he has the feeling she doesn't. Anyway, he's only half-listening because his attention is focused on the tiny ball of mucous stuck to the hair in her nostril. Emily notices where he's staring and becomes self-conscious and covers her mouth and nose with her hand.

"What?" she asks through her hand.

He leans closer and whispers, "You have something in your nose."

"Oh, my God!" she whispers and walks quickly out of the room and returns a few minutes later. "Thanks," she says.

He watches her as she searches his eyes. What is it he sees in her expression now? For sure, she looks thankful to him for having helped her avoid embarrassment, but there's something else, a mixture of apprehension and hopefulness. He thinks he was right about her friends, that she doesn't have a lot of them or maybe even any. "Hey, what are friends for?" he asks and sees her smile for the first time. "Anyone ever tell you the freckles on your right cheek look like the Big Dipper?" She looks surprised and shakes her head. "It's nice. I like it." He sees she's flattered and blushes." "You look cute when you blush," he says and sees the rosy hue of her cheeks and neck deepen. He likes Emily. They're going to get along just fine.

It's been over a week since Julie appeared in the bedroom doorway that night and Trey's been wondering what's going on with her and why she hasn't done anything. It's one of those afternoons arriving home from school that feels like he's the only one in the house, but passing by Julie's bedroom he sees through the partly open door that she's sitting on the bed with one foot up on it, blowing on the pink nail polish she's painting on her toes to match her fingernails. She looks up at him and smirks. "Hey, lunch tray!" he hears her call and walks back and stops at the door.

"Just the person I want to see," she says and screws the top on the bottle of nail polishes and places it on the nightstand. "Come in and shut the door."

Trey steps into the room and closes the door behind him and takes off his backpack and sets it down on the floor and stands there, waiting to see what she has planned. She puts her other foot up on the bed and her arms around her legs and looks at her toes and wiggles them and then looks at him and cocks her head.

"It's pretty fucked up dontcha think?" she asks.

"What?"

"Letting your little sister jerk you off? Do you guys do that every night?"

"No." They didn't for a few nights afterward but resumed the practice, always as a result of Kim's pleading. She can't seem to get enough of playing with him and watching him come. He'd be lying if he said he doesn't enjoy it and he knows they have to stop, but he's not sure yet how and their having to share a bedroom isn't helping matters.

"Don't you have a girlfriend?"

"No."

"Maybe it's time you got one."

Emily comes to mind and he realizes that, surprisingly, he's never involved her in any of his masturbatory fantasies. It's not that he doesn't find her attractive, but for some reason he's just never thought of her as anything other than a friend and cotillion partner. He sees Julie's staring at his crotch and that her smirk is gone and she raises her eyes and looks at his.

"So here's the deal. You're gonna do whatever I want or I'm gonna tell. Got it?"

"Like what?"

She stands and unbuttons the waistband of her shorts. "Like kiss my ass," she says and unzips her shorts as she turns and pulls them and her underpants down around her ankles. She turns and puts her hands palm down on the bed and sticks her ass out toward him and looks back at him over her shoulder. "Go on! Do it!"

He admires her ass and legs, still a little baby fat but hot and now he notices the pimples and the stubble and here and there the tiny nicks on her legs from shaving and she seems more like a real person and less like the monster he imagines her to be when he isn't coming on her face in his fantasy and he wonders why this, of all things, is what she wants him to do? If she thinks he views the prospect of kissing her ass humiliating or disgusting she miscalculated. In fact, he's looking forward to it.

"What are you waiting for?"

He drops slowly to his knees and puts his hands on her cheeks and spreads them and brings his face close to her skin. He studies the curlicues of strawberry blonde hair ringing her asshole and the little tuft of hair between her legs and runs his hands slowly upwards on her cheeks, feeling the soft hair against his palms and he can smell the faint odor of shit as he brings his lips to the inside of her cheek and kisses it and then does the same to the other. He feels her body shudder. "You and your sister are fucking perverts," he hears her say and feels her pushing back against his mouth now. He pulls his head back slightly and watches her search for his mouth with her ass and smiles and places his fingertip lightly on her rim and traces it round and round while he gives her cheeks tender kisses and feels her begin trembling. "Ungh," he hears her say, her head down now, and sees her bring her hand to between her legs and begin stroking herself, faster and faster until she swings her head to get her hair to one side and looks back at him over her shoulder, her eyes barely open and her face flush. He sees her begin rubbing herself furiously and he brings his mouth to her asshole and kisses it and keeps his mouth on it. He feels her body shaking and hears a howling, shrieking sound he's never heard before, the type of sound he imagines animals deep in the forest make, a wild sound that's both scary and exciting. The sound gets louder and louder and finally trails off and she lowers herself onto the bed. He stands and looks down at her and she rolls over on her side and looks up at him. He expects to see her smirk but she doesn't. In fact, she looks confused and conflicted, like she's pleased he did what he was told to do, but not that he obviously enjoyed doing it.

"Get out and shut the door."

He sits at the small desk in the bedroom reading *Lord of the Flies,* William Golding's novel about a group of well-mannered English schoolboys whose plane crashes while attempting to evacuate them during the war with Germany, stranding them on a deserted island and it isn't long before they descend into savagery. He's just finishing the part where Simon has discovered the bloody fly-covered head of a sow Jack and his band of hunters have put in the forest on a stake and Simon has a terrible vision, during which the head seems to be speaking to him and tells him that he'll never escape the evil on the island, that it doesn't exist without, but within him and each of the other boys and Simon travels to the beach to tell the others what he's seen and heard and finds a feast underway, put on by Jack and his band, and everyone is in a state of chaotic revelry — even Ralph and Piggy have joined in — and when they see Simon's shadowy figure emerge from the forest they fall on him and kill him with their bare hands and teeth.

Trey can't help thinking about cotillion. What's the point of learning the proper way to introduce yourself and shake someone's hand and walk down a receiving line and dance when just below the surface we're all savages? Learning that stuff doesn't change human nature. In fact, it's purpose seems to be to mask it, to make everyone believe that who we are as human beings is somehow better than who we really are and he remembers what Henry said about polite society, that it's people who smile as they hurt each other. Well, if he's going to be hurt by someone he'd much rather see the hurtfulness on her face.

He hears his mom and Kim arrive home and Kim comes into the bedroom in her soccer outfit carrying her backpack and sports bag with her school clothes in it and plops them on the floor and herself face down on the bed. "What's up?" he asks. "Nothing," he hears her say into the pillow. "Yeah, right. What's up?" She pushes her face deeper into the pillow and he thinks he hears her crying, but he's not sure and then she slowly rolls over and he sees she is crying, although she's trying hard not to.

"They called me a boy," Kim says.

"Who?"

"Some girls on the other team."

He knows part of the reason why. Kim's a great athlete and the best striker in her soccer league. "You won, right?"

She nods.

"They're just jealous." He can see this doesn't make her feel any better and she slowly rolls over again and pushes her face back into the pillow. How cruel can you get? He wonders if the girls were smiling when they said it.

Lying in bed in the dark, he feels the change in the atmosphere in the bedroom. He knows Kim is pretending to be asleep. That much is usual, but he senses she doesn't have playing with him on her mind, that she's still hurting from what the girls on the other team said. He could see she was all afternoon and at dinner and while doing her homework at the desk and reading in bed and he saw it in her expression when she said good night and turned off her light. Oddly, he doesn't feel like masturbating, despite the fact that he now has hot new images to conjure up as a result of his encounter with Julie. He's concerned about Kim and wishes there were something he could do to make her feel better about herself, but he doesn't know what that might be. He's seen how reassuring words are. Not very. "You awake?" he asks. There's a long pause before he hears her say, "Yeah." "Still thinking about what they said?" he asks. "Yeah," he hears her say. "C'mere," he tells her. He sees her hesitate and knows it's because she doesn't want to play with him, but isn't sure if that's what he wants, so he says, "Just c'mere," in a way he knows will put her at ease and she rolls over and climbs out from beneath the covers and tiptoes to his bed and he holds back the covers in a way he knows she'll understand means he wants her to get in and lie beside him and that's all and she does and he covers them and they lie facing each other in silence for a while.

"Do you think I look like a boy?" she finally asks. "Be honest."

"No."

She searches his eyes. "I don't believe you."

"I'm being honest. You just don't look as girly as most girls do. It's no big deal." He wishes he hadn't said that last part because it is a big deal to her, a very big deal.

"So you think I'm ugly."

"No! That's not what I meant."

"I don't know why I look the way I do. I just do. I can't help it."

"There's nothing wrong with you. You're fine." He can see in the dim light that her eyes are glistening with tears.

"Then why did they say that?"

"They're ignorant assholes."

"It still hurts."

"I know." He searches for something else to say to reassure her, but words seem useless at this point. He could go on telling her she's fine and there's nothing wrong with her all night and she still wouldn't believe him and would still be hurting. The only other thing he can think to do is comfort her and he puts an arm around her and draws her close to him and she snuggles against him with her forehead against his shoulder and her hands tucked under her chin. "Can I stay here a while?" he hears her ask. "Yeah," he says and doesn't care who opens the bedroom door and turns on the light.

Art's almost done with the little finish work there is remaining in the solarium. He happily agreed to stay late to finish up when Bud asked him to and has been taking his sweet time, hoping that Joanne will arrive home. He's thinking that if she doesn't by the time he finishes, he just might wait for her and pretend to be finishing up when she does. He's pleasantly surprised to hear the garage door opening and listens to her enter the house and drop her keys on the kitchen counter and walk toward the solarium and turns to see her leaning against the doorway, admiring the room. She's as attractive as he remembers her being and is wearing a navy blue business suit this time.

"This looks great," Joanne says and looks at him. "Wanna beer?"

They sit in the solarium sipping their beers and chatting. Joanne tells him she's an investment analyst at PACBOND, the bond trading company in Newport Beach. Art says he knows of it. She tells him she's divorced and fine with living alone. He tells her he's married but separated and that he and his wife began experiencing difficulties in the marriage when the construction boom ended and he couldn't find work and money became a problem and the marriage finally couldn't take the strain. He knows she knows he's telling her a sanitized version of the story and the way she's scrutinizing him as she listens makes him feel she's analyzing him the way she does investment strategies at work and that she's probably already concluded she's dealing with a loser. He sips his beer and sees her studying his face.

"You're a handsome guy," she says. "You should take better care of yourself."

He smiles. He's sure she meant this as nothing more than friendly advice, but it's nice to hear that she thinks he's handsome, despite the wreck he's made of his appearance. June was the last person who told him he was, but that seems a long time ago now.

He sits at the bar in the XXXotic with the other regulars, sipping his beer and listening to Ramon, who he's always considered a squirrely character. Ramon's going on about how his brother in San Bernardino is making bank selling meth, how he cooks the shit in his own kitchen and it costs him peanuts to make the stuff and how he's got a supplier in Mexico who gets him all the ephedrine and pseudoephedrine he needs – none of this buying Sudafed at the pharmacy and having them take down his personal information – and how they're stupid to be slaving away working shit jobs making chump change when they could be making bank cooking and selling crank and he should think about it, his brother could set them up. Art's been listening, but not really paying attention. He's been staring at Chi's refelection in the mirror behind the bar. She's sitting a few stools down chatting up a new face.

He's gotten to know her pretty well and found out what the "it" that turns him on so much is really all about. She looks innocent enough, but she's a real operator. She says she has a boyfriend in Westminster and that they're engaged, but he's never seen the guy and even if he does exist and she is engaged, it doesn't stop her from hustling. For twenty bucks she'll suck your cock, for fifty you can fuck her in the pussy and for a hundred you can fuck her in the ass. The motel room down the street is on you. He's availed himself of her services many times and he probably will again later on and which he'll spring for he doesn't know, but the prospect of having sex with her, far from being exciting, has become tiresome and depressing, as has listening to Ramon's pitch and everything else going on in his life.

Talking with Joanne was a bright spot in his otherwise typically dreary day. It was nice talking with someone who actually understood what he was talking about when he explained his love of stochastic calculus and she thought it was cute when she asked him what his current read was and he told her a reread of *The Fractal Geometry of Nature* by Benoit Mandelbrot. What is it that's so appealing to him about randomness and the fragmentation of things? Is it that he feels so fractured and out of control? Probably. Well, maybe he's not so unpredictable. He's always been able to count on himself to fuck things up. Maybe he never matured enough to be in an adult relationship. Maybe he's just too selfish. That doesn't seem right, though, since he doesn't even seem to care enough about himself to take care of himself. Maybe he's just lost and has given up hope.

He remembers when he was a kid the way his father used to get on his mom about doting on him, claiming she was spoiling him rotten when all she was doing was what mothers naturally do, showing him love and affection, the same love and affection she probably showed his father when they first met, but that he either couldn't or wouldn't accept anymore. Is that it? Did his mom over-compensate, showering enough love and affection on him for two people? Maybe his father is right. Maybe he is just an overgrown baby. His father's a prick but he's not stupid. "Wouldn't you?" He hears Ramon ask and sees him leaning toward him, leering. "What?"

"Fuck her?"

"Who?" Art asks and sees Pedro's expression change to one of disbelief.

"The solarium chick, man!"

"Yeah. I guess so," Art says and sips his beer and turns his attention back to Chi. He watches her smile and cover her mouth as she laughs and stroke the new face's forearm and imagines having sex with Joanne. He can see the two of them together easily enough, but they're like frozen stick figures because he can't see a realistic set of circumstances that would lead to her having sex with him. She's a different person than Chi. It's not a simple matter of pulling money out of his wallet and handing it to her. There'd have to be a reason why she'd want to and he glances at himself in the mirror and doesn't see one. He notices the new face put money on the bar and stand and Chi stands too. The new face heads toward the entrance and Chi toward the back to throw some clothes on and meet the guy out front and with the two of them gone, Art thinks of June, as he inevitably does as the night wears on and he's past the point of having had too much to drink.

June is the everlasting reminder of what a colossal fuck up he truly is and nothing will ever remove the shame he feels at having let her and Trey and Kim down so completely. He doesn't see June that much anymore, only for a few moments when he picks up or drops off the kids and then not always. Sometimes he arrives at Walt's to find them waiting outside. He likes to think it's because June knows how much he hates the fact that she's living with Walt and sends the kids outside so he doesn't have to come anywhere near Walt, but he knows the real reason is that he's an embarrassment to her and she doesn't want Walt to see him.

He remembers the day he and June first met, the summer after he graduated from high school. He was surfing with friends by Huntington Beach Pier and it was a gloriously sunny day and a good day for surfing with good sets and the pier above was crowded with people, many of them leaning on the railing watching the surfers and he noticed this one hot chick wearing a pink sailing cap and pink tube top and white short-shorts and wrap-around sunglasses standing with a friend, also pretty hot, and he couldn't be sure, but he had the feeling she was watching him and the more time went by, the more he was sure she was. He was pretty tan and buff then with shoulder-length hair and he thought why shouldn't she be watching him? He saw them turn away from the railing and begin strolling out toward the end of the pier and he told his buddies he was taking a break and went looking for them. He found them at the end of the pier standing with their backs to him, watching the Asians and Hispanics fishing there, usually without much luck, and he walked up behind them and said, "Hey," and they turned to face him and he saw they were both holding ice cream cones and that hers was peppermint chip. He couldn't see her eyes behind the dark lenses, but he knew hers were on his. She licked her ice cream, slowly, and there was something about the way she did, showing lots of tongue, that really turned him on. They introduced themselves. Her name was June and her friend's Tammy. They made small talk and it turned out June lived in Florida and was visiting Tammy and was going back in a few days and he asked her if she had to, if she had a job to get back to and she shrugged and said, "No, not really," and he invited them to join him and his friends that evening for a few beers and told them where they'd be and they said maybe they'd stop by.

He'd never felt as anxious as he did that evening standing at the bar with his friends, staring at the entrance, hoping they'd show up. When they finally did he was completely flummoxed. He'd always been confident that women found him attractive and enjoyed being with him and they'd always seemed to, but now he was worried about fucking up, embarrassing himself by saying or doing something stupid or nonsensical and he didn't even know June. It was a new feeling and he couldn't shake it. June and Tammy spotted him and he waved them over and Tammy was smiling, but June wasn't and for the first time she removed her sunglasses and put them on the top of her head and he looked at her hazel eyes and noticed the flecks of gold and the way she was looking at him and she seemed strong and confident in a way no other woman he'd ever met had and he was speechless. The two women were quickly welcomed into the group and bought drinks and were engaged in conversation and seemed to be enjoying themselves and June didn't look at him, but kept her eyes on whichever of his friends was talking to her and it occurred to him that if he didn't make a move soon, she might find someone else to her liking and his opportunity would be lost. It was a weird situation and getting weirder by the moment. He was the one who'd invited them, but that didn't seem to count for much with either of them and especially with June. He couldn't think of anything to say to her that wouldn't sound lame. The conversation was going along fine without him, so he decided not to say anything and just go quietly outside for a smoke, which he did, without anyone noticing, or so he thought, but soon June was standing by his side and held up her fingers forming a V and he put a cigarette between them and lit it for her and they stood for a while smoking and looking up at the evening sky.

"So, what's with you?" she finally asked.

He looked at her and gazed into those gold-flecked hazel eyes of hers.

"I thought you liked me," she said.

"I do."

"Could've fooled me."

"It's hard to explain."

"Give it a try."

"I'm head over heels for you." He watched her eyes as she studied his. He wouldn't have been surprised if she'd burst out laughing and walked away but she didn't and kept her eyes on his.

"You don't waste any time," she finally said.

"I'm afraid of losing you." He saw her eyes widen slightly and the corners of her mouth turn up slowly and realized it was the first time he'd seen her smile.

"You don't have me yet," she said.

He tossed his half-smoked cigarette aside and took her in his arms and kissed her and it was a kiss unlike any he'd ever given and her kiss felt unlike any he'd ever received and as far as he was concerned they could have stayed that way forever and he had the feeling she felt the same. They finally drew their heads back and gazed at each other's eyes and he saw that smile of hers again that he'd already come to love. "Like camping?" he asked.

"Not much."

"Road trips?"

"I get car sick. What do you have in mind?"

"I have a trip planned to visit national parks. Wanna come?" He watched her mull over his offer, keeping her eyes on his, and counted the number of times, three, she brought the cigarette to her lips and she tossed it aside and blew the smoke out very slowly.

"Sure," she finally said.

She called her folks the next day and told them she'd be staying and a week later they set off in his pickup with a camper top and a bed in the back and all sorts of provisions, including a healthy supply of Dramamine and good weed and it was the weed, it turned out, that did the trick where her car sickness was concerned. They giggled their way from Orange County to Joshua Tree and then to the Grand Canyon and Zion and Bryce and Yellowstone. They laughed themselves silly each evening by the fire and then in the back of the pickup making giggly passionate love high on pot and they were on the road for almost a month and got to know each other well, the way people do in circumstances like that, dealing with inconvenience and discomfort and the unexpected, like when a tire blew on the way to Bryce and the pickup nearly turned over.

At the beginning of the trip they were both very conscious about hygiene, washing themselves each morning and showering whenever they could, but as the days went by they were less concerned about it and sometimes only brushed their teeth in the morning and the smell of their bodies filled the air in the back of the pickup and became stronger each night when they made love and they liked the smell, it was their smell and it was sweet.

At the end of the trip as they headed down the 5 from Yosemite back toward Orange County, he had only one thought on his mind, wanting to spend the rest of his life with this marvelous creature with the gold-flecked hazel eyes and wonderful laugh who'd happened into his life and whom he loved deeply.

He wanted to ask her to marry him and kept waiting for the right moment and it finally arrived about a half-hour after they'd stopped to get a bite to eat at a McDonald's in Fresno. She got that look on her face he'd come to know meant she was about to fart and she lowered the window and lifted one cheek off the seat and smiled ecstatically as she let a noisy one rip and they both laughed. "Marry me," he said. She looked at him as she raised the window and he could tell she'd also been thinking about what happens next. "I will if you keep getting pot this good," she said and they laughed again and that was that.

When they returned he stayed with his parents and she stayed with Tammy and about a month later, with his father's assistance, he bought the small house in Fountain Valley and he and June moved in together and he began working construction jobs, which were plentiful and well-paying, and she got a sales job at Macy's at South Coast Plaza and each evening after work they'd stay in or go out to a bar or a movie and it didn't matter what they did because they were happy just being together.

He remembers his parents' reactions when he told them he and June planned to marry. They were both extremely interested in who she was but he knew for very different reasons. His mom was always interested in meeting his friends and almost invariably liked them and it was no different when she met June. The very first thing his mom said to her was, "You have the most beautiful eyes," and he saw June blush and knew they'd be fast friends from that moment on. His father, on the other hand, predictably grilled her as diplomatically as he could manage about her family and upbringing and when June told him her father was ex-Air Force and worked for Florida Power & Light in Homestead and her mom was a housewife, he could see by the slight rise of his father's right eyebrow and slight lengthening of the flat line of his mouth that he estimated them to be one step up from trailer trash and that's pretty much how he treated her parents when they came to attend the wedding.

His mom wanted June's parents to stay with them, an idea he knew his father disapproved of, and when he conveyed the invitation to June's dad Blaine over the phone he had the sense that Blaine was reading the situation pretty well. Blaine said they didn't want to be a bother and would stay at a motel. He'd spoken with Blaine and Carla on the phone a number of times and they struck him as easy-going good-natured people and that's just how he found them to be when they arrived. His mom liked them immediately and told them she welcomed their daughter into the family with open arms but, of course, his father remained cool and aloof and had a hard time talking with them. He could tell his father felt they had nothing in common, other than that their children planned to marry, and also that his son was marrying beneath himself and his family. He, on the other hand, felt Blaine and he had a lot in common.

They enjoyed hitting the bars in the evenings and Blaine kept him in stitches with a seemingly endless supply of stories about his hijinx in the Air Force. By far, his favorite story was the one about the time Blaine and his buddies who worked with him on the flight line decided to play a practical joke on this guy Harris from Lincoln, Nebraska, who returned to the barracks stumbling drunk each night. One night they waited for him to collapse unconscious on his bunk and they laid him on the sofa in the rec room and carried it out to the runway where a C-141 Starlifter was preparing to take off and put the couch on the runway in the dark at a point where they knew the plane would be airborne, but still low overhead with its giant engines roaring and they waited at a safe distance to see what Harris' reaction would be. "Sent him and the sofa flying!" Blaine said with glee. "Man, did we get shit for that!"

June's sister April and her husband Jack arrived for the wedding from Alaska where they live far off the road, relying as little as possible on government and the services it provides. Their house is a large cabin they built themselves using wood from trees they felled and lathed themselves and the fact that they have electricity and running water is Jack's doing – April reluctantly agreed to be tied to the grid – and this, according to April, was one of the only times that Jack prevailed in their never-ending contest of wills. Most of what they eat they either grow or hunt and it's only as a last resort during the dead of winter that they grudgingly make the long trip to the nearest town to buy provisions. It happens infrequently and April said that even one trip is one too many as far as she's concerned.

The dynamic between April and his father was fascinating to watch. April's a few years older than June and while you can tell they're sisters, April has a hardness to her features and bluntness to her personality that June doesn't. She has a way of putting you on notice without saying a word, as she did him when they first met and then his father, that she doesn't take shit from anyone. He was fine with it, but his father was visibly uncomfortable in her presence, like he knew he'd met someone who didn't give a rat's ass what he thought or did or had to say and couldn't quite figure out how to deal with it. He had to hand it to April. He'd never seen his father squirm the way he did and it was fun to watch.

He remembers standing with June and April and Jack on the sidewalk outside the terminal at John Wayne Airport. Jack had said his good-byes and hugged June and was busy putting the luggage in the line at the Skycap station and Art and April hugged and she stepped back and gave him one last look and she didn't have to say anything. He got the message: take good care of her baby sister or else. Why April hasn't paid him a visit yet is beyond him. Ever since he and June separated he's been expecting her to show up at any moment with a large hunting knife in her hand and he wouldn't blame her if she did.

He glances up at the mirror and sees not April walking into the bar but Chi, alone. He hopes the new face got his money's worth, whatever it was.

Trey was born – it was June's idea to name him after his father, a sweet idea, but one he resisted and finally agreed to just to make her happy – and then two years later Kim. Everything was still going fine. He was never out of work, in fact, he could pick and choose jobs and afford to turn down the less well-paying ones. He could also afford to take the family on vacation.

The first was to Southern Florida when Trey was six and Kim four. They stayed in a motel near Blaine and Carla in Homestead. On the way to the motel from the airport they toured some of the significant places in June's past. They walked around Coral Palace, the fantastic stone creation of Latvian immigrant and jilted lover Edward Leedskalnin who built it singlehandedly. June told them it was a place where she and her friends liked to hang out and later told him, giggling, that what they really liked to do there was get high on whatever they could get their hands on. Trey and Kim marveled at the place and then their mom's elementary school and high school, representing as they did her life before they were born, when she was a kid like them. He could tell by the expressions on Trey's and Kim's faces as they listened to June's description of living through Hurricane Andrew, huddled with her parents and sister in the bathroom holding a mattress over their heads, and the devastation it caused, almost wiping the community off the map, that they had a hard time getting their heads around it.

They'd spend one day at the beach and the next sightseeing. They visited Knaus Berry Farm and the kids stuffed themselves with black bottom cake. They toured the Fruit & Spice Park and they stuffed themselves with exotic fruit and nuts. They took the Boca Chica Key & Lighthouse boat tour, which was nice, but not such a big hit with the kids since it wasn't centered on food. On the way back from the tour they stopped at a stand by the side of the road and bought a bag of boiled peanuts and Trey and Kim polished them off by the time they got back to the motel and spent most of that evening in the bathroom taking turns puking their guts out. They were ready for more in the morning, though, and so it went: a trip to the Everglades one day and back at the beach the next.

Each evening when the kids were finally asleep he and June would step outside the motel room and walk to the far end of the parking lot and stand together in the hot, humid night air and smoke a joint and joke about this or that goofy roadside attraction they'd seen or whacky personality they'd met, June a little uneasily because she'd grown up there and these were her people, after all, and she'd listen, rapt, as he'd let his mind roam freely, his ideas unwiding like yarn from a skein, her favorite being that they were destined to meet because there's a Berry

Farm beginning with K and a fantastic structure built single-handedly by an obsessed immigrant in both Southern Florida and Southern California – he'd grown up with Watts Tower, built by Italian immigrant Simon Rodia, and Knott's Berry Farm – and they'd giggle and hug and kiss and walk back to the room and undress and climb into their bed with the creaky springs and try not to make too much noise as they made love. They couldn't have been happier.

The day before their departure Blaine took him and the kids fishing for red snapper on a boat owned and operated by his friend Grady, an ex-Air Force buddy from Oyster Bay, Alabama. Art fished until he'd had enough and enjoyed lounging in the stern with Blaine and Grady, drinking beer and talking while the kids fished. Grady, a big, balding barrel-chested man whose fair skin was tanned almost as red as the snapper, struck him as a typical laid-back Southerner until Blaine asked him how his daughter was doing and Grady got even redder in the face and launched into a tirade about what a good for nothing son of a bitch his deadbeat son-in-law is and how what he wants to do is kick the shit out of him, except he knows it would upset his daughter, and listening to Grady, he imagined how he would feel if Kim got stuck with a guy like that and figured he'd feel pretty much the same way and want to do the same thing. All fathers would, including Blaine, as easy-going as he is. He tried to imagine what it would be like if Blaine ever felt that way about him but just couldn't see it, couldn't imagine a scenario that would result in his father-in-law feeling that way. Grady went on and on about what an asshole his son-in-law is and how he wishes his daughter had never met the son of a bitch and Art noticed Blaine glance at him and he couldn't tell from Blaine's expression whether he was thinking, Please excuse my friend here, or, I hope your paying close attention to what my friend here is saying. It could have been either and he suspects it was a bit of both.

He notices that Ramon has left as have most of the regulars and that the few girls left in the place have changed into street clothes and are sitting together at a table in the corner counting their cash and chatting and having a drink before closing. Chi comes out of the back in her street clothes and walks over to him and sits on the stool next to him and leans close to his ear and he feels her hand on his thigh. "Hey, baby. Want something?" he hears her ask.

Good question. He wants something, all right, something better than what Chi has to offer but he'll settle for it. He tosses enough money on the bar to cover his drinks and a tip and stands and walks out with Chi to the motel down the block. He rents a room for an hour and they both undress without looking at each another and she sits naked in the middle of the bed, watching him as he takes his wallet out of the back pocket of his jeans and five twenties out of the wallet and walks over and hands them to her and she takes them and counts them and puts them on the table by the bed and turns around and waits for him on her hands and knees. He climbs on the bed behind her and spreads her cheeks and looks at her asshole, which always strikes him as impossibly small, and he knows he should probably be wearing a condom — for all he knows she's HIV positive— but he can't be bothered. He just wants to fuck her without having to look at her face and he's happy to see he's not having a problem getting hard and slowly works his cock into her ass. He puts his hands on her hips and pumps a few times but being in her there feels cold and unresponsive, which makes this dull act seem even duller and he withdraws and enters her pussy, which feels just as unresponsive, but at least warmer. What the fuck, she can keep the hundred.

All that love and affection his mom bestowed on him, all those high hopes she had for him. And look at him now. He hasn't seen or spoken with her in a while, although he knows she and June keep in touch and June takes the kids to see her from time to time. Despite everything that's happened, his mom and June have maintained a relationship that couldn't be closer if they were biological mother and daughter. He's happy about that. June needs all the support she can get being stuck in a relationship with a guy like Walt. It occurs to him just how disingenuous his concern for June is. He was the one who set in motion the circumstances that ultimately caused her to get involved with Walt. He was an out of work drunk and unfaithful and deserved to be kicked out and she had the kids' best interests in mind and needed help from someone and Walt was there and willing to take them in. According to June, Walt's first wife was a drug addict and he divorced her for his daughter's sake. He's sure there's more to the story and he can't really blame Walt for putting his own spin on things. He's been doing it himself all his life and especially so since that fateful day, September 15th, 2008.

He was having a few beers with his buddies after work, as usual. ESPN Sports was on one large flat screen and CNN on another and the financial news hadn't been good for some time, but now CNN was reporting that Lehman Brothers, the fourth largest investment bank in the country with $10 trillion in market capitalization and 25,000 employees worldwide, had filed for bankruptcy and he can't recall what his buddies were talking about because he was listening intently to hear what the pundits on CNN were saying over the din in the bar and he had the strong sense that good times in the construction industry would soon be coming to an end and he'd be unemployed and he asked himself what he'd do if that happened. Sell cars? Stock shelves at Ralph's? Greet people at Wal-Mart? He liked to think that he didn't care what his father thought about the path he'd chosen and up until then he didn't have to, but now it seemed pretty clear, given the fear he felt as he listened to the reporting on CNN, that he'd been fooling himself all along. He did care, it did matter and the prospect of being reduced to asking his father for financial assistance filled him with dread. His father already viewed him as a failure, but at least he was a failure who could provide for his family and his father paid him grudging respect for that, but if he were no longer able to provide, what then? There'd be nowhere to hide from the truth.

Sure enough, not long after, the project in Irvine came to an abrupt halt and everyone was laid off and so began the real test of his character. What he should have done was take any job, no matter what, to keep money coming in and his family together. At least he would have maintained his self-respect and the respect of June and the kids. June tried to be supportive and she and the kids wouldn't have cared what he did, but he felt like a total fuck up and that his father had gotten the best of him and he began spiraling down, settling for unemployment benefits and not really looking for work and spending more and more time with his buddies at the bar until that's all he did. His father helped out with the mortgage payments until his roll in the sack with Landis put an end to that. June had every right to kick him out.

He's aware that he's been pumping Chi for some time now and that she hasn't moved or made a sound. He looks at her, on her elbows and knees with her head down and her forehead pressed into the pillow. She could be an inflatable sex toy and might as well be. He imagines there probably are more selfish ways for two people to use each other, but not much more. He's had so much to drink that he barely feels connected to his body and doesn't really feel like coming but figures he probably should now and get it over with. He'll be doing them both a favor. A few more thrusts and he comes and Chi climbs off the bed without looking at him and walks quickly into the bathroom closing the door behind her. He dresses and listens to the toilet flush and the water running in the sink and Chi emerges and dresses without looking at him. She takes the bills from the table and folds them and stuffs them in the front pocket of her jeans and picks up her bag and slings it over her shoulder. "All set?" he asks without looking at her.

He drops the key in the drop box outside the office and they walk in silence back past the now dark bar to the parking lot around back where their cars are parked. He notices a black SUV in the corner of the lot and as he and Chi approach their cars, all four doors open and it seems to him there are a lot of men climbing out, all Vietnamese and shorter than he. The driver, probably Chi's boyfriend, is walking quickly toward her and shouting angrily at her in Vietnamese and she's shouting back at him and now the guy is slapping her in the face and then punching her. The way the guy crouches in front of her and throws punches makes Art think he fancies himself a ninja.

Chi's curled up on the ground now, shrieking and trying to protect her head and "Ninja" is trying to kick her in the stomach but can only manage to kick her legs and two of his friends begin shouting at him in Vietnamese and pulling him away and Art's aware that the rest of the men are now positioned beside and behind him. He knows he should be more concerned about the situation and what's likely about to happen but he's just too drunk to care or do anything about it. With "Ninja" restrained, Chi gets to her feet and takes a few wobbly steps toward her car but her legs buckle and she falls straight down on her ass, hitting the ground hard, and sits there sobbing with her face in her hands. "Ninja" breaks free of his friends and walks quickly over to her and gives her one more hard kick in the ribs that leaves her sprawled on the ground, then turns and walks toward him, reaching into his pocket as he comes. Art feels the men surrounding him grab hold of his arms and hears them talking among themselves in rapid-fire Vietnamese and now "Ninja" is standing in front of him and his face looks like an angry cat's.

"You like fucking my girl?" "Ninja" asks. "Huh?"

Art can't think of anything to say, nothing would make any sense or difference. He sees "Ninja" is holding something in his hand but can't quite make out what it is. He sees the kick coming and the next thing he knows his groin is exploding with pain and he goes limp, but is being held up by the men surrounding him. He feels something drawn quickly across his cheek and they let him fall to the ground and begin kicking him furiously and when they've had enough they leave him lying there and he turns his head and watches them go, taking Chi with them. They climb in the SUV, "Ninja" behind the wheel, and the doors slam shut as the lights come on and the engine starts with a roar and the tires screech. He sees the SUV coming straight at him and manages to lift his head and roll over, but not fast enough to get his hand out of the way and he doesn't feel anything as the front tire runs over it but it hurts like hell immediately afterward. He watches the taillights disappear as the SUV rounds the corner of the building with its tires screeching and then the reflection of the taillights on the wall of the building across the alley and then they're gone. He sits up and holds his throbbing hand and realizes that both hands are covered with blood and he can feel the cut in his cheek now and touches it and it's deep and there's a lot of blood. "Shit," he says and gets himself to his feet and staggers toward his car.

So, here he is, in an empty parking lot behind a bar in the dead of night, drunk and in pain with a crushed hand — he assumes it is, although he can still move his fingers slightly — and a slashed cheek, having been worked over by an angry Vietnamese boyfriend a head short than he. He knows this is precisely where he should be, where he's allowed life to take him and deserves to be. It feels like the end of something, but he's felt this way in the past and been surprised by how much more he was willing to take, how much lower he was willing to sink.

He hopes what comes next is the beginning of something that will somehow lead to being with June and the kids again. At the moment, though, the distance from here to there seems infinite and as bad as here is, he's used to it. He looks up at the night sky. November is his favorite month in Southern California. The weather is cool and crisp and reminds him of early September in New England and the fact that the days are shorter eases his conscience about having his first drink of the day before noon.

CHAPTER 4

Monday morning and you could shoot a cannon ball down the corridor in South Coast Plaza and not hit anyone. It's the type of day most people in retail dread, but it gives Henry the opportunity to catch up on the stack of charge-sends for customers he's accumulated over the weekend. This charge-send business is a blessing and a curse. If he doesn't have an item, he can get it from the catalog or another store. If the catalog has the item it's quick and easy. If not, it can be a tedious time-consuming process of calling each store until he finds one that has what he needs and then he has to rely on whichever associate is assisting him to come through. Most of the time they do and everything goes smoothly, but occasionally they don't and the result can be a very unhappy customer and sometimes a complete disaster. He's not obliged to track down merchandise for customers. It's a service offered as a courtesy and most customers are patient and appreciative of the time and effort it takes, but not all and it's this small group of people that can sometimes make the business of charge-sends a matter of "no good deed goes unpunished." He's on the phone with an associate at another store when a tall man who looks to be in his mid fifties with combed-back, wavy light brown hair wearing a Tommy Bahama shirt and dress trousers and Ferragamo slip-ons and sipping something from a Starbucks cup comes sauntering toward him and seats himself in a chair opposite him. "I'll be right with you," Henry says.

The man nods and smiles. "Take your time," he says and puts the cup on the desk and crosses his legs.

The charge-send request taken care of, Henry hangs up the phone and extends a hand across the desk and they shake. "Henry. What can I do for you?"

"Alan. I understand you're the man to see about having a suit made."

Henry gestures toward the row of fabric books on the shelf behind him. "You've come to the right place."

"Used to wear suits all the time for business, but I haven't in years. Don't have to anymore."

"What business are you in?"

"Used to be a developer. Commercial properties. Now I just invest."

"In?"

"Other people's projects, all over the world."

"Travel a lot?"

Alan nods. "That's how I met my fiancée, in Italy."

"Whereabouts?"

"Milano."

"Ah," Henry says raising his eyebrows and smiling slightly. Of course, she would be *Milanese* and Alan would use the Italian name of the city. It's clear that Alan's as enthralled by his fiancée as he once was by Laura. "Do you speak Italian?" he asks in Italian.

" A little, " Alan responds haltingly in Italian. "I'm learning the language. I hope to be fluent one day."

"*Bravo!*"

"Been there?" Alan asks.

"I have."

Alan smiles and shakes his head. "They're something, the *Milanese*. Consider themselves part of Northern Europe and everything south part of North Africa."

"I know."

"Call Italians in the south 'children.'"

Henry nods. "What type of suit do you have in mind? I imagine this is for your wedding?"

"Getting married in Bali in August."

"Something light then."

"Yeah. I'll have to wait for my fiancée to decide on the fabric."

"Of course. Her name?"

"Feronia."

Ah, the goddess of fertility and abundance. Henry's curious to see if the name suits her. Laura's certainly didn't, as he discovered. While she was attractive, like her Roman goddess namesake Larunda, Laura was far from loquacious and was extremely secretive.

"Should be here soon," Alan says and rolls his eyes. "Left her in Loro Piana."

"You're a brave man. Let's get you measured."

Henry chats with Alan in the fitting room as the tailor measures him. He learns that Alan's a native Southern Californian, born and raised in Los Feliz. His father, now retired, was a businessman and Alan followed in his footsteps, attending USC and then the Marshall School of Business. At a friend's urging he got his realtor license and went to work at the friend's agency, which specialized in high-end properties and catered to celebrities. Alan and his friend went in on a development project of another friend's and it paid off handsomely, so much so they decided to get into the development business themselves and things took off from there. Alan married his college sweetheart and they have three children, two girls and a boy, grown now and the oldest, one of the daughters, married with a child of her own. He and his wife had their problems through the years, as all couples do, but he was otherwise happily married or thought he was until he was in Milan meeting with a group of Italian businessmen to discuss a development project in Dubai they were promoting and he was introduced to Feronia at a dinner party. She was also married at the time, although her husband wasn't with her. Alan looks at him in the three-way mirror.

"Ever been seduced?" Alan asks.

Henry smiles. It must be something in the water in Milan. "I have."

"It's the damndest thing, isn't it?" Alan says. "Never saw it coming."

"*Ciao, amore!*" Henry hears from behind him. He recognizes the precise business-like accent, unlike that of the Romans, which Laura once described as a "life is beautiful drawl." He turns and sees Feronia, a very attractive, carefully made up, well-coifed, expensively dressed and bejeweled woman who looks to be in her late forties posed with shopping bags from Loro Piana and Tiffany and Louis Vuitton in hand. Abundance personified and the complete opposite of Laura who never wore makeup or a dress, at least not that he ever saw, but always a simple shirt or tee shirt and jeans and black ballerinas.

"They told me I'd find you here," Feronia says.

"This is Henry, honey."

"*Ciao!*" she says, "Nice to meet you!"

Henry smiles and nods and gestures toward one of the upholstered leather chairs. "Likewise. Make yourself comfortable."

She sits and arranges her bags around her. "Aiyee! This place is filled with Arabs wearing headscarves! I keep waiting for a bomb to explode!"

It's been so long, but both the accent and the attitude are familiar. Henry glances at Alan in the mirror and sees his apologetic expression and shrug.

"They're shoppers, honey," Alan says, "just like you."

"Still! And these American sales people! They know nothing!"

Henry feels that same visceral reaction he felt when pronouncements and judgments like these came out of Laura's mouth. He learned then to simply keep smiling and say nothing. Really, when prejudice is this deep-seated, what is there to say and what good would it do anyway?

He escorts them to the desk and chats with Feronia and learns that her former husband is a financier, that she has two children studying at university in Italy and that she descends from German nobility on her father's side. The details are different, but her story is similar to Laura's. He places fabric books containing swatches of cloth he knows will be suitable for the suit in front of them on the desk and leaves them to look through them while he continues with the business of charge-sends on the phone. He watches them interact and sees the same dynamic at play that he once experienced with Laura. Each time Alan ventures an opinion about a fabric, Feronia makes a face and dismisses it. In the end, of course, all the samples are of her choosing and he checks the availability of each and some aren't available, much to her displeasure, but her three top choices are; one a light gray wool solid, another a tan wool glen plaid and another a khaki Irish linen. He watches Alan finger the tan fabric swatch.

"I like this one," Alan says.

Feronia purses her lips and furrows her brow. "Hmm...I think the Irish linen."

Henry smiles and mentally shakes his head. There you have it. The Irish linen it will be.

It's been a long time since he's thought about his relationship with Laura, but having met and spent time with Alan and Feronia, he naturally does now as he sits during his lunch break on the bench by valet parking, smoking and eyeing the people coming and going and the two attractive young French-speaking girls sitting on the bench opposite, both slender with short blonde hair and wearing oversize sunglasses. They sip frappaccinos and nibble on cookies as they chat and each time he glances at the wild-eyed, unshaven and slightly disheveled-looking man about his own age who's sitting on the bench to his right he finds him looking at him like there's something he desperately wants to say or ask.

Looking back on the time just prior to his meeting Laura, it seems obvious to him now that he was ready for a change in his life. He'd met Claire at the computer company where he worked as a writer for a couple of years and married her to escape his college girlfriend Anise. It was a ridiculous reason to marry someone and unfair to Claire, but that's who he was then. He left the computer company and started his own marketing communications company and while it was doing well servicing the needs of high tech clients, he was spending far too much money on carousing and cocaine and was worn down by his debauched lifestyle and finally it was the drug deal gone wrong in the bank parking lot behind Ryles Jazz Club in Cambridge that finally caused him to take a hard look at what his life had become and where it was headed.

What a wake up call that was. He was sitting in his car waiting for Oscar, the Guatemalan drug dealer he'd been buying coke from for months, and his girlfriend Teri to show up. What a pair those two were; Oscar, a quiet stick of a man who spoke almost no English and whose crooked nose reminded him of a question mark, and Teri, a pudgy buxom white girl with piggish features and the personality of a truck driver and a penchant for wearing tight-fitting clothing and showing a lot of cleavage — she always reminded him of a sexy bratwurst about to burst its casing — and who did all the talking for Oscar. They were late, as usual, and when they finally arrived so did the Cambridge Police in a swarm of marked and unmarked cars. They'd obviously been watching Oscar for some time and this just happened to be the moment they decided to descend on him. They emptied Oscar's pockets and found packets of cocaine and handcuffed him and Teri and drove them off and the Boston Irish detective who was in charge of the operation asked him to step out of the car and questioned him and listened to his story about how he was a business owner and was only in the parking lot to make a call on his cell phone and that he lived in Lexington with his wife and two sons and was active in Scouts and the detective listened patiently to his story and when he was finished said, "You might want to think about what will happen to your family if you're arrested on drug charges," and let him go. Why he did he'will never know, but it was one of those moments in life when you glimpse the awful consequences that might have been and that makes you think maybe there is such a thing as fate and getting arrested just didn't happen to be his. In any event, that incident focused his mind.

He reigned in his carousing and coke use and he and Claire made a half-hearted attempt at couple's counseling and met once a week with a woman recommended by one of Claire's friends. The woman sat in front of a wall displaying framed diplomas and certificates and he had the sense that while she was trying to appear impartial, she really had Claire's and the boys' best interests in mind and he had his suspicion confirmed during one of the last meetings when the subject of alimony was being discussed. The woman had asked Claire to list all of the household expenses and arrive at an amount she felt she needed to maintain her and the boys' then current standard of living and Claire did and it seemed a surprisingly inflated figure to him. He explained to the woman that his income depended on his work for clients and sometimes he was flush with project work and other times not and he couldn't guarantee a steady stream of income or that he could make alimony payments in the amount Claire was asking on a regular basis and the woman just looked at him coolly and said, "Then I guess you'll just have to figure out a way to make more money." He resented the comment bitterly at the time but smiles now remembering it. She was right and, really, all he had to do was stop throwing away money.

Having given up on couple's counseling, he and Claire were resigned to the fact that divorce was inevitable. Claire stubbornly maintained her position that it would happen when the boys went off to college, but he didn't want to wait that long and knew that he didn't have to, that all he had to do was file for divorce, but he couldn't bring himself to do it and didn't understand what was holding him back and thought that maybe a therapist could help him figure it out and began meeting each Wednesday afternoon with Warren, the husband of yet another of Claire's friends.

Warren was a gentle soft-spoken man with a bushy moustache who always seemed to be wearing the same outfit at each meeting: a brownish-green plaid shirt open at the collar, brownish tweed sport coat, khaki trousers and burgundy penny loafers. Warren also sat in front of a wall displaying diplomas and certificates and each meeting began in precisely the same way with Warren asking, "So, how was your week?" He would spend the rest of the hour doing most of the talking, telling Warren about this and that going on in his life and the first few meetings were tolerable, but he soon tired of telling pretty much the same story each week and things became so monotonous that he suggested to Warren that they record one of the sessions and Warren could listen to it each Wednesday afternoon and he'd mail him a check. Warren was amused by the idea, but he could see in his eyes that he was worried he might be losing a patient and income.

He'd always wanted to learn Italian. His dad spoke the language fluently, having been raised in the Bronx by his grandmother who spoke only Italian in the home, but he didn't speak Italian in their home. Had he, he would have learned the language easily as a kid, the way you can hum a tune after hearing it for the first time. Instead he learned it the hard way, as adults do, through study and practice. He doesn't blame his dad and understands why he didn't. His generation of Italian-Americans saw no reason why their children should speak the language of the old country. After all, that's why they came here, to get away from it.

Whatever the language the two young women sitting at the table in Café Paradiso in Harvard Square that day were speaking, he knew it wasn't Italian, although it sounded a lot like it, only mushier. He sipped his cappuccino and waited for the lesson to end and finally the student gathered up her books and stood and left and he introduced himself to the teacher and asked what language they'd been speaking and the woman said, "Portuguese." He asked if she taught Italian and she said she didn't, but a friend did and wrote down Laura's name and phone number for him. He remembers looking at the number and feeling good about himself for finally doing something about learning the Italian language. It felt like taking a step in the right direction in his life. If he could have foreseen where that step would lead, would it have made a difference? Probably not. He doesn't believe in fate but what happened next seems a lot like it now.

He watches the French-speaking girls collect their things and stand and walk away toward the bridge over Bristol Street. He glances at his phone and sees it's time to head back to the store and sticks his cigarette in the ashtray beside the bench and stands and puts the phone in his inside coat pocket and turns and sees the man sitting on the bench looking up at him with narrowed eyes.

"Nice suit," the man says.

"Thanks."

"Brooks Brothers?"

"You know your clothing."

"Got a closet full of 'em. Used to wear 'em all the time when I was a broker."

"What do you do now?"

"Whatever I damn well please." The man leans forward and puts his elbows on his thighs and holds his clasped hands in front of him. "This country's going to hell in a handbasket."

"You mean this debt ceiling crisis business?"

"I mean every damn thing from top to bottom. It scares the hell out of me and I don't have a thing to worry about financially."

"It's not the same country we grew up in, that's for sure."

"You have kids?"

"Two sons."

"I have a son and three daughters. So what do you tell them?"

"They're going to be dealing with this mess a long time."

"That's what I tell my kids. It makes me sick. Got a card?"

Henry takes one out of his coat pocket and hands it to him.

"Henry, huh? Dale. Maybe I'll come see you. I could use something new for special occasions."

"Give me a call," Henry says.

"I'll do that.

Henry notices Dale looking at something behind him and looks over his shoulder and sees a silver Bentley Mulsanne pulling up.

Dale stands and puts out his hand. "My ride's here. Gotta go. Nice meeting you."

"Likewise," Henry says and watches as the liveried driver gets out and walks around to the rear passenger door and holds it open for Dale. Henry smiles and shakes his head. Just another example of why it's a bad idea to judge people in Southern California from their appearance. He remembers the day a man with wild hair and a sunburned face wearing a polo shirt and shorts and flip-flops appeared in Men's Suits one Saturday afternoon looking like he'd slept on the beach. As it happened, he'd just been surfing in Huntington Beach and is the CEO of a large local financial institution and now one of his best customers. Dale waves as the car pulls away and he waves and turns and walks back toward the store.

He passes the carousel filled of parents standing next to their kids on the horses, all going round and round, and sees the slender young woman, Vietnamese he thinks and probably a college student, under the canopy of balloons with her long black hair and black horn rim glasses and cute pug nose and uniform of red shirt and black pants. He asks her in passing as he always does, "How's the balloon biz?" and she says, "Great!" as she always does and as cheerily as ever. He's passed her countless times and doesn't even know her name. He's purposefully never stopped to chat and get to know her better. Her smiling enthusiasm is like a beacon in his life, as important and anonymous as a runway light and better left that way.

He eyes the sheep above the store entrance and thinks that the simple fact of the matter is that he and Laura were both in limbo in their lives and using each other for their own purposes, she to free herself from what she felt to be the tyranny of her husband and he to atone for his treatment of Claire and Anise.

His old friend Bohdan comes to mind as he walks past the sport coats and notices a tan check like the one Bohdan used to wear and probably still does. Bohdan and his wife and kids moved onto the street in Lexington a few houses down not long after he and Claire and Gene did and they became good friends. Bohdan, a physicist, views things rationally. Henry was raking leaves one fall day when Bohdan walked up to him wearing his tan check sport coat, slightly hunched over with his hands stuck in his back pockets in that way of his, and told him that his wife Marta, ten years his junior, had just informed him that she wanted a divorce because she thought he'd become "too old." Bohdan raised his eyebrows and shrugged and said, "Maybe she's right." When Henry told him about the job offer in Southern California and that he was going to accept it and that preparing for the move would give him the opportunity to get rid of a lot of junk he'd accumulated through the years, Bohdan raised his eyebrows and said, "Be careful what you throw away."

He'd been planning to throw away every last reminder of Laura, but when the time came to do it he reviewed the contents of the thick manila envelope, read her notes and looked at her drawings and they seemed like precious mementoes he couldn't part with and packed them up to take with him, knowing he'd never open the envelope again and he hasn't. Still, the mementoes are like the memories. While he hasn't looked at them and the memories seldom come to mind, they're like an incurable non-fatal disease, an inseparable part of him that permeates his being.

CHAPTER 5

June watches in despair as the three Chinese women rifle through the piles of neatly folded blouses and sweaters on the display tables, unfolding each item that catches their eye and holding it up for inspection and consensus on whether it will fit whomever they're buying it for back home. It's called an "Asian Invasion" in retail and as racist a term as it is and as much as June dislikes it, it describes perfectly the mess these people can make when they descend on a table of neatly folded clothes. She politely requested that they not unfold everything they lay their hands on, but the women ignored her and proved unstoppable and so she's just left them alone, resigned to the fact that she'll have to refold everything when they leave, just as she is to the fact that she'll have to return to Walt's at the end of the day.

It was criminal what the bank did, telling her they were considering her request for a loan modification and then foreclosing on her. Declaring bankruptcy didn't prevent it and only ruined her credit. She probably could have found a small apartment for them she could afford, but with a BK and foreclosure on her credit history no one would rent her one. It doesn't seem right and she understands perfectly well now why April and Jack feel the way they do and have chosen to live the way they do. It's not just government they despise, it's the capitalist system, which they strongly believe is designed to enrich a few at the expense of many and it's hard to argue with them. She's living proof. From time to time the thought crosses her mind to do as they did, move to Alaska and live off the road as inexpensively as possible and rely on government services as little as possible, but she knows it's not in her. She's not really cut out for that type of life and the idea of raising Trey and Kim that way just seems wrong. Anyway, she's with Walt now, so she's stuck where she is, at least for the time being.

She glances over at the escalators and sees two teenage girls stepping on it and rising up toward the next level. That's the way it used to be. You stepped on the escalator in kindergarten and rode it up through elementary school and high school and college and it took you up to a job and a career and as long as you stayed on it continued lifting you up and if you stepped off, you were considered exotic and maybe you ended up in a loft someplace creating art or in a cabin in the woods writing books, but you still lived a pretty good life. It's not like that anymore. These days it's more like being on a moving walkway at the airport. You step on and it takes you forward through an economic landscape that's as flat and bleak as the Texas panhandle and if you step off, you end up living out of your car or in a homeless shelter. It's all just gone terribly wrong.

She wonders how Tammy's doing. It's been a while since they've seen each other and she makes a mental note to give her a call. They've been best friends since third grade and it was Tammy's mom Ceil, an OR nurse, who encouraged them both to think about making nursing a career. There's a shortage of nurses, she told them, and nurses make good money. The work can be emotionally draining, but it's worth it. June and Tammy had heard so many of her mom's stories about work that they felt they were well ahead of the pack when it came to learning how to be nurses. Tammy was hell bent on living in Southern California and took off right after high school graduation to establish residency so she could apply to a school in the Cal system a year later. June wanted a change of scenery too. She'd lived in Southern Florida all her life and felt that if she attended nursing school there, she'd never get out. She and Tammy planned to relocate together, but June's mom was diagnosed with ovarian cancer and her dad was sick with worry and she stayed. She made a deal with herself that if things felt good when she visited Tammy, she'd relocate and meeting Art sealed it.

He looked so confident and in control on his surfboard, but less so when he was standing in front of her and even less so later that evening in the bar with his friends. It seemed to her he was a lot like her, searching for someone to pull himself out of himself and get himself moving in the right direction and when he suggested the trip to visit national parks, as much as it didn't appeal to her, she agreed because it seemed to her that it would do them both good.

She looks up from the sweater she's folding and sees the three woman walking toward her holding armfuls of blouses and sweaters and chatting among themselves, probably Mandarin, and she has a pretty good idea what's about to happen from past experience with shoppers from China. One of the women drops her pile on the counter and holds up a blouse and narrows her eyes.

"What cost?" the woman demands to know.

"Thirty-nine ninety-five," June says and watches the woman scowl and look at the price tag and back at her disapprovingly.

"No discount?"

June shakes her head. She knows they understand English and shopping customs here well enough to know the deal. There are no sale signs on the tables they've been ransacking, so the women know the items are full price. This little game of pretending to be ignorant to try to get a discount is all too familiar. They try to wear you down to the point where you finally give in, but it's important to her not to let them, to stand firm. It may be a small thing, but to her it's doing her part to save the country from being sold cheap to the Chinese. The woman looks disapprovingly at her and says something to her companions and picks up a sweater and holds it out to her.

"What cost?"

"Seventy-nine ninety-five." The woman's look of incredulity comes as no surprise. She's seen it countless times before.

"No discount?"

June shakes her head. Again the woman looks disapprovingly at her and so it goes with each remaining item and then each item in the next woman's pile and the next's until they finally walk away in disgust, chattering among themselves and leaving the pile of rumpled clothes on the counter for her to refold. The sad and maddening thing is that with the value of the Yuan versus the dollar, even had they paid full-price for the merchandise it still would have been a bargain for them. So, this is America now, this is what we've come to, the world's bargain basement. She knows it's no one person's fault, that everyone caused it to happen as the result of stupidity, selfishness and greed and it's a bitter lesson, but she's not confident that anyone's really learned anything from it or that anything's going to change anytime soon and she suspects most people in the country feel the same way she does. The people she feels sorriest for are Trey and Kim and their generation. It's going to be up to them to clean up the mess they've been left. Some legacy.

She picks up a sweater to refold. At least Tammy stuck to her plan. She went to Cal State Fullerton and became a licensed RN and got a job at Children's Hospital Orange County in Newport Beach where she's been working ever since. It's not that June changed her mind about wanting to be a nurse. When she began working at Macy's, her intention was to work there until she established residency, but eight months later she was pregnant with Trey and she put nursing school on the back burner. Then Kim came along and nursing school sort of fell off the back of the stove somewhere. She tells herself it was just life happening, but remembers the feeling of giving up her dream. She didn't want to, but couldn't help it and didn't know why she was and didn't like watching it slip away and she doesn't blame anyone but herself. Art kept encouraging her to apply to nursing school and was perfectly willing to bear more than his fair share of the parenting responsibilities, but she just kept putting it off and putting it off until finally there was no more discussion about it. She went back to Macy's when Kim was old enough for day care and she's been stuck here ever since. It's an okay company and her co-workers are nice enough, although the topics of conversation never seem to change and the talk is pretty shallow, the type of idle chitchat people engage in just to kill time and get through another day.

Of all the things she misses about Art, that's what she misses most: their conversations. They could talk forever about anything and not just when they were stoned. For a guy who didn't go to college, Art knows a hell of a lot about a hell of a lot. It's surprising how much he knows. Well, maybe not so surprising, given how much he reads. He always had a pile of books on the nightstand, biographies and books about history and mathematics, his passion, and they used to read together in bed and she could tell by the way he'd say, "Huh…," that something he was reading had really captured his interest and she could count the seconds until he'd say, "Get this," and put the book face down on his stomach and explain to her whatever it was he'd found so interesting. He always made it interesting to her and she wonders why he doesn't just teach because he'd be a great teacher.

When he was working and the money was coming in he could deal with the fact that his father felt he was a big disappointment, which she the first time she met Arthur senior. She could see Art and his father were engaged in high-level psychological warfare. It was fascinating to watch and Art held his own pretty well, but she felt sorry for him, sorry that he had to deal with a father like that. It seemed to her that she and Art could weather just about any crisis, but she was totally unprepared for what happened to him when he lost his job and couldn't find work. Day by day she saw the self-confidence draining out of him and she tried to be encouraging and supportive but it didn't do much good. He began hanging out with his buddies at that bar in Westminster and coming home later and later, always drunk, and she hated to keep after him to ask his father for financial assistance — she knew her parents' and April and Jack's financial situations, so she didn't bother to ask them — but she was desperate and he finally did and she could tell that in doing so he felt his father had won the war, that he'd been right all along about his being a failure. A part of him was broken and he wasn't the same Art after that. He was some other Art, an Art she didn't know and didn't find very attractive and didn't feel close or connected to.

It was this other Art who decided to get back at his father by fucking his wife. She was shocked when Arthur called to tell her about it and her anger when she confronted Art about it surprised her more than it did him. She found herself verging on violence and she shouldn't have said the things she did to him, screaming with the kids in the house.

After he left and the bank foreclosed she and the kids stayed in the house until a man showed up one day and said he'd bought the house at auction and showed her the paperword to prove it. He said he felt sorry for them and would give them a week to leave, but that if they weren't out in a week he'd have the sheriff evict them.

Eileen would have taken them in, but June was so furious with Art and distraught about her situation that she wasn't thinking straight and couldn't bring herself to call her. Asking Eileen to take them in seemed like making her pay for Art's mistakes and making her do that seemed as unfair to June as the bank foreclosing on them. She didn't even bother calling Tammy, who lives in a one-bedroom apartment. Instead she called the people at the rescue mission and they took them in.

The other residents were nice and the people who run the place are very compassionate and understanding, which made living there bearable and Trey and Kim took it in stride.

Walt came up to her at work a few of months later with a bunch of black socks and three packs each of white extra large V-neck tee shirts and boxer shorts and asked if she could ring them up. They got talking and he seemed like a nice guy, very soft-spoken for such a big man. He was handsome with chiseled features and in good shape. She noticed him glancing at her bare ring finger – she was so angry with Art that she removed her wedding band when he left – and he asked if she were married or dating someone and she lied and said she wasn't and he asked her out on a date. She knew he had romantic intentions, but romance was the farthest thing from her mind. She felt lost and wanted companionship.

She met him at the restaurant. She didn't share much about herself with him, other than that she had two kids. She learned that he'd been in the Army and served in Iraq and then Afghanistan and was a mortician and divorced and lived with his teenage daughter in his home in Costa Mesa. Hearing this her immediate thought was that with only Walt and his daughter in the house, there was probably a spare bedroom the kids could share and if she had to sleep with him, so be it. She'd had enough of the shelter.

Then on one of their dates he shared with her that he didn't like living alone, that he'd much prefer having a partner and asked how she felt about it? She considered her answer carefully. In fact, she was fine with living alone, just not at the shelter and as far as having a partner was concerned, where had that gotten her? She knew Walt wanted her to move in with him and her only reason for doing so would be to get herself and the kids out of the shelter. She felt that if she were going to, though, he should know about Art and losing the house and staying at the shelter because he'd find out sooner or later. So, she said she didn't like living alone, either, and also preferred having a partner and told him the story. He was very sympathetic about her situation and said there was a bedroom her kids could use and she felt relieved, but it wasn't long after they moved in that he began acting like he he was doing them an enormous favor letting them live in his house.

Her dad used to joke that he always wanted daughters but knew that girls could be difficult and the only reason she was so easy — one out of two wasn't bad — was that he'd made a deal with the Devil when she was born and that he'd be spending a fiery eternity in his skivvies as his part of the bargain. Now she knows what the real deal feels like and it's no joke.

"Hey," she hears Art say and looks up from her folding to see him standing in front of the counter with a bandage on his left cheek and his right hand in finger splints and also bandaged. She reaches out instinctively to touch his cheek but catches herself and puts her hand to her mouth. "Oh, my God! What happened to you?" Art looks just like a guilty kid who's misbehaved and is waiting to receive the scolding he knows he deserves.

"Long story."

"Were you in an accident?"

"Yeah, sort of." He fidgets with the price tag on one of the unfolded sweaters. "Listen, I'm not so sure it's a good idea to take the kids Saturday."

"Why?"

"I don't want them to see me looking like this. I look like hell."

She shrugs. "They've seen you in a lot worse shape."

He knows she meant this as a simple statement of fact and it's true, but it hurts all the same. "I was gonna take them to Trestles."

"So take them! They can surf and you can get some color. You can use it." She picks up another sweater to fold. "Are you working?"

"Bud's got something coming up, a teardown in Corona Del Mar. Some people still have money."

"Good. They can spread it around."

He picks up a rumpled sweater from the pile and lays it flat on the counter and begins folding it, keeping his eyes on it. "I'm thinking of going back to school and getting my teacher certification," he says and knows she's looking at him. "I spoke with Mom about it. She's willing to help financially but I don't want to burden her. I might talk with Dad. He'd love having that conversation."

June stares wide-eyed at him. He said this so casually, but what she's just heard is important. It's the most important thing she's heard him say in a long time. She knows what it means to him to have to go back to his father and ask for money, especially after everything that's happened between them, and she knows Art's waiting to hear what she thinks about the idea and that he wants and needs her approval and encouragement. "It's a good idea," she says softly. "It can't hurt."

"No, it can't. Anyway, it's worth a try." He places the folded sweater on her pile. "So, there you go." He looks up at her and sees her looking at him curiously, like she's trying to figure out which Art is the one standing here in front of her. He can't blame her for wondering. "Who was that guy who helped you with Trey's cotillion clothes?"

"Henry, at Brooks Brothers."

"Maybe I'll pay him a visit. I can use some new clothes. How's everything with you?"

She shrugs and looks down at the sweater and continues folding it. "Same old."

He hates seeing her this way, sounding so defeated and looking like she's out of dreams and hope and resigned to a life that isn't going to get better. "See you Saturday," he says.

She glances up at him. "Yeah," she says and looks back down at the sweater.

Art eyes the dangling sheep above the entrance to Brooks Brothers and is reminded of his childhood in Cambridge when his father was teaching economics at MIT's Sloane School and would take him on the occasional trip across the Charles River to Brooks Brothers on Newbury Street in Boston's Back Bay to replenish his supply of button-down dress shirts, which is all he wears to this day: solid white and solid light blue and dark blue hounds tooth check, worn open collar. It's comforting to know that after all these years and despite all the tumultuous events that have occurred and are still unfolding you can still walk into Brooks Brothers and buy the same button-down shirts his father did forty years ago. His first special occasion outfit, a navy blue blazer and light gray trousers and black penny loafers, was purchased at the Newbury Street store. How old was he then? Twelve? He got a lot of wear out of it until he finally outgrew it and then they moved to Southern California and he gravitated toward surf culture and that was the end of Brooks

Brothers clothes for him. This is the first time he's set foot in the store at South Coast Plaza, but the wall of neatly stacked dress shirts and the tables with piles of neatly folded dress trousers and the racks of sport coats and suits are all familiar to him and a part of him feels right at home. A young woman walks up to him eyeing his bandaged cheek and hand.

"May I help you?" she asks uncertainly.

"Is Henry here?"

She nods toward the rear of the store. "Older man with short graying hair."

Art finds him going through the suits hanging on the rack, checking them for size and putting any that have been misplaced back where they belong. Henry turns and takes him in at a glance. Art can imagine the impression he's making, his bandaged cheek and hand aside, sartorially: cheap Hawaiian print shirt, faded and worn jeans and flip-flops, none of it Brooks Brothers. "Henry?"

Henry smiles warmly and shakes his hand. "Yes. What can I do for you?"

"Art. I need a make over."

"What do you have in mind?"

"Not sure. I don't really need a suit."

"Sport coat? Nice shirt and trousers? That sort of thing?"

"Yeah, I guess so."

Henry lays out a couple of sport coat and trouser combinations, placing shirts and ties with them. He studies Art's face as he inspects them. The clothes seem to remind him of something, but he can't tell from Art's expression if the memory is a pleasant or unpleasant one. "Have you shopped at Brooks Brothers before?"

"Long time ago, when I was a kid, with my father, in Boston, before we moved here."

"What's his name?"

"Arthur Hollinswood."

"Ah!" The last time Henry saw Arthur was when he and his young Southern bride-to-be Landis visited the store to order a suit for the wedding. They struck him as a most unlikely couple and having spent an hour or so with them he was left with the feeling that the marriage would neither last long nor end well. "He's a customer of mine. Give him my best when you see him."

"I will. We don't see each other that often."

Henry can tell by Art's tone of voice that there's a story there and definitely not a pleasant one.

"You know my wife June, at Macy's."

"Yes!" Henry wonders how June's doing with that big guy — what's his name? Ah, yes, Walt. He glances down at Art's wedding band. So, they're still married. Interesting. "I helped her with your son's cotillion outfit. Trey, right?"

"Good memory."

"Nice kid. How's he doing with cotillion? Enjoying it?"

Art shrugs. "As far as I can tell." He fingers the "40% Off" tag attached to the sleeve of one of the sport coats and notices the others have the same tag on the sleeves and he knows that's why Henry selected them. Given his appearance, Henry probably assumes he doesn't have a lot of money to spend on clothes and he's right. "Nice discount."

"The shirts and trousers are on sale too," Henry says.

Art glances at him and looks down at the outfits. "Do you have these in my size?"

"They are your size: 40 Regular coat; $15^{1/2}/33$ shirt; 35 waist trouser."

"Last time I checked I was a 33."

Henry smiles. "I'm sure you were. Which would you like to try on?"

Art points at the tan sport coat, navy blue pants and white with blue stripe button-down shirt combination.

"Good choice," Henry says. "It's a smart-looking outfit." He gathers up the clothes and escorts Art to a dressing room and calls the tailor shop.

Art studies himself in the three-way mirror and he has to admit that, bandages and all, he looks pretty good in the clothes. He may be a fuck up, but he's at least a well-dressed one. There's a difference and he can feel it. Of course, the sleeves of the coat need to be shortened a bit and the trousers hemmed, as Henry told him they would, but it's spooky how well everything fits without Henry having measured him. He figures if you spend as much time sizing people up as he does, you get to the point where you don't have to measure them. The guy's good. He looks at Henry in the mirror, standing behind him by the counter with an alteration ticket in hand as they wait for the tailor and notices he isn't wearing a wedding band. "Ever been married?" Art asks.

Henry nods.

"Just didn't work out?"

"I used to tell myself that. Things usually don't work out for a reason. I was it. I think I'm better off alone."

Art looks at his bandaged cheek and hand and hair, which needs cutting, and eyes, which look bloodshot, and the skin beneath them, which looks puffy. There's his reason and, unlike

Henry, he's definitely not better off alone. In fact, left to his own devices he's been doing a pretty good job of destroying himself. The tailor arrives and comments on how well everything fits and marks up the clothing and leaves and Art turns to Henry and grins. "That was easy."

Henry smiles. "It always is when you begin with a good fit, just like with relationships. That 'good fit' part can be tricky, though. You and June still on good terms?"

"Yeah."

"Still love her?"

"Yeah."

Henry raises his eyebrows. "Going to try to win her back?"

"Yeah."

"Good for you! I admire you. It takes courage."

Art heads to the dressing room to change. Joanne telling him he's handsome, June clearly impressed that he would put aside his pride and ask his father for help, Henry telling him he admires him — He thinks of where he was when he was sitting in the park lot behind the XXXotic, having been roughed up and run over, and where he is now and thinks that maybe, just maybe things are moving in the right direction.

Art earmarks the page and puts the biography of Tycho Brahe down on the blanket and looks out at Uppers, the best break today at Trestles. He spots Trey up on his board riding in and then Kim lying flat on hers paddling back out. There's something endearing to him about Brahe, the Sixteenth century Danish nobleman astronomer who made the most accurate and comprehensive astronomical and planetary observations in his time, using really only the naked eye. Sure, he built large astronomical instruments to assist him in his measurements, but the telescope hadn't been invented yet. It wouldn't appear until a couple of years after his death in 1601.

Brahe was good, but despite his extensive observations and precise measurements and the attempts on the part of his assistant Johannes Kepler to persuade him otherwise, he held stubbornly to his belief that the sun orbited the earth, believing that the earth was just too sluggish to be continuously in motion. He went to his grave satisfied that he was right.

We see what we want to see and overlook the obvious, as he knows from his own experience. He used to believe that the world revolved around him when, really, he's spent his entire life orbiting his father, negotiating his way around him. He believed stubbornly that he knew better than his father and that the path he'd chosen was the right one. His desire to prove his father wrong made him blind to the fact that he was putting his family at financial risk and to what it was doing to June. He saw what he wanted to see.

Why is he so concerned about his father's approval and love? Where is it written that his father has to love him? Why should he? For as long as he can remember, certainly since he was thirteen or fourteen, when his father cooled noticeably toward his mom, he's done nothing but spite him, deliberately disregarding his advice and seizing every opportunity to disappoint and humiliate him. Fucking Landis was simply the icing on the cake. How would he feel if Trey treated him that way?

He sees Trey paddling back out and Kim timing the wave over her shoulder and then paddling quickly to get herself into position and now she's up and gliding across the face of the wave, just outrunning the curl. He smiles. She's good. They both are. He taught them well and instilled in them a love of surfing and it's a love that binds the three of them together. There's nothing like that between him and his father. Sure, they both love to read and they both love science and mathematics, but those are things they enjoy by themselves in their own separate worlds. It's not like they get together to have a few beers and discuss String Theory, although they used to talk when he was younger.

He was mystified when he was kid by how scientific discoveries are made and remembers having a conversation with his father about Watson and Crick and their discovery of the double helix. His father said you have to have the proper frame of mind, a mixture of intellectual curiosity and rigor and, above all, the ability to recognize the truth when you see it and not let preconceived notions get in the way. "As they say in ballet and yoga," his father said, "'it's okay to hold a pose, until it hurts.'" He touches the scab on the still tender wound on his cheek. Shit if his father isn't right. Something Henry said about relationships comes to mind, a lesson he said he learned too late: "You can be happy or you can be right." Shit if Henry isn't right too.

He watches Trey come running toward him with his board, making his way around the sunbathing couples and families gathered under umbrellas.

Trey plop himself down on the blanket.

"Drink?" Art asks.

"Sure."

Art takes a sports drink from the cooler and holds it out to him and watches him unscrew the cap and take a long sip. "So, how's it going, buddy? Everything okay?"

Trey shrugs in a way he knows his dad understands means there's a lot going on in his life and he's not sure he wants to talk about it right now.

"Hey, I saw Henry at Brooks Brothers. He asked after you."

Trey glances at his dad. "Yeah?"

"Nice guy. He asked how cotillion's going. I said I think you like it."

"It's okay."

"How're the kids?"

"Okay."

"Know any of them?"

Trey shakes his head. "Well, one person, sort of."

"From school?"

Trey nods.

"Guy? Girl?"

"Emily."

"What's she like?"

"Shy. I don't think she has any friends."

"Cute?"

"Yeah, especially when she blushes." Trey glances at his dad's bandaged hand and the scar on his cheek and looks out at Kim. He didn't buy the story about an accident on the job. His dad's really careful and he's never been injured at work. It's possible, of course, but he can't see how trying to catch a falling 4x4 could have resulted in those two injuries. It just doesn't make sense. "So what really happened? How'd you get hurt?"

"In a fight."

Trey looks skeptically at his dad. He tries to imagine him in a fight but can't see it. His dad's such a laid-back soft-spoken person. Even when things were really bad between his dad and mom and they'd argue, his dad never raised his voice and when they had that last argument, when his mom was screaming at him, the only voice he heard was hers. "Who with?"

"With whom," Art says and grins as Trey rolls his eyes, which he always does when he corrects his grammar.

"Whatever."

"Some woman's boyfriend."

"Why?"

"She's his girlfriend."

Trey glances at his dad's cheek and hand again.

"He had a knife and ran over my hand. I think he wanted to run me over but I got out of the way in time, mostly."

Trey stares wide-eyed at his dad. With those few details he can picture the scene, but still has a hard time seeing his dad in it. "Who is she?"

"Just someone I know."

"Do you have a girlfriend?" Trey asks, hoping to hear no.

"No."

Trey believes him. He knows how his dad feels about his mom. He can see it in his eyes whenever he comes to pick him and Kim up or drop them off and he and his mom are together talking. He's not so sure how his mom feels, though. He thinks she still loves his dad, but she's harder to read. "Do you love Mom?"

"Yeah."

"Why don't you get back together?"

"It's not that simple."

"Because we're at Walt's?"

"There's that, but there's more to it."

"Like what?"

"I'm not so sure Mom wants to get back together."

Trey looks out at Kim again and sees her cut back nicely across the face of the wave and duck as she enters the curl and then cut back again. It's a difficult move. Compared with that their parents getting back together seems pretty easy. He looks at his dad. "Why don't you ask her?"

Art grins. "Maybe I will."

Trey searches for Emily in the crowded hall on his way to science lab. They never have time to do more than stop briefly and say hi to each other, but he enjoys seeing her and knows by the way her expression brightens when she sees him that she enjoys seeing him. They've become pretty good friends. He figures he's the best friend she has at school, maybe outside school too. Just when he's beginning to think she stayed home sick today he sees her down the hall, walking toward him slowly with her head down and hugging her books to her chest and she looks really upset about something. He stops in front of her and sees her looking at him with an expression that's a mixture of guilt and shame. "Hey, what's up?"

"I can't talk now," Emily says and looks down at her shoes. "I'll see you at cotillion."

"Sure," he says and steps aside to let her pass and watches her walk off down the hall with her head down.

It seems they've been practicing this waltz routine forever and Trey's not paying much attention to his partner but keeps glancing over her shoulder at Emily, who's paired up with another boy and he sees her doing the same thing, glancing over her partner's shoulder at him. He knows that, like him, all she's thinking about is being done with cotillion for the evening so they can spend the last fifteen or so minutes together while they wait for their moms to arrive to pick them up. She looks in better shape than she did this afternoon, but he can see she's just pretending to be composed. Finally the music ends and Missus Pantages thanks everyone for coming and he walks over to Emily and they move away from the other kids. "So what happened?"

"You know Kurt, in Mr. Broussard's home room?"

"Yeah." He knows Kurt, all right. He's a jerk, big for his age and a real bully who likes to throw his weight around and enjoys picking fights with smaller boys. He was suspended earlier in the year for sending a kid to the hospital to get his lip stitched up. He keeps as much distance between himself and Kurt as he can. He sees that expression of guilt and shame again and can't wait to hear what it has to do with Kurt.

"I went to the movies with him Saturday afternoon," Emily says and sees Trey's disappointment and quickly adds, "He's friends with my friend Allison's boyfriend. She asked me to come with them so her mom would let them go. She said her mom wouldn't let the two of them go alone."

"Whatever. So what happened?"

"There were hardly any people in the theater and Allison said she and her boyfriend were going to sit by themselves, if that was okay, and I said sure. I mean, what else could I do? She just left me there with him."

"And?"

"We watched the movie a while and then he put his arm around me. I asked him to take it away but he didn't. And then he started feeling me up and I told him to stop and that if he didn't I was going to leave, but he wouldn't let me go and I didn't want to make a scene, so I just sat there and let him touch me. And he didn't stop with my boobs, either. It was awful." She searches Trey's eyes for some sign of sympathy and understanding and not seeing any looks down at her shoes. "He told me not to tell anyone. He said I'd be sorry if I did."

Great. So she tells him. How stupid could she be? What did she expect? She got what she deserved. He knows being angry with her and blaming her is wrong. If he's afraid of Kurt, how must she have felt?

Emily looks up pleadingly at Trey. "You're the only person I could tell. I knew you'd understand."

He's trying to. It isn't easy, but he's trying. He notices parents arriving and sees his mom enter the room and then Emily's mom a few parents behind her with that phony smile on her face. When their moms first met they were friendly toward each other, but lately Emily's mom seems standoffish and he doesn't know why and he's pretty sure his mom doesn't, either, and if his mom's bothered by it, she doesn't let it show.

June walks up to them and smiles at Emily, who's looking down at her shoes. "Hi, Emily," she says brightly.

Emily forces herself to look up at her but has a hard time looking in her eyes. "Hi, Missus Hollinswood."

"You're looking beautiful, as always."

"Thank you," Emily says weakly. She feels awful. Trey's mom is always so nice to her, always complimenting her like this. She's pretty sure Trey and his mom don't know that her mom snooped on them. She hates her mom for what she did and doesn't know what she'd do if Trey and his mom should find out. She already feels guilty and ashamed because of what happened with Kurt. She can't imagine how she'd feel if that happened. "Let's go, Emily," she hears her mom say and turns and follows her toward the door and looks back over her shoulder at Trey. "See you tomorrow."

"Yeah." There's something going on between Emily and her mom. He doesn't know what, but he knows there is and he can see what it's doing to her.

June pulls into Walt's driveway and stops. "Emily's always so sweet. She didn't seem herself this evening. Is anything wrong?"

"Yeah, her mom," Trey says and stares at the garage door. "Do you miss Dad?"

June reaches up and presses the button on the garage door opener and sits back with her hands in her lap and looks at him. "Why do you ask?"

"He misses you."

"Did he tell you that?"

Trey nods and watches the garage door disappear into the track in the ceiling. The garage light is on and there's Walt's black SUV and there's the empty space next to it where his mom parks her car. It all seems so homey, but it doesn't feel homey at all. Every time she pulls in and the garage door closes behind them he feels like he's back in prison. Maybe a little less so since things changed between him and Julie, but not much.

"Sure I do, honey," June says to make him feel better. She knows he and Kim want their parents back together, but she's not sure if she wants Art any closer to her than he is now.

Trey looks at her. "You guys should get back together," he says and keeps looking at her until she looks away. He looks back at the empty space next to Walt's SUV. He hears his mom sigh and she noses the car into the garage and reaches up and presses the button on the remote and he listens to the garage door begin clattering loudly overhead as it closes behind them, sealing them in.

The way Kurt's coming at him in the hall with a buddy on either side, Trey knows, the way he just knows these things that they're on a collision course. Each time he makes a small adjustment to pass to the side of the three of them they counter to keep him squarely dead ahead. What he should do is just move to the side and stop and let them pass, but it's too late for that now and the three bear down on him and the next thing he knows he's bouncing off the lockers and then lying flat on his back on the floor looking up at Kurt, who's scowling down at him.

"Watch where you're going, asshole," Kurt says, "and tell your friend to keep her big fucking mouth shut."

Trey watches them walk off down the hall. No one, of course, comes to his assistance. In fact, it's as if he doesn't exist. He gets unsteadily to his feet and looks around. Where the fuck's the hall monitor and what the fuck's with Emily? Some friend she is.

All day his mind is focused on meeting her in the hall at room change. He's still smarting from his encounter with Kurt. He doesn't think his shoulder is dislocated but it sure feels like it is. Finally she's in front of him, hugging her books to her chest and looking down at her shoes. "How'd he find out?" he asks.

Emily looks up at him on the verge of tears. "Kurt bragged to Allison's boyfriend about what he did and her boyfriend told her and she asked me if I were going to tell anyone and I said no, that I only told you because you're my best friend and I trust you. She must have told her boyfriend and he must have told Kurt. I knew I shouldn't have told her. I'm sorry."

Trey stares at her and shakes his head and walks away and makes a mental note to be very careful about trusting anyone from now on, no matter how close a friend she seems to be.

CHAPTER 6

Brett takes a square white envelope out of his backpack and hands it across the aisle.

"What's this?" Trey asks.

"Dude, your invitation!"

Trey looks at the front of the envelope and sees it's addressed to him with a stamp in the upper right corner.

Brett shrugs. "I told my mom not to bother with the stamps."

Trey opens the envelope and removes a stiff white card and reads what's printed on it in raised black letters. He's cordially invited to celebrate Brett's sixteenth birthday and join him for a day of fun at Six Flags Magic Mountain. He can bring a friend and transportation will be provided. "Holy shit!"

Brett grins. "I told you."

It was months ago that Brett first told him he was planning a killer sixteenth birthday party and that his parents were down with it, but then a long time passed without Brett mentioning it and he figured it was because the party wasn't going to happen, but now here's the invitation and it's for real. "Outstanding!"

Trey says and sees Brett smirk, not the way Julie does, but a friendly smirk.

"Gonna bring Emily?" Brett asks.

Trey looks back down at the invitation. "Yeah, I guess," he says, but he's not sure about Emily. Her situation just seems to keep getting worse. He'll ask her, of course, she's the only girl he can think of to ask. He puts the invitation in his backpack and thinks about his and Brett's friendship and how they both benefited from Brett's bad luck.

Brett was a grade ahead of him at school. The summer before last he went off to camp in Maine and got really sick. Trey can't remember the name of the place, Winny-Wonga-Minny-Tonga, something Indian-sounding like that. They thought Brett had a really bad case of the flu, but the camp nurse recognized his symptoms – the rash on his feet, his sensitivity to light and sound – and had him taken to the hospital where they did tests and determined he had spinal meningitis. They pumped him full of antibiotics and actually had to put him in a coma so his body could fight the disease. According to Brett, at one point his heart stopped and they had a hard time getting it started again. They ended up having to amputate a few fingers from his right hand and his right foot below the knee, but he pulled through and didn't suffer any brain damage, at least, Brett likes to joke, none that anyone can notice. Still, he required so much physical therapy that his parents decided to keep him out of school for a year and that's how he and Brett ended up in the same homeroom sitting across the aisle from each other and became good friends. Brett told him he really didn't have any good friends before. He's kind of a loner to begin with and a geek who loves writing computer programs and while everybody loved playing the games he created, no one wanted to hang with him. The other good thing that happened as a result of Brett's missing a year is that he met Tracy.

Trey's known her longer than Brett, since third grade. Tracy's always been smart, but she wasn't much to look at back then. Over the last few years she's changed a lot and now she's pretty hot and her IQ is way up there in the genius range. She's on track to graduate a year ahead of them and plans to go to Stanford or MIT. Brett plans to go to whichever school Tracy does and he won't have any problem getting in, either. They're both really smart and they both share the same wicked sense of humor, which makes hanging with them a lot of fun. This outing at Six Flags should be a blast and Trey's looking forward to telling Emily about it. He's never invited anyone on a date before and as first dates go, this one should really be something.

Emily stares wide-eyed at the invitation. "Wow! I'd love to go! I'll have to check with my parents. I can't see why they wouldn't let me go. I'll let you know tomorrow."

"Sure," Trey says. She holds out the invitation to him and he holds up his hand. "Keep it and show it to them, just so they know it's for real."

"Good idea," Emily says, nodding. "Thanks! See ya!"

He watches her walk off down the hall and look back at him over her shoulder, smiling and waving the invitation in the air. Why wouldn't they let her go?

It's another afternoon arriving home from school that feels like he's the only one in the house. He knows Kim's at soccer and his mom and Walt are at work, but he's never quite sure about Julie. Sometimes she hangs with her boyfriend after school, at least that what she says she does, and sometimes not.

If he were Walt, he'd make her get a part-time job after school like most everyone else her age, although jobs are hard to find these days. Still, he'd make her do something other than sit in her room all afternoon painting her nails. On the other hand, he has to admit that it's fun playing this game they have going and it's gotten a lot more interesting. She lets him fondle her tits and stroke her between the legs now and he knows just how to do it to make her come and he's still amazed at that sound she makes when she does and wonders if the neighbors can hear her. She still acts like she's doing him a big favor letting him play with her body, but he knows she enjoys it as much as he does and looks forward to it and even prepares herself for him now with a flowery fragrance. It's a great game of pretend and he isn't going to be the one to spoil it. He walks down the hall and sees the door to her bedroom is ajar, which is the way she leaves it now when she wants him to know she's home. He stops and opens the door a little wider and sees her sitting on her bed pointing what looks like a real gun at him.

"Bang!" Julie shouts.

He's on the floor with his arms covering his head, relieved that she was only messing with him, but pissed that she's laughing hysterically. He uncovers his head and looks up at her. "You stupid bitch!" he yells and gets to his feet and walks toward her as she smirks and points the gun at him again. He sees it's a real gun, all right.

"Scared the shit out of you didn't I!" she says, looking smug.

He pushes the gun aside. "Don't point that at me. Where the fuck did you get that?"

"It's my dad's. He keeps it in his nightstand." She picks up one of the bullets from beside her on the bed and holds it up. "It's empty. See?"

He slaps her hard – he's surprised how hard – and knocks her off the bed onto the floor. She loses her grip on the gun as she covers her head with her arms and he picks it up. She tries to get up, but he hovers over her and slaps her hard again and again each time she tries to get up and she finally stops trying and turns her head cautiously to the side to look up at him. He straddles her and points the gun at her head and he's beyond angry now, he could kill her. He presses the barrel to her forehead. "Fuck with me again and I'll make sure it's loaded and blow your brains out! Understand?" He sees a flash of defiance in her eyes and presses the barrel harder against her forehead and the defiance gives way to fear and her eyes fill with tears. "Do you?"

She closes her eyes and sniffs and nods.

He finally has her right where he wants her, cowering on the floor at his feet. Just for good measure he pulls the trigger and her body jerks at the sound of the click. It's confusing, though, because while he's relishing the moment, he's also disappointed in her for having pulled this stupid stunt on him. He thought they'd arrived at a new place in their relationship and was beginning to really like her.

He has a bad feeling about the fact that Julie hasn't appeared at the dinner table. She's been in her room with the door closed all afternoon and Walt's called her a couple of times and now he's standing in the dining room doorway and clearly losing his temper.

"Julie!" Walt calls. "Get in here! Dinner's getting cold!"

Trey looks up at Julie as she enters the dining room and sees the bruise on her left cheek. He glances at Walt and sees him staring at Julie's cheek as she sits at the table.

"What happened to you?" Walt asks.

Julie picks up one of the serving dishes and glances at Trey as she puts a slice of roast beef on her plate. "I got hit with a medicine ball in gym class."

Trey glances at Walt and sees he's not buying the story and looks back at Julie and sees she's keeping her eyes on her plate.

"You what?" Walt asks.

Julie shrugs. "I wasn't looking," she says without looking up.

Trey glances at Walt again and sees him staring at her in disbelief and doesn't seem to know what to say.

"How the hell…?"

Trey feels uneasy and he's relieved to see Walt's appetite finally win out over his curiosity. Julie's keeping her eyes down as she eats and Trey can't quite read her expression. She doesn't look angry or hurt. She looks like she has a lot on her mind and is thinking things through. He's thankful she covered for him, although she probably did to save her own skin. She'd get shit from Walt if he found out she was playing with his gun. Trey has the feeling their relationship is about to change again, but no feel for how.

Emily turns the corner at the other end of the hall and even at a distance he can see her glum expression and knows she's not going. She hands him the invitation and looks down at her shoes.

"I can't go," Emily says weakly.

"Why not?"

She shrugs.

"It's a birthday party. Brett's parents will be there." He feels foolish trying to reason with her. It's just like her parents to prevent her from having a good time for no reason at all. She looks up at him and he sees that same expression of guilt and shame he saw about Kurt. "You mean they won't let you to go with me. That's it, isn't it?" He sees she's reluctant to answer. "Isn't it?"

"I guess," she finally says.

"Why? What have they got against me?" He sees she's having a hard time getting whatever it is she has to say out.

"They know you stayed in a homeless shelter," she finally says.

How the fuck did her parents find out about that? "We lost our house," he says angrily. "We needed a place to stay. That's what it's there for." It dawns on him that Emily's mom works in the school district administration and has access to student records. It isn't right that she shared his personal information with Emily, but what's he going to do about it?

Emily looks back down at her shoes. "I'm sorry."

Trey watches her walk off slowly down the hall. She should be sorry, but he feels sorrier for her. It's shameful what her parents are doing to her and pathetic that she seems powerless to do anything about it.

Brett narrows his eyes and shakes his head. "Dude, that's totally illegal."

"Yeah, whatever." Trey gazes out the window. As angry as he is about it, he can't blame Emily. It wasn't her fault. It's her snoopy mother's fault.

"Anyone else you can ask?"

"I'll think about it." The only other girl Trey knows that he could ask is Julie and he's not at all sure she'd agree to go with him, but he figures it's worth a try. Going to the party alone would definitely suck.

He isn't sure if Julie's home and sees her door is closed and knocks lightly on it. "Yeah?" he hears and opens the door just enough to see her sitting on the bed painting her toenails, as usual. "Hey," he says stepping into the room.

"Whaddya want?" she asks without looking up.

"My friend Brett's having his birthday party at Six Flags on Saturday. Should be fun. Wanna go?"

She glances up at him and looks back down at her toenails. "Can't find a date?"

"My friend's parents won't let her go."

"Why?"

"They think we're trash because we stayed in the shelter."

She looks up at him. "Ouch."

"Yeah. Whatever. Anyway, do you?"

She looks down at her toenails and shrugs. "Sure. Why not?"

He takes off his backpack and puts it on the floor and walks over to the bed and sits next to her. "Listen, I'm sorry I hit you."

"Don't be. I deserved it. So what's up with your girlfriend?"

"Her mother's a jerk."

"So? She can't stick up for herself?"

"It's not so easy." He wants to point out that Julie's living pretty much under Walt's thumb but doesn't.

"I guess not." She wiggles her toes. "Like the color?"

"Yeah." What does it remind him of? He can't put his finger on it, but it's something good. "What's it called?"

"'Sinful Cinnamon.'"

That's it, cinnamon. Who comes up with these names?

"So," she asks and rests her chin on her knee and looks at him, "how should I look?"

"I dunno. However you want."

"Do you want me to look hot? Do you want to impress your friends?"

"I don't need to impress anyone."

She searches his eyes a moment and looks back down at her toenails. "I'll think of something."

Julie finally makes her entrance in the kitchen and Trey's impressed. He glances at his mom and Kim and sees they are too. Julie's struck the perfect balance with her clothes and makeup. She looks hot, all right, tastefully so and he knows exactly what the boys' reaction will be when they see her. They'll wish she were their date.

"You look beautiful, Julie!" June says, smiling.

The compliment delights Julie and she feels herself blush. She spends so much time on her appearance trying to make herself look as attractive as possible, hoping to be complimented, but no one has until now. She smiles sweetly at June. "Thanks."

It's the first time Trey's seen Julie blush and her sweet smile. She's like a different person. He glances at Walt and sees him looking at Julie with narrowed eyes and it's clear Walt's not at all happy about sending his daughter off on a date with him. Julie said her dad would need convincing, but not to worry, that it wouldn't be a problem and she was right. She definitely knows what she's doing when it comes to getting her way with her father.

Walt jiggles his keys impatiently. "Let's go."

The boy's reaction to Julie is just what Trey predicted. He sees envy in their expressions and resentment in the girls', but Julie smiles that sweet smile of hers and introduces herself to everyone and acts like she's everyone's best friend and gradually puts them all, and especially the girls, at ease and she and Tracy are chatting away like new best friends and he's impressed by how smoothly she's handling the situation. It's a side of her he hasn't seen before and it makes him feel proud to be with her.

They climb into the bus and Trey and Julie and Brett and Tracy make their way to the back seat. Julie and Tracy sit next to each and immediately continue their conversation and Trey sits beside Julie and Brett beside Tracy. The driver plugs in the iPod Brett gave him with a compilation of his favorite road songs and AC/DC's *It's A Long Way To The Top If You Want To Rock And Roll* begins blasting out of the speakers and off they go north on the 55 to the 5 north toward Los Angeles and on up into the hills north of the city toward Valencia.

Julie and Tracy have been chatting non-stop and Trey's been content watching the scenery go by. Julie's turned toward Tracy and the thing he finds really interesting is that she's been holding his hand the entire time and seems to be enjoying doing so and every now and then when too much time has gone by without her having paid any attention to him, she's given his hand a squeeze and turned toward him and smiled sweetly, just to let him know she hasn't forgotten him, and then turned back toward Tracy and he's been totally cool with that. It feels like the most natural thing in the world, like they've known each other forever and have the confidence to be able to pay attention to other people and not say anything at all to each other and still feel completely connected. It's the first time he's experenced it with anyone and it feels great.

He sees yet another side of her at Six Flags. She insists on going on only the max rides, the most heart-stopping and stomach-dropping, of which there are plenty, yet she's absolutely terrified from the moment the ride begins until the moment it ends. They go on as many of them as they can and each time it's the same. She screams the entire time and when the ride finally ends throws back her head and laughs and can't wait to go on the next one. The rides are pretty terrifying to him too but seem so much more so to her that he feels the need to not let his fear show and tries his best to hide it. He thinks he knows why she enjoys these rides so much. He's pretty sure it's because of all the years spent living cooped up with her tight-ass controlling father who doesn't encourage her to do anything or make anything of herself, which is why she spends so much time in her room painting her nails. He knows she's longing to be free of Walt and is biding her time until she graduates from high school, when she says she plans to go to college and move out. As terrifying as the rides are to her, they seem to make her feel truly alive and free.

By the time everyone climbs back into the bus for the ride back down to Orange County it's late in the evening and it's been a fun, but long and exhausting day and there are plenty of yawns. As soon as Trey and Julie take their seats in the back of the bus next to Brett and Tracy, Julie wraps her arms around one of his and leans her head against his shoulder. It's been a pretty amazing day for him. He knew he and Julie would have fun, but he had no idea things would turn out so well. She's been absolutely the perfect date and genuinely seems to enjoy being with him and it gives him the courage to ask her about things he's been wondering about. "Have fun?"

"Hm-hmm," Julie purrs.

"What's Brad like?"

She lifts her head and peers at him. "Why do you want to talk about Brad?"

"Just curious. He's your boyfriend, right?"

"Brad's a jerk. He's only interested in sex. I'm done with him. Anything else you want to know?"

"I guess not."

She snuggles back against him.

He knows he should probably leave things where they are, but he's still curious. "Where's your mom?" He sees her lift her head again and he can tell by her expression, angry and hurt, that her mom is a sore subject.

"I don't know and I don't care."

"Why?"

"She left and I've never heard from her. End of story."

"How old were you?"

"Ten."

"What's her name?"

"Irene."

"Where's she live?"

"I dunno. My dad knows."

"Do you miss her?" He sees Julie struggling to answer the question, like she's not really sure how she feels about her mom or does and doesn't want to admit it to herself.

"I told you. She left and I haven't heard from her. What kind of mom is that?"

He guesses the kind of mom who either didn't care about her or was scared to death of Walt. He can't believe her mom didn't care about her. "Aren't you curious about her?"

"Why are you?"

"I dunno. I just am."

She lets go of his arm and sits back and crosses her arms and legs and swishes her foot. "Do me a favor. Mind your own business."

"Sure," he says and watches the iridescent blue streaks her toenails are making in the darkness. He hears Tracy ask Julie if she's okay and Julie say, "Yeah," but she's still swishing her foot like an angry cat's tail and he regrets having spoiled an otherwise perfect day by being so nosy, but not really. The closer they've gotten, the more curious he's become about her mom and it was perfectly natural to ask about her. He just wasn't expecting her reaction. Well, what's done is done and he can't take it back. The swishing slows.

"I'm sorry," Julie says. "I try not to think about her."

"What was she like?"

"Nice, when she wasn't high."

He glances at her and sees her staring out the window. He's relieved she's talking with him again, but her mom's drug use feels like a dangerous subject and he wisely says nothing.

"I think she lives in San Diego," Julie finally says.

"Do you want to see her?"

She glances at him and stares out the window again. "I dunno."

They ride the rest of the way in silence and the bus drops them off at the house and they say their good-byes to everyone and wish Brett Happy Birthday again. They climb out and walk slowly hand in hand along the path toward the kitchen door and Trey feels Julie pull him to a stop and turns and sees her smiling sweetly at him.

"I had a great time," she says. "Thanks for inviting me."

"Thanks for coming."

She pulls him to her and puts her arms around his neck and brings her lips to his and Trey puts his arms around her and they close their eyes and enjoy a long sweet kiss in the darkness.

The thing that surprises him most about the day happens when he's lying in bed masturbating. He knows Kim's probably listening, but that's all she does anymore. He's not picturing the usual scenes, but just thinking about Julie in the limo with her arms wrapped around his and her head resting against his shoulder and when he feels himself about to come he doesn't picture her on her knees in the bathroom begging him to come on her but the two of them in bed in each other's arms making love and when he comes he feels completely different this time, not like a selfish, sex-obsessed teenager, but like a lover delighting in pleasing his partner. He wipes himself and wads up the tissue and sticks it under the mattress and as he lays his head on the pillow Emily comes to mind and he realizes it's the first time she has all day.

Trey's been wondering whether Emily would have the courage to face him and as he watches her approach him in the hall he sees her curiosity about the party has given her just enough to do it.

"How was it?" she asks glumly. "I bet you had a great time."

"Yeah. It was fun."

"Did you go with anyone?"

He can see she's hoping the answer is no, but she asked. "Yeah, Julie." He sees she's surprised and perplexed.

"I thought you didn't like her."

"I didn't. She's actually really nice."

"Isn't she, like, seventeen?"

"Yeah." Emily looks crestfallen. Well, that's what you get when you let other people run your life.

She looks down at her shoes. "I'm glad you had a good time."

He watches her walk off slowly down the hall, not so much walk as drift. Lately there seems to be less and less of her there each time he sees her.

She's barely there at cotillion and is trying her best not to make eye contact with him as they practice the steps to the new waltz they're learning with their partners. He wants to feel sorry for her but can't quite bring himself to. After all, she's allowing herself to be victimized by her parents and he's begun to think she must like the way it feels. He's never known anyone like her and he's thankful he does because she serves as a reminder of the importance of sticking up for himself. It really is too bad about her, though. She'd be a great person if only she'd develop some backbone. He's not surprised when "polite conversation" time arrives to see her hang with a group of girls instead of with him and stand with her back to him. "What's up with Emily?" he hears Douglas ask. "Dunno," Trey says and glances at Eddy, who never misses an opportunity to be crude, and sees him grin.

"I bet she's on the rag," Eddy says.

Douglas makes a face. "Dude, you're disgusting."

"Hey," Eddy says, "girls act weird when they are. My sister turns into a total bitch."

Trey sees parents arriving and then Emily's mom with that phony smile on her face and his mom not far behind her and the parents chat among themselves and his mom stands with her car keys in her hand chatting with Douglas' mom and one of the other girl's father but Emily's mom isn't interested in chatting with anyone and he sees her motioning to Emily to leave and his mom turns and smiles at Emily as she passes and says, "Hi, Emily," but Emily doesn't say anything or even look up and his mom looks at him and he can see she's puzzled by her behavior.

June starts the car. "Did something happen between you and Emily?" she asks.

Trey stares out the windshield. "Her parents think we're trash."

June looks at him wide-eyed. "What?"

"Her mom found out we stayed at the shelter." He can feel his mom looking at him and he can tell she's struggling with what to say, but she doesn't say anything and finally looks away and they both sit staring out the windshield, listening to the sound of the idling engine.

"I'm sorry," June finally says.

His mom's voice sounds weak. "There's nothing to be sorry about. We needed a place to stay."

June stares at the haloed glow of the streetlight and then at a star shining faintly in the evening sky above it. This isn't the way life's supposed to be but she feels powerless to do anything about it. She wishes she could be like Trey, not let things get to her, stay positive and keep moving forward, hoping for a better future, but she can't and it's grinding her down.

Should he confront Emily or ignore her when he sees her in the hall? Trey's still undecided. One moment he thinks he'll ignore her and the next he thinks he'll confront her and he keeps going back and forth about it in his mind and when he turns the corner and sees her walking slowly toward him with her head down, hugging her books to her chest, he feels his anger rising and knows he has to confront her and stops in front of her. "Hey," he says and she looks up at him like a wounded animal.

"Hey," Emily says weakly.

"So, you were pretty rude to my mom." He sees her lower lip quivering.

"I'm sorry."

"Listen, I don't give a shit what your parents think about me and my family, but my mom has always been nice to you and she doesn't deserve to be treated that way." He sees her eyes filling with tears.

"I'm sorry."

"So why did you?"

"I don't know! I'm sorry!"

He glances at the kids who've either slowed or stopped to watch this hallway drama and decides he's done with it. "Get a life, Emily," he says and walks off leaving her standing there and wishing he hadn't said that. She would if she could and obviously can't. He's beginning to really worry about her.

CHAPTER 7

It's amazing to Trey how Julie's changed. She's been like a different person ever since the party. He hasn't seen a hint of a smirk, only tender looks and sweet smiles. His mom commented to him about how nice it is to see Julie looking so happy and so did Kim. The only person who's unhappy about it is Walt, who seems more pissed off than ever about everything. Trey smiles when he remembers the time, not so long ago, when he would arrive home in the afternoon and hope Julie wasn't there, but now he hopes she is and as he enters the kitchen and hears music coming from her room his smile widens. He sees her door is open and stops and looks in. She's sitting on the bed with her knees up and her chin resting on them, staring down at a piece of paper in her hands and he has the feeling she's been waiting for him. "Hey," he says.

She glances up at him. "Hey."

"What's up?"

"Come in and shut the door."

He steps into the room and shuts the door and takes off his backpack and puts it on the floor. She puts the piece of paper on the nightstand and her feet on the floor and holds her arms out to him and when he stops in front of her she unbuttons the waistband of his jeans and unzips them. He smiles at this pleasant surprise and watches her pull his jeans and boxers down around his knees and take him in her hand and begin gently stroking him and it only takes moments before he's hard. She takes him in her mouth and he closes his eyes and tilts his head back and puts his hands lightly on the back of her head and enjoys the feeling of her sucking and her tongue moving in circles around him and he's never felt anything so good in his life. Whoever this Brad is, he's a total loser for not having treated her better. Did she do it this way with him? Maybe she didn't want to make him feel this good.

She slowly pulls back her head and lets him free and smiles up at him sweetly as she takes off her tee shirt and bra and shorts and underpants and tosses them aside and lies back on the bed and holds out her arms to him again. He lies on top of her and she spreads her legs and guides him in. "Don't worry," he hears her say softly next to his ear, "I'm on the pill." They move together as he thrusts and he feels her lifting her butt off the bed and raises himself up as she does and when he's gazing straight down at her she wraps her legs around his waist and clasps her hands on the back of his neck and hangs from him with her eyes shut tightly and her mouth wide open and he feels her tightening around him inside and then coming and he comes too. He moves to pull out but she presses her legs tighter around his waist and puts her hands on his butt and pulls him to her.

"Stay inside," she says, "it feels good."

He lowers himself onto her and rests his head on her shoulder and they stay that way until he feels himself withdraw and then lies on his side facing her. She rolls on her side and they gaze at each other's eyes.

"First time?" she finally asks.

"Yeah."

"I'm glad it was with me."

"So am I. You?"

She looks at him sadly and shakes her head. "It felt like the first time, though."

It occurs to him that unlike before when she's come, she didn't make a sound. "Why didn't you make any noise?"

She searches his eyes. "I dunno." She takes the piece of paper from the nightstand and hands it to him. "My dad sends her money each month."

He reads the address and phone number and looks at her. "Let's go."

"I dunno."

"Maybe my dad will take us or we can take the train." He sees she's anxious and uncertain and she searches his eyes again.

"I dunno. I'll think about it."

Art listens to Trey as they stroll with Kim along Huntington Beach Pier out toward the end. When he's heard Trey out, he narrows his eyes and purses his lips. "Ya gotta be careful with stuff like this."

Trey looks up at his dad. "She can see her mom if she wants to."

"Sure she can, but that's her business. If you get involved it's another story. Obviously, her parents aren't on good terms and her dad doesn't want her to have anything to do with her mom. If she sees her, he's going to find out. That's one thing. If he finds out you were with her, that's another. And if he finds out I took you, that's another still. Think about Mom."

"So you won't help?" Trey asks.

"Hold on, buddy. I didn't say I wouldn't help you. I'm just saying you need to think twice about it. Who knows what kind of shit could happen? What if Walt kicks you out?"

"Fine with me," Trey says.

"Me too," Kim says.

Art looks at them and smiles and shakes his head. "So when did you and Julie become pals? I thought you didn't like her?"

"I got to know her better," Trey says.

"She's nice," Kim says and glances at her fingernails and toenails. She'd never worn nail polish before and it was nice of Julie to offer to paint them. She was reluctant to let her at first until Julie suggested black, which seemed kind of cool, about as far away from pink as you can get. She's been checking out the nails of the girls and women and she's the only one wearing black. It feels nice, special.

They find the usual collection of Asians and Hispanics arranged in small groups around the end of the pier by the railing and usually their lines are in the water and their buckets empty and they're just passing the time, hoping the stray halibut or mackerel or rock fish will happen along, but it's a new moon and the sardines are running and the scene is one of bustling activity. Each time one of the fishermen reels in his line there's a wriggling silver sardine on every hook and they can't haul them in fast enough. They watch an elderly Vietnamese man plop his catch on the deck and his elderly Vietnamese wife bend over and begin removing the fish from the hooks and tossing them into their large, half-full, white plastic bucket. Art feels for the fish and he can tell by Trey's and Kim's expressions that they do too. They know what it's like to be pulled unexpectedly out of a comfortable and familiar world into an uncomfortable and unfamiliar one. He fingers the scar on his cheek and wonders what's become of Chi. She's probably back at the XXXotic, dancing and turning tricks. It's not important. What's important is that he's determined to make that misadventure his last, not only because he's trying to turn his life around but also because he has the feeling he won't be so lucky next time. They watch the wriggling sardines being reeled in and tossed into buckets until they've seen enough and walk back along the pier. Art puts a hand on Trey's shoulder. "Keep me posted, buddy."

Julie stares at the graphic of the earth on the screen as Trey types in the address on Google Earth and clicks on the magnifying glass icon and they watch as the earth begins slowly turning toward the Western United States and the view quickly zooms in to Southern California and San Diego County and San Diego and stops at an aerial view of the location in Pacific Beach. Trey continues zooming in and now they're looking at a street view of a white two-story apartment building and he does a 360 of the street and they see it's lined with similar buildings and they end up back at Julie's mom's building.

"Remember what she looks like?" he asks.

"Yeah, sort of. I think my dad threw out all the pictures of her. I've looked everywhere for them but can't find any."

"You look like her?"

"I dunno. A little, I guess."

"Whaddya think?"

"It's scary. I don't know anything about her now. I don't even know if she wants to see me."

"Why not ask her?"

Julie looks down uncertainly at the phone number on the piece of paper in one hand and then her phone in the other.

Trey shrugs. "The worst that can happen is that she says she doesn't want to see you."

She glances at him and looks back at the number. "That's what I'm afraid of. Maybe it's better not knowing."

"It's your call. Anyway, my dad said he'd help us."

She looks at him apprehensively. "That's nice, but I dunno. My dad will be really mad if he finds out your dad was involved."

"He's gonna be mad anyway."

"Yeah, but it'll be worse." She looks down at the phone. All she has to do is make the call, but her fear of not knowing what the outcome will be is overwhelming, almost paralyzing. She tells herself that things are fine the way they are, that she's gotten along fine without her mom all these years, so why contact her now and risk causing trouble? Even worse, why risk finding out that her mom doesn't want to see her or have anything to do with her, that she's perfectly happy without her in her life? It seems to Julie there are a lot more reasons not to make the call than to make it. It would certainly be easier not to.

She can't lie to herself, though. She knows she wouldn't be sitting here staring at her phone if she didn't really want to find out, one way or another. She knows what will happen if her mom has no interest in seeing her. She'll just go on living the way she's been living and it will be sad, but that will be the end of it. The truly scary thing is that she doesn't know what will happen if her mom does want to see her, how seeing her will change things and what the repercussions with her dad will be. The idea of making the call seems like running blindly off a cliff without knowing what, if anything, is below. Why would she do that to herself? Yet everything seems to have led her to this moment when that's just what she wants and needs to do. She punches in the number and places the call and puts the phone to her ear and listens anxiously to the rings. "Hello?" she hears and is surprised by how familiar her mom's voice sounds. "Mom?" she asks tentatively. A long moment of silence passes and she can hear voices in the background.

"Julie?" Irene asks with surprise.

"Yeah, hi!"

"Oh, my God!"

Julie hears her mom's muffled voice. She must be talking to someone else with her hand over the phone.

"Hold on a second," Irene says.

Another long moment passes and as Julie waits for her mom she feels pretty good now about having made the call. Her mom naturally sounds surprised to hear from her and, most important, happy.

"How are you?" Irene asks.

"Fine. You?"

"Fine. I'm with a client, so I can't talk long."

"What do you do?"

"I'm a manicurist."

Julie glances at her nails and smiles.

"It's so good to hear from you! Does your dad know you're calling?"

"No. Listen, I'd like to see you." Julie waits to hear what her mom has to say and not hearing anything fills her with worry again. Is her mom hesitating or just being distracted?

"Sorry," Irene says, "we're busy. Sure! Just let me know when. I'm off Thursdays and Sundays."

"Maybe next Sunday. I'll check the train schedule and let you know."

"Okay. I've gotta go, honey. Great hearing from you! What a pleasant surprise! Love ya!"

"Love ya too," Julie says and looks at Trey, who's been watching her and listening to her side of the conversation and is smiling at her. She feels her eyes filling with tears and wipes her eyes with the back of her hand. "I can't believe it. It's like a dream."

"I'm really happy for you."

She smiles sweetly at him. To think she resented Trey coming into her life. How fortunate and grateful she is that he did. If not for him, she wouldn't be feeling the way she is now and looking forward to seeing her mom. She leans forward and puts her arms around him and kisses him tenderly and gazes at his eyes. "I know. Thanks."

They hold hands and watch the coast glide by as they head south on the train past Trestles and the twin domes of the San Onofre nuclear reactor, which always look to Trey like two gargantuan tits, and through Camp Pendleton toward San Diego. The plan is pretty simple. His dad picked him and Julie and Kim up at Walt's and the story is that they're going to spend the day at the Orange County Fair in Costa Mesa. His dad and Kim are, but his dad dropped him and Julie off at the station in Irvine and will pick them up later when they return. His dad seems okay with covering for them, but Trey knows he's going way out on a limb getting involved like this and if anything goes wrong and Walt finds out, it isn't going to be good. He tells himself there's nothing he can do about it now, but that doesn't make him feel any less uneasy.

With each passing mile Julie feels herself drawing closer to the beginning of a new chapter in her life. She doesn't know what it holds in store, but she's hopeful that it will be filled with good and positive developments, although you never know how things will turn out. What can seem promising at first can just as easily turn out otherwise, so, as hopeful as she is she still feels uncertain and a bit apprehensive about what comes next. Her journey's begun, though, and there's no turning back.

The train slows as it enters the station in San Diego and noses forward next to the platform. Julie scans the people waiting there and as the train comes to a stop sees a woman with strawberry blonde hair just like hers and knows instantly she's her mom. Her mom's wearing sunglasses and a tee shirt and shorts and espadrilles and has a big canvas bag slung over her shoulder and is scanning the windows of the train. Julie waves and catches her mom's eye and her mom sees her and smiles and waves back.

She steps down from the train and walks quickly to her mom, who's beaming at her and holding her arms open wide. They throw their arms around each other and hug rocking back and forth and Julie's eyes fill with tears. She's longed to feel her mom's embrace for so long and it feels wonderful.

Irene steps back and puts her sunglasses on her head and looks Julie up and down. "Look at you! My baby's all grown up!" Julie sniffs and wipes her eyes and Irene hugs her again and rubs her back and smiles at Trey and puts out a hand to him. "Irene. Nice to meet you."

"Trey. Nice to meet you too." He's been studying Julie's mom's face and eyes and smile and she and Julie sure look a lot alike, the way he and his dad do.

"So, what do you feel like doing?" Irene asks.

"I dunno," Julie says, "whatever, you decide."

Irene grins. "Let's go to the beach and get ice cream. We'll make it up as we go along."

They sit on the wall by the boardwalk, watching people on the beach, walking along the shore, wading in the surf. "People come here everyday to watch the sunset," Irene says, "like they do in Key West, only here sometimes you can see a green flash when the sun sets."

Julie turns her cone slowly as she licks and looks at her mom. "Have you?" She sees her mom looking at the horizon and can tell by her eyes that what she sees is a bad memory.

Irene nods. "It's rare, but I've spent a lot of time sitting on this wall watching the sunset."

Julie hears the sadness and pain and regret in her mom's voice and feels concern.

Trey hears it too and knows the time has come for Julie and her mom to be alone. He pushes himself off the wall and lands on the sand and turns and looks at them. "Going for a walk. Be back soon."

Irene nods and watches him walk across the beach toward the shore. She likes him. He's a smart kid. "He's nice," she says.

"If it weren't for him I wouldn't be here."

Irene glances at Julie and looks back at Trey. "I'm glad you are."

"I was afraid to call."

Irene stares at the horizon. "You have more courage than I do."

"Why'd you leave? You just disappeared."

"That was the deal, honey."

"Why? What happened?"

Irene looks at her and searches her eyes. "Has your dad told you anything?"

Julie shakes her head.

"I'm not surprised. I'll be honest with you, honey. I wasn't a very good wife and I wasn't a very good mother. I was a mess."

"I kind of remember."

Irene stares at the horizon again. "I was pretty depressed after I had you. Not about you, about...I dunno, life, my life. Anyway, I was on anti-depressants for a long time, but they didn't help much. And then I started hanging with a friend who's boyfriend was a tweaker and we'd do meth at her place and it made me feel better, at least it took my mind off feeling depressed." She looks at Julie and searches her eyes again. "You wanna hear this?"

Julie nods.

"Anyway," Irene says, looking back at the horizon, "I started drinking at home to come down from meth and that went on for a long time and, naturally, your dad wasn't happy about the situation." She looks at Julie. "You know he was in the Army, right?"

"Yeah," Julie says. "I don't know anything about it, though. He never talks about it."

"He never talked about it with me, either, except to say that he suffers from PTSD. He was in Iraq and Afghanistan.

"What's PTSD?"

"Post-Traumatic Stress Disorder. A lot of the troops suffer from it. I don't know how you can go through that shit and not." Irene shrugs and looks at the horizon. "Anyway, he has anger issues and my doing drugs made him really angry. He tried to convince me to get into rehab, but that was the last thing I wanted to do and we'd argue and fight and sometimes things got really physical and it got to the point where I knew if I stayed with him, he'd either kill me or I'd kill myself, so I left. The deal was if I disappeared, he'd help me financially. I didn't really have a choice at the time. I was too messed up to work and support myself."

"Why'd you move to San Diego?"

Irene looks at her and raises her eyebrows. "You don't remember Gramma Doris and Grampa Earl?"

Julie squints at her mom. "Sort of. Not really."

"Yeah, the last time you saw them you were, what, four, maybe five? We never saw much of my family. They live here. This is where I grew up. See much of your dad's family?"

Julie shakes her head.

"I'm not surprised. I didn't see much of them either. They only came to visit once, when your dad and I got married. Anyway, I got into rehab here and finally got straight. It wasn't easy but I did. And then I got my license and I've been working as a manicurist every since. It pays the bills."

"Does Dad still send you money?"

Irene shakes her head. "Not anymore. Hasn't for a long time. I don't need his help anymore."

"Then it doesn't matter if he finds out."

"Not to me, honey, but I'd think twice about telling your dad you came to see me."

Julie shrugs. "I know he'll be mad."

Irene can tell that Julie hasn't seen the worst of her dad's temper. She remembers vividly the day she was dropped off at home, still cranked out of her mind, and walked into the kitchen to find Walt sitting at the table staring at his hands, waiting for her. He took one look at her and got up and grabbed her by the hair and forced her to her knees and dragged her to the stove and opened the oven door and stuck her head in the oven and turned it on. She'll never forget her feeling of utter terror. She struggled to pull her head out, but he kept kicking her in the ass and forcing it back in, like she was a dog he was intent on killing. Why he didn't she'll never know. "Just be careful," she finally says.

Julie nods and wraps her arms around her mom's arm and leans her head against her shoulder. "I've missed you."

Irene puts her hand on Julie's arm. "I've missed you too, honey. There hasn't been a day that's gone by that I haven't thought about you and wondered how you were doing."

Julie sees her mom's getting teary.

Irene looks at her and wipes her eyes with the back of her finger. "I'm sorry."

"It's okay."

"I let you down. I feel so ashamed."

"Don't," Julie says and squeezes her mom's arm. "There's no need to. I love you."

"I love you too, honey, more than I can say. I don't know how you can forgive me."

"You did what you had to do, Mom."

Irene reaches into her bag and fishes out a tissue and blows her nose and wipes her eyes and looks tenderly at Julie and shakes her head. "My baby, all grown up."

Julie nods toward her mom's bag. "Do you have pictures? I can't find any. I think Dad threw them all out." She sees her mom's expression brighten a bit.

"Sure I do!" Irene says and takes out her wallet and opens it.

Julie snuggles against her mom and puts her cheek against hers and looks down at the pictures in the plastic sleeves. There's one of her mom and her when she was a baby. They're on a beach with the ocean in the background and her mom has her sunglasses up on her head, just as she does now. Her mom's smiling and holding her between her legs with her arms around her.

Irene smiles. "You were just a peanut. I think it was your first time at the beach."

The next one is of the two of them when Julie was a little older. She's standing and smiling and her mom is crouched down beside her and smiling and there's Cinderella Castle in the background.

"First trip to Disneyland," Irene says.

Julie's older still in the next one, sitting on a pink bike with her hands on the white handlebar grips and there are pink ribbons streaming from them and her mom is standing behind her and leaning forward with her hands on her hands and they're both smiling at the camera.

"Your first bike."

"You look pretty happy."

"Yeah, I was then."

Her mom turns to the next picture and Julie sees the two of them, sitting at a table outside at some theme park. She's holding up a hamburger in both hands, which looks almost as big as her head, and there's a rollercoaster behind them in the distance. She's smiling at the camera, but her mom is staring at it blankly.

"Knott's Berry Farm," Irene says. "I wasn't having a very good day."

Julie sees in the few remaining pictures that her mom's smile has gone and been replaced by an expression that looks increasingly confused and troubled and lost.

"It was a bad time," Irene says softly.

Julie hears the sadness and pain and regret in her mom's voice again and looks at her. "You must have felt awful, Mom." She flips the pictures back to the first one taken at the beach and they look at it and smile and press their cheeks together. "I want you back in my life, Mom. I don't care what Dad thinks or what he does. I want you back." Her mom looks at her and searches her eyes again, like she's trying to find in her the courage and strength she'll need to be a mother again. Julie feels relieved and happy and smiles when she finally sees her mom nod slowly and smile back.

"I'll try my best, honey."

"Can I keep it?" Julie asks, nodding at the picture.

"Sure, honey," Irene says and takes it out of the sleeve and hands it to her and Julie kisses her on the cheek and rests her head on her shoulder and gazes down at it. "Thanks, Mom," Irene hears her say and the happiness she feels at having her daughter sitting here next to her, listening to the sound of her voice, feeling her body pressed against hers close enough to smell her hair and skin is unlike anything she's felt before and makes her think that maybe the hell she's been through and put everyone close to her through, especially Julie, was worth it. It seems crazy to thinks so, but maybe it was. She looks up to see Trey standing in front of them, studying them and grinning.

"You two should check yourselves out in a mirror," Trey says. "People tell me and my dad that all the time."

CHAPTER 8

Henry stands just outside the yellow caution tape watching the workers on the lifts install the glass siding on the new Forever 21 store by the entrance to South Coast Plaza near valet parking. The contrast between the workers and the shoppers entering and exiting the plaza is striking. Here are the workers — all men with the exception of one woman, who's dressed like the rest of the men and could be mistaken for a man when her back is turned — who build the temples of consumerism, wearing hard hats and work shirts and vests and jeans and carpenter belts and heavy work shoes, and there are the shoppers, mostly girls and women of all ages, the older ones trying to look as young and attractive as possible and all dressed in the clothes they've purchased at the various temples the workers have built. Soon they'll have a new one to worship in and it couldn't be clearer about the image it's selling, as impossible as it is. He sees one worker, a handsome young Hispanic who's standing with a walky-talky in his hand looking up at the men on the lifts and the man glances at him and smiles and walks over and looks him up and down admiringly.

"Lookin' sharp," the man says.

"Work clothes." Henry's noticed the workers have been putting in long days lately. "When's the store opening?"

"Tuesday," the man says.

Impressive. Only a few days away and there's still a lot of siding to put on. "Any incentive in the contract?" Henry sees the man's expression change to one of disgust.

"Those days are over. We're lucky to have the work. We're coming from Riverside to do this job."

What a hellish commute that must be. "Good luck," Henry says and strolls back toward the benches by valet parking to have a smoke. He sits in his usual spot next to the ashtray and notices a white pickup pass by and park. He just glimpsed the people in the truck, a man driving and a woman in the passenger seat, but something about the man looked familiar and sure enough it's Art and he's wearing the outfit he sold him. His companion is an attractive young brunette wearing a white silk tee and black tight-fitting jeans and black wedge sandals. Art sees him and waves and he waves back and they walk over to him and he stands and shakes Art's hand. "Nice to see you, Art." Henry notes in a glance the young woman's shapely arms and legs and long slender fingers and toes, all of which he finds very sexy.

"Same here, Henry. This is Joanne."

Henry shakes Joanne's hand and enjoys the feel of those long slender fingers. "A pleasure," he says and admires her face, in particular her eyes, which are a lighter shade of brown than any he's seen before and her smile, just slightly turned up at the corners and framed by adorable dimples.

Art spreads his arms wide and looks at Joanne. "Henry's doing."

She looks at Henry and nods. "Good job."

It's nice to see that Art's been working on his appearance, beyond his wardrobe. His hair is nicely cut, he's clean-shaven and the scar on his cheek is faint enough now to look dashing and distinguished. His hand seems to have healed well too. Henry knows from the posters in the plaza that Blue Man Group is performing at the Segerstrom Center for the Arts across Bristol Street. "Blue Man Group?" he asks and Art nods. "They're wild," Henry says. "I saw them in Boston twenty-five years ago. Those Blue Men are probably retired now. You'll enjoy it."

Joanne cocks her head and looks thoughtfully at Henry. "What do retired Blue Men do I wonder?"

"Worry about their declining health and the high cost of medical care."

"Of course," she says.

He sees that adorable dimpled smile again. "Nice meeting you. Have fun."

"We will," Art says and waves.

Henry waves and sits and watches them walk up and over the bridge until they're out of sight. He looks at the workers on the lift who are carefully maneuvering another large pane of glass into place and then at the shoppers passing by beneath them who don't look up or even seem to notice the activity around them and shakes his head and smiles.

Good for Art for taking better care of himself. Joanne strikes him as a sharp person and a good influence. Is she just a friend or more than that? Well, it doesn't matter. All that matters is that Art's decided to move forward, rather than continue spiraling downward. He's been there himself and knows it isn't easy and that there's no telling where moving forward will take him. For himself, he's arrived at a place where he's content being alone. The idea of having someone to share things with in life does have its appeal, but he wonders if he wouldn't make a mess of things again. Maybe some people just aren't cut out for it. As Laura used to say, *"Meglio soli che male accompagnati,"* "Better alone than in bad company."

He heads back to the store and glances at his reflection in the plate glass window as he passes Boudin's restaurant by the plaza entrance and sees the image of a dapperly dressed graying older man. Handsome? Desirable? Well, it's not for him to say. When he looks at himself in the mirror these days he sees a man staring back at him who looks uncannily like his paternal grandfather in the one picture he has of him that was taken when his grandfather was around the age he is now. He didn't know his dad's dad very well, but he remembers him as being a quiet reserved man, much like himself, who lost his wife early and remained a widower for the rest of his life. His own mother's experience was the same. Maybe being alone is in his blood.

Art and Joanne stroll back across the bridge toward South Coast Plaza. Joanne smiles and shakes her head. "Henry was right. They're wild."

"What're you up for?"

"Pool."

"Sorry?"

"Shoot pool and drink beer."

"The Q Club's not far from here. I take the kids there sometimes."

"I know the place. Let's go."

Art leans against the counter and sips his beer and scans the room filled mostly with kids in their late teens and early twenties. The two couples at the table next to theirs look to be in their late twenties and are better dressed and are probably young professionals. He studies the back of Joanne's body as she leans over the table in front of him and lines up her shot. He likes the way she wiggles her butt slightly as she does and he can picture it without those jeans on and maybe he'll see it and maybe he won't, but he's not going to make any moves. He's happy just being here with her and wants to get to know her better and doesn't want to run the risk of making a fool of himself. She takes her shot and he watches the nine-ball disappear into a corner pocket. He smiles and shakes his head and puts the rack on the table. "You're cleaning my clock."

She grins and takes the balls out of the pockets and rolls them toward him and looks at his wedding band. "Still love her?"

He glances at her and catches the balls as she sends them his way and places them in the rack. "Yeah."

"What are you going to do about it?"

He rolls the rack back and forth and presses his fingertips against the balls to tighten them and carefully removes the rack and places it under the table. "I dunno."

She places the cue ball on the table in her preferred break spot, just slightly to the right of the head spot on the green felt directly in front of her and leans over the table and wiggles her butt as she lines up her shot. She draws back her cue and sends the cue ball smashing into the diamond-shaped cluster of balls and watches as the one and five roll into pockets and the other balls come to rest with the nine an easy shot into the far right corner pocket. She turns and looks at him. "Why not?"

"I'm working on it."

She sinks the nine and grins at him as he smiles and shakes his head again and she puts her cue on the table. "I'm gonna have a smoke," she says and slings her bag over her shoulder.

They step outside onto the walkway between the buildings and find a few other people standing and chatting and smoking. They put some distance between them and she fishes her pack of cigarettes and lighter out of her bag and takes out two cigarettes and gives him one and lights them both and they stand smoking and looking up at the narrow slice of nighttime sky overhead. "What are your kids names?" she asks.

"Trey and Kim."

"How old are they?"

"Fifteen and thirteen."

"Nice kids?"

"Yeah, they're great."

"Bet you're a great dad."

"I try. I'm supposed to be the parent, but I get the feeling sometimes they know more about what's going on than I do. I haven't been a very good role model."

"Don't be so sure."

He glances at her. "Marriage just didn't work out?"

She searches the sky. "My ex wanted kids. He knew I didn't. That was the deal but he tried to convince me to have them after we were married. I finally had enough of his pestering me about it. There were other problems we coldn't seem to work through but that was the biggest."

"What type of guy is he?"

"Nice. Plastic surgeon. Works in my dad's practice. That's how we met." She glances at his cheek. "They can take care of that if you want. I kind of like it, though." She traces the scar lightly with a fingertip. "It's edgy." She draws on her cigarette and blows out the smoke slowly and thinks about his plan to get his teacher certification and his reluctance to ask his father for financial assistance. "I wouldn't think twice about asking my dad for money if I needed it for a good reason, whether or not he loved me. I'm his daughter, right?"

"I guess."

"If your kids needed money, you'd give it to them, if you could, wouldn't you, no matter what?"

"I guess."

"Don't let your pride stand in the way. Besides, helping you might be just what you both need."

That thought hadn't occurred to him and now it has him thinking.

They step back into the room and find the two young men from the table next to theirs leaning against their table, holding their cues and chatting, and the two young women sitting on stools at the counter, also chatting. The men move away as they approach.

"Sorry," Michael says.

Joanne smiles. "No problem." She looks at Art and raises her eyebrows. "Had enough?"

He grins. "Best five out of seven."

"You're a glutton for punishment." She picks up her cue and chalks the tip and glances at the young woman with the short dyed-black hair and red horn-rimmed glasses who strikes her as cutely nerdy. The necklace she's wearing catches her eye and she leans her cue against the table and walks over to her. "Excuse me, I couldn't help noticing your necklace. It's beautiful, very unusual. Where'd you get it?"

Kaitlin fingers the pendant nervously and glances at Michael, who's watching Keith line up his break shot, and then at Beth, who takes her bag and stands and walks toward the rest rooms. "Germany, Munich."

Joanne moves closer. "Mind if I have a look?"

Kaitlin tenses. "No, not at all." She holds out the pendant for her inspection and hopes she doesn't notice the way her hand is shaking slightly.

"I love the chain. The work is so delicate, so intricate. Are they oak leaves?"

"Yes."

"They're so tiny, and the enamel work.... Is it a plane?"

"Yes, well, no," Kaitlin says and glances at Michael and Keith again and sees they're chatting about something. "An eagle."

"I bet there's a story behind it."

"It's based on a medal they used to give glider pilots. My friend who made it flies them. It's her passion."

"Interesting." Joanne looks at her and smiles. "Joanne. Nice meeting you."

"Kaitlin. Nice meeting you too." She sips her beer and watches Joanne walk to her table and pick up her cue and lean over and break and send the nine-ball straight into a corner pocket. She overheard the comment Joanne made to the man she's with that he's a glutton for punishment. Maybe he is and maybe he isn't. You never know about people and Magda's a perfect example.

Magda intimidated her when they first met at her family's cottage in Berchtesgaden. She'd never met anyone as intense and opinionated and found it unnerving listening to her at dinner go on and on about the sorry state of the world and the hypocrisy of politicians and the sheepishness of society. Magda clearly rankled her parents. Her mother would sigh and her father would frown.

After dinner Magda accompanied her and Manfred on a long walk and other aspects of her personality emerged. She would stop on the trail and stare transfixed at something — the view, a rock formation, a particular leaf —and they'd stop and wait for her and when she rejoined them she seemed to be in a trance.

When they returned from the walk the three of them sat at one end of the porch with the rest of the family at the other, enjoying the view and the evening air. Magda was wearing the necklace, which Kaitlin been admiring and she commented about it, just as Joanne did. That's when she learned that Magda makes jewelry and that the necklace was inspired by her grandfather's Glider Pilot of the German Air Force medal. Magda said that whenever they visited him she would take it out of the drawer where he kept it and sit next to him, admiring it as he told her about the history of gliders and the important role Germany played in their development.

"He was passionate about gliders," Magda said, "like many of the boys and young men in Köln, where he grew up, and they appropriated that passion and turned him into a fighter pilot, which he didn't want to be but, you know, he had no choice. None of them did," she said, staring at the evening sky and shaking her head. "They stole everything good about us as a people and turned us into monsters." She looked admiringly at her parents and uncle and aunt sitting at the other end of the porch. "They had it hard," she said. "They were faced with having to live down the past while the entire country was in denial. It's thanks to them that we're happy and proud to be German again. We're not free of the past, but we're no longer enslaved by it."

The three of them drove to Wasserkuppe and Magda took her soaring aloft and it was her most exhilarating experience ever, looking down at the ground far below and listening to the sound of the wind against the canopy, and by the time Magda brought them safely back to earth and they climbed out and stood on the tarmac hugging each other, she felt an immutable bond had formed between them and that they would always be close, no matter what.

It was when they were back at the cottage and she and Manfred were ready to drive back to Munich and were saying their good-byes that Magda removed the necklace and put it around her neck without saying a word. Her relationship with Manfred was still platonic then and when she thinks back on it, she doesn't know how they managed to keep it that way for so long.

They didn't say much on the ride back to her hotel and when they arrived and he parked the car, she knew what was about to happen and welcomed it. He'd kept her at bay with kissing and cuddling and she'd come to understand that toying with women was a perverse pleasure of his and she shouldn't have allowed herself to be used like that, but she couldn't help herself. Now she sensed he'd reached the point in his little game where it was time to claim her and she knew it would be good, maybe not as good as that animal love she'd imagined, but she wasn't disappointed.

The moths diving into the porch light come to mind. It was great, all right, for what, an hour? Those sixty minutes have complicated her entire existence and she's still trying to figure out what to do about it.

"You're up," she hears Michael say and realizes she has no idea what's happened in the last few minutes. She glances at him and puts her beer on the counter and stands and stares uncertainly at the balls on the table. "Solids," she hears him say.

Joanne's still wondering how the evening will end as Art turns onto her street. She knows he loves his wife and wants her back, but she also knows he's attracted to her and was probably staring at her wiggling butt all evening. He's a man, after all, and she gives him high marks for having behaved like a perfect gentleman. She senses that whatever else might happen, her friendship is the most important thing to him and that he doesn't want to compromise it by being forward. She's gotten to know him pretty well in the short time she's spent with him and has the feeling that having sex with her would be good for him, good for his self-esteem and a step in the right direction toward getting his wife back. It's ironic, but there it is. He's a nice guy and a good man, just adrift, as she is in her own way.

She should be dead and would be without the cocktail of drugs she takes each day. As it is she's enjoying relatively good health. For all the thinking she's done about it, she's no closer now to understanding the psychology of someone who's HIV positive knowingly infecting other people than she was when she first learned she has the disease. The thing she finds bitterly ironic is that he was just what she'd hoped he'd be: handsome and intelligent and charming. He might as well have put a gun to her head and those of the three other women he infected and blown their brains out. To think that she was so looking forward to studying abroad for a year at the Sorbonne and fantasizing about having an affair with just such a professor. What a fool. Well, she got what she deserved for being careless, but there's no justification for what he did and she gets no satisfaction from the fact that his disease progressed to full-blown AIDS and finally killed him. So, now she lives with her "friend", as she took to calling it, and always will, just the two of them for as long as she has left. She knows it will probably be pneumonia that finally does her in, as it does most people, but it's her friend who killed her emotionally and psychologically and turned her into one of the walking dead, a real life zombie.

She looks at Art as he brings the pickup to a stop at the curb in front of her house and smiles when he looks at her. She can see in his eyes that he'd like to be invited in. He has nothing to worry about. She'll make sure of that.

Kaitlin plops down on the sofa and tucks her legs under her and watches Michael head toward the kitchen. Why doesn't he ask? He knows her well enough to know something's up, so why doesn't he ask her about it? Is it that he doesn't care or doesn't want to know? She can't believe he doesn't care. "Beer, babe?" she hears him call from the kitchen. Enough beer. "Glass of wine!" she calls.

If he did ask, what would she tell him? She honestly doesn't know. Sure, she could tell him she's been sleeping with a colleague in Munich, but all that would do is hurt his feelings and probably anger him and if he asked the next logical question, whether she loves the guy and what she plans to do about it, she'd have to say that she honestly doesn't know and where would they be then? Of course, his reaction could be to simply end the relationship. He'd have every right to. Maybe he feels the same way Beatrice does, that it's better not to know how your partner feels about other people.

Michael hands her a glass of white wine and sits in the chair facing her and puts his feet on the coffee table and crosses his legs and holds up his bottle. "Cheers," he says.

She yawns and holds up her glass. "Cheers."

"Tired, huh?"

"Still jet lagged."

"They're grinding you pretty hard."

She shrugs and sips her wine. "No more than they're grinding you." She looks over his shoulder at the framed picture on the wall of the two of them smiling and hugging in swimsuits on the beach in Maui on a trip they took with Keith and Beth. "Beth's having a hard time with her new job." she says. "She's really struggling, putting in long hours trying to make it work."

He shrugs. "We all are."

"Everyone we know is in the same boat. What's the point?"

He smiles. "You are tired. It's not a sprint, babe. It's a marathon."

She yawns again. "I guess." It's his favorite analogy. He's right, of course, but he's the marathoner. She's always been a sprinter.

"Every generation goes through this. Our parents did and their parents."

"Seems to me they had a brighter future ahead of them. I don't see things getting better in this country anytime soon. We could be looking at this mess a long time."

"I'm sure things looked just as bad to them, but they had hope and kept going."

"I guess you're right." She places her glass on the coffee table and sits back and crosses her arms and looks at him and sighs. "Happy?"

"Yeah. You?"

She's been happier. This trying to deal with having strong feelings for two people business is wearying. She shrugs. "Yeah."

"Keep me posted."

She gazes at him. This is what she loves about him most, his trust and confidence in her that she has their best interests at heart and in mind and is holding up her end of the relationship. In the beginning that responsibility seemed weightless, but now it feels heavy and she's not sure she can continue carrying the weight. She's reminded of what he shared with her about his training to run marathons, that when he first began he felt he couldn't run the distance, that he reached a point where he felt he couldn't go any farther and knew that if he stopped then, he'd be failing himself, that he had to keep putting one foot in front of the other and run through the pain. It was a test he felt he had to pass and did. Maybe Manfred is her test. Maybe if she can get past him she'll be able to go the distance with Michael. She looks over his shoulder again at their smiling faces in the pictures on the wall. She knows she's being selfish and she knows how she'd feel if she learned that Michael was sleeping with someone else. She'd be hurt and probably wouldn't ever feel the same way about him or be able to trust him. It's only natural. She yawns and looks back at him and sees him smiling at her.

"C'mon, babe," he says, "it's late and you're beat."

She watches him stand and walk toward the kitchen. Is she beat? She's in over her head emotionally and struggling, that's for sure, but she's determined to sort things out. She's exhausted, but not beat, not yet anyway.

"It's a totally different vibe," Magda said of Berlin, a city she prefers to Munich and where she lives and Kaitlin can feel it as they stroll arm in arm down Freidrichstrasse toward Quartier 206, the upscale shopping center where the most important of the several boutiques that carry Magda's jewelry is located. The atmosphere in the city feels electric. She knows Berlin's history, that it's been through the fire and risen like a phoenix from the ashes and recreated itself. It feels like a city that isn't afraid to take chances. She listens as Magda tells her about Quartier 206.

"You wouldn't believe it now, but not so long ago this part of Berlin was considered déclassé. The wall came down, but there was this 'anti-East' mentality among people living in the West. They were against development. And then this investor had the idea to build Quartier 206 and got I.M Pei to design it. You know, now when people think of Berlin they think 'hip' and 'trendy' and 'cutting edge', all of which is true, but the old guard can be real stuff shirts and when Quartier 206 opened they were appalled! They called it a monstrosity! The investor had a hard time getting renters. Beh." Shes shrugs as they near the entrance. "Now they all flock here like sheep. Wait till you see the interior space!"

Kaitlin takes in the Art Deco-inspired atrium with its sweeping staircase leading up to the upper levels and tilts back her head and looks up at the glass-ceiling high overhead. "Wow! It's spectacular!"

"It's really something, eh? Come on. We'll take the elevator up and the staircase down."

Magda introduces her to Brigitte, the statuesque, elegantly dressed and icily polite boutique owner and she's struck by the color of Brigitte's hair, which is just long enough to be combed straight back, and eyebrows. If there's a color called "Impossibly Platinum" this is it. They walk over to the display case containing Magda's jewelry and Kaitlin studies the pieces. There are a dozen or so necklaces on display and they're all beautiful, but one in particular catches her eye. The central design element of the disc-shaped enamel pendent is unmistakably a swastika and it's ringed by what appear to be flames or rays of light. "I see an American Indian influence in that one," she says, pointing to it.

"Yes!" Magda says. "When I was a kid we vacationed in the American Southwest. I fell in love with New Mexico and the art. One of the shops in Santa Fe carried a lot of Navajo art and there was this one beautiful rug that used swastikas in the border design. It was the first time I'd seen a swastika used in a context other than as a symbol of Nazism. I'll never forget the experience. I didn't know how to react to it, how to feel, what to think. I'd been taught to hate this symbol, but here it was used in a totally different context, as part of a beautiful design, and that's when I became fascinated with symbols and the power they have over people. I learned that the swastika is an ancient symbol, that its use probably originated in ancient India and that the word 'swastika' comes from the Sanskrit words 'su-', meaning 'good' and 'well', and 'asti', meaning 'being.' So, 'well-being', completely the opposite of what I knew it to mean: Hitler, Nazism, the worst aspects of human nature. This piece is my way of reclaiming the symbol."

Kaitlin's been gazing at the pendant as she's been listening to Magda. What is it she sees represented in it? "I think 'light'...'understanding.'"

Magda smiles. "Good! Manfred had read *1984* and said I should read it and I did. It was a revelation. I knew exactly what Orwell was writing about, what he was trying to warn the world about, that if you let other people appropriate symbols and language and use them for their own nefarious purposes, you will wake up one day and find yourself enslaved. I've been hypersensitive about it ever since. I can't watch ads on TV. They infuriate me. I'm mystified why people enjoy being deceived by them."

"Some of them are very clever and entertaining."

"Precisely. So was Goebbels. I listen very carefully to what politicians have to say. It drives me crazy that people don't seem to care that they lie through their teeth. I can't be the only one who sees it."

"You're not."

"Then why do we do nothing about it?"

"It's not so easy. And it isn't just politicians."

Magda nods at the brooch. "Brigitte is very brave to display this piece. I give her a lot of credit. Strictly speaking, it's illegal to use the swastika in Germany and she has some very influential people in her clientele."

"Will it sell do you think?"

Magda shrugs. "If it does it will be to a tourist, maybe from Argentina. Come on," she says, putting her arm around Kaitlin's and leading her away, "there's a great Viennese pastry shop just down Friedrichstrasse. We'll make our grand exit down the staircase."

Kaitlin sips her coffee and studies Magda's face. Manfred has his father's blue eyes and square jaw and full lips while Magda has her mother's oval-shaped face and brown-almost-black eyes and thin nose and lips. She should wear her hair longer. It's too severe cut so short. It would soften her look and help take the edge off her personality. She notices Magda's staring at her engagement ring.

"What's he like, your fiancée?" Magda asks.

"Nice, very sweet."

"Does he know?"

Kaitlin looks down at the island of tiny bubbles on the surface of her coffee. They seem huddled together for protection against – What? She nods. "I'm pretty sure he does."

Magda glances up at her. "And he hasn't said anything?"

Kaitlin shakes her head.

"Ah. He's either very understanding or also seeing someone, possibly both."

As much as Kaitlin thinks she's gotten used to Magda's bluntness, this comment unnerves her. "I don't think he is," she says and hears the defensiveness in her voice.

"You might never know. How would you feel if he were?"

Kaitlin considers the question and of all the feelings she imagines she would feel one stands out. "Betrayed."

Magda smiles and shakes her head. "We humans are funny. We think we're above nature or beyond it somehow. I think in many ways nothing has changed since we crawled out of the mud and probably never will. Even when we're living on Mars, we'll still be silly imperfect humans." She raises her eyebrows and grins. "Well, life is going to be very interesting for you now."

"What do you mean?"

"With Manfred there." Magda realizes from Kaitlin's expression that her brother hasn't bothered to tell her. It's just like him. He has his own ideas about what is and isn't important in relationships and has broken more than a few hearts as a result. She hopes he doesn't break her friend's.

What are the odds that Beatrice would be on her flight? Whatever they are, Kaitlin's delighted and relieved to see her sitting in the gate area. She must not be doing a very good job of hiding the fact that she's in a high emotional state and needs to talk and unburden herself because Beatrice looks at her with surprise and then concern and puts the document in her bag and stands and leads her by the hand to get her seating assignment changed so they can sit together.

"White wine," Beatrice tells the flight attendant.

Kaitlin glances up at the attendant. "I'll have the same." She looks at Beatrice and sees her looking at her with narrowed eyes.

"Why didn't he tell you?" Beatrice asks.

Kaitlin shrugs. "He said he'd been meaning to but just hadn't gotten around to it." She hears Beatrice make that "tsk" sound.

"But he told his sister."

"Yeah." The flight attendant hands them their glasses and Kaitlin sips her wine and watches Beatrice out of the corners of her eyes take an even longer sip and put her glass down and stare at it.

"What type of man is he?" Beatrice asks.

"Self-centered. I didn't see that side of him."

"What did you see in him?"

"Mostly his interest in me I guess. He's handsome, charming. He pursued me. It was flattering. I wasn't thinking."

Beatrice fixes her eyes on Kaitlin's. "It's easy for that to happen when you're six thousand miles from home."

"I feel like a complete fool."

"No. If you were a complete fool you'd still be interested in him."

"I know the way you feel about sharing things with your partner, that some things are better left unsaid, but I think I should tell Michael about it."

"If you feel it's a risk worth taking, then do."

"Yeah, I do. I don't know if it'll make our relationship stronger or end it. I'm ready for either I guess. It's all Magda's doing. She's so passionate about truth and honesty."

Beatrice eyes Kaitlin's necklace. "That's an interesting necklace. Very unusual."

"Magda made it. She makes jewelry."

Beatrice leans closer and inspects the pendant. "Is it a plane?"

"Yes, well, no, an eagle. It's a long story."

Beatrice wonders if Manfred's sister might not be just as self-centered and controlling as he is in her own way and senses that Kaitlin is wondering the same thing. She studies her eyes. She wanted children but wouldn't have them with Roger. It would have been selfish and unfair to the children to bring them into that realationship and by the time she met and married Arnold they were both older and well into their careers and really didn't have time to devote to being parents and decided they were perfectly content as they were, just the two of them enjoying life together. She's mentored and counseled many young professional women, but she feels motherly toward Kaitlin, concerned that she's allowed herself to come under the influence of people who don't to have her best interests in mind but can't see it. She looks tenderly at Kaitlin and puts her hand on her forearm and sits back slowly. "We have plenty of time. So, tell me about Magda."

CHAPTER 9

Trey's still thinking about his encounter with Emily in the hall earlier that afternoon as he walks home from school. She's been different lately, even more quiet and withdrawn, but today she seemed downright depressed and the fact that she's taken to wearing long sleeve shirts, which she's been doing ever since she returned from a week out of school, supposedly away with her parents somewhere, is troubling to him. Is she cutting herself? He's heard about kids with low self-esteem doing that. He wanted to ask her if she were but felt it was too personal a question. He's concerned about her, though, and hopes she isn't. Anyway, if she were her parents would know. Her mom's so controlling, how could she not? They'd do something about it, wouldn't they?

He turns the corner onto his street and sees Walt's black SUV parked in the driveway, which is odd. It's just past four and Walt usually doesn't arrive home from work until six-thirty or later and the fact that he's parked in the driveway means that he isn't home to stay, that he just stopped by for some reason.

As soon as Trey enters the kitchen he hears Walt's raised voice coming from Julie's room. He's going on and on about her having gone behind his back and how he thought he could trust her and how this is the thanks he gets for everything he's done for her. Trey's not sure whether he should walk down the hall to his room and make his presence known or leave quietly and wait outside somewhere until Walt leaves. He decides to leave and walks down the block in the opposite direction than the one he knows Walt will head in when he returns to work, if he returns to work. How did he find out?

Trey reviews everything that happened that day from the time his dad picked them up to the time he dropped them off and can't see anything that would have made Walt suspicious. Did Julie's mom tell him? He can't imagine she did. He sees Walt appear from around the side of the house and walk quickly toward his SUV and get in, slamming the door. Even from this distance he can tell that Walt's furious. He hears the SUV start with a roar and watches it back out of the driveway and take off down the block with its tires squealing and sees the break lights come on at the corner as it slows, but it doesn't stop and turns the corner, accelerating rapidly and disappears and he listens to the sound of the engine fade and waits a few more minutes before walking back to the house.

He finds Julie lying face down on her bed and takes off his backpack and puts it on the floor and sits on the bed beside her. "Hey," he says. She looks up at him and he can see she's been crying. He doesn't think Walt hit her, at least not that he can see. "What happened? How'd he find out?"

"I'm so fucking stupid. I used my debit card. I should have paid for the tickets with cash."

"So, he knows about my dad?"

She looks up at him guiltily and nods.

"It's okay. He was probably going to find out anyway, sooner or later."

"I wanna go live with my mom."

He's surprised by his reaction. It wasn't that long ago that he considered Julie a spoiled brat and a jerk and now he feels closer to her than anyone else. The prospect of living in this house without her here seems awful, but he understands how she feels. "You should. Have you spoken with her about it?"

She nods and looks down at her hands.

"What's she think?"

Julie shrugs. "She says she's okay with it, but I know she's uneasy, and not just because of my dad."

He thinks of his dad and his struggle to be a good parent. He knows his dad doesn't think he's doing a very a good job being one, but he is as far as Trey's concerned, despite everything, and he knows Kim feels the same way. "She'll do fine."

Julie looks up at him. "I'll miss you if I go."

"I'll miss you too."

"I wish you could come with me."

"I'll come visit."

She moves closer to him and curls up on her side and rests her head in his lap and he puts his arm around her shoulder and they stay that way without saying anything awhile until he hears her ask, "Do you think life's fair?" Good question. He's aked himself the same question. Around the time things really got bad with his parents he found himself thinking it wasn't, but something about that didn't feel right and lately he's come around to thinking that life's neither fair nor unfair, that it simply is. "I dunno. It doesn't seem so sometimes." He gives her shoulder a squeeze and she nestles her head deeper into his lap.

He lies in bed in the dark staring at the ceiling and waiting. He's unsettled by how afraid Kim is. She knows the sound of every car on the street as well as he does. When they moved to Walt's they made a game of lying in the dark identifying the sound of the neighbors' cars. This one is the FJ Cruiser that belongs to the people three houses down. It's the husband's car. He comes home late from work. Its engine sounds deeper and its lights appear brighter and a different color against the bedroom wall than his wife's Ford Escort and Kim knows that as well as he does, but as the sound of the approaching car grows louder he hears her ask fearfully, "Is that him?

It's almost midnight and still no sign of Walt, which is really unusual. He only goes out with his buddies once in a while and when he does he's never out this late. Trey has the feeling that something bad is about to happen. He doesn't know what but he feels the same way he does just before an earthquake. There's that moment when everything seems to freeze, when there's no motion and no sound and then the earth suddenly drops beneath him with a rumbling "whoosh" sound and when it passes he feels lucky to be alive. As often as he's experienced earthquakes living in Southern California he's never gotten used to them. It isn't possible to get used to something like that. At least with earthquakes there's only a moment of uncertainty and the shaking only lasts a few seconds. He has the feeling that whatever's about to happen will be as scary as an earthquake but last a lot longer.

Finally he hears Walt's SUV round the corner and pull into the driveway and the clattering of the garage door opening and he glances at the clock on the nightstand: 12:06. It seems to take forever for the door to go up and then he hears the door of Walt's SUV slam shut and the clattering of the garage door as it closes. He knows that Julie and his mom are lying in their beds just as he and Kim are, staring at the ceiling, listening and waiting and wondering. He hears Walt enter the kitchen and drop his keys on the counter and then walk down the hall and into his bedroom and close the door. "He's mad," he hears Kim say and then, "I'm scared," and watches her pull back the covers and climb out of bed and pad over to his bed and sit on it next to him with her knees together and her shoulders hunched and hands jammed between her thighs. He sees her turn and look down at him and even in the dim light he can see the fear in her eyes and that she's trembling.

"Think he'll do anything?" she asks.

"I dunno," he says and gets out from under the covers and sits on the bed beside her. "Probably not." He can tell she doesn't believe him. Before long they hear the muffled sounds of Walt's and their mom's voices coming from their bedroom, low at first, but growing louder and it's Walt's voice they hear over their mom's now and he's shouting at her about your fucking husband this and your fucking husband that and that shit son of yours and how they can all get out of his house and go to hell and Trey can't take sitting here listening anymore and stands and heads toward the hall. He hears Kim say, "Don't!" and feels her grab his arm but he pulls free and keeps going.

He finds Julie standing in the hall outside her bedroom with her back to him and he can tell by the way she's standing, with her hands to her mouth by the looks of it, that she's scared too. She hears him coming and turns to face him.

"Trey, don't!" Julie says.

She tries to hold him back but he breaks free and keeps going. "Leave me alone!" he hears his mom scream as he arrives at the closed bedroom door and then a sound like a bag of cement being dropped on the floor.

He opens the door and sees Walt standing in the bathroom doorway with this back to him, hunched over and swaying and screaming at his mom to get out and Trey can tell by the sound of his voice that he's been drinking. He steps into the room and sees his mom on her back on the floor, crying and cowering with her arms in front of her face. He glances at the nightstand on Walt's side of the bed and scampers across the bed to it and opens the drawer and takes out the gun and turns to see Walt facing him now and coming toward him and he's never seen him look this way, like a wild animal.

"I'll kill you!" Walt screams. "You fucking shit!"

Trey sees his mom behind Walt, struggling to get to her feet. She looks horrified and her cheek is bruised and he looks back at Walt who's towering over him now with his hand in a fist and his arm back ready to hit him. For an instant Walt seems frozen and then he snaps into motion and Trey sees his fist coming toward him fast and he points the gun at his chest and pulls the trigger.

He opens his eyes and has no idea where he is or what he's looking at. All he can see is a blurry field of dingy white, like the fog sometimes at the beach. He can hear people's voices in the distance and tries to turn his head to look around, but can't.

A man's face he doesn't recognize comes into view and the man peers down at him.

"Hey, buddy."

The man sounds like he's a lot farther away than he is. Trey watches him hold up a penlight and turn it on and shine it in one of his eyes and then the other. He sees the EMT patch on the man's blue shirt sleeve and realizes that he's on his back staring up at the ceiling and remembers being in Walt's bedroom and pointing the gun at his chest and pulling the trigger and seeing Walt's fist coming at him and that's the last thing he remembers. Did he kill him? Shit! What if he did? He realizes that he can't move his head because it's in a brace. He sees the EMT looking down at him again and feels a pat on his arm.

"You're gonna be okay."

He sounds closer now, more like the way he should sound. Trey sees a female EMT appear in front of him and now he's being lifted up and rolled along and he realizes he's on a gurney being wheeled out of Walt's bedroom and out of the corners of his eyes he sees Julie and Kim standing in the hall by the bedroom door. They still look scared and they're dressed like they're going somewhere and then his mom is walking beside him holding his hand and he sees her bruised cheek and black eye and she's dressed like she's going somewhere too. He watches the ceiling fan in the living room pass by and then the lintel of the front door and then the night sky is above him and he can see red and blue and white lights flashing in the trees along the sidewalk. The gurney comes to a stop beside an EMT van and now his dad is standing beside him next to his mom and they're both looking down at him.

"Hey, buddy," Art says, "how ya feelin'?"

"Okay. Where's everybody going?"

"You and I are going to the hospital to get you checked out. Mom and Kim and Julie are going to Nana's."

"Where's Walt?"

"Dunno. He took off."

"I didn't shoot him?"

Art smiles and shakes his head. Strictly speaking, no. "It wasn't loaded."

Kim runs upfield on offense on what she hopes will be a breakaway. She's keeping her eye on Hilary, her teammate and the right forward who's running up the right side of the field kicking the ball in front of her with Laguna Canyon's right midfielder beside her and right forward in hot pursuit. This is a play they've run so many times they don't even think about it anymore. Hilary will find a way to get the ball to her in the middle of the field and all she'll have between her and the goal will be the fullbacks and the goalie. She's not concerned about most of the fullbacks in her school's league. She can handle herself against them and once past them it's just her and the goalie and an almost certain goal. Knowing how to finish breakaways is her specialty as a striker, but Laguna Canyon's center fullback is different. They've faced each other a few times before and while Kim's been able to get past her it hasn't been easy. She's good and Kim watches her move into position in anticipation of her getting the ball. Hilary puts on a burst of speed and feeds the ball to her in the middle of the field and she sees the center fullback coming toward her, but not too fast. She's smart this girl.

Kim pushes the ball to the right and sees the center fullback moving to the right with her. She fakes right and heads back toward the center but the center fullback is right there with her and forcing her to the left and the approaching right midfielder, not at all where she wants to be. Time to go for it.

She does a stutter step left and then right that puts the center fullback off balance for a second and kicks the ball between the girl's legs and runs around her and now it's just her and the goalie who's running out of the goal toward her with her arms spread wide. As the goalie plants her feet, Kim sets up the ball and kicks it off her right foot just out of reach of her outstretched hand and watches the ball sail toward the right side of the goal bending left and land in the net.

She hears her teammates' cheers and those of the parents on the sideline rooting for her team and she and the center full-back exchange glances. They know who they are, each the best player on her team and Kim the better of the two. She feels a bond between herself and this girl as she does with all of the best players in the league, like they're sisters.

"Hey," Kim hears and looks up from stuffing her things into her sports bag to see the girl standing there. In a way it's as if she's looking at herself. The girl has the same short hair and the same wiry build and stands the same way she does, squarely on both feet with her arms hanging at her sides. What she notices the girl has that she doesn't are three silver studs in the crescent of her right ear. "Hey," she says.

"Cyd."

"Kim."

"I know your name. Everyone does. Think you'll get league MVP?"

Kim shrugs and turns back to stuffing things into her bag. "I do," she hears Cyd say as she zips it up. She stands and hoists the bag and slings the strap over her shoulder and looks at Cyd. "There're a lot of players who could, including you."

Cyd grins. "You're better. Just admit it."

"Okay. I'm better." Kim begins walking toward the parking lot and hears Cyd following her and now she's walking beside her.

"We should hang," Cyd says.

"Why?"

"We're a lot alike."

Kim glances at the three studs in Cyd's ear. "How?"

"I dunno…I can't explain it."

"You don't even know me."

"That's why we should hang, to get to know each other better."

Kim stops and so does Cyd and she waits a moment to see if Cyd has anything else to say and sees she doesn't. "I'll think about it," she says and walks toward the parking lot. "Hey," she hears Cyd say and stops and turns and sees Cyd walking toward her and notices the folded piece of paper in her hand.

"Here," Cyd says holding it out to her, "get in touch."

Kim takes it and Cyd grins and turns and walks away.

Nana Eileen is going on about what a great player she is and how proud she is of her and Kim's not really listening. She's focused on the folded piece of paper Cyd gave her, staring down at in her hand and trying to decide whether or not to unfold it and read what's written on it. If she doesn't everything will remain just as it is, which is fine with her, but if she does she has the feeling that things will change in unexpected ways and perhaps in ways not to her liking. She's still unsettled by Cyd's seeming to know more about the two of them than she does. Why is Cyd so interested in her? Because she's a better soccer player? That doesn't feel right. How are they alike, beyond the fact that they're both the players on their teams? The urge to see what's written on the paper finally proves irresistible and she unfolds it and reads Cyd's contact information and sees that she's on Facebook.

She tunes into her grandmother for a moment and hears her say she might be the next Brandi Chastain. It's not the first time she's heard Nana Eileen say this and thinks as she always does that the last thing she wants to do is rip off her jersey and show everyone in the Olympic stadium her sports bra and then pose nude in a men's magazine, but she knows Nana Eileen means the part about how Chastain inspired the next generation of girl soccer players to play hard and dream big and, yeah, she's benefited from people like Chastain but she's not interested in being a role model like her. She plays the game for the sheer joy of being able to get around defenders as good as Cyd anytime she wants. Other than that, she's not trying to prove anything to anyone.

She sits at the computer in her bedroom, finishing up creating a Facebook account. She's a newcomer to this business, but Cyd seems to be an old hand at it and sure does have a lot of pictures of herself with her friends in the photo gallery on her Facebook page. There are photos of them at The Block, at Fashion Island, at South Coast Plaza, at a friend named Maura's birthday party, at another friend named Courtney's birthday party, at Cyd's own birthday party, on and on. There are only girls in the photos and they all have the same tomboyish look. In fact, they all look pretty much like herself, except they're also wearing three silver studs in their right ear, just like Cyd. She sees Cyd's online and is tempted to send her an instant message but hesitates. She has the same reservations about doing it that she did about opening Cyd's note but the urge to send her a message proves just as irresistible and she types one and sends it:

checking out ur pics. what's w the studs?

She stares at the screen and waits for a reply and enough time goes by that she thinks maybe Cyd's too busy messaging with her friends. She clicks through a few more photos while she waits. There's a series of three of Cyd and someone named Allie on the beach in Laguna Beach. Allie's wearing a bikini and Cyd a white tee shirt and they're cheek to cheek and smiling and the photos were obviously taken by Cyd holding out her phone. Allie's the only one of Cyd's friends who doesn't look like the rest of the girls. She has blonde hair held back by a pink barrette and is wearing a thin silver chain around her neck and no studs in her right ear but tiny diamond-looking studs in her earlobes. She's pretty and looks very girly and the way Cyd looks compared with Allie she could be her boyfriend. Cyd's reply appears:

in thing.... how r u? :-)

This is why she was reluctant to send Cyd a message in the first place. Now that the conversation's begun she doesn't know where it will go. Until this moment she's dealt with Cyd as an opponent on the soccer field where she understands her well and is able to negotiate her way around her, but now she's dealing with her off the field as a person and is uneasy about who Cyd is and what her interest in her is and especially so now, having seen the photos on her Facebook page. What's confusing is that as much as she wants to just end the conversation and sign off, she finds she can't and doesn't want to and stares at the screen, feeling like a moth staring at a flame and finally takes a deep breath and types her reply and sends it:

u sure have lots of friends n hang a lot.

I do n we do. u kicked my butt today. |-(

i play 2 win.

I do 2. post some pics!

don't have any.

we'll take some! :-)

who's allie?

She stares at the screen and waits for Cyd's reply. She waits a few moments longer and is about to send Cyd a message saying she has to go when it appears:

girl i knew....

did she move?

Another long moment passes and finally Cyd's reply appears:

no....

something happen to her?

no.... let's talk about u. :-) into boys?

Reading this makes her uncomfortable. She thinks she knows where Cyd's headed with this question and isn't sure how to respond and settles for:

idk.

girls?

as friends?

more....

idk.

ever liked a girl?

no.

think u could? :-)

It's a scary question and she honestly doesn't know how to answer. She could say she doesn't think so but she doesn't really know, or she could say she thinks she could but doesn't know that, either, and isn't sure she wants to be attracted to a girl. Any answer would only encourage Cyd to continue asking scary questions. She's not ready for this and types and sends her reply:

gotta go.

come hang! u'll like my friends. i know they'll like u.

i'll think about it. bye.

bye. ;-(

She lifts her fingertips off the keycaps and sits back in her chair and exhales slowly and stares at the screen. Can she cancel her account? You must be able to. Maybe she just won't sign in to Facebook anymore. That way she won't have to deal with Cyd's scary questions.

Art walks through University Town Center on the UCI campus toward the restaurant to meet his father for lunch. He's surrounded by college students and sees a young woman wearing a white UCI soccer uniform walking toward him with a canoe paddle slung over her shoulder. The incongruous paddle brings to mind the camping trip with his father to Saranac Lake that summer when he was eight.

It was a beautiful sunny day when they arrived at the lake and put in and loaded their provisions in the canoe and set off, but by the time they reached open water and began making their way toward the islands where the campsites are located, the weather had turned. A massive bruise-colored thundercloud was towering over the hills in the distance and coming in their direction and now it was a matter of trying to outrun the storm and find an unoccupied campsite and get their tent set up before the downpour. They finally spotted one and were about fifty yards from shore when the rain began and by the time they reached shore and turned the canoe over and managed to get their provisions and themselves under it, everything was soaking wet and they sat there listening to the sound of the rain pattering on the bottom of the upturned canoe and splattering on the ground and he remembers sitting there hugging his legs with his nose pressed against his knees and looking at his father and seeing him looking at him with a big grin on his face and asking, "Having fun?" He wasn't having fun at all, he was miserable, cold and wet and shivering, but he felt that letting his father know how he really felt wasn't the right thing to do, that it would disappoint him, so he nodded.

It wasn't until they were back home and he reflected on all the things they'd done together that he realized he'd had a great time: canoeing through the locks to get from one lake to the next, hooking what he thought was a big fish that turned out to be a small fresh water clam, fishing along the shore from the canoe one evening, ready to call it a day when his father decided to make one last cast and hooked an enormous pike that leapt out of the water the way he'd only seen fish do on TV, then poaching it over the campfire and thinking it was the most delicious thing he'd ever tasted. In fact, he'd had the best time of his life with his father, precisely because of the cold and discomfort and the fact that they'd roughed it together. Why did they stop doing things like that? He was, what, fourteen when they last went camping together in the Sierras? Maybe he'll ask him.

He enters the restaurant and spots his father sitting alone at a table in the corner of the restaurant, his reading glasses halfway down his nose, perusing the menu. He could be reading a colleague's paper for peer review. He'd look the same. To see him sitting there in his button down, blue, hounds tooth check Brooks Brothers shirt, the very picture of a college professor, you'd never guess his passion is the outdoors and that his idea of a really good time is to trek into the wilderness and camp for a week or build an igloo and sleep in it in sub-zero conditions. "Hey, Pop," Art says, pulling back a chair.

Arthur glances at his wristwatch and frowns and removes his reading glasses. "You're late."

"Yeah, sorry. I had to take care of something." Art sits and watches his father's expression change to one of curiosity as he slowly folds his glasses and puts them in his shirt pocket. "Overdue license renewal," he says with a shrug.

Arthur shakes his head. "Same old shit." He notices the scar on Art's cheek and narrows his eyes. "What happened to you? Bar fight?"

"Yeah, sort of."

"Somebody's husband? That seems to be your MO."

"Listen, Pop, how about if we call a truce, just for this afternoon?" Art's aware of the waitress standing at his side and looks up at her and can tell by her deliberate smile and the way she's looking from his father to him that she senses the tension between them. She has that experienced look about her that comes from years of dealing with people and reading them quickly and he figures that to her looking at the two of them is like looking at a flashing yellow "Proceed With Caution" sign.

"What can I get you?" the waitress asks Art.

"Sierra Nevada Pale Ale."

She nods and looks at Arthur and raises her eyebrows.

"Another, and ask the bartender to make it dirtier this time."

"Will do," she says and turns and walks away.

Arthur looks at Art's shirt and sport coat. "Nice to see you're taking an interest in your appearance. You looked like hell."

"Henry sends his best."

Arthur nods. "Good man."

Art watches his father drain his martini and set the glass down, a drinking glass rather than a martini glass as his father has long preferred. He's always wondered if this is just an affectation on his father's part, a way of making himself seem somehow more manly or if he uses a drinking glass as a practical matter, to keep from spilling his drink as the evening wears on. It's probably a bit of both. His father's always been a hard drinker, unlike, it would seem, whoever designed the martini glass. Art has to agree with his father that whoever it was never had more than one.

"Have you spoken with your mother lately?" Arthur asks.

"Yeah, a few days ago."

"How's she doing?"

"Fine. When's the last time you spoke with her?"

"Been awhile. I only hear from her when something needs repair. Apparently the house is holding together."

Art's surprised by his father's tone of voice. Not a hint of bitterness or sarcasm. Has time finally drained the reservoir or did he just forget himself? If his father's preoccupied it has to be with worries about Landis and if he's bitter about anything it should be the irony of his situation.

Art knows his father's side of the story, that his mom let herself go to seed like a typical Catabrigian in the mid-Seventies and that as the Women's Liberation Movement gained strength he saw his male colleagues turning into a bunch of eunuchs and was damned if he was going to let that happen to him and when his mom came under the influence of her women friends in that "warren", as his father called it, they grew apart.

His mom never talked much about their Cambridge days and it wasn't until his father moved out of the house that she shared her side of the story with him. According to her, it was his father's womanizing that ultimately ended their marriage. She said he'd probably always been seeing other women but that she only became aware of it a year or so after he was born and when she confronted his father about it he became furious and told her to mind her own business. She didn't divorce him because she didn't have the courage and that realization got her thinking about how insecure and subservient to his father she was and she decided that she needed to go to work on herself, to gain self-confidence and become more self-reliant. She joined a women's support group and that infuriated his father even more. He called her and her new friends a bunch of "closet lesbians" and it was remarkable to her how such an otherwise intelligent man could be so ignorant about the women's movement and so intolerant and dismissive of it. She said she's no psychiatrist but thinks it's because his father's mother was such a strong-willed woman and strict with her boys. What his father wanted to be was a Forest Service Ranger but Gramma Eloise would have none of it and insisted he become a college professor like Grampa Harold and his father was really rebelling against his mother and taking out his latent anger and frustration and resentment of her on women, in general, and herself, in particular. She felt like she was dealing with a spiteful five-year-old. She could have left him but decided to stay in the marriage for Art's sake, at least until he went off to college.

Sad to say, there were a lot of couples with kids then who were in the same situation. She wasn't surprised when his father announced that he wanted a divorce. She knew he was having an affair with Landis and by then she was ready to leave him anyway. "Your father's met his match with that woman," his mom said. She said almost felt sorry for him. Almost.

The waitress arrives and places their drinks on the table and picks up Arthur's empty glass and looks at Art. "Ready to order?" she asks.

"Give us a few minutes," he says. She nods and walks away and he looks at his father and picks up his glass and holds it out to him. "Cheers," he says and studies his father's eyes as he stares at the glass, trying to decided what to do. He knows his father's still angry and bitter and resentful, but there's a reason he returned his call and agreed to have lunch. He doesn't know what it is, but he suspects his father wouldn't be here if everything were peaches and cream with Landis.

Arthur finally picks up his glass and holds it out and they clink. "Cheers," he says and takes a long sip.

"I was thinking of that trip we took to Saranac Lake. Remember that pike you caught?" Art sees his father's expression brighten a bit. "I'd only seen a fish leap out of the water like that on TV."

"I can you see you sitting under the canoe during that rainstorm, water dripping off your nose. You looked pathetic."

Art smiles. "I was miserable. Why'd we stop doing things like that together?" He sees his father's eyes narrow and his expression change as quickly as the weather did that day on the lake.

"All you were interested in was surfing and getting high with your buddies at the beach. You might recall you turned down a couple of invitations to go camping."

"Yeah, I guess I did."

"It was painful watching you waste so much talent and ability. I tried to help, but you fought me every step of the way."

"Well, I'm not here to fight with you, Pop. I'm here to ask for your assistance."

"With what?"

"Money. I want to get my certification and teach." Art watches his father's eyes slowly widen.

"I'll be damned. You cuckold me and ask for money."

"Yeah, well, my friend Joanne says helping me might be just what we both need."

Arthur narrows his eyes. "Who's Joanne?"

"An analyst at PACBOND."

"What's she doing with you?"

"Fair enough. I want June back."

"You're screwing Joanne and you want June back?"

"I didn't say I was screwing her."

"You didn't have to."

"It doesn't have anything to do with my feelings for June."

Arthur studies him. "Teach, huh? Math?"

Art nods.

"I'll think about it," Arthur says and picks up his menu and takes his glasses out of his pocket and unfolds them and puts them on halfway down his nose.

Art scans the list of burgers, searching for one with bacon and bleu cheese, his favorite. "She might be right," he hears his father muse.

CHAPTER 10

Eileen looks at the faces of the handful of special education students seated around her, all with mild to moderate mental retardation and listening intently to the story she's reading them with various expressions of wonderment, and smiles as her gaze settles on Abby's. As much as she tries to feel the same about these children, Abby is her favorite. What is it about this young girl with the pale blue eyes and blond hair done up in short pigtails that stick out on either side of her head and whose features bear the unmistakable characteristics of Down syndrome that is so endearing? Is it the way Abby gazes at her so trustingly, or the way she smiles from time to time for no apparent reason when she hears a word that sounds particularly funny to her, or the way she'll appear at her side when she's working with one of the other children and put her arms around her and hug her, or the way she's quick to take her hand and hold it tightly when the class is walking together in a group, or the way she calls her "Messy Golliwog" and then giggles? All of the above and she feels grateful to have Abby in her life. The fact is that Abby's lucky to be alive. Eileen's all too familiar with the statistics. The vast majority of pregnancies where a prenatal diagnosis shows the fetus has Down syndrome are terminated. It's shocking and she thinks should be criminal.

Fortunately for Abby her parents, a firefighter and a nurse, are both devout Catholics and the thought of denying Abby her right to be born and enjoy life as fully as possible never occurred to them. In fact, they love her all the more because of her disability. They consider her blessed with simplicity and serenity and when she thinks about it, she has to admit that there are advantages to living life as Abby is, always in the present, unconcerned about the past and future, always seeking love and seizing every opportunity to give it. We could all do well to be more like Abby.

Eileen sips her tea in the teacher's lounge and peruses the article about a newly developed Special Ed teaching methodology. "Hi," she hears Betty say and looks up to see her place her mug on the table and pull back a chair and sit. "Hi," Eileen says and smiles as she takes in the effect Betty has prepared for the world today. Just as Abby is her favorite student, Betty is her favorite colleague. She's smart and witty and has a knack for adding just the right touches to her appearance to enhance her natural beauty. With her high forehead and prominent cheekbones and almond-shaped eyes and long delicate nose and full lips, Betty reminds her of an African queen, a role she imagines she'd have no problem playing. Today's touches are that she's wearing her hair pulled back to accentuate her face and large gold disc earrings and a gold chocker necklace. As Eileen always does, she marvels at how youthful Betty's face looks and what great shape her skin is in. They're about the same age, but Betty looks easily ten or fifteen years younger.

"Coming Saturday?" Betty asks, bobbing her teabag.

"I guess so. I'm getting tired of going to parties alone."

"You won't be the only singleton," Betty says and looks at Eileen mysteriously. "Who knows? You might meet someone."

Eileen wonders what the air of mystery is all about. "I'm not sure I want to. I'm so used to being alone now I don't think I'd be very good company."

Betty eyes her and presses the teabag against her plastic spoon and places both on the napkin on the table. "Maybe you just need to meet the right person." She sips her tea and eyes Eileen as she does.

"Maybe," Eileen says skeptically. "You're the math teacher. What are the odds of that happening?"

"Wouldn't venture a guess, but it's always possible."

Eileen smiles sadly. "Yes, anything is.... I remember hearing that all the time when I was a kid and believing it. And then as time goes by you realize that not everything is possible, that some things just aren't, that they're never going to happen."

Betty frowns slightly. "You sound down."

"Just tired. I haven't been sleeping well lately."

"What's going on?"

"Worried about the family, as usual. Lots of issues."

"Every family's got 'em. I could write a book about mine."

"Yes, but when it's yours.... "

"Reggie's brother will be there. He'll be in town on business."

So, that's what the air of mystery is all about. Betty's mentioned Reggie's brother before, but only in passing. "Roland, right? He lives in D.C. doesn't he?"

Betty nods. "When he got out of the Army he and a couple of his Army buddies formed a consulting company. They specialize in technology transfer from the R&D environment to DOD. He's here meeting with some company in Irvine."

"Staying with you?"

Betty shakes her head. "The Hyatt in Newport Beach. He likes his privacy."

Eileen conjures up a mental image of Reggie, an academic she greatly admires and a man she considers strikingly handsome, and tries to imagine what his brother would look like. "Do they look alike?"

Betty grins. "Different flavors of the same good thing. He's more reserved than Reg. I guess it's the military thing, but he's nice. You'll like him."

"I look forward to meeting him."

It takes Eileen a few moments in the shower to get used to the spray of just-shy-of-too-hot water on her back and when she does, she turns and enjoys the feel of it on the front of her body and steps forward and tilts back her head and turns it from side to side, enjoying the feel of it beating against the skin of her face. She really was planning to pass on this party but she's intrigued by the prospect of meeting Roland, in fact, has been thinking about it all week since her conversation with Betty. She's not really sure what she's expecting or hoping will happen, other than meet him and make his acquaintance. Betty never mentioned his status, but she assumes he's either single or divorced, in any event, available. She catches herself. What does it matter? She's being silly. Well, to be honest, the prospect of meeting him is making her feel a bit like a schoolgirl and she remembers this feeling of anticipation from that time in her life long ago when it seemed filled with romance and mystery. Why not just enjoy it? It's been ages since she's felt this way and she didn't think she ever would again. It's harmless fun and her little secret and he probably has bad breath.

She turns off the shower and steps out onto the rug and begins toweling herself dry, studying herself in the mirror above the sink as she does. She wraps the towel around her head and moves a little closer to the mirror and stands facing it with her arms at her sides and inspects herself. So, there she is, a sixty-two-year-old woman with a body to match, a bit heavier and more saggy in places than it used to be but not unattractive, at least she doesn't thinks so. Her face is still pretty, although not as youthful-looking as Betty's. The crow's feet and bags under her eyes are more pronounced and her skin doesn't have that natural glow that Betty's does.

She turns sideways to the mirror and inspects her tummy and breasts, then turns back the other way. Not bad. There's more tummy and sagginess in her breasts than she'd like, but overall, not bad. She's fortunate she doesn't have large breasts. If she did they'd really be saggy now.

She turns and looks over her shoulder at her back and butt. There's more weight on the hips and thighs than she'd like and a few too many creases under her buttocks, but when all is said and done, not bad. She could be in far worse shape. Of course, whether Roland will find her attractive is another matter entirely and there isn't much she can do about that. All she can do is make the most of what she has and hope for the best.

She sits at the vanity massaging her forehead and cheeks and neck with skin crème. She examines what little there is of makeup and crèmes and lotions on the table. She's never used them much. When a teenager she wore very little makeup and then she went through her "Cambridge phase" when she deliberately tried to make herself look plain. She really did let herself go then. She's not excusing Arthur's behavior and the awful way he treated her, but she certainly didn't help matters. What husband wants to come home to a plain-looking wife?

She eyes the still unopened bottle of toilet water Kim gave her as a birthday present. She picks it up and unscrews the top and sniffs. The scent is subtle and smells the way the air does just after a summer rainstorm. She pours some in her palm and rubs her hands together and then over her shoulders and arms and breasts and finds herself lingering on her breasts and feels her nipples getting hard and sees their erectness in the mirror and is surprised to feel herself getting aroused, but shouldn't be, after all, the way she's touching herself. She touches herself every morning when she bathes and always without giving it a thought, but the prospect of meeting Roland and the evening ahead has her thinking and apparently feeling sensual and sexy. She looks at herself in the mirror in mock astonishment. "Naughty girl," she says.

She takes the "sexy black dress" June insisted she buy out of the closet. She remembers the day she bought it, standing in front of the three-way mirror, studying herself uncertainly with June standing beside her grinning at her in the mirror and all she could think was why on earth should she buy it? She hasn't needed one in years and when she did own one she only wore it a handful of times, mostly with Arthur when they were dating and then to the occasional faculty soiree after they were married. June insisted, though, so she bought it and as she stands in front of the mirror modeling it she's glad she did. She turns sideways and bends a knee slightly and runs her hands down the sides of the dress and looks coquettishly at herself over her shoulder and bats her eyelashes. How perfectly silly.

She sits at the vanity again and studies herself in the mirror as she massages vanishing cream into the skin of her face to hide the blemishes and discolorations as best it can. Maybe she'll apply just a touch of mascara and eyeliner too. Why not go all out? Satisfied with her eyes, she paints her lips with rose-colored lipstick, the color she uses whenever she wears lipstick, which is rarely anymore. She presses her lips together and rolls and purses them and puts the cap on the canister and places it on the vanity and gives her face a final inspection in the mirror. Not bad. So what if all this has been for no one's benefit but her own. It's been fun pampering herself.

She enters the kitchen to a collective "Wow!" from June and Trey and Kim, who've been waiting for her.

"You look beautiful, Mom!" June says.

"Thank you," Eileen says and looks at Kim who looks awe-struck, like she can't believe what she's seeing. Has she really become such an old frump?

"You should dress up more often, Nana," Kim says.

"I guess I haven't had a reason to, dear."

"So who's the lucky guy?" Trey asks, grinning.

Eileen touches her hair nervously. "No one," she says unconvincingly and glances at June and sees her wink.

Betty steps back from the doorway and cocks her hip and puts a hand on it and looks Eileen up and down. "Well! Look at you! Lookin' good, girl!" She steps forward and they hug. "I was beginning to think you weren't coming."

Eileen steps back and admires the effect Betty's created for the evening. She's looking radiantly sexy in that "earth goddess" way of hers. She's wearing her shoulder-length hair down, gold and ebony earrings that dangle in an inverted pyramid pattern, a matching necklace, a skintight off-the-shoulder black tube dress cut low revealing plenty of cleavage and black high heel sandals. "You look fantastic, as always," Eileen says and looks past Betty at the crowd gathered in the living room. She recognizes a dozen or so colleagues and as many newcomers. "He's running late," she hears Betty say close to her ear and starts. Is it that obvious?

She mingles and finds herself stuck in a group that includes a short squat woman who introduced herself as Jean and her taller pear-shaped husband Paul and a tall willowy blonde named Peg whose features strike her as horsey. She's not surprised to hear that Peg is from Prides Crossing, horse country north of Boston. She's been listening politely to their views about the mess the country's in as a result of the financial crisis and home foreclosures and now they've gotten around to the local offshoot of the Occupy Wall Street movement, Occupy Orange County, and it all sounds to her like one long depressing rant. What she wants to do is excuse herself and step outside for some fresh air.

"It's an eyesore," Jean says disgustedly about the tent encampment on the triangle of land in front of City Hall in Irvine. "I don't know why they let those people stay there."

Paul looks at Jean wistfully. "They're just like we were when we protested against the war in the Sixties."

Eileen glances at Peg and sees she's clearly displeased with Paul for suggesting these people are anything like they were then.

"Most of them are homeless," Peg says. "They're just a bunch of socialist freeloaders who expect the government to put a tit in their mouths and feed them."

Eileen hasn't heard a Brahman accent like Peg's since the Cambridge days, with that intonation that seems to coat every utterance with condescension as it leaves the mouth, but she remembers it well and hearing it again puts her on edge and causes her to clench her teeth just as it did then. If Peg ever did have a tit in her mouth it probably wasn't her mother's but a wet nurse's. Who the hell does this haughty bitch think she is?

Eileen's driven past the encampment at City Hall many times and seen the mostly young scruffy-looking people holding up handwritten signs proclaiming, "We Are the 99%!" and, "Tax Wall Street!" She understands their frustration. Several neighbors on her street lost their homes to foreclosure and she's seen the beating her mutual fund investments have taken as the markets have plunged and she resents the fact that CEOs at financial institutions are paid obscenely high salaries while their banks refuse to use the government bailout money they've received for lending. She's not so much worried about herself as she is Trey and Kim and the mess they're being left. "Excuse me," she hears Betty say behind her and turns to see her and Reggie standing there and she's puzzled why he would have changed clothes.

"This is Roland," Betty says with an impish grin. "Did I mention they're twins?" she asks with mock surprise and gives

Eileen's shoulder a playful shove and laughs. "Silly me. Guess I forgot."

Roland smiles and takes Eileen's hand. "It's a pleasure to meet you."

His voice is deeper and richer than Reggie's and hearing it and seeing the way he's looking at her, like she's the most beautiful woman he's ever laid eyes on, has quickened Eileen's pulse. "Nice to meet you too," she says and knows she's staring at Roland, but can't seem to take her eyes off his. Like Reggie and the number of other Jamaican men she's met through the years, Roland is handsome and polite, but he's also charming in a way she's never experienced and if the warmth of her cheeks and neck is any indication they must be beet red.

"Shall we?" Roland says, nodding toward the patio and offering his arm.

"Yes, let's," Eileen says, wrapping her arm around his. He escorts her out into the cool evening air and pulls two chairs together and they sit and sip their wine and admire the full moon. "It's beautiful," she says. "Do you know which it is?"

"Full Worm."

"The Man in the Moon always looks so worried to me."

He chuckles softly. "When you consider what goes on down here, it's no wonder."

"How long were you in the military?"

"Thirty years."

"Were you an officer?"

He nods. "Retired a full colonel."

"What did you do?"

He looks at the moon a moment and then at her. "Let's just say I served my country."

"Was your work secret?"

He smiles. "I hear you're a Special Ed teacher."

She nods.

"I admire you. It's hard work."

It's charming of him to say so. She can only imagine how difficult and probably dangerous his work in the military was. "I love what I do. The children really are special."

"Do you have kids?"

She nods. "A son."

"On good terms with your ex?"

"Reasonably. We don't talk all that often, only when we need to. You?"

He smiles and shakes his head. "Never been married."

"Just didn't want to?"

He narrows his eyes a bit and studies the moon. "I dunno. The idea of marriage has always struck me as bit too claustrophobic."

"I think it seems that way to everyone, to one extent or another. It's something you have to get past, or used to." Listen to her, the authority on marriage. How ridiculous she must sound.

He smiles and puts a hand lightly on her forearm. "Just not for me. Don't hold it against me."

She smiles nervously. She can't remember the last time she's been touched affectionately by a man and the center of her being now seems located under his palm. Her only thought is that he please not take his hand away. "I won't."

"Another glass of wine?"

"Sure." She hands him her glass.

"Be right back."

She gazes at the moon feeling pleasantly elevated by the one glass of wine. She seldom drinks at all anymore and then only a glass of wine at Betty and Reggie's parties. She drank more in the early years with Arthur. She remembers how she used to get. She would sometimes say and do things at parties after her third drink she regretted later. She still has the same metabolism she did back then so she'll be careful.

Roland returns and hands her her glass and sits and crosses his legs and asks her about her family and listens, sipping his wine, as she tells him about what's been going on with Art and June and makes no mention of Arthur. She asks him about his family and sips her wine as he tells her about his parents in Kingston who are enjoying their old age, well-cared for by family there, and how he doesn't see them as often as he'd like but will make an effort to now because who knows how much time they have left and when he's finished so is the wine in her glass and she's feeling tipsy. "How long are you in town?" she asks.

"I fly out early Monday morning." He puts his hand lightly on her forearm again. "Have dinner with me tomorrow. Are you free?"

She hasn't felt like it for a very long time but she does now, as much because of the wine as his company. "Yes. I'd love to."

"I'm staying at the Hyatt in Newport Beach. Meet me there at eight. Okay?"

She nods and stares at his eyes. They have a way of holding hers and she knows the time has arrived for her to leave because she's having difficulty looking away and finds her eyes straying to his lips and she wants to put hers on his and whatever happens after that would be fine with her. "I'd better be going. It's been a long day. I think I've had a little too much to drink."

He smiles and leans forward and pats her hand. "I'll see you to your car."

She enjoys the feeling of Roland's arm around her waist as he escorts her – no, guides her and he's doing it so well – through the crowd in the house. She feels like she's glowing and knows she's probably smiling a little too broadly but doesn't care. It's a wonderful feeling. She thanks Betty and Reggie at the front door and can see by their expressions they're happy for her. They're such dear friends. "Here we are," she says, arriving at her car.

"You going to be okay driving?"

She nods and smiles up at him. "I'll be fine."

He smiles and draws her to him and looks into her eyes and strokes her cheek with his fingertips. "I've enjoyed meeting you."

She gazes into his eyes. "And I you." It's silly, but she imagines herself to be Scarlet O'Hara being tipped backward and going limp, draped on Roland's arm and she watches his eyes coming closer and feels his lips on hers and he's still looking into her eyes but she closes hers and, no, he doesn't have bad breath. It's sweet.

Arthur puts down the paper he's been reading, one of particular interest to him presented at the conference in San Francisco, and removes his reading glasses and folds them and puts them in his shirt pocket and rubs his eyes. He would have much preferred to return yesterday after the conference but friends of his he doesn't see that often convinced him to stay over and have dinner yesterday evening. He was alarmed but not all that surprised to hear that Landis' reputation for promiscuity has spread far and wide. His colleagues shared this news with him as delicately as they could, but it hit hard. He hates being gossiped about and remembers this feeling from the Cambridge days.

He looks down at the Santa Monica Mountains and the Channel Islands off the coast. They'll be on the ground at John Wayne soon. The time has come to do something about her, either find a way to rein her in or divorce her. As wearying as the idea of divorcing again is, if it comes to that he will. He won't be made a laughingstock, anymore than he probably already is.

He turns on his phone as the plane taxis toward the gate. His call to Landis goes directly to voice mail and he leaves her a message letting her know he's back.

He enters the condo and closes the front door. "Landis!" he calls. The place is oddly quiet. Where the hell is she? Who's she screwing now? He sees the folded piece of paper with his name on it propped up against the lazy Susan on the island in the kitchen. "Shit," he mutters and picks it up and unfolds it. He knows what he's about to read and is furious with himself for not having seen it coming:

Arthur,

He can hear her drawling voice in his head, sounding like an effort is required to muster enough energy to utter each syllable:

Sorry to be such a sneak about leaving, but the time has come for me to go and I thought it best to do so when you were away, for obvious reasons. We've always been honest with each other, so I won't stop now. Frankly, you've been acting a little too old for me lately. You just seem tired and preoccupied and less virile than when we first met. I know you have a lot on your mind, not the least of which are my shenanigans, but I don't think what's happening to you has anything to do with me. You're just plain getting old, Arthur, and you aren't much fun to be with anymore. You're so concerned about being in control of your life, but I think you've met your match with aging. You can't accept it, but it's not going to stop and there's nothing you can do about it. So, it's better that I go. Send any papers I need to sign to my parents. Take care of yourself, Arthur.

Landis

P.S.: You have shirts at the cleaners.

He looks up from the note at the Lazy Susan and eyes the glass container of olive oil and the sugar bowl. He wants to throw things, just to break them, but what's the point? He'd only make a mess, which he'd have to clean up, and possibly damage the walls, which he'd have to pay to have repaired. Breaking things won't help or change a thing. The thing that's already broken is his spirit and while no amount of vodka will repair it, a glass now will calm him down a bit and he pours himself one and damned with the olive juice and tosses it back. Another can't hurt, either, and he refills the glass and walks into the bedroom and finds Landis' closet doors open and the closet empty. He pulls open each of the drawers of her dresser and they're all empty too.

He notices the framed photograph of the two of them on her nightstand and picks it up and sits on the side of the bed and stares down at it. It was taken on their honeymoon trip to the Turks and Caicos Islands. They're sitting on the beach with their heads together smiling at the camera and he can see the tiredness from the night before in their eyes. It was her idea that he take Viagra, which he did reluctantly and only to humor her. He has no problem getting or sustaining an erection, but she wanted to see if it made a difference and it did. They fucked until dawn – as languid as she is, she's plenty energetic in bed – and then dragged themselves to the beach to sleep and recover and this picture was taken late in the afternoon when they were beginning to feel themselves again and ready for more. Where did the man in this photograph go? It would be the one thing she'd leave behind. It's all the damning evidence she needs to prove she's right. He feels used up and discarded and alone in a way he hasn't before and appreciates for the first time how Eileen must feel. What a complete fool he's been.

Kim sits at the kitchen table watching her grandmother move about as she fixes herself toast to have with her tea. Nana Eileen slept late, which is unusual for her, and is still in her bathrobe, also unusual at this hour of the morning. Her grandmother's been telling her about the party last night at Betty and Reggie's and it seems that she had a really good time, especially meeting this man Roland, and in between the details Kim hears her humming softly, which is really unusual for Nana Eileen. She watches her place her mug of tea and plate of jam-covered toast on the table and sit across from her. "Does he live around here?"

Eileen takes a bite of toast and sips her tea and slowly shakes her head. "Washington, D.C."

"Too bad," Kim says and sees her grandmother shrug. "I bet he's handsome," she says, grinning.

Eileen looks at her and smiles. "Very. Roland is Reggie's brother."

"No way!" Kim's met Betty and Reggie and she knows her grandmother thinks Reggie's really handsome and she does too, but Nana Eileen with a black man?

Eileen nods. "They're twins."

This piece of information amazes Kim. She imagines her grandmother with a Reggie look-alike, the two of them smiling happily. It's a nice image. Why not?

"We're having dinner this evening."

"Wow! You must really like him!"

"I do. He's very nice." Eileen takes another bite of toast and her phone rings. She looks at the screen and is surprised to see it's Arthur. Why would he be calling? She swallows and picks up the phone. "How are you, Arthur?"

"Not well. Landis left me."

"Oh, dear. I'm sorry to hear that."

"I bet you are."

"There's no reason for sarcasm, Arthur." She glances at Kim. "Excuse me, dear," she says and stands and walks outside to the patio. "Is this why you're calling? To tell me Landis left you?"

"Of course."

"But why?"

"Who else am I going to call? No one else gives a damn about what's going on in my life, unless it's to gossip."

"But, Arthur, what makes you think I do? After the way you treated me? After everything you've done? Really, I'm surprised at you."

"You were no saint, Eileen."

"I never claimed to be. So what are you going to do?"

"What can I do? I'm going to try to get on with my life."

"Well, whatever you do, don't drink too much. That won't help anything."

"Don't lecture me about my drinking, Eileen!"

"Arthur, calm down. Shouting at me isn't going to do any good."

"I'm sorry. I'm just upset. Anyway, I want to see you."

"Why?"

"To talk."

"About?

"For Chrissake, Eileen, about what's happening to me. Who else am I going to talk with?"

"A therapist. I think that would be better."

"Fuck therapy! It's nothing but bullshit!"

"I don't know, Arthur. I don't think it's a good idea."

"Well, think about it."

"All right. I'll call you in a few days. Take care of yourself, and make sure you eat."

"I will."

She stares at the phone. He's unhinged. To think she used to love and respect and admire him. Well, she still respects his intellect, there's no denying that, but love and admiration? Those feelings departed long ago. He's still the frightened little boy he's always been, only now more than ever. Why he thinks talking with her about the mess he's made of his life will do any good or that she'd even want to talk about it is beyond her. As intelligent as he is, at the moment he seems delusional. She can't help feeling sorry for him, though. She doesn't like to see anyone suffer, although Arthur certainly deserves to. He brought this on himself. Well, she'll think about meeting with him but that can wait. At the moment she's thinking happily and only about seeing Roland again this evening.

She touches the hair at the back of her neck nervously as she walks toward the entrance to the Hyatt. It was June's idea that she wear it up, which she hasn't since she was in her early twenties, and then only occasionally. She's never thought she looks good with her hair up but June insisted she does, that it shows off her face and neck to good effect and, as important, that it will give her a new look to present to Roland. "Men like to be surprised," June said. "It keeps them interested." She hopes she's right.

Roland looks smart in his black and white check sport coat and gold turtleneck sweater as he walks toward her in the lobby. Judging from the smile on his face, he seems pleased with what he sees. He takes her hand and gives her a kiss and steps back and admires her.

"You look great," he says. "I love your hair up."

She feels herself blush and touches the hair at the back of her head nervously again. "Thanks. I'm glad you like it."

"There's a nice restaurant on the water in Newport Beach. I thought we'd go there."

"Great!" Anywhere would be fine with her. Food is the last thing on her mind.

She listens through dinner to Roland's explanation of the business he and his partners are engaged in. It all sounds very interesting and important to national security and she's trying her best to be attentive but her thoughts keep straying to their embrace and kiss on the sidewalk last night and she can't help wondering what will happen after dinner and how the evening will end. She knows how she'd like it to end, but she's not sure how they get from here to there or what she has to do to make it happen. She's not very practiced at this sort of thing and isn't very cunning.

He lifts the bottle. "More wine?"

"Please."

He studies her eyes as he refills her glass. "You look like you have a lot on your mind."

"Do I?" Is it that obvious?

He smiles and nods. "Want to talk about it?"

She takes a sip of wine and puts down her glass. It's her second and she's beginning to feel elevated and uninhibited. Even so, she's always been uncomfortable talking about her emotions and the idea of sharing what she's feeling now with Roland is beyond her. She searches for something to say and Arthur's phone call is the only thing that comes to mind. "My ex called today to tell me his wife left him."

He frowns. "Sorry to hear it."

"It's probably for the best. She's much younger and wasn't good for him."

"What type of person is he?"

"Arrogant...self-centered...insensitive...."

He chuckles and shakes his head. "He has to have some good qualities. You fell in love with him, right?"

She did, of course, but doesn't want to admit it, which she knows is foolish and finally nods.

"So, what type of woman does he need?"

"A mother."

"That's the problem with men. They want a lover but need a mother."

She knows her expression looks adoring and hopeful and probably ridiculous to him, but she can't help it. "Not all men."

He grins. "What type of woman do you think I need?"

"Someone who'll go anywhere with you...do anything with you...."

If he didn't like and respect Eileen as much as he does and know that she's had a bit too much to drink, he'd ask her if she thinks she's that woman, but he spares her. She'd probably say yes and he doesn't want her to make a fool of herself, anymore than she probably feels she already has. "It always feels that way in the beginning doesn't it? You're a romantic."

"What's wrong with that?"

"It's dangerous."

"I can't imagine that would bother you."

She's feeling a little unsteady on her feet as she takes Roland's offered hand and steps out of the car in front of the Hyatt. He tips the valet and they stroll arm in arm toward the entrance. "How're you doing?" she hears him ask and looks at him and smiles. "Fine."

"Sure you're up for a nightcap?"

She nods.

They sit at a table in a corner of the lounge and he orders them each a glass of port. She clinks his glass and takes a sip. She's always liked port. Arthur introduced her to it as an after dinner drink when they were dating. She's glad Roland suggested it. She places her glass on the table and looks at it and the amount of port remaining in it. It's such a small glass and there's not much left. That's good. There wasn't much to begin with so it can't do all that much damage.

It occurs to her that she's drunk more in the last two days than the last ten years. It's been fun, a welcome break in her humdrum existence, but she's not sure she could live this way day in and day out. She has the feeling that Roland does, though, that he's out every evening with someone, just like this. He's a player, all right, and she's sure he has a stable of admirers back in D.C. who are only too willing to spend the evening with him when he calls. Well, she's the one he's with now. That's all that matters. She has him all to herself.

She finishes her second glass of port and thinks again of how she'd like the evening to end but still can't see how to get from here to there, short of throwing herself at him, which she can't see herself doing. "It's getting late," she says. "I should probably be going." She waits to see what his reaction will be, hoping it will be to suggest that she stay the night.

He motions to the waiter for the check. "Working tomorrow?"

She shakes her head. "Spring break."

"Ah, good. You can sleep in."

Almost certainly alone, judging from the way he's treating her, like a perfect gentleman. Maybe it's because she's a close friend of Betty and Reggie's that he's handling her with kid gloves and keeping a respectful distance. Maybe that's it, or maybe it's that he just isn't all that interested in her, beyond having dinner and drinks afterward. Is she really that undesirable? He sure charmed the socks off her and seemed to enjoy kissing her last night. Well, whatever the case, she isn't very good at this game.

The waiter returns with the check and Roland's credit card and she watches him sign the check and put his credit card in his wallet and his wallet back in the inside pocket of his coat.

He looks at her and smiles. "All set?"

She's sure her adoring and hopeful expression looks even more ridiculous to him now, but it's all the ammunition she has and she's running out of time. She nods and stands and feels even unsteadier on her feet and Roland offers her his arm. She wraps hers around it tightly and he guides her through the lobby toward the entrance. "Thanks for a lovely evening," she says and can hear the disappointment in her voice. What a fool he must think she is.

"Thanks for joining me. I had a great time."

She watches him hand the valet her ticket and the valet run off into the darkness. She stares at the two moons in the patch of sky between the plam trees and tries to focus and bring them together, without success. She feels Roland's arm around her waist.

"You sure you're okay driving?"

"No, I'm not. I thought I was."

"I'll get you a cab."

She gazes at his lips and then into his eyes and doesn't care now how ridiculous she looks. "I'd rather not go home like this. Do you mind if I stay?" She sees him smile and slowly shake his head and she rests her head on his shoulder. The valet pulls up in her car and she watches Roland walk over and hand him a tip and take back her ticket. "Thanks," she hears him say, "put it back."

She sits on the side of the bed, her hands at the back of her head, removing the pins June so carefully placed in her hair to hold it up and gazes at Roland as he calls the front desk and puts in a wake up call and places the receiver back in the cradle. "Are you always such a gentleman."

He grins and slowly shakes his head.

"Good," she says and lets down her hair, "I was beginning to wonder."

She doesn't often remember her dreams and when she does, they seem full of meaning, as this one does and she wants to remember it and hopes it won't dart away like a shadowy fish just beneath the surface of the water when she wakes.

She's walking through the surf on a beach with a man who must be Roland in what must be Jamaica, or what she imagines to be Jamaica, never having been there. She's walking closest to the water and she's aware of Roland walking by her side, but each time she turns her head to look at him he's just out of sight and all she sees are the sandy beach and the palm trees bordering it. The waves grow stronger and the surf more powerful and she's aware of the sand beneath her feet giving way and with each wave that breaks on the shore she sinks deeper and tries to reach out to Roland for help, but can't find his hand and she's sinking under the water and feels herself being swept out to sea.

She opens her eyes and remembers the dream but not where she is and looks at the unfamiliar furniture and pictures on the wall and feels completely disoriented until she remembers that she's in bed with Roland in his hotel room and smiles as she remembers their lovemaking.

She picks up her head and looks over her shoulder, expecting to see him there next to her, but he's gone. Of course, she remembers he had an early flight. She climbs out of bed, aware of her nakedness — she can't remember the last time she slept nude — and sees a note propped up against the lamp on the desk and her valet parking ticket beside it. She begins reading the note as soon as she's able to make out the words:

Eileen,

Didn't want to wake you. You were sleeping pretty soundly. You looked cute.

She picks up the note:

Had a great time last night. We'll have to do it again the next time out there. Should be in a couple of months. I'll keep you posted.

Love,
Roland

She stares at the word "Love." It's such an easy thing to say. It occurs to her just how skillful Roland is at the game. Would he really have put her in a cab and sent her home? She doesn't thinks so. He wanted the evening to end the same way she did and he didn't have to ask her to stay the night. He knew that all he had to do was remain gentlemanly and let her desire and alcohol do the rest. Maybe that's his thing, never having to ask to get what he wants. She should probably feel foolish for having allowed herself to play so easily and obviously into his hands, but she doesn't. She doesn't mind at all being his latest conquest. She got what she wanted and she'd never made love like that with anyone and he certainly seemed to enjoy it. It was well worth it. She glances at the clock on the nightstand. It's late and she'd better get going before housekeeping arrives to make up the room.

CHAPTER 11

Joanne rides the escalator up to the second level. The dangling sheep above the store entrance comes into view and she remembers her last visit to Brooks Brothers. The store was in Fashion Island in Newport Beach then and she was buying a Father's Day present for her dad. They closed that store in 2000, so it's been more than ten years. Jesus, she never would have imagined she'd be measuring the passage of time in decades, at least not since her friend came into her life.

She steps off the escalator and is greeted by a sculpture, one of several she's passed, this one a cute and nicely ironic Hello Kitty constructed entirely of tuna fish cans. It's part of the annual Festival of Children hosted by South Coast Plaza. She considers Henry Segerstrom, the man who built this place on one of his family's lima bean fields and the Segerstrom Center for the Performing Arts across Bristol Street, to be not only an entrepreneur and philanthropist, but also a true visionary, as she does Donald Bren, the Chairman of the Board of The Irvine Company. Segerstrom was determined to bring high-end shopping and culture to Orange County and did, just as Bren was determined to turn the 94,000-acre Irvine Ranch into the most desirable real estate in Southern California and did.

Most people associate the spirit of The West with cowboys and movies about them and think that it died when Westerns fell out of favor. She has to admit the statue of Duke Wayne outside the terminal at John Wayne Airport does look a bit forlorn, but the spirit never died. It lives on in people like Segerstrom and Bren. She knows other visionaries will come along.

She wishes she were as optimistic about politics. She's come to view presidential elections as laughable and the cast of characters seeking the nation's highest office comical. It would be funny, if not for the fact that one of them ends up in the Oval Office. Well, we'll survive. We always do. She eyes the sheep above the entrance as she enters the store and thinks the entire country is in the same state right about now, just hanging and waiting to see what happens next.

She meanders slowly down the women's side of the store, stopping to check out the business outfits. Nice, conservative, which is what you'd expect from Brooks Brothers, but smart and fresh. She wonders why she doesn't shop here. Probably the lingering stereotype that only bluestocking women wear Brooks Brothers clothes.

She arrives at the back of Women's and sees Henry sitting at a desk across from a customer in Men's. She catches his eye and he smiles and waves and she smiles and waves back. She wanders slowly through the racks of men's suits while she waits for him to be free. She recognizes many of them from work. It's a weird experience, like being at work and not seeing the men, only their suits.

"Hello again," she hears Henry say and turns to see him standing there smiling and she sees the same look in his eyes she did when they first time met. She has the feeling those eyes have seen a lot. "Hi, Henry," she says, smiling. "Nice to see you again."

"Shall we," he says, motioning toward the desk.

She studies the graceful movement of his body as she follows him and he pulls back a chair for her and she sits and watches him sit across the desk from her and notices the way his fingers delicately intertwine as he clasps his hands in front of him.

"A suit is a great idea for a birthday present," he says. "Your dad will be delightfully surprised and truly appreciate it. He's one of my favorite customers and one of the only men I know around here who loves double-breasted suits. I admire him for it."

"Well, you probably know he grew up in Baltimore and went to Johns Hopkins and lived in D.C. East Coast culture."

Henry nods. "Let me show you some of the fabrics he's selected."

She watches him select several fabric books from the shelf lined with them behind him and set the books on the desk and sit and she smiles as she studies his face and watches his hands and fingers as he opens each book and goes through the swatches until he finds the one he's after and she fancies him a wizard about to turn something lifeless into something miraculously alive. Finally he has her dad's selections arranged before her. Each fabric is different and they all look equally nice and she knows she's out of her depth and looks at him and raises her eyebrows. "Which do you recommend?" she asks and sees him smile and nod. He moves one of the books closer to her and she sees the fabric looks warm gray or cool tan, she can't decide which, and has a slight sheen to it. It reminds her of glistening skin. He holds the swatch out to her.

"Feel it."

She does and smiles as she feels its silkiness. "It's luxurious."

He nods. "A silk-wool blend and a very nice one. Each time your dad comes in to choose a fabric for his next suit he always lingers over this one, more so than any of the others. It's one of the first he selected years ago but he always passes on it. When I asked him why he said it's too self-indulgent. It's what's called in Italian *un piacere,* 'a pleasure', something you see passing by a shop window that catches your eye that you just have to have, but your dad hasn't been able to bring himself to do it. I know he'd love it. It would look great on him."

She grins and sees Henry grin too. She feels like a gleeful co-conspirator. "Let's do it! This is fun! I'm so excited!"

"Now you know why I love what I do."

She thinks about her meeting with Henry as she drives home. Making people look great and feel great, making them happy, that's what he does. There's a lot to love about a job like that and he obviously loves his work. It was such a pleasure talking with him. She had the feeling she could share anything with him and he'd understand, that nothing would surprise him. She hasn't felt this happy and excited about something in a very long time. She didn't think she could anymore, but she does and realizes she hasn't stopped smiling since she left the store. *Un piacere*.... That's what it is, all right.

Her house is the only one on the street that's dark, as usual, but it looks particularly so this evening as she pulls into the driveway and feels particularly empty as she enters the kitchen from the garage and turns on the lights. She tosses her keys on the counter and pours herself a glass of white wine and sits in the solarium in the dark gazing out the windows at the night sky. She's conscious of the space surrounding her, as usual, and can feel it against her skin, but it seems larger this evening and she feels particularly alone in it now. She can't get the image of Henry's face and hands and fingers as he touched the fabrics out of her mind and she's still picturing them as she lies in bed in the dark only he's not touching the fabrics now but her unfeeling body, bringing it miraculously back to life.

The corridor in South Coast Plaza is crowded this Saturday afternoon. There seems to be a never-ending stream of people and Joanne sits on a bench a ways down from Brooks Brothers, watching people pass by while keeping an eye on the store entrance. When she called earlier she was told that Henry usually takes his lunch break around 4 pm but she knows that could change if he's assisting a customer. No matter. She'll wait.

She woke the morning after she met with him with the strong desire to be close to him. Given their age difference, she naturally wondered whether it was because she viewed him as a father figure but quickly dismissed that idea. She's not sure what he represents to her, beyond revitalization, or how she feels about him, but he's not a father figure, that's for sure. All week she's thought about what it is she wants to have happen between them and she's not sure about that, either. Something.

She notices a man who reminds her of Art and wonders how he's doing. She hasn't seen him in a while. He seems to have drifted in and out of her life as most people do, which is fine. She hasn't wanted anyone close to her or to be close to anyone, until now. The last time she saw him she listened wide-eyed to his story about what happened between his wife and the guy she was living with and the guy hitting his son and his son trying to shoot him. Wild! She agreed with him that as bad as what happened was, it was probably all for the best. His wife and kids are at his mom's now, so maybe that will bring them back together. Events can turn in remarkable ways. You just have to let things happen and see where they take you. She hasn't in a long time. She's kept her life on a tight reign and is excited by the prospect of loosening up. It's a feeling she hasn't experienced in a long time.

She sees Henry walk out of the store and head toward the escalator. She stands and follows him, keeping her distance, down the escalator, through the crowd by the balloon vendor and the carousel, past the people at the restaurant tables inside and outside the entrance. She sees he's headed toward the stairs that lead up to the next level and the benches by valet parking and figures that's where he's going, to sit quietly and pass the time watching people. If she follows him there'll be no way to avoid his seeing her, so she turns and quickly walks back inside and through the plaza to the entrance on the other side of valet parking by that new store, Forever 21, where she can watch him at a distance unobserved. She walks outside, careful to keep people between her and Henry and finds a spot behind a palm tree where she can sit with without being seen and watch him by leaning forward slightly and peering around it.

How silly. At work she's respected and relied on for her clear-eyed analyses of investment strategies and here she is spying — yes, there's no other way to describe it — on a man she's met a couple of times and to whom she feels strangely attracted, but about whom she knows very little and it reminds her of the Peeping Tom phase she went through when she was twelve or thirteen, when she and her friend Arissa would sneak through backyards on summer evenings to spy on neighbors in their homes and most of it was pretty boring to watch, but thrilling in a way because the people didn't know they were being watched, which was the point, after all. They finally hit the jackpot with Alex Bracken, the hunky blond high school junior down the block who was into weightlifting. They would sit in the dark and watch him do reps in his bedroom wearing only his boxer shorts and they could have sat there watching him all night if he'd kept it up. It was silly, but fun.

She takes out a cigarette and lights it. As busy as it is by the entrance, Henry is alone over by valet parking, sitting quietly with his legs crossed, looking around at the office buildings across Bristol Street and the sky above them, at the people by the plaza entrance where she is, drawing now and then on his cigarette. Even at this distance she can see the fingers of his hand quite clearly and the way he holds his cigarette, delicately, as it seems he does everything. When he finishes his cigarette he moves his hand gracefully to put it out in the ashtray beside the bench.

What's he thinking about? Some customer's suit, his ex-wife, his sons? She learned that much about him during their conversation at the store. His girlfriend? Does he have one? She has the feeling he doesn't, that there's no significant other in his life and that he's content being alone. He has that air about him. Well, maybe not content. Maybe he's made peace with the fact that he's alone, just as she has. What would he think if he noticed her sitting here spying on him? That she's a nut case? She doesn't think so. She knows he'd understand and probably better than she does.

She sees an attractive young Asian woman, Japanese she thinks, with long black glistening hair walking toward the valet parking area. The woman's wearing a tight-fitting short black skirt and oyster-colored silk blouse and black Jimmy Choo heels and has a zebra print Jimmy Choo bag slung over her shoulder. She's holding a Nordstrom shopping bag in one hand and a phone to her ear in the other. It's silly, but she feels jealous and the nearer the woman gets to Henry the stronger the feeling grows. She watches the woman sit on the bench opposite him and put down her shopping bag and hold the phone away from her ear and ask him for directions to where she is, judging from her hand gestures, and the woman listens and then nods and waves at him and sits back and puts the phone to her ear again and she feels relieved that they're no longer talking. It's just too silly.

Henry glances at the palm tree over by Forever 21 and looks back at the attractive young Japanese woman. He can't remember the last time he thought about the Rockport period in his relationship with Anise but this situation brings it to mind. She was still living in the rooming house in the Back Bay where he lived before moving to Rockport, to put some distance between them. Anise was as intelligent as she was attractive and had a "built-in bullshit detector", as Hemingway called it, which he hadn't developed. Toward the end of their living together she would walk up behind him and read over his shoulder what he'd written on the page in the typewriter and shake her head and sigh and walk away. It strained their relationship to the breaking point and rather than have it end in an ugly scene, he decided to move out.

She would occasionally come up for the weekend and they saw each other regularly at the dialysis center in Brookline where they worked as therapists on the graveyard shift. The money was good, but he was attending the graduate writing program at Boston University during the day and was getting very little sleep. He wondered whether his inability to produce any good writing was the result of his state of chronic fatigue, but knew that wasn't the reason. It wasn't as if the job didn't provide him with plenty of good material, either. The patients were quite a cast of characters and represented a fairly broad cross-section of society. They were all on a transplant list, waiting for a kidney and their chance to live dialysis-free. Some made it while others died waiting. Most were resigned to being hooked up to a machine twice a week for the rest of their lives and made the best of it. There was a story there, all right, just waiting to be told, but he wasn't up to telling it. He was surprisingly good with needles and his sterile technique was excellent, so he was given the most difficult patients, obese diabetics, some with hepatitis and all with glass-like veins buried deep in subcutaneous tissue. He still doesn't know how he was able to find and hit those veins, but the feeling was like extending his brain to his fingers. The same thing happens when he touches a woman's body. It's a wonderful feeling for them both. He can tell.

He'd been living in Rockport about six months when the older woman in the apartment next to his moved out. The apartment was vacant a couple of weeks and he arrived home one day to find the new tenant moving in. It was Anise. He was flabbergasted and flattered and her bold stroke resulted in a rekindling of their relationship, but the flame it sparked was the kind that sometimes blazes up in a fire just before it goes out and soon they were seeing more of each other at work an hour away than they were living next to each other.

It was summer and Rockport was swollen with tourists, as it is every summer, some spending a few days in a motel and others two weeks or a month in a rental property. Shelly's family was among the latter. He met her in the center of town on a walk early one sunny Saturday afternoon. She was standing outside an ice cream shop with a cone of vanilla ice cream in her hand gazing at the people passing by and smiling, as if just being there were the greatest pleasure she'd ever experienced. She looked to be in her late teens and had long wavy black hair and dark brown eyes and fair skin and shapely arms and legs and ample breasts. She was wearing khaki shorts and a white tee shirt and deck shoes. She struck him as wholesome and inexperienced and he imagined the fun he might have teaching her a thing or two. He introduced himself and they chatted. She told him she was from Ohio, where he can't remember, nineteen and a freshman in college, where he also can't remember, and that this was her family's first visit to Rockport. He asked her what she'd been doing for fun and she said going to the beach and taking the occasional trip to Boston. They'd walked the Freedom Trail and gone on a duck boat tour, that sort of thing. He asked her if she'd like to have dinner that evening and she said sure, she'd love to and gave him directions to the house they were renting.

He arrived around seven to pick her up and found Shelly and her mom, who struck him as an older plumper version of Shelly with the same big smile, waiting for him out front. He told Shelly's mom he was taking her to the Red Barrel in Essex, just down 128, and that he'd have her home around eleven. Her mom smiled as she listened and she had that look in her eyes that let him know she knew what was up.

"Have fun!" her mom said.

He was careful to open the door for Shelly and smile and wave to her mom as he walked around and got in behind the wheel and he had the distinct feeling as he drove away that her mom was sending her off for the expressed purpose of having that summer fling she'd been longing to have, that rite of passage that turns an innocent teenager into an experienced young woman.

They chatted over dinner and she listened wide-eyed as he told her about the road trip he and his brother were about to go on from New York to San Francisco where his brother had been assigned to the Presidio and that they'd be driving his brother's Austin Healey Sprite.

"Wow! she said. "What a great adventure! I'd love to take a trip like that!"

She seemed to have arrived at a point in her life where she was ready and eager to experience everything and all through dinner he envisioned her naked on the bed in his apartment and wondered what she would be like and just how innocent she really was. You never can tell about girls from the Midwest.

He'd met some wild ones. He asked if she had a boyfriend back home.

"Sort of," she said, "not really. We're just good friends."

She asked if he had a girlfriend and he said he'd recently broken up with her and she asked why and he shared with her a brief account of his and Anise's relationship, which, of course, was completely one-sided and ended with his arriving home one day to find she'd moved into the apartment next to his.

"Wow!" she said, "She must really want to be with you."

"Yeah," he said, "but it's creepy."

They were ready to leave and just waiting for the waitress to return with his change when his high school buddy Jim appeared at their table looking disappointed and miffed. He had no idea Jim was in the restaurant and was surprised to see him and puzzled by his expression. He'd introduced Anise to Jim and his wife Donna when the two moved from New York to Boston and the three formed their own friendship. Jim said he and Donna had come up at Anise's invitiation and Henry wasn't surprised to hear that the Red Barrel had been her suggestion since he'd introduced her to it and it became her favorite restaurant. Jim said they'd been sitting in the next booth and couldn't help overhearing their conversation. "Way to go," he said, "you broke her heart." Jim would later have an affair and divorce Donna. So much for moral superiority. He remembers watching Jim leave and thinking how remarkable it was that he'd been so focused on charming Shelly that he hadn't noticed Anise and Donna leave, which they must have before Jim. Talk about having your brains in your balls.

Back at his apartment he led Shelly to the bed and they embraced and kissed and he remembers how firm her body felt as he caressed it and how white her skin was when he removed her clothes, so white it seemed to glow in the darkness. He kissed his way down to between her legs and she parted them and ran her fingers through his hair as he made love to her with his mouth. She moaned with pleasure and he could tell she wanted to make more noise and was holding back, either out of modesty or concern that other people in the building would hear, probably both, and he said, "Don't hold back." That was all the encouragement she needed. She wrapped her legs around his head and grabbed his hair and pulled him to her and ground herself against his face and began bucking and when she came he was sure that any second there would be loud banging on his apartment door, possibly even from a neighbor down the street.

As delightful as making her come was he was exhausted by the effort, but she wanted more and he lay on top of her and entered her and they gazed at each other's eyes as they made love. She was smiling at him dreamily and he remembers her look of surprise when he suddenly withdrew and straddled her face and put his cock in her mouth and as wonderful as her sucking felt and the sight of her doing it was, he remembers thinking as he emptied himself into her how irresponsible it was of him to risk transmitting whatever it was he had.

He hadn't been feeling well for about a week. His feeling of malaise had begun with belching that produced an aftertaste in his mouth like celery salt, of all things, and then a feeling of fatigue set in that was different and deeper than the one from lack of sleep. Every motion was an effort. Why it never occurred to him that he'd accidentally infected himself at work, probably hastily stripping the tubing and needles from one of the dialysis machines to ready it for the next patient, he'll never know. When he arrived at his mother's house in upstate New York to begin the road trip his brother opened the front door and took one look at him and said, "Holy shit! You're jaundiced!" which his brother knew something about having contracted malaria in Viet Nam.

He spent the next month in the hospital flat on his back recuperating from hepatitis B. and when he finally returned to Rockport Shelly and her family had long since returned to Ohio. He regretted what he'd done and wondered how she was. He still regrets and always will.

Someone else was now living in Anise's apartment. Where she'd gone he didn't know and wouldn't find out at work since he was on disability leave from the dialysis center. He had the feeling she was still in town, though, and finally ran into her on one of his painstakingly slow and exhausting walks to the center of town to get some exercise. She was with a guy in his early twenties who she introduced as Tommy and who didn't say a word. She told him she'd moved to an apartment a few blocks away and he knew the one she was talking about.

The next time he ran into her she was alone and told him that Tommy was a townie who worked on the fishing boats and he could tell she was relishing rubbing his nose in the fact that this blue-collar type was fucking her now. He knew it was irrational but he felt jealous.

He began taking walks late in the evening to see if Tommy's pickup truck was parked in front of Anise's apartment and it always was. He would stand in the darkness and stare at the closed blinds in the bedroom window until the light went out and then linger, imagining the two of them in bed. He knew every inch of Anise's body and all the things she liked to do and have done to her and just how she liked having them done and when he imagined her doing these things with Tommy he felt more than jealous, he felt violated. He knew he was acting and reacting crazily but he couldn't help himself. He had to let it play out and it finally did when he arrived at her apartment late one evening and stood in the shadows staring at the bedroom window and saw the light go out and imagined Anise and Tommie in bed and all the things they were doing and the next thing he knew the streetlights went out and it was dawn.

A cab pulls up and he watches the Japanese woman stand and sling her Jimmy Choo bag over her shoulder and pick up her Nordstrom shopping bag and walk to it and get in. As the cab pulls away he notices Joanne pull her head back behind the palm tree. He has no idea what she's up to, but whatever it is he's sure it doesn't have anything to do with her dad's suit.

The air feels cool against Henry's skin as he steps out onto the balcony and takes a cigarette from the pack and picks up the lighter. He eyes the blue sky and wispy clouds, a typical late fall early morning in Southern California. He lights his cigarette, the first of the day, and inhales and blows out a stream of smoke and scans the cars parked in the residential parking lot across the street. He's familiar with them all and their owners and their schedules. They won't be racing off this morning. It's Saturday and they'll be sleeping in. He's the one who'll be headed to work and he wonders what new developments in Joanne's game of surreptitious observation the day might bring. He still can't figure out what she's up to and tries to resist thinking she's attracted to him. That's the conclusion an old fool would come to.

He steps outside on his afternoon break and looks around and thinks that if she's observing him, she's doing a good job of keeping out of sight. He reaches the top of the stairs at Valet Parking and is pleasantly surprised to see her sitting on the bench directly across from the one he usually sits on, her legs crossed, smoking and waiting for him. She's wearing black jeans and boots and a light blue sweater against the cool breezy day. She looks up at him as he approaches. Her expression is a mixture of anticipation and apprehension and she keeps her eyes on his as he sits on the bench, but as he reaches into his coat pocket for his phone he sees she's now looking at his hand and follows it with her eyes as he takes out the phone and places it on the armrest and reaches into his shirt pocket for his pack of cigarettes and lighter and takes out a cigarette and lights it and puts the pack back in his pocket and the lighter on the armrest beside the phone. She doesn't seem to want to talk but just be here with him and now she's looking at his eyes again and he studies hers and thinks he sees something in them he recognizes. Maybe it's the same obsessiveness that drove him to stand staring at Anise's bedroom window all night.

He'd like to ask her what her interest in him is, beyond having a suit made for her dad? He'd like to tell her how flattered he is by her spying on him, how much he's enjoyed their little game, how beautiful she is and how struck he was by her fingers and toes that day they first met and how fortunate he feels that she's come into his life and that he feels toward her something he hasn't toward anyone before, that what he wants to do is take her in his arms and please her and care for her. Does she know what he's thinking? She looks like she does.

He watches her stand and walk toward him and feels his skin tingling as she stops beside him and sticks her cigarette in the ashtray, her hand dangling only inches away. He looks up at her and sees her gazing down at him, her expression now a mixture of hope and fear. He wants to reach out and take her hand and give it a reassuring squeeze and he's certain that's what she wants and is waiting for him to do, but he hesitates. The distance between them is small, but the consequences of closing it now seem enormous.

As enjoyable as their little game has been until now it's been just that, a game and a harmless one, but the moment contact is made everything will change. It won't be a game anymore and the possibility of being disappointed and hurt and of disappointing and hurting will be very real. In a way he wishes they could always remain this way, in a state of perfect anticipation and possibility, but he recognizes this for what it is: lingering emotional cowardice and the fear of failing, yet again.

He reaches out and takes her hand and gently squeezes it and thrills at the feeling of her hand squeezing back. She smiles and turns and walks away and for a moment he's uncertain whether words were spoken between them.

He's still thinking about their encounter as he arrives home, half-expecting to find her waiting for him at the door to his apartment. At this point nothing would surprise him. He turns on the lights and pours himself a glass of beer in the kitchen and takes a long satisfying sip. He changes into shorts and a polo shirt and hangs his suit in the bedroom closet and slides the closet door shut and looks at himself in the mirror. He tries hard to see an old fool looking back at him but doesn't. They're beyond that now and he knows it's only a matter of time before she'll appear and reminds himself that he doesn't need redeeming. Whatever happens next it won't be about that.

He sits at the dining room table and turns on his laptop and sips his beer as it starts up and clicks on the novel document. It's ironic that when he so wanted to write a novel for selfish reasons he couldn't to save his life and now that he's begun writing again after a forty-year hiatus for no reason other than the sheer joy of writing it's effortless. It's life's doing. Forty years of living have worked on him the way wind and water work on rock, smoothed the hard places and made him sufficiently humble to be able to remove himself from between the writing and the reader and he's grateful. He begins reading what he's written from the last chapter break to get the sense of it but his mind is on Joanne and he wisely closes the document and takes his beer and steps out on the balcony to have a smoke.

He sees a black Mercedes CLK convertible parked by the curb across the street and a silhouetted figure standing under the streetlight. He smiles and takes a cigarette from the pack and picks up the lighter and lights it. He watches her light a cigarette and they stand smoking and gazing at each other and when they've finished their cigarettes he watches her get in her car and drive slowly toward the gate and steps back inside to open it.

He's waiting for her at the front door and she seems nervous and uncertain as she enters and puts her bag down inside the doorway. He pours her a glass of white wine and waits for her in the living room on the couch while she wanders slowly through the apartment. He listens as she moves about and watches her in his mind's eye, stopping to look at pictures of his sons and parents on the wall, tilting her head to read the spines of books on the shelves – she'll undoubtedly take note of the large Italian-English dictionary and Italian grammar books and novels – sitting on his bed with her hands palms-down the bedspread smoothing it, opening the closets and fingering the fabric of his suits. He hears her enter the kitchen and pictures her inspecting the collection of postcards and snapshots and silly magnets holding them on the refrigerator door. He hears her behind him walking toward him and watches her perch uneasily on the edge of a chair across from him with her back straight. She slowly brings her glass to her lips and sips her wine, keeping her eyes on his. He has no idea what to say and feels relieved and thankful when she speaks.

"It's crazy, huh?" she asks.

"What?"

"The way I'm acting. Irrational."

He shrugs and smiles. "Emotions can be." She doesn't seem satisfied with his answer.

"Obsessing about someone? Spying on him?"

"I've done it."

"You have? Who was she?"

"My college girlfriend."

"Huh." She takes another sip. "What was your major?"

"English, Creative Writing."

"Published?"

"A few short stories."

"Still write?"

"I didn't for a long time, forty years."

"What got you writing again?"

"My mom's death."

"Short stories?"

"I wrote four of them, each longer than the last. I was half-way down the first page of the fifth and realized it wasn't going to be short."

"A novel?"

He nods.

"About?"

He shrugs. "Life."

"It's good that you're writing again. Divorced?"

He nods.

"So am I. What's your ex's name?"

"Claire."

"On good terms?"

"We have a better relationship now than when we were married."

She nods. "Your boys are handsome. One looks like you and I'm guessing the other looks like his mom. See them often?"

"Not as often as I'd like. Gene, my older son, is in Seattle. He's the one who looks like me. Frank lives in Massachusetts. Kids?"

"No. My ex wanted them." She wants to leave it at that but sees he's curious why she didn't. "Don't get me wrong. I like kids."

He sips his beer and studies her. She's like a dam ready to burst.

"Speak Italian?" she asks.

He nods.

"My French has gotten rusty. I saw the books. Take lessons?"

He nods again. "I ended up having an affair with my teacher. She was married and had two young daughters. It was something I told myself I'd never do."

"What's her name?"

"Laura."

"How'd it happen?"

"She seduced me. It was thrilling." He sees her raise her eyebrows and sit back and cross her legs, eager to hear the story. He's happy to see her relaxing. "We'd meet a couple of times a week at her home. I was very respectful of her and viewed her as my teacher, nothing more. As the weeks went by we got to know each other. Her husband was a doctor, a researcher. She'd received her Baccalaureate in architecture but hadn't pursued it as a profession. In fact, since arriving from Italy, the only thing she'd done, other than take care of the kids, was give Italian lessons to earn what she considered her own money and this seemed to be a point of contention between her and her husband. According to her, he kept urging her to do something with her education and she kept resisting and slowly the picture emerged of a young wife who felt suffocated by her controlling husband. Her parents adored him and considered him a great catch. I only met him once and he seemed like a nice guy. He was here in the U.S. on an H-1B visa and she didn't have a green card, so she was dependent on him. Get the picture?"

"Yeah."

"So one day during a lesson she asked me how things were going with my divorce. I'd shared with her that while I wanted to as soon as possible, my wife's position was not until our younger son graduated from high school. Laura mentioned that she'd been thinking about divorcing her husband. It came out of nowhere and she didn't say anything more about it. A few weeks later she asked me if I'd like to go see *Kika,* Pedro Almodóvar's new film."

"I loved that film!"

"I naturally assumed she meant with her and her husband and I said sure, I'd love to, and she said maybe we could go after the next lesson and see the early show. Her husband's office was in Cambridge, not far from the theater where the movie was playing, so I said I'd drive and that way she could ride home with her husband. She looked at me with a surprised expression, like I'd missed the point entirely, and said, 'He won't be coming. He's in Italy.'"

Joanne grins. "The plot thickens."

"It seems pretty obvious doesn't it? It wasn't at all to me at the time, which shows you how respectful of her I was." He shakes his head and smiles. "So, I'm thinking we'll go see *Kika* and maybe have dinner afterward and talk about the film, maybe in Italian, kind of an extended lesson. My first inkling that she had other things in mind was when we were watching the film. I'd be laughing with everyone else and I'd glance at her and she'd be staring intently at the screen and I got the feeling she wasn't watching the movie."

Joanne nods. "The wheels were turning."

"We went to a restaurant on the waterfront afterward and had dinner and talked about this and that, in English, and she had a couple of glasses of wine, which according to her was a lot for her. We took a walk out to the end of the wharf afterward and stood there in silence, smoking and watching the light in the lighthouse out in the harbor sweep round. I looked at her and saw she was looking at me and knew by her expression what she wanted and I was only to willing to oblige."

"Lets have a smoke," Joanne says.

They step out onto the balcony and she lights her cigarette and draws deeply and gazes at the moon, looking like a snake's eye fixed on her. "So what happened?"

"We kept on with the lessons for a while, but things were different. She was too preoccupied, too emotionally fraught to teach. She'd spend the hour covering sheets of paper with intricate drawings."

"I bet you kept them."

He nods.

"I'd like to see them."

"Sure. Anyway, we lasted about eighteen months. I helped her move out of the house and into a duplex and I knew she was just using me, that it wasn't about us, but her. She brought out the Boy Scout in me. When I'd finally had enough I walked away with a clean conscience. It was the first time that had ever happened."

"Did they divorce?"

"Separated. I don't know if they ever divorced. They're back in Italy now. I did shortly after I stopped seeing her. I've lived alone ever since."

"Happy?"

"Resigned."

"I know the feeling. I'm HIV positive."

He isn't surprised to hear this, curious about how she became infected, but not surprised that she has the disease. It's an important piece of the puzzle he's been putting together in his mind, the most important one so far and it explains a lot.

"I had a fling with a professor at the Sarbonne. He knowingly infected me and three other women."

"Charming."

"He was charming. He died of AIDS. Ever since my friend came along—"

"Your friend?"

"That's what I call it. I've felt like I'm living in the grave."

"I did the same thing once."

"What?"

"Infect someone. I'm pretty sure I did. I wasn't feeling well at the time. I didn't know what I had. Turned out to be hepatitis B. I've always regretted it and wondered what happened to her."

"That's different."

"Think so? In New Hampshire they call it 'picking fly shit out of the pepper.'"

She smiles. "That's good. I've never heard that." She looks back at the moon and draws on her cigarette and inhales deeply and blows the smoke out slowly. "Ever been in love?"

He hesitates. It's important to be honest with her. "No."

"Neither have I. I'm not sure it matters."

"You might be right. Anyway, I've made a mess of every relationship I've been in."

"Maybe you just weren't ready for a one."

"You might be right about that too."

"Maybe you weren't with the right person. Maybe there is no right person. Maybe there's no such thing as love, just benevolent self-interest." She stubs out her cigarette in the ashtray. "I'm picking fly shit out of the pepper aren't I?"

He smiles at her. "Like a real Emmett."

She stares at the moon again. That snake's eye looks malevolent, like all the dark forces at play in the universe are channeled through it and focused on her. She was bitten by that snake once and its venom worked its way throughout her body and numbed her to life and she's felt that way ever since, or did until she met Henry and felt life stirring in her again.

"So what happens next," he asks without looking at her, "now that the game's over."

"I dunno. Maybe I just wanted to talk with you and get to know you better. Maybe I want something more. I dunno." She looks around at the stars. "I feel so disconnected, like I'm not even here in the present, like the light from a distant star that's still shining long after the star is gone. I'm as resigned to being alone as you are, Henry, and as unhappy about it. I'd like to be with someone I can just be quiet with." She looks at him. "Know what I mean?"

He nods.

"I should probably go."

He watches her search his eyes anxiously, but hopefully.

"Shouldn't I?"

He smiles and reaches out his hand and she takes it.

She lies on the bed propped up on an elbow, watching him undress and, yes, he has an older man's body, but she can see that it hasn't changed much through the years. He's slender and toned and moves gracefully and she bets he plays tennis or runs or once did. She holds out her hand to him as he climbs on the bed and he takes it and she draws him to her and wraps her arms around him and pulls him close until they're pressed against each other and she feels the warmth from his body warming hers. It brings to mind pleasant memories of

Thanksgivings and Christmases at her dad's parents' home in Baltimore. Her grandparents always had a crackling fire going in their big fireplace and she would lie on the rug in front of it with their speckled border collie by her side, just as Henry is now, and gaze at the fire, just as she's gazing at Henry's eyes now. She brings her lips to his and presses gently and feels his pressing back and his arms tightening around her and she thinks that if they went no farther than this it would be fine with her but, of course, they both want more. She's felt numb for so many years, but now her skin feels alive to his touch and she thrills as he caresses her breasts and strokes her stomach lightly with his fingertips and her body shudders in anticipation of where she knows he'll touch her next. "Get a condom," she whispers.

He nuzzles her neck. "I hate condoms."

"You have to."

"Don't have any."

"I do, in my bag."

"It wouldn't be making love then, would it?"

It's just what he would say and she knows he means it. She brushes his cheek with her fingertips. "Get one."

They sit on the balcony sipping their first cup of coffee of the day. Henry admires the large yellow blooms of the hibiscus in the glazed blue pot on the table between them, their petals unfurled in the morning sunlight. The blooms' vermilion centers and long yellow stamens tipped with vermillion anthers remind him of their lovemaking.

Joanne sits with her feet up on the chair, her long slender toes curled over the edge, studying one of the sheets of paper covered with Laura's intricate drawings done in the tight precise hand of someone who's spent many hours at a drafting table. Henry shared with her how Laura finally set the hook. He forgot his books at her house when they left to see *Kika* and didn't realize it until the next day. He called her to see if he could stop by and pick them up. According to him, he really was intending just to pick them up and leave. Sure, Laura said, she was home and he could stop by anytime. She greeted him at the door wearing a sarong. It was the first time he saw her wearing anything other than her usual plain shirt or tee and jeans and ballerinas. She had his books waiting for him on the coffee table in the living room and followed him as far as the couch. He picked them up and turned and saw her standing by the couch looking at him intently and as he walked past her to leave she asked, "What? No kiss?" So he kissed her and she unwrapped the sarong and let it fall and they kissed their way onto the couch and then onto the floor and that was that.

She draws on her cigarette and studies Laura's rendering of a hieroglyphic-looking eye around which in tiny letters, like the motto on an official seal, is printed, YOU WATCHING ME WATCHING YOU WATCHING ME WATCHING YOU, suggesting a never-ending activity. Beneath it is a good likeness of Henry's mouth and printed in tiny widely spaced letters along the contour of the upper lip is, YOUR LIPS ARE, and along that of the lower lip, ALL I SEE! She places the sheet of paper beneath the others and sees on the next a detailed rendering of his forearm, the sinuous veins bulging and written in large letters at the bottom of the page, ABBRACCIAMI! the meaning of which she can guess. Laura's extreme cast of mind is evident in all the drawings and it strikes her as verging on mania.

Henry said that after he and Laura made love she told him that if he'd turned down her invitation to go see *Kika,* that would have been the end of the lessons and she wouldn't have wanted to see him again. He said he knew Laura had strong feelings for him, but that her fear of losing her children was stronger and that, in the end, their relationship was really all about his helping her to stand up to her husband and establish her independence from him. She was using Henry to serve her purpose and he knew it and allowed himself to be used. He said he did it to redeem himself for his selfishness in the past. She looks at him and raises her eyebrows. "She's really something."

"She was stressed, fearful and suspicious."

"Ever see her again?"

"Once, on my first trip back east. We had dinner at her place and I spent the night. We didn't make love. We had sex. I was happy to see her in my rear view mirror the next morning."

If only it were that easy, just driving away. She knows Laura will always be with him the way her friend will always be with her. It's fine. She can live with them both. She puts the sheets of paper on the table and looks around. "What a gorgeous day. To bad you have to work. Every weekend, huh?"

He nods. "That's when people are shopping."

"How'd you end up at Brooks Brothers anyway? I've been meaning to ask."

"A client and friend of mine from Silicon Valley landed at a privately held company here in Irvine. He was president. The founder wanted to take the company public and my friend asked me to come out and be VP of marketing and help shephard the company through the IPO. It was a great offer and I needed a change of scenery. We raised $55 million and the founder began buying up companies and overreached. Four years later the company was saddled with debt and first my friend and then I was politely asked to leave, which was fine with me. I had a great severance package and was done with marketing by then and wanted to switch gears, although I didn't know what I wanted to do. I needed some white dress shirts and walked into Brooks Brothers at South Coast Plaza and felt right at home. I'd shopped at the Newbury Street store in Boston for years and knew all about the clothes and the company. What appealed to me most about working there was the prospect of meeting people and getting to know them and building lasting relationships. I've met hundreds and have heard some fascinating stories."

"I bet." She looks around the balcony and glances back over here shoulder. "It's a nice apartment. How long have you lived here?"

"Since I arrived in Ninety-nine."

"I've got more house and income than I know what to do with. Why don't you live with me? You could write full-time."

He smiles and shakes his head. "You're too much."

"What? It's a great idea!"

"I appreciate the offer. It's a tempting one. It's funny."

"What?"

"In the past I would have considered it meddling in my life. I don't."

"Well, that's a good thing, isn't it?"

He nods.

"You do as you please, Henry, but I'm going to tell you what I think and how I feel. You want that don't you?"

"Of course."

"I'm done not caring about anything. So, when do I get to read the novel?"

He grins. "When I've finished it."

She knows all about waiting. That's all she's been doing for the longest time, waiting for the end to arrive. Waiting for Henry to finish his novel feels different. It's the first time she's felt happy about waiting for something in years. She gazes contentedly at the clouds and sips her coffee and smiles. It feels nice having a reason to be alive again.

CHAPTER 12

The hills and houses atop them pass by as the train speeds through San Juan Capistrano headed toward San Diego. Trey's been looking forward to visiting Julie ever since his dad drove her and her stuff down to her mom's in San Diego a few days after they all left Walt's. His dad and Walt talked things over and decided the best thing to do was just let the matter drop and move on. His dad said Walt told him he suffers from PTSD and that's why he got so angry and became violent. Trey's not excusing Walt for what he did but he feels sorry for him now. He wouldn't have thought it possible but he does.

He's been wondering about what's been going on with Julie. He can't put his finger on it but she's changed somehow. He can hear it in her voice when they speak on the phone. Something's happened that she hasn't shared with him and he's hoping to find out what it is. He misses her as a friend, but he can't deny that he also misses their afternoons together in her room. They've been his masturbatory fantasy every since she left and he also can't deny that he's hoping they'll have sex. Her mom's working, so maybe they'll spend some time in her bedroom the way they used to.

He looks down at the bulge in his pants and squirms in his seat and glances at the woman sitting across the aisle with her nose in a book. Just thinking about having sex with Julie makes him hard. He closes his eyes and leans back in his seat and tries to think of something else but his mind is filled with images from their past encounters and they won't go away. Shit! He's has to take care of himself before he comes in his pants. He gets up and makes his way gingerly to the restroom, hoping that no one will look up at him and notice how curiously he's walking, bent over slightly and a little bow-legged, trying to minimize the bulge.

He spots Julie waiting for him on the platform as the train glides to a stop and smiles and waves at her. She smiles up at him and waves back. She looks the same, dressed in a tee shirt and shorts and flip-flops and she hasn't done anything with her hair, but he has that feeling again that she's changed somehow.

He steps down from the train and they walk quickly toward each other, smiling and spreading their arms wide. They hug and rock back and forth and he realizes just how much he's missed the feel of her body in his arms pressed against his.

Julie steps back. "It's great to see you!"

"You too."

She takes his hand and they walk toward the parking lot. "I thought we'd hang out at PB. It's not far from the apartment."

"Great," Trey says.

They catch up as they head toward her place. He tells her that Brett and Tracy say hi and are looking forward to seeing her again and that maybe the four of them can get together when she comes up for a visit, that his dad's still working construction jobs whenever he has the opportunity, but that he's begun taking courses at Cal State Long Beach to get his teacher certification, that his mom and dad are spending more time together now and that his dad is still living at his friend's apartment, but comes to pick up his mom and they go on dates now, you know, sort of starting out fresh. He's pretty sure they'll all end up living together again and thinks it's really only a matter of time.

She asks how Kim's doing and he says fine but that she's still struggling with her self-image and she laughs and says she'll never forget that night she turned on the light in their bedroom and saw the two of them together, Kim with his cock in her hand, jerking him off, and she'll never forget the look on their faces. Do they still fool around with each other like that? No, he says, that stopped when they moved into his grandmother's and they each finally had their own bedroom again, although when they were living in the same bedroom at her father's with no privacy he got used to masturbating knowing that Kim was lying awake listening to him and sometimes watching. That's how that whole business got started. When you think about it it was really no big deal. It was like sex education.

She asks how Emily's doing and he tells her that she took a week off from school and said she was away somewhere with her parents, but that he doesn't believe it and she's been wearing long sleeve shirts ever since she returned and he's concerned that she might be cutting herself. Maybe he's completely off track but she's seemed really down lately, sort of depressed, like she's on meds. She hasn't been to cotillion. Something's going on with her but she doesn't share anything with him anymore. When they run into each other at school now, they barely say anything to each other. That's too bad, Julie says. Maybe her parents are suffocating her and she's struggling to get out from under them. He says that's what he thinks too and that he hopes she makes it.

He sees the apartment is smallish but that Julie and her mom have their own bedrooms. When they arrive at Julie's she takes him by the hand and he looks around as he follows her happily to the bed. He recognizes the pictures and posters and some of the bric-a-brak from her old bedroom. He notices a snapshot of some guy stuck in the frame of her vanity mirror. That's new. She turns and sits on the bed in front of him and begins undoing his pants and pulling them down. He sees her looking at the round moist stain on his boxer shorts and she looks up at him and grins.

"Did you come in your pants?"

"Almost, on the train, thinking about you. I had to take of myself in the restroom." She shakes her head and pulls down his boxer shorts and takes him in her mouth and he closes his eyes and tilts his head back and savors the feeling of once again having her lips wrapped tightly around him and the warm insides of her mouth as she sucks and her tongue licking the head of his cock as she does. He's immediately hard and if she keeps going like this, it won't be more than a few moments before he comes, but she takes her mouth away and he opens his eyes and looks down at her and sees her looking up at him almost sternly.

"Wait," she says. "Get undressed."

He's not sure he can wait but he pulls off his clothes and watches her pull of hers and lie on her back on the bed and spread her legs and he lies on top of her and feels her hand wrap around him and guide him inside. "I missed you," he hears her say softly next to his ear. "I've missed you too," he says. As much as he wants to hold back he knows he can't. The anticipation has just been too great. He'll be lucky if he lasts more than a few thrusts before coming. He pulls back his head and looks down at her, not wanting to disappoint her but feeling helpless. She smiles up sweetly at him and puts her hands on his butt and pulls him to her with each thrust.

"It's okay...come...," she says softly, "but don't stop...keep going...it doesn't have to end...you'll see...."

He kisses and sucks her breasts and moves his body to her body's rhythm and feels himself coming.

"Good...come...but keep going...," she says a little louder.

He does and is surprised to find he's still hard and thinks he can sustain it.

"That's it! Keep going!" she says louder still.

With each thrust he feels her lifting her ass higher off the bed, wanting him to penetrate deeper.

"Good! Long strokes! Just like that!" she says urgently.

He's thrusting so hard he's afraid he'll injure her but it's just what she wants and he continues thrusting and watches as her mouth opens wide. She looks like she's about to scream or is screaming at a frequency he can't hear and now he feels his thrusts being met by hers as she impales herself on him. She never did this before and it feels wonderful. He feels her coming and her body's undulations gradually slow and she settles back down on the bed. She opens her eyes and gazes up at his and reaches up and clasps her hands at the back of his neck and draws him down to her. "Thank you," he hears her whisper in his ear.

They sit on the wall at Pacific Beach, staring at the horizon, neither wanting to speak first. It's an awkward silence and Trey anticipates by Julie's expression and body language that he's about to find out what's changed with her and isn't going to like what he hears. He guesses the reason she's reluctant to speak is because she doesn't want to hurt his feelings.

"So, I met someone," she finally says.

It's pretty much what he was expecting to hear. "Great," he says glumly.

She looks at him angrily. "Don't get mopey on me."

"Some guy at school?"

"Yeah." She looks back at the horizon.

"How old is he?"

"Eighteen."

He would be older. "What's his name?"

"Erualdo."

It's the icing on the cake. He loses out to a Hispanic. He knows it's wrong to think that but there it is. "So why did we have sex?"

"I knew how much you wanted to."

"So, a sympathy fuck," he says and knows it was a dopey thing to say but he couldn't help himself. She turns on him so violently that he flinches and puts an arm in front of his face.

"Stop being a jerk and listen to me! I want you to be a part of my life." She looks back at the horizon. "You and I have been through a lot together. You're like a brother to me. I need you to get past the sex part." She looks at him. "Okay?"

"Yeah, no problem." Even as he says it he wonders if he can. He's never been asked by someone to put his desire aside and remain friends. It doesn't seem like an easy thing to do but his experience so far in life is that nothing about it is. He thinks of his mom and dad and everything they've been through and where they are now. Maybe it never ends. Maybe growing up takes a lifetime.

"Hey, Yulita," he hears a young man with a lilting voice say and turns to see Erualdo walking up to them. He's smiling and looks even older and more handsome than he does in the picture stuck in the frame of the vanity mirror. Looking at him, Trey feels every bit the fifteen-year-old. He sees Julie smile sweetly at Erualdo and put her arm around his waist and it's not the same sweet smile she shows him. It's different. There's more to it and he can see by her expression that her feelings for Erualdo are different too, deeper. She looks truly happy in a way he's never seen her before. He'd be a jerk not to be there for her. He smiles and puts out a hand to Erualdo. "Trey," he says, shaking Erualdo's hand, "nice to meet you."

"I've been looking forward to meeting you," Erualdo says.

Trey glances at Julie and sees her looking at him hopefully and knows she's waiting to see if he'll step up and be the friend she wants him to be. He winks at her and sees she's relieved and smiles. He admires her skill at handling delicate situations again and even more so now because she's actually brought him around to almost feeling happy she met Erualdo. He wouldn't have thought it possible.

He watches the gray Navy vessel heading south just off the coast as the train speeds north through Camp Pendleton. It's boxy but moving fast and he guesses its purpose is to deliver troops and equipment to the shore during an assault. He sees helicopters rise from its rear deck and land inland and armed Marines in battledress jump out. He knows just how an enemy would feel seeing this coming its way. It's how he's felt all day and still does to a certain extent, under attack emotionally.

He thinks back on the time he and Julie spent in her bedroom and realizes now that she was gently instructing him in the art of lovemaking and also who's been instructing her. The damndest thing is that as much as he resented Erualdo and wanted to dislike him he couldn't. He's a genuinely nice guy, very polite and smart and Trey really enjoyed talking with him.

Erualdo told him his family is from San Cristóbal de las Casas in Chiapas, Mexico, and he was three when they arrived in San Diego legally and they're citizens now. He's going to be a doctor and devote part of his time to working with the poor peasant framers back home. He's spent time working in the program assisting the doctors. He says he loves the work and that it's his calling. He returns from time to time to visit his grandmother and aunts and uncles and cousins and is looking forward to introducing Julie to them and the country. It may be a poor state, he said, but it's beautiful and filled with people who appreciate its splendor. Really, it's a jewel, like no other place. Erualdo invited him to come with them sometime. How could he not like the guy? He saw the way Julie looked proudly at Erualdo when he talked about his plans for the future. It made him realize that he hasn't been thinking about the future at all, that he's just been drifting along. He'd better wake up and start thinking about what he wants to do with his life. He's not going to be a fifteen-year-old forever.

Art starts the truck and looks at Trey. "So, how'd it go, buddy?"

"She has a boyfriend."

"Meet him?"

"Yeah. She wants me to be her friend."

"And?"

Trey shrugs. "I guess."

"What's he like?"

"Nice guy, actually a great guy. He's good for her."

Art grins. "Damnedest thing, huh?"

Trey nods. The good part is that Julie's more confident and happier now that she's living with her mom and has Erualdo in her life. The bad part is that as important as he was in helping to reunite her with her mom, Erualdo's the leading man in her life now and he's just a friend, a good friend, but a friend. He's happy for her but he's still hurting and the idea of no more sex with her isn't helping any. He knows he'll get there eventually, but still....

Trey's pleasantly surprised when he sees Emily in the hall at room change. Her eyes are bright and she's smiling and walking briskly toward him and she looks like she can't wait to share good news with him. "Hey, what's up?"

"I'm going to the movies Saturday. Wanna go?"

"Sure." He see's she relieved to hear it. She was probably worried he was still mad at her about the Kurt business and her stupid mom's snooping and the way she treated his mom. "Where?"

"Edwards Metro Pointe."

"What movie?" He sees her searching his eyes and has the feeling he's missing something.

"Meet me in the lobby around two. See ya there," she says cheerily and walks off down the hall.

He checks out the movie posters in the theater lobby as he waits for Emily to arrive. One movie, *The Rays of the Setting Sun,* looks like a real yawn. The poster shows a group of people dressed in early Twentieth century costumes seated and standing in what he imagines is an English garden. The people stare out from the poster with supremely bored expressions. He reads the blurb: "A touching portrait of British polite society in the period just prior to World War I." Polite society. It's a yawn, all right. He feels a hand take his and turns to see Emily standing there and the first thing he notices, besides her smile and bright eyes, is that she's wearing eyeliner and lipstick and a little makeup, not enough to cover her freckles and the Big Dipper on her right cheek, just enough. He's never seen this Emily before and smiles. "Hey."

"Hey," she says cheerily.

The next thing he notices is that she's wearing a short skirt, unlike all the other girls in the lobby who are wearing shorts. "So, what movie are we seeing?" He sees her searching his eyes the way she did in the hall when she invited him and he has the same feeling that he's missing something.

"Come on," she says.

She begins leading him toward the theaters but he stops her and she turns and looks at him.

"What?" she asks.

He nods toward the concession stand. "Want anything?"

"No."

They walk hand in hand to the end of the hallway and arrive at the theater where *The Rays of the Setting Sun* is playing and he stops her again and looks at her in disbelief. "You really want to see this?"

"Yes," she says firmly and leads him into the theater.

The movie is in progress and they stand just inside the doors for a few moments looking at the screen until their eyes adjust to the darkness. An older man with a bushy white moustache twirled at the ends and an attractive young woman are sitting in a garden talking. The older man is wearing a British military uniform and the young woman a lavendar dress with an embroidered collar buttoned up to her throat and a hat with a wide brim decorated with a yellow ribbon tied in a bow. The woman's hat is tilted just enough to almost cover one of her eyes and she tells the man that although she misses her fiancée dreadfully, she's relieved that he's in India out of harm's way and the old soldier looks at her sorrowfully and sighs and tells her to expect him home soon now that war with Germany seems inevitable.

Trey looks around and sees the theater is almost empty, just a handful of older couples sitting mostly in the middle of the theater. He feels Emily's grip tighten on his hand and he follows her up the side aisle all the way to the back row and then all the way over to the last two seats in the right corner. She's still holding his hand as they sit and stare disinterestedly at the screen for a few moments and then he's aware that she's turned her head and is looking at him. He looks down at their hands, glowing in the pale blue light, and the long sleeve of her shirt and slowly slides his hand back from hers to the hem of her sleeve and begins pulling it up but she stops him with her other hand. He looks at her and sees the uncertainty in her eyes and smiles reassuringly and keeps smiling until she smiles back. He looks down at her wrist again and continues pulling up her sleeve and turns her wrist over and sees a thin dark scar about two inches long. He strokes it lightly with his finger and looks at her and she offers her other wrist for his inspection, turning it over for him. He pulls up the sleeve and sees a similar scar. He takes her wrists in his hands and brings them to his lips and kisses first one scar and then the other and looks at her and sees her eyes are glistening with tears. She reaches up and places her hand gently on the back of his neck and draws him to her and they kiss. She guides his hand to her breast and he cups it gently and feels her arch her back and press her body against his hand as he fondles her. How stupid could he have been not to see that this is what she had planned? Probably for the same reason he's never involved Emily in any of his masturbatory fantasies. This Emily is so unlike the Emily he's known.

He draws back his head and sees her searching his eyes like she's worried he's going to stop and he smiles and sees the worry leave hers eyes and she places her hand on his again and guides it down and under her skirt to between her legs and he's surprised to find she isn't wearing any underpants. He has to hand it to her. She's done a great job of planning. She slides her butt forward to the edge of her seat and parts her legs and he brushes and twirls the wisp of soft hair on her mound and gently strokes her and she parts her legs wider. The look of pleasure on Emily's face is a joy to see and he'd gladly keep stroking her like this forever, but he feels her pressing harder against his hand and knows she wants him to stroke harder and faster and he does and feels her hand on his fingers, moving them toward her opening and pushing them in and he strokes her inside and out. He can tell by the way she's rising up out of her seat and meeting his strokes now that she's about to come. She bites her lip and shuts her eyes tightly and he feels her thrusting against his fingers and gazes at her face. She looks different than Julie when she comes. He's only seen the two of them and he imagines everyone does, himself included.

They sit for a while, Trey with an arm around her shoulders and Emily resting her head against his shoulder, and finally she straightens up in her seat and looks at him and grins and reaches over and puts her hand on the lump in his shorts and squeezes it.

"You're turn," she whispers. She unbuttons and unzips his shorts and fishes him out of his boxers and wraps her hand around him and begins stroking him.

He doesn't want to make a mess on his clothes. "Do you have tissues?" he whispers.

"Don't need any," she says and slides out of her seat to her knees.

They walk hand in hand toward the lobby and he isn't surprised to hear that she was really at Children's Hospital that week she was away and that she's seeing a therapist.

"Every Wednesday," she says.

"What's it like?"

"We talk for an hour, sometimes with my parents there."

"Is it doing any good?"

"Yes. They've backed off. They were totally freaked when I cut my wrists."

"Did you really want to kill yourself?"

She shakes her head. "I wanted them to think I did. I was desperate to make them see what was happening to me."

"You shouldn't cover up the scars. Why hide them?"

"My parents said I could have plastic surgery. I don't know. Maybe I will, maybe I won't. I'm not ashamed of what I did."

"Can you do stuff now?" He sees a new expression on Emily's face, filled with confidence and determination.

"Yes. They have to let me. That's the deal."

He smiles. "Good." It'll be fun getting together with Brett and Tracy and bringing Emily home to meet his family. "Coming back to cotillion?"

She shakes her head. "I'm done with people telling me what to say and how to act."

"Good for you."

"It isn't easy but I'm trying."

"I'm there for you," he says and squeezes her hand.

"I know," she says and squeezes his back. She grins impishly. "That was fun."

He grins back. "Way more than the movie."

CHAPTER 13

Kim's spent the afternoon with Cyd and her friends at Fashion Island, wandering around and stopping here and there to check out the window displays in the shops and comment on them the same way they do people. She and Cyd have been walking side by side just as Maura and Brit and Courtney and Trish have been, although they haven't been holding hands.

She didn't sign into Facebook again until a few days after that first message exchange with Cyd and when she did, no sooner had she arrived at her own page than an instant message popped up from Cyd saying hi and she responded and they chatted about this and that, how their day had gone, what they were up to, what they thought about the teams they were playing next. She was relieved and appreciative of the fact that Cyd didn't bring up the subject of girls being attracted to girls again. It put her at ease and she enjoyed having someone to chat with about things and began looking forward to their daily exchanges and as the weeks went by it felt like she and Cyd had become good friends. So when Cyd invited her a few weeks later to hang with her and her friends at Fashion Island it seemed only right to accept the initiation. Why not? It would be nice to finally meet some of the people she'd only seen in Cyd's photo gallery.

She's gotten to know them and they all seem nice, typical young teenage girls just like her friends, a little shy and self-conscious and awkward and quick to giggle. They've certainly been nice to her, welcoming her into the group like she's always belonged. That doesn't happen all the time when you meet new people. They've chatted about movies and TV shows and celebrities and music they like and so on, all normal stuff. She wonders if they've all had the same conversation she did with Cyd about girls being attracted to girls and if they have, how they feel about it. They seem to her to be a group of friends enjoying hanging together and except for the handholding business nothing they've said or done has led her to believe they're anything more than just friends.

They stop at Häagen-Dazs and carry their cups of ice cream over to a fountain and sit on benches and check out the people. A woman carrying a Bloomingdale's Big Brown Bag passes by walking quickly toward the store, obviously to return something, and her two young daughters are walking as fast as they can to keep up. The woman's honey-colored shoulder-length hair glistens. She's wearing tortoise shell Wayfarer sunglasses and a pink polo with the collar turned up and khaki shorts and light brown wedge sandals and the two girls are dressed the same as their mom and have the same glistening honey-colored shoulder-length hair. The group watches them in silence and when the woman and her daughters are a safe distance away

Brit says, "Oh, my God, that is so Fashion Island!" and the other girls giggle.

Kim looks at Brit. "The malls are all the same."

"No way!" they cry.

"The Block is so ghetto," Courtney says, "and South Coast Plaza is all mixed up, but Fashion Island is so –"

"Newport Beach!" they cry.

"I feel sorry for them," Maura says. "They're gonna grow up to be just like their mom. They'll marry some rich guy and spend the rest of their lives shopping."

Kim puts another spoonful of Chocolate Chip Cookie Dough ice cream in her mouth and squints at Maura. What's wrong with that? Her family lost their house and then had to live in a shelter and then with Walt and now they're living with her grandmother. They've never had a lot of money. That's why she took to wearing Trey's hand me downs and gets the same cheap haircut he does, to help save money. No one told her to. She just did and doesn't complain about it. Her mom barely makes enough to get by and rarely buys anything for herself. Kim loves her dad, but what's wrong with marrying someone who has money and living in a nice house and being able to afford things?

"Cyd says you're a really good soccer player," Courtney says.

Kim feels herself blush. "I try my best."

Cyd nudges her. "She'll probably get League MVP," she tells the others.

Kim sees Trish smile and lean toward Courtney and whisper something in her ear and Courtney smiles and looks at her.

"Trish thinks you look cute when you blush," Courtney says. "So do I."

Everyone giggles and Kim feels her blush deepening. She's embarrassed to be the center of attention but at the same time it feels nice to be complimented. No one's ever told her she looks cute, other than her parents and grandparents and that's different. She feels Cyd's hand on hers and glances at her and Cyd smiles and leans closer and gives her hand a squeeze. She listens to the girls chat about this and that and comment on passersby and she's not at all uncomfortable with the fact that her fingers and Cyd's are now intertwined and when she glances down at them they look nice that way. It's the first time she's held someone's hand affectionately. There's the same reassuring feeling she used to feel when she held her mom's or dad's hand but it's different somehow.

She and Cyd spend the rest of the afternoon walking hand in hand and by the time they're walking toward valet parking to meet her grandmother, it feels to Kim like holding hands with Cyd is the most natural thing in the world.

"Thanks for coming," Cyd says.

"It was fun meeting everyone. They're not just pics anymore."

"Let's get one of us," Cyd says and stops and takes her phone out of her bag. They put their arms around each other's waist and their cheeks together and Cyd holds out the phone and takes the picture. "One more. Ready?"

Kim nods and feels Cyd's cheek pressing harder against hers and Cyd's arm tightening around her waist.

"Got it."

They huddle together to check out the pictures. Kim looks at the first one and then the second and makes a face. "I look awful. I always do in pics."

Cyd nudges her. "You look cute. I'm the one who looks awful." She puts the phone in her bag and takes out a gift-wrapped book and hands it to her. "Here, for coming."

The gift surprises Kim and she holds it in both hands and stares down at it. "Thanks."

"Open it later."

"What's it about?" Kim asks and looks up to see Cyd grinning at her.

"You'll see."

Ever since Cyd gave her the book unwrapping it to see what it's about has been the only thing on her mind. She wanted to wait until the right moment and here she finally is sitting on her bed, leaning back against her pillow with the book in her lap. She feels her body tingling in anticipation of finding out what it's about and while she's eager to, she's also enjoying the feeling of not knowing. What if she never unwrapped it? It'd be great to feel this way forever, always in suspense but, of course, that's not going to happen. She picks it up and carefully removes the tape from the wrapping paper — it's important not to tear it — and unwraps the book and sets the wrapping paper beside her on the bed and turns the book over and looks at the cover. She reads the title, *That Summer With Sarah,* and sees an illustration of two girls holding hands, just a close up of their forearms and hands and they're standing beside a pond in the woods. She isn't surprised it's about girls liking girls. She reads the author's name, Penelope Goldthwaite. The last name strikes her as funny and even feels and sounds funny when she tries to pronounce it. She turns the book over and reads the synopsis:

Jenny Paterson is a shy awkward fourteen-year-old who has moved with her parents into a new neighborhood. Jenny feels unattractive and is having difficulty making friends until she meets Sarah, who lives a few houses down, when she returns from a vacation with her parents in South Africa. Sarah, Jenny learns, is free-spirited. As the two girls confide in each other and their friendship blossoms they give expression to feelings that seem to come naturally to Sarah but are a revelation to Jenny, who never suspected she could feel the way she does about a girl. Having discovered their strong feelings for each other the two girls struggle with what they mean and what to do about them. Are they just going through a phase? Are they lesbian? Is it possible for them to feel the way they do about each other and not be? The two girls struggle to answer these questions as they explore their sexuality and in so doing discover their sexual identity.

She looks at the photograph of Penelope Goldthwaite. Her narrow face and bird-like features remind her of Miss Patti's, the soft-spoken school librarian who always seems to be on the verge of a nervous breakdown. She reads the "About the Author" write up beneath the photo:

Penelope Goldthwaite is an award-winning author of books for young LGBT teens. Ms. Goldthwaite, who is lesbian, learned from personal experience the difficulty LGBT teens have in coming to grips with and embracing their true identity, sharing it with family and friends and ultimately gaining acceptance and support. LGBT teens face many challenges. They are subject to social isolation, truancy, running away, poorly developed dating skills, low self-esteem, self-hatred, alcohol and drug abuse, harassment at school and home, feelings of inferiority, depression, threats of suicide and eating disorders. All too often LGBT teens are shunned by their families and forced to live on the streets, often resorting to prostitution to survive. Ms. Goldthwaite's hope in writing her books is that they will serve as a steadying hand on the shoulder, a much needed hug that will help give these special teens the encouragement and strength they need to become the healthy people nature intended them to be.

She puts the book in her lap and stares down at it, her mind racing. Is Cyd gay? Is that why she gave her the book, to let it tell her what she can't? She doesn't think she is. The only lesbians she knows, other than people on TV, are the two girls at school who say they are and don't hide the fact. Cyd doesn't look or act like either of them. Okay, so she and Cyd are tomboys. They're into sports and aren't interested in looking girly and aren't interested in boys. Does that make them lesbians? She doesn't think so. Did Cyd give the book to Allie? She probably did and it probably freaked her out. Given the way Allie looks in the photos and the type of girl she probably is, it seems it would have and that's probably why Cyd doesn't want to talk about her. Does Cyd even know who she is? Probably no more than she does herself. It seems they're both trying to figure themselves out. She leaves it there for now and turns to the first chapter and begins reading.

By the time she hears Trey arrive home from seeing a movie with his friends Brett and Tracy she's a few chapters into the book and has learned a great deal about Jenny and feels she knows her well. In a way their circumstances are similar. They've both had to move with their families due to financial difficulties, although Jenny's parents' relationship seems to be fine so far. Her father was laid off from his job in sales due to the financial crisis and was lucky to find a new less well-paying one and had to move his family at their own expense. They've had to really tighten their belts but he's thankful he's been able to continue to keep a roof over their heads and put food on the table.

Jenny is an only child and has always been shy and considers herself unattractive because she's tall and skinny and the fact that she's experiencing a growth spurt that's making her feel more awkward than usual isn't helping her already low self-esteem. She's met two girls her age who live on her street, Cindy, a cute blonde who seems obsessed with her own appearance and Missy, a pretty brunette whose father owns an insurance agency and is mayor pro tem of the city, a fact Missy never tires of mentioning. They haven't exactly become friends but the two girls allow Jenny to hang with them and they've taken to calling her "Stick", the nickname of the skinny girl with glasses and braces in the *PreTeena* comic strip. Jenny doesn't like the nickname but tolerates it. She hasn't met Sarah yet, although she's heard a lot about her from Cindy and Missy, nothing complimentary. Sarah's "strange" and "weird" like her parents who both teach at the local state college. According to Cindy and Missy nobody on the street really likes them. People are just polite to them. Jenny will see soon enough when they return from their vacation. Kim glances up and sees Trey poking his head in the doorway.

"Hey," he says, "I need to use the computer."

She wishes now she'd chosen the smaller bedroom so the computer and desk would be in his room. She doesn't need all this room anyway. Maybe they can swap. "Sure," she says and turns her attention back to the book.

He glimpses the cover as he walks to the desk and sits and turns on the computer. "What're you reading?"

"That Summer With Sarah."

"Lemme see."

She holds up the book a moment so he can see the cover and puts it back in her lap and continues reading.

That's what he thought he saw, a picture of two girls holding hands. This is interesting. "What's it about?"

"Two girls who become great friends."

"I guess," he says.

She doesn't like his tone of voice and tries to ignore him.

"Where'd you get it?"

"My friend Cyd gave it to me."

"The girl you were at Fashion Island with?"

"Yeah."

It's getting more interesting by the moment. "She likes you, huh?"

Kim looks at him and narrows her eyes. "We're friends, okay?" She doesn't like his prying and insinuating but has the feeling this is only the beginning of it and there's a lot more to come. If it makes her feel this way she can only imagine how it makes LGBT teens feel. No wonder they have so many problems.

She stares at the road ahead as she rides home with her mom from soccer practice. She knows it's coming, she can feel it and she knows her mom is struggling to find a way to ask her about the book as casually as possible, the way she asks her how school was each day.

"Anything you want to talk about, honey?" June finally asks.

So, here it is. "No. Why?"

"I couldn't help seeing the book your reading."

Kim feels like screaming that's because she left it on the nightstand and isn't trying to hide anything! "What about it?"

"Is it assigned reading?"

"No. My friend Cyd gave it to me."

"Oh! The friend you were at Fashion Island with?"

"Yeah."

"It's an interesting book to give you. Why do you think she did?"

This is so lame. "She thought I'd like it."

"Do you?"

"Yeah." Kim waits for her mom's next question. She knows what it will be and there's no way to ask it delicately, which is why she's still waiting.

"Does she like girls?" June finally asks.

Good. Now they're getting somewhere. "Yeah."

June glances at her. "You know what I mean."

"I dunno. Does it matter?"

June shrugs. "I dunno, honey. I guess not."

That didn't sound very convincing. "What if I liked girls? Would it matter?"

Would it matter? June would like to think it wouldn't but it would and she suspects she feels about it the same way any mother would, concern for her daughter's psychological well-being and the burden living her life as part of a small community of people who are viewed by the rest of society as "different" would place on her and sadness for Kim that she'd probably never experience the joy of having children and disappointment for herself that she'd be denied grandchildren. She's knows she's being selfish but there it is. "No, honey, it wouldn't."

Kim glances at her mom. That didn't sound very convincing, either, and she can see in her mom's eyes that it would matter, a lot.

She reads in bed as Trey works at the computer. She's about two-thirds of the way through the book. She could easily have finished it by now but hasn't wanted to rush through it at her usual pace. She's wanted to read it slowly to really get inside Jenny's and Sarah's heads and try to understand how this relationship of theirs changes from being one of two girls who become friends and feel like kindred spirits to something more, something sexual.

They met about a few chapters back and took to taking walks in the nearby woods to a pond that Sarah found on her explorations shortly after her family moved into the neighborhood. There's a big rock overlooking the pond and that's where they sit and share their thoughts and feelings with each other and discuss every aspect of their lives. It's been all talk until now but this chapter feels different. Sarah's usually the talkative one, going on and on animatedly about whatever pops into her head as they walk to the pond, but today she's quiet and Jenny knows something's bothering her. When they arrive at the rock, instead of sitting on it facing each other with their legs crossed as they usually do, they sit side by side with their knees drawn up and their arms wrapped around their legs and their chins on their knees and instead of chattering away as they usually do, they stare at the reflection of the trees on the still surface of the pond:

"Can you feel it?" Sarah finally asked mournfully.

"What?" Jenny asked, looking at her with concern.

"Fall," Sarah said, not taking her eyes off the reflection of the trees. "It'll be here soon. I can smell it, taste it.

Jenny smiled and looked back at the pond. "The leaves haven't even started turning."

"Before you know it we'll be back in school," Sarah said. "No more lazy days and long walks in the woods."

"We'll still be able to do that," Jenny said encouragingly, trying to lift her spirits.

Sarah looked at her and searched Jenny's eyes for some sign that she had even an inkling of how she felt toward for her. She'd done such a good job of keeping her feelings bottled up that she thought probably not and her sadness deepened. She picked up a pebble and threw it in the pond and the two girls watched the reflection of the trees dissolve in the expanding ripples. If I wait for her, Sarah thought, I could be waiting forever. Why not try to change things? It's in the air. "I didn't tell you about the best part of the trip," she said, grinning at Jenny.

"More animals?" Jenny asked, happy to see Sarah's grin.

"Even better. We visited a Himba village."

"Are they a tribe?"

Sarah nodded. "They're the most beautiful people I've ever seen, especially the women. They don't cover their breasts and their breasts are…." She picked nervously at her toenail and searched for the right word. "Amazing!" she said, looking up wide-eyed at Jenny.

"How?"

Sarah modeled them with her hands. "Big and pointy!" she said and they giggled and Sarah bumped Jenny's shoulder with hers. "So why do we cover ours up?" she asked.

"It's colder here," Jenny said, avoiding Sarah's eyes and shifting nervously.

"It's pretty warm now," Sarah said and poked Jenny's arm with an elbow. "Let's be Himba women! This pond is our sacred place and we'll do the Himba Pond Dance!"

Jenny looked around. "Someone might see us."

"In all the times we've been here have you ever seen anyone?"

"No, but —"

"C'mon," Sarah said, leaping to her feet and pulling her tee shirt over her head.

Jenny looked up at her, astonished. "You're crazy!"

Sarah reached down and grabbed Jenny's arms and pulled her to her feet. "C'mon! Let's dance!" she said, undoing her bra and tossing it on her tee shirt.

Jenny couldn't help staring at Sarah's breasts. She'd always wondered what they looked like and there they were, two firm mounds with perky nipples and rosy areolas, just as beautiful as she'd imagined them.

Sarah stuck her hip out and put a hand on it and gave Jenny a stern look. "Are you gonna dance or not?"

"Yeah," Jenny said uncertainly, slowly removing her tee shirt and tossing it aside. "I am," she said, slowly undoing her bra and tossing it on her tee shirt.

Sarah began gyrating wildly and singing the Himba Pond Dance song, making up lyrics as she went along. "Hoo-hoo-yaa-yaa, naa-naa-waa-waa!"

Jenny responded, repeating after Sarah and they grabbed each other's hands and hopped more than danced in circles. Round and round they went, Sarah singing a made-up verse and Jenny repeating it.

"You-ou are-are my best frie-end!"

"I think you are beau-ti-fu-ul!"

"I-I want to kiss-iss you-ou!"

They stopped spinning, both getting their balance and catching their breath. They stood looking at each other's flush faces and breasts, now glistening with sweat. Jenny's didn't look anything like a Himba woman's to Sarah. They were small with inverted nipples but they looked to her like the most beautiful breasts in the world. She knew she'd have to be the one to make the first move and stepped forward, keeping her eyes on Jenny's. She slowly put her arms around Jenny's waist and brought her lips to hers and kissed her, gently at first, but harder as she felt Jenny respond. She felt Jenny tense as she placed her hand on her breast and began caressing it. A bird screeched in the woods nearby and Sarah felt Jenny jump and want to pull away but she tightened her hold around her waist and pressed her lips harder against hers and caressed her until she felt Jenny relax and press back. She thrilled when she felt Jenny place her hand tentatively on her breast and begin caressing it.

"Need the computer?" she hears Trey ask and looks up at him. "Yeah, leave it on," she says and watches him leave the room and puts down the book. She's aware of the moistness between her legs as she climbs off the bed and sits at the computer and notices in the browser that she has three email messages waiting, which is surprising since she seldom uses her email. The first one is from a girl whose name she doesn't recognize. She opens it and sees it's from Facebook and reads the message:

have fun w ur lezzy friend at fi?

She starts. Who is this person? She clicks on the girl's name and goes to her Facebook page where she finds no photo posted and no information. She returns to the message and deletes it and opens the next email from another girl whose name she doesn't recognize and reads the message:

r u a girl or boy?

This girl also has no photo posted and no information on her Facebook page. She deletes the message and reads and deletes the next, similarly hurtful from another girl she doesn't know. A message from Cyd appears:

how r u? c the pics? :-)

no.

check em out!!!

She goes to Cyd's page and sees several photos from the new series she's posted. The first two are the two Cyd took when she was about to leave Fashion Island. There they are with their cheeks pressed together and their arms around each other smiling at the camera. She types and sends off her message:

getting ugly comments from girls who have.

just delete em.

Right. Like that will make the whole thing go away. She types her reply and sends it off:

already have.

Are they girls at her school? Girls on other soccer teams? She's frightened by this anonymous attack and feels helpless to do anything about it. Another message from Cyd appears:

finish the book?

no.

get 2 the hpd?

yeah, this evening.

what do u think?

What does she think? She thinks Cyd wants to do it with her. Why with her she doesn't know and she's not sure how she feels about it. She's never kissed a girl or a boy and no one's ever touched her. She didn't think anyone would want to. It's not that she hasn't thought about it and wondered how it would feel. She knows it would feel good. Just look at Trey. She types her reply and sends it off:

> Idk. ever done it?

> no.... want 2 w u!!! come sleep over!!! :-)

Sleep over? If she does she does so knowing full well what Cyd has in mind and there won't be any backing out once she's there:

> i'll think about it. gotta go. talk tomorrow.

> XOXOXO!!!

She stares at Cyd's string of Xs and Os and tries to understand what she's afraid of. Is it the fact that Cyd's a girl? She didn't have a problem holding her hand at Fashion Island. In fact she liked it. It felt good. Is it the idea of kissing her? What's the big deal? She can easily imagine them doing that and just as easily imagine the two of them touching each other. Maybe it's something else. She shuts down the computer and climbs back into bed and picks up the book and continues reading:

"That feels nice," Sarah said, encouraging Jenny's touch with the movement of her body as she massaged one of Jenny's inverted nipples. "Do they come out?"

"I dunno," Jenny said, embarrassed and blushing. "They never have."

Sarah grinned. "I bet I can get them out," she said and wrapped her hand gently around the underside of Jenny's breast and kissed her areola, then placed her mouth over it and began gently sucking. She felt Jenny's body thrill at the sensation and heard the air whistling softly between her slightly parted lips as she breathed in and out. She pulled Jenny slowly down onto the rock and felt her place her hand on the back of her head and pull her gently to her, encouraging her to suck harder. Good, Sarah thought, she's getting into it and enjoying herself and she hoped the pleasure Jenny was experiencing was as great as her own in pleasing her. She sucked and sucked and finally felt Jenny's nipple pop out and drew her head back and looked at it. "Wow!" Sarah said, grinning. "Look at that!"

Jenny stared down at her nipple. To her amazement it was rosy and long and standing proudly erect. She'd always thought her nipples, if and when they ever did emerge, would be unremarkable like the rest of her, but here was a most remarkable nipple, longer than Sarah's!

"I bet it feels great to finally be free," Sarah said.

"It does," Jenny said, admiring it.

"Now the other one," Sarah said.

Jenny nodded and watched Sarah cup her breast with her hand and put her mouth on her areola. Jenny closed her eyes and smiled and slowly stroked Sarah's hair as she enjoyed the feeling of her sucking. Sarah's hand felt nice on her stomach, moving slowly in circles around her navel, but it startled her when she felt it moving lower down and for a moment she panicked. Her instinct was to stop Sarah, but thinking about it the idea of stopping her now seemed silly. She'd already let Sarah suck out one of her nipples and was encouraging her to suck out the other, so why make her stop now? Jenny knew from the tingling between her legs that her body wanted Sarah's hand to continue on its way, that it couldn't wait for its arrival, so why should she let her inhibitions stand in the way of her pleasure? No one had ever paid attention to her the way Sarah was now. It would be a shame to stop her. She felt Sarah's hand moving down the front of her baggy shorts to the top of her leg and then to the bare skin of her thigh. She thrilled when she felt it move slowly beneath the leg of her shorts and up her thigh toward her crotch.

"Hmm," Sarah said, feeling Jenny's nipple pop out in her mouth and she leaned back to admire her handiwork. "There!" she cried triumphantly.

Jenny looked down at the now proudly erect nipple and then at its twin and then at Sarah. "Thank you," she said softly.

"My pleasure," Sarah said and put her hand on the back of Jenny's head and gazed at her lovingly as she brought her lips to Jenny's. They kissed gently, tenderly at first with their mouths closed and then more ardently as they opened them. The tips of their tongues met and began exploring the inside of each other's mouth and Jenny felt Sarah's fingers arrive between her legs and begin lightly brushing the hair on her mound. She parted her legs wider, encouraging Sarah to play with her to her heart's content.

Good, Sarah thought, open up for me, like a flower opening to the morning sunlight. She was surprised and delighted to feel Jenny's hand on her thigh and parted her legs eagerly, inviting her exploration. The two girls slowly laid back on the rock, kissing as they did, and turned their bodies to face each other. They kissed and caressed each other's breasts and stroked each other between the legs feeling happy and content and complete as they never had before and they wished they could stay that way forever. They knew it was just wishful thinking but that's what they wanted and if they could have, they would have.

She stares down at the page and feels her body more than tingling now and especially so between her legs. So that's what the Himba Pond Dance is all about. She knew the chapter would end this way, with the two of them touching each other, maybe not exactly like that, but touching. She places the book on the nightstand and turns off the light and settles under the covers on her back and closes her eyes and imagines herself and Cyd in the scene. Who would she be? Jenny, of course. She pulls up her tee shirt and caresses her breasts. How would it feel if they were Cyd's hands? How would it feel if Cyd were sucking her nipples? She slides a hand down inside her underpants to between her legs and parts them and begins stroking herself. She imagines Cyd's hands doing the stroking and her body shudders with pleasure and she brings herself to that point she's able to reach now where she feels her body wanting to orgasm. She isn't able to yet, although she knows she's close and that it will happen soon and that if they really were Cyd's hand stroking her she would now. She wants them to be, more than anything and, yes, that's what she's afraid of.

CHAPTER 14

Kaitlin rides her mountain bike behind Michael as they head up yet another hill on the road in Big Sur and it's remarkable to her how his pace never slows. She doesn't know how he does it. It's the same going up hills as down and he just keeps putting one foot in front of the other. She's not a runner but she is in pretty good shape. Even so, she knows she couldn't do it. It takes a certain type of person, a certain attitude and mental discipline, the ability to tune out everything around you and just focus on repetitive motion, on keeping going and that's not her, or at least it hasn't been. Her experience with Manfred has deepened her appreciation of Michael's love of long-distance running in particular and his approach to life in general. Just keep going, steady on through good times and bad. She studies his broad shoulders and back, his arms and thighs and calves pumping away. It's people like him who get things done, who get an idea in their heads and won't give up until they either realize it or die trying, who just keep moving forward, no matter what.

It was her idea to spend the weekend in Carmel just up Highway 1 from where it all began. They haven't spent time like this together in a long time and here they are enjoying a glorious afternoon. They have dinner reservations at Dametra Café where they ate that evening after the race before returning to the campsite in Big Sur and then taking that walk and making love on the hill overlooking the Pacific. She wanted to have dinner there to tell him about Manfred. She just wants to come clean and whatever happens happens. She looks at the large dark disk of sweat on his back plastering his shirt to his skin across his shoulders. It turns her on and she squirms on the seat.

She stands in front of the full-length mirror in their room in the bed and breakfast putting the finishing touches on her outfit and listening to the rush of water in the shower and imagines the way Michael's body looks as he turns this way and that, washing and rinsing himself off. She decided to wear the same red halter top and skinny blue jeans and black high heel sandals she did the first time they met. It worked then, so why mess with a good thing? She doesn't often wear makeup, only on special occasions and this is definitely one. She leans closer to the mirror and smoothes her pomegranate lipstick with her pinky and studies her face. Just enough blush on the cheeks, a nice mocha foundation on the eyes and just a hint of eyeliner. No need for mascara. She never uses it. Her long thick eyelashes have always been one of her best features. She looks at herself and purses her lips and bats her eyelashes and decides against wearing her clear lens red frame glasses this evening. She doesn't want anything to come between their eyes.

"Hey, sexy," she hears Michael say and looks at him in the mirror, leaning against the bathroom doorway and smiling at her with his arms and legs crossed and a towel wrapped around his waist. She's been feeling horny all day and the way looking at that body of his is making her feel now they might not make it out of the room. She glances down at Magda's necklace on the table beside the mirror and picks it up and holds it out to him. "Help me with this, baby," she says. It's silly, of course. She doesn't need help putting it on but she's feeling coquettish as well as horny and guilty. It's an odd mixture.

If she's going to come clean she wants him to be in the best possible frame of mind. She wants to begin with him wanting her. Whether or not he will afterward remains to be seen. She sees him smile and watches him sidle over to her and take the necklace and stand behind her and look at her in the mirror as he lays the pendant carefully on her chest and drapes the strands as carefully around her neck and fastens them. He wraps his arms around her and presses his cheek against hers and she places her hand on his forearm and smiles. She looks at her herself in the mirror and sees the guilt in her eyes and knows he can too. Even so, she can see by the look in his eyes that he's feeling as horny as she is and would just just as soon skip dinner and hop in bed right now.

He gives her a squeeze and kiss on the cheek. "You look great," he says.

She watches him walk away to get dressed. So far, so good.

She puts down her menu and looks at him. "It all looks delicious. I remember I had a hard time choosing an entrée the last time we were here."

"I think I'll have the cioppino."

Hmm...mussels...good sex food. She grins. "Me too."

They chat through the meal. Michael's dad has been diagnosed with a quite treatable form of prostrate cancer but, still, he's concerned. They've found malignant tumors in both of Kaitlin's mom's breasts and she's contemplating having a double mastectomy. Breast cancer runs in her family and how would he feel if she were diagnosed with breast cancer and decided to do the same? It wouldn't make any difference to him. They're decided on the Royal Hawaiian in late October. She'll get in touch with the hotel and begin making arrangements. They should probably go see Henry at Brooks Brothers and get Michael's suit squared away and Keith should do the same. There's no reason to put it off until the last minute. She doesn't know what she wants to wear yet, something simple, she'll think about it. She and Beth had lunch and Beth seems to be doing better, not as stressed out as she was, which is good. She reminisces about when they first met and how self-absorbed she thought he was until she realized after the race that it was just part of his pre-race mental preparation, about how bright the moonlight was when they took that walk and how beautiful the Pacific looked when they reached the top of the hill and how she opened up to him as she never had with anyone before and how wild and wonderful their lovemaking was and how she'd never been on top with anyone and how exciting and sexy it felt, riding him like a cowgirl and she'd never come so long and hard before. The waiter clears the dinner plates and asks if they'd like dessert and they order the chocolate cake and cappuccinos. She takes a deep breath and sits back and crosses her arms and looks at him. "I know you know."

"What?"

"That I'm seeing someone, or was."

He nods.

"Why haven't you said anything?"

He shrugs and fidgets with his dessert fork. "I figured you'd tell me about it when you were ready."

"I've never done anything like that before."

"What?"

"Cheat on someone. And you of all people!"

"Maybe that's why you did."

"What?"

"You knew I'd understand."

Damn it! He's right! He gave her all the rope she needed to hang herself. He must think she's a complete fool and now she feels even guiltier.

"So what happened?"

"I don't know. He was just so interested in me. I guess it went to my head. I wasn't thinking."

"I mean to end it?"

She shrugs. "I realized he was just toying with me. He's very self-centered."

"What if he weren't?"

She stares at him. He would ask that question. It's the right one to ask, the one that goes to the heart of the matter, the one she'd be asking him if the shoe were on the other foot and the one she hoped he wouldn't ask. Well, there's no point lying to him now. "I don't know." She waits for his response feeling uncomfortable and shifting nervously in her seat, but he just looks at her with his usual understanding expression. "Talk to me, Michael."

He shrugs. "What's there to say? These things happen." He looks at her as the waiter places their cake and cappuccinos in front of them and sees she's upset and fighting back tears.

"I feel like shit," she says, dabbing at her eyes with her napkin.

"It's okay. Take it easy."

"Why is it so easy for you to forgive me? I'm not sure I could forgive you."

"I'd be surprised if you didn't. Hey," he says, shrugging, "you had a fling."

Is that what it was? A fling? She didn't think so at the time and it doesn't feel like one now. What it feels like is a mistake she isn't done paying for. At least she got it off her chest and he's still here, sitting across from her, smiling at her.

They stroll hand in hand along the dark empty street back toward the bed and breakfast. She's still wondering why he was so understanding and quick to forgive her and about the way he dismissed her relationship with Manfred so casually, calling it "a fling", as if having flings is perfectly normal and acceptable for people in a relationship. Could it be? Being the unfaithful one, she's in no position to ask, but she's curious and thinks she's prepared for his answer. "Have you been with anyone since we've been together?"

He knows her well, knows how important the issue of fidelity is to her and how deeply her own infidelity has affected her and how she's still agonizing over it. It took a lot of courage for her to tell him about it. It would be so easy to lie to her, but he feels he owes it to her to be honest. "Once."

She thought she was prepared but suddenly feels just as she told Magda she would: betrayed. She wants to let go of his hand and stop but forces herself to keep going and try to remain calm. "Who was she? Anyone I know?"

"No. Keith and I were having drinks after work at South Coast Plaza one evening and there was a group of women who'd been shopping and were having drinks."

So, Keith knows. At least he didn't tell Beth, otherwise she'd have heard about this. "Young? Old?"

"Young. They looked like trophy wives. Anyway, this one woman couldn't take her eyes off me. She and her friends left and she was waiting for me outside."

"Just standing there?"

"No, sitting at a table in the dark."

"And you just happened to see her?" She knows she sounds accusing and has no right to be but can't help herself.

He looks at her and smiles patiently. "Katie, she was waiting for me. She made her presence felt."

"I bet she looked hot."

"Very."

"Way hotter-looking than me."

He looks at her and sighs. "Katie...."

She tries to rein in her anger and hurt get herself back under control. She wants to hear the details. "So what happened?"

"We got a room at the Westin and fucked our brains out."

Wow! It really is true that women need a reason but men only need a place, as if she didn't know that already. "What's her name?"

"She never mentioned." He grins. "By the way, she paid for the room."

She feels herself losing it again. What's he grinning about? What an arrogant asshole! She wants to slap him. "Oh, that's good! So how was it?"

"Wild! She wanted anal sex."

This stuns her and she stops and lets go of his hand and he stops and turns to face her. "You fucked her in the ass?"

"Yeah."

She doesn't know why she's even more angered and hurt by this revelation but she is and now she can't contain her rage. "You fucked a perfect stranger in the ass?"

He glances around the street. "Katie, keep your voice down."

She flails her arms at him but he catches her wrists and holds them tightly. "Fuck you!" she screams. She hears chuckling coming from across the street and sees a couple in the shadows strolling along the sidewalk looking at them. She looks at Michael and feels tears streaming down her cheeks and sniffs and steps forward and puts her arms around his waist and presses her face against his chest. "I'm sorry," she says and feels his arms tightening around her and his kiss on the top of her head. Well, they're even.

They lie in bed in each other's arms, cuddling and stroking each other tenderly the way they always do when they begin their lovemaking, but she's still thinking about Michael's revelation. The surprising thing is that unlike with Josh, she doesn't feel at all betrayed by Michael. She knows he didn't have any real feelings for that woman other than desire and lust, which is all she felt for Manfred. In fact, she feels angry with herself for not having paid more attention to Michael's needs as a sexual partner. She needs to be more adventurous. She's not so sure about anal sex, though. Like every kid growing up she had it drilled into her head that the hole in her behind was exit only and off limits and that letting a guy stick his thing in it would be painful, as her only experience with anal sex was on her one and only date with that jerk in college. She'd had too much to drink and he entered her behind before she knew what he was doing and it was excruciatingly painful. Clearly he didn't know what he was doing, but it was enough to put her off ever wanting to try it again. She told Michael about the experience, which is undoubtedly why he's never brought up the subject of anal sex. Maybe it would be different with Michael. The woman at the Westin sure seemed to enjoy it. Maybe there's more to it than just having a cock rammed in your ass. She owes it to him to at least try it, doesn't she? She knows he likes it. "Why haven't we done it? Why haven't you asked me if I wanted to?"

"I figured if you wanted to you'd tell me."

"Did the woman at the Westin tell you?"

"Yeah."

"So now I am," she says.

She sips her coffee and nibbles her croissant and can't stop grinning. What an absolutely amazing experience that was. Her rear is still tingling pleasantly. The bright morning sunlight feels warm against her skin and all she wants to do is sit here and bask in it and gaze at Michael as he surveys the morning scene, checking out the people passing by their sidewalk table. It was nothing like that other time. Michael was so focused on making her feel relaxed and comfortable, taking his time, making sure at each step of the way that she was comfortable and the feeling was pleasurable. Was it ever! She had multiple orgasms! Making love like that, on her knees with her ass in the air and back arched and head down — Well, she felt incredibly sexy! Like a wild animal! The fact that not twenty-four hours ago anal sex was the farthest thing from her mind and now she can't stop thinking about it and is looking forward to doing it again makes her giggle.

Michael looks at her and smiles. "What?"

She pokes his leg with her toes and grins. "You know." She feels him tickle the sole of her foot and giggles again and pulls her foot away. It occurs to her that she owes what happened last night and her happiness now to Magda. It was Magda's passion about honesty that encouraged her to talk to Michael, which led to what happened. More than anyone she can think of Magda would appreciate and enjoy hearing about the experience. She fishes her phone out of her bag and types and sends off the message:

amazing anal sex last night!!!
:-o.... :-P.... ;-).... :-)

Magda eyes the chiseled torso of the gorgeous young man sitting between two attractive young women on the far side of Brigitte's heated pool. A model? Maybe, although she won't find out this evening even if she does have sex with him. That's the rule at their now famous parties: no talk, just sex. The parties were her idea. She and Brigitte and Keir were at yet another boring party and the conversation was particularly banal and tedious. So much talk and most of it a regurgitation of what people had been told by the news media or about topics of no consequence, like football. When they finally made their escape and were driving to Brigitte's to spend the night together, Magda said, "Wouldn't it be nice to have a party where the rule is no talk, no opinions about politics, no talk about football, no talk at all." Brigitte and Keir thought it was an intriguing idea and asked what people would do? The idea just popped into her head and she blurted it out. "Have sex! Take Ecstasy and fuck!" Brigitte suggested they could use her pool. It was brilliant. What better venue than her heated pool in the backyard of her home on a quiet tree-lined street in an exclusive neighborhood in the Berlin suburbs? They could enjoy privacy and no one would know what was going on behind that high brick wall or care, for that matter. They invited only their closest friends to the first party, like-minded people who embraced the idea wholeheartedly and it was a wild success. Word spread and now friends of friends of friends pester them for an invitation.

This young woman with the Mohawk that looks like a zebra's main sitting on her left and whose clit she's stroking is very cute. She likes the way the young woman responds to her touch and the fact that she's not clean-shaven, but has a nice hairy bush between her legs, which is refreshing. Maybe she'll spend more time alone with her later before she joins Brigitte and Keir to sleep in late, as they always do.

The young man on her right with his hands between her legs knows what he's doing. He's already made her come twice and she's been stroking his cock, which is stiff as a rod, for what seems forever but he shows no signs of coming anytime soon. It's probably the drug. It can have that affect.

She gazes across the pool at Keir with a pretty young man on either side of him and then Brigitte with an attractive young woman on either side of her, as they planned for this evening, to keep things interesting. She shuts her eyes and enjoys the feel of stroking and being stroked. Didn't she hear her phone?

She removes her hand from between the young woman's legs and reaches back and picks it up and checks her messages and smiles as she reads Kaitlin's. Good for her!

Kaitlin hears the ethereal-sounding ring tone she chose for Magda and picks up the phone and reads her reply:

happy for you! with?

Of course, with Manfred here Magda would ask. She hasn't told her that she's done with her brother and he obviously hasn't, either, which isn't surprising. She taps and sends off her reply:

michael!

Magda settles back in the pool and closes her eyes and feels the young woman take her hand and guide it back to between her legs and press it against her hairy bush. Good. Take what you want. She reaches over and finds the cock of the young man to her right and wraps her hand around it again and begins stroking it. It's still stiff as a rod and she's a little surprised the woman on the other side him didn't claim this marvelous plaything while it was available. Well, she must have her hands full with something else.

She looks at the young woman to her left and sees her gazing at her rapturously and feels her pressing her fingers against her opening. "Make me come," the young woman whispers, "inside." She frowns. "Shhh," she whispers and slides two fingers into the young woman, who presses eagerly against her hand. She feels the man to her right put his hand on her leg at the top of her thigh and she parts her legs, inviting him to play. The situation is wonderful, simply wonderful. She smiles and settles back against the side of the pool with her eyes closed and enjoys the radiating waves of pleasure emanating from deep within her as they move through her body. She glances at the woman beside her and sees her watching her the way a dog watches its mistress, waiting for a sign of what to do next. She stands and takes the young woman's hand and places it on the man's cock and turns and puts her elbows on the side of the pool and spreads her legs. She sways her ass and looks back over her shoulder at them and sees the young man now positioning himself behind her. She reaches back and guides him in in honor of her friend and picks up her phone and texts Kaitlin:

good! can't wait to meet him!

"Who're you texting?" Michael asks.

"Magda."

"What're you up for?"

She looks up at him and grins and pokes his leg with her toes. "You know." She sees him grin and feels him tickle the sole of her foot again and she giggles. As much as last night was an amazing revelation, so is the fact that it might never have happened if she hadn't been led astray by her desire for Manfred and Michael hadn't had sex with that woman at the Westin and they hadn't told each other about it. If anyone would appreciate the irony of it all, Beatrice would. She hopes she sees her again soon. Beatrice already feels more like a mother to her than her own mother.

CHAPTER 15

Eileen places her salad fork on the side of her plate and looks at Arthur with raised eyebrows. "I think the idea is preposterous."

Arthur stares at her a moment and then looks down at his salad and puts another forkful in his mouth and chews slowly. "Why? You used to love camping."

"I do, although I haven't been camping since the last time we went and that was ages ago." She takes a sip of sparkling water and looks around at the other diners. "Anyway, I've met someone." She doesn't have to look at him to know the way he's looking at her now.

"Really? Who?"

He seems genuinely surprised to hear she's involved romantically. Well, she can't blame him. He was the only man in her life for so long and there hasn't been anyone since they divorced. She looks at him. "His name is Roland. He lives in D.C. He's an ex-Army officer. His company provides DOD with new technology."

"Interesting. How'd you meet him?"

"One of Betty and Reggie's parties." Arthur knows Betty and Reggie. They had dinner together a few times toward the end of the marriage and although he considered them her friends, he liked them and enjoyed the conversation, especially with Reggie. She keeps her eyes on his. She wants to savor watching his expression as she shares the next piece of information with him. "He's Reggie's twin brother." She smiles and knows she looks smug and sees his eyes narrow slightly.

"If he's anything like Reggie he must be charming and handsome."

Isn't it just like him, all men, really? After having treated her so badly for so many years and then dumped her — there's no more delicate way to put it — he now looks like a hurt little boy because there's another man in her life, and a black man at that. "He's utterly charming and even handsomer I think." Okay, maybe she shouldn't rub his nose in it, but she's relishing doing it and, after all, it's tit for tat.

Arthur stabs an artichoke heart with his fork. "So, back to the trip. Do a little fishing, a little hiking…."

"What is it, precisely, you're trying to prove, Arthur? I mean, I know you're hurting because Landis left you, but why are you trying to involve me in your life now?"

He eyes the fork tines entering and exiting the artichoke heart, like the motion lines of a bullet in a cartoon, and looks up at her. "I dunno…reconnect as friends? I've known you longer than I've known anyone. You know me better than anyone, probably better than I know myself. That's valuable, isn't it? Isn't that worth preserving?"

"We don't have to go camping to be friends, Arthur."

"Anyway, we're not getting any younger. We're both at that age where we can see how much lonnger we have left, if we're lucky. We know what that amount of time feels like and how quickly it'll pass. Having someone close to you to share things with is important, don't you think?"

How sad he looks. "I think you're terrified of aging, Arthur. I think that's why you wanted Landis in your life, to distract you from it, and I think that's what this newfound interest in my being your friend is all about. Don't fool yourself."

He narrows his eyes. "You've always been pretty sharp, pretty insightful. Maybe you're right. Maybe I am afraid of getting old. So what? I wouldn't be the first person."

"That's not the problem, Arthur. The problem is how you're dealing with it, which isn't very well."

"I think I'm being pretty reasonable. All I'm asking is that you go camping with me, for old time's sake. We can sleep in separate tents if you like."

Poor Arthur. He's so defeated. "I don't know. It just seems like such a silly idea."

"Think about it."

Betty looks thoughtfully at her teabag as she dips it in her cup of hot water. "Heard from Roland?"

Eileen shakes her head.

"Huh.... I know he enjoyed meeting you."

"Well, I'm sure he's been very busy."

"Yeah, that's probably it."

"And I imagine he has other women friends. I'd be surprised if he didn't."

"I'm sure he does...."

"What's on your mind?"

Betty presses the teabag against her plastic spoon and places them both on her napkin. "Oh, I don't know.... You two seemed to click. It would be nice if something came of it."

"Something did. We had a great time together."

"I know. Something more...."

"Like what?"

"I dunno...."

Eileed rolls her eyes. "And Roland accused me of being romantic."

"I just want you to be happy. That's all."

"I don't have to be in a relationship to be happy, Betty." Eileen's struck by just how disingenuous that sounded.

"Today's his birthday," Betty says.

"Oh! I didn't know."

"Yeah, I figured you didn't. I'm taking Reggie out to dinner."

"Maybe I'll call and wish him Happy Birthday," Eileen says and sees Betty's expression brighten, as she knew it would. It's surprising how much of a matchmaker she's become.

"Great idea! Do!"

Roland savors the buttery consistency and aged taste of his medium well-done filet mignon and watches Charlotte cut off another piece of hers, bloody, the way she likes it. He reaches for his glass of champagne and takes a sip and watches her place the piece of steak delicately in her mouth and close her eyes and chew slowly, happily and contentedly. She's his type of woman: a politically well-connected and influential advisor to the National Security Committee and the Defense Intelligence Agency with a high security clearance, in her mid forties, attractive and elegantly dressed, a good conversationalist and a Southerner with a bawdy sense of humor. Of all her attributes, though, it's the cat in her he enjoys most and he can almost hear her purring as she chews. She's white, as most of the women he's intimate with are, and is perfectly happy, as he is, with their "no questions asked" relationship. She's a tigress in bed and he's looking forward to enjoying that aspect of her later.

She places her fork on the side of her plate and takes a sip of champagne. "How'd it go? Anything interesting?"

"Their developing technology that could ultimately be used to provide a unit commander on the ground a complete history of everything associated with his location: friendlies and unfriendlies, past engagements and outcomes, political affiliations. Neat stuff."

"Yeah, a few companies are developing similar technology. We'll see who crosses the finish line first." It's an unspoken agreement between them that she'll help him however she can in the competition for government contracts, but only if his horse is a winner. She won't taut a nag.

His phone rings and he takes it out of the inside pocket of his blazer and looks at the screen and sees it's Eileen. "Be right back." He stands and walks toward the front entrance with the phone to his ear. "Hi, how're you?" he asks brightly.

Eileen looks at the darkening late afternoon sky through the trees in the backyard. He sounds cheery, like he's out celebrating and she feels guilty now about disturbing him. "Fine. I just wanted to call to wish you Happy Birthday."

"Thank you. That's sweet of you, baby."

She starts. Did he just call her "baby"? No one's ever called her that. In all the years she was with Arthur he never used any term of endearment in addressing her, not "honey" or "sweetheart" or anything other than her name, which was fine with her, but she's not sure how she feels about being called "baby." It doesn't seem to suit her and how telling it is that she should feel that way. "Doing anything special to celebrate?"

"Just having dinner with a friend. A birthday treat."

"Oh! I'm sorry I disturbed you. I'll let you get back."

"You're not disturbing me. It's great to hear from you, baby."

There it is again. Why does it seem like he's addressing someone else? And why didn't he call her that when he was here? Maybe he's a different person when he's home in D.C.

"So how're things?" he asks. "What's going on?"

How are things? What's going on? Well, she's back to her humdrum existence and the only noteworthy thing going on is Arthur and his silly invitation to go camping. She doesn't want to mention it but really doesn't have anything else to say. "My ex wants me to go camping with him."

"Huh. That's interesting."

"We had lunch. He's having a hard time dealing with the fact that his wife left him."

"That's understandable."

"I think what's really bothering him is that he's getting old. He isn't handling it well."

"Also understandable. Sounds like he wants to reconnect and make amends."

"I'm sure that's it, but I'm not sure I want to."

"That's understandable too. Well, it's your call, baby."

There it is again and now she's sure she doesn't like being called "baby", doesn't like the sound of it at all and she's also sure that's what he calls all his women friends in D.C.

"You do have your son and his family as a mutual concern. That's important. It's worth it for their sake."

"I'm sure you're right."

"This idea of going camping reminds me of team-building exercises. You learn how to trust each other by working together on projects. They work."

Why is he being so encouraging? Does he want something to happen between her and Arthur? He's being perfectly reasonable and everything he's saying makes perfect sense and, honestly, she doesn't want to be just another one of his women, but still.... Is she that disposable? Now she regrets having called. "I'll let you get back to your dinner. Happy Birthday!"

"Thanks, baby. Take care."

She puts the phone on the patio table and stares at it. She's left with the strong feeling that she's both making a fool of herself and being made a fool of and more so the latter now. It's funny, but in all the years with Arthur, for all his womanizing, she never felt this way. She was well aware of what he was up to and he never tried to hide it and she made the conscious decision to stay with him for Art's sake, but this feeling, it's new and different and she doesn't like it at all.

Roland pulls in his chair and reaches for his glass. "That company in Irvine."

Charlotte raises an eyebrow and reaches for hers. She'd be very surprised if it were the company in Irvine calling. More likely it was a harem member calling to wish him Happy

Birthday. She knows him well, better than anyone, his body language and facial expressions and tones of voice. She knows his appetites and how to satisfy them. That's why she's his favorite and spends the lion's share of time with him. The other women are sideshows in his life. She's the main attraction, just as her mama was in her daddy's life. She learned from her daddy that men like to roam and from her mama that the best thing to do is let them and pay it no mind. She looks at Roland suggestively. "I've got a little birthday surprise planned, suguh. I just know you're gonna love it."

He grins and shakes his head and chuckles. "I'm sure I will, baby, I'm sure I will."

Eileen plops down an armful of supplies by the firepit in the campsite and straightens up and takes a deep breath and exhales and breathes in deeply again and looks around at the ruggedly beautiful landscape of the Golden Trout Wilderness high in the Eastern Sierras. They're at around ten thousand feet and the air is thin and she can feel the affect it's having on her breathing when she exerts herself. When they hike to the first of the Cottonwood Lakes tomorrow in pursuit of native California Golden Trout, they'll be at eleven thousand feet and the air will be even thinner and the going slower and more difficult. That's why they're here, of course. "If it isn't difficult," Arthur said as they set out on the Precipice Trail to climb Cadillac Mountain on their first trip to Acadia National Park in Maine as a dating couple, "it isn't worth doing." That's why they always took the route along the Knife Edge to the summit of Katahdin and the Hedgehog trail to climb Monadnock in New Hampshire, a relatively easy climb by any other route. If it isn't difficult, she learned, it isn't worth doing.

Being the smitten and eager to please new girlfriend she was then, she was determined to prove to her new boyfriend that she could climb any trail he could and hike as fast as he could and make herself at home in the same miserable conditions he could, that is, until she realized not long after they were married that her willingness to do these things was simply the price to be paid for the privilege of being with him. It didn't seem to bring them any closer together. It wasn't long after Art was born that the first rumor of Arthur seeing other women made its way back to her and she began sending him off alone on his camping trips and to this day doesn't know whether he went alone or with one of his women and it doesn't matter now anyway.

"One tent or two?" she hears him ask and turns to see him leaning into the open back of the SUV and looking at her over his shoulder with an expression that shows no discernible preference for their sleeping arrangement. "One will be fine," she says and sweeps the hair off her forehead and walks back for another armload of supplies. "I'm sure you'll be on your best behavior."

He narrows his eyes and peers at her as he removes the tent bag and the Coleman stove and lantern from the back. "What makes you so sure?"

She reaches in for the cooler. "Don't be silly, Arthur. You know the rules."

"Leave that. It's heavy."

She yanks it onto the tailgate and tests its weight and, yes, he's right, it's too heavy. It must be the thin air. She picks up a bag of food instead.

She stares into the fire as she sips an after dinner brandy, mesmerized by the dancing flames. They were able to get in a short but brisk hike before sundown, which Arthur didn't consider real exercise but was plenty for her. It was strenuous enough at this altitude. She remembers how much she used to enjoy this aspect of their camping trips, sitting around the fire after a day spent hiking or climbing, feeling the warmth of the fire and the dull ache in her muscles and joints, satisfied that she'd pushed herself hard and kept up. That was when she still had something to prove to Arthur. It seemed so important at the time. Now she has nothing to prove to him, nothing at all. She glances up at him and sees him staring into the fire, his face lit dramatically and the flames reflected in his eyes. She remembers when the fire in his eyes came from within. Is it still there, smoldering, or is it dead?

"I give you high marks for coming," he says without looking up. "For a while there I didn't think you were."

"I wasn't going to, but the more I thought about this silly idea of yours it seemed sillier not to. After all, I enjoy camping, and I don't hate you, Arthur."

He glances up at her. "That's good to hear. How're things with your beau?"

"He's not my beau. He's a friend, an acquaintance."

He raises his eyebrows. "I thought it was more serious than that."

She's reluctant to say anything more about it and hesitates. What difference does it make? None, really. She shrugs. "We had a fling. That's all."

He studies her face as he sips his brandy and tries again to imagine her with Reggie's twin brother. He can picture Roland and Eileen together, but she's not the Eileen he knows. She's more — What? Earthy. He wouldn't mind seeing that side of her himself. "Well, I hope it was fun."

"It was, delightful." She gazes at the fire and finishes her brandy and he holds up the bottle and she holds out her cup and watches the brandy pour into it and taps the cup against the neck of the bottle as the level nears the brim. She sips and gazes at the fire and is reminded of the ones they used to have in the small fireplace in their apartment in Cambridge when their relationship was young, before they were married. They would sit together reading in the evening. She worked her way through all his books, taking them on one author at a time. He had everything Hemingway had written and she read it all, first the short stories and then the novels, as Arthur had suggested, and her favorite and the one she found most touchingly and sadly revealing about men was the short story "The Three-Day Blow": Two friends, Nick, the son of a doctor, and Bill, the son of a painter, sit by the fire in Bill's dad's cottage drinking whiskey and talking about baseball and favorite books and authors and fishing and hunting and the fall wind blowing steadily as they get purposefully drunk and only then are able to get to the heart of the matter, their fear of commitment to women and being done in by marriage.

Of all the writing Arthur had collected Hemingway's reminded her most of him. Arthur struck her as something of a

Hemingwayesque character, with his love of the outdoors and roughing it and drinking and his tendency to get moody when he drinks. She saw a lot of the two characters in "The Three-Day Blow" in him, wanting and needing the companionship of a woman but reluctant to be in a relationship with one for fear of losing his independence. Arthur said "The Three-Day Blow" was a boozy story, the type of story only a drunk could or would write and that Hemingway had probably written it when he was on a bender or recovering from one. Maybe he was right. He would know. Boozy or not, to her the story put its finger nicely on the eternal dilemma women pose to men, that they can't live with them or without them. It was certainly true in Arthur's case. Roland's comment about men wanting a lover but needing a mother comes to mind. Is that what this is all about? She takes a sip of brandy and looks at Arthur. "You should've followed your heart and been a ranger."

He looks at her. "If I had we never would have met."

"You never know. I might have camped in your park."

"What are the odds that would have happened do you think?"

"I wouldn't venture a guess, but anything's possible." She takes another sip and stares at the fire. "Do you think you would have been better off?"

"What?"

"Had we never met?"

"No."

She's surprised by the quickness and certainty of his answer. "Why?"

"I can't think of another woman who would have put up with my bullshit the way you did. You could have made my life a living hell, but you didn't. You had every right to, though, and I wouldn't have blamed you if you had."

She knows this is high praise coming from him but doesn't feel flattered. "So that's it? You loved me because I was long-suffering?"

"No, I loved you for who you are. There's a lot more to you than that."

She looks back at the fire and sips her brandy. "You sure had a funny way of showing it."

"I made a mess of it, that's for sure."

"Why didn't we have pet names for each other?"

"I guess we're not that kind of people."

She looks at him and raises her eyebrows. "What kind of people?"

"Mushy, lovey-dovey."

"Really! I remember you being very mushy and lovey-dovey when we first met. All those love notes you used to leave tucked around the apartment for me to find?"

"That was different."

She smiles and shakes her head. "You're still just a shy, tongue-tied little boy when it comes to expressing your emotions, Arthur. Admit it."

"I still love you and want you back."

She looks back at the fire. "I think it's the brandy talking. I think what you're looking for is a mother."

"I had a mother. She's dead and gone. I don't need someone to wipe my nose and ass. I want a companion in life, someone to share things with, someone I enjoy being with, someone who understands me."

She looks at him and studies his face. His features are heavier and his eyes seem more tired now, but she sees the same honest and vulnerable expression she remembers from long ago. Is that the fire reflected in his eyes or is it the flicker of something within? She's not sure and maybe it's just that she's had too much brandy but at the moment he looks a lot like the man she fell in love with. "You're breaking the rules, Arthur," she says and sees that impish grin of his. It's been a long time since she's seen it, since he's shown it to her.

The sun is just rising above the ridge in the distance and they've been on the trail two hours, both with backpacks loaded with food and fishing gear, Arthur leading the way at his usual pace and Eileen trying hard to keep up, which she's managing to do, but with difficulty, as she expected. She isn't in the shape she once was, that's for sure, and the air keeps getting thinner as they climb higher, which isn't helping matters. It doesn't seem to be bothering Arthur, though. She watches his body moving with that same rhythm she remembers, a sort of rolling gait, walking on the outsides of his feet, "the way Indians do," he once told her.

They're almost across the meadow and she can see the trail ahead, rising up past the tree line to bare rock. How does he do it? He had more brandy than she did last night but it doesn't seem to have affected him in the least. She woke with a headache and he was already up and had gotten the fire started and was busy making breakfast, bright-eyed and humming to himself. He's always been that way the next morning, no matter how much he's had to drink.

She's still not sure how she feels about his revelation last night. Does he really love her and want her back or is he just feeling lonely and desperate? She thought she didn't have any feelings for him, but now she's not sure. She does feel comfortable being with him, the way she used to. They know each other so well. But what's that? Just familiarity. Still....

They pass the tree line and there's no discernable trail that she can see, but Arthur seems to know where he's headed and she just follows him, looking for the best place to plant her boot as she tries to keep pace. She takes her eyes off the trail for a moment and looks at his back and glimpses the valley coming into view beyond and feels her boot sliding out from under her. She reaches out for something to grab hold of as she tries to regain her balance but there's only air. She sees him stop and turn as she falls and hears him call her name as she begins tumbling down the rock face, completely out of control and not knowing when or if she'll stop. She abruptly does when she bangs into a boulder and bounces off it and lies dazed and hurting on her back. She's aware that the part of her body that hurts most is her right ankle, which is surprising, since her shoulder bore the brunt of the collision, and she's sure it's sprained and possibly broken. She hears him scampering down to her and he's soon kneeling by her side.

"You okay?"

She tries to move her leg and grimaces. "My ankle."

"Hold still." He unties her boot and carefully removes it and rolls down her sock and inspects her ankle. It's bruised and swollen. He probes gently around the contusion, feeling for broken bone. "Just sprained I think."

"I'm sorry, Arthur. How clumsy of me. I've spoiled everything."

He looks at her. "Don't apologize to me, Eileen. You're the one who's injured and hurting and you haven't spoiled anything. Fuck fishing."

She watches him, studying his expression as he removes his backpack and unzips the side compartment where he keeps first aid supplies and takes out medical tape and two splints to immobilize her ankle. She remembers just such an incident occurring early in their relationship, turning her ankle on the trail up Mount Madison in New Hampshire in the Presidential Range, which ended their weekend plan to summit it and neighboring Mount Adams. She knew by Arthur's stony silence and expression that he was displeased with her and was fully expecting him to react the same way now, but his comment took her aback and she can't see anything in his expression other than what looks like genuine concern for her.

"Let's get that pack off you."

She sits up and he helps her out of it. "I'll be okay," she says. "I'll make it back. It'll be slow going but —"

"Don't be ridiculous. You're not walking back."

"What do you suggest?" She watches him fasten a water bottle to his belt and begin filling the pockets of his fishing vest with as many energy bars as they can hold.

"I'll carry you. I'll come back for the packs."

She stares at him wide-eyed. "Now who's being ridiculous? It's at least three miles back to camp!"

He turns and crouches down in front of her. "Put your arms around my neck."

"This is crazy, Arthur!"

"Come on. Don't argue."

She sighs and wraps her arms tightly around his neck and clasps her hands and works her way up to a standing position, bobbing to keep her right foot off the ground. He heaves her onto his back and she presses her legs as tightly as she can around his waist. "You'll never make it, Arthur," she says and immediately regrets having said it.

They've come far enough now that she's beginning to think he will make it and the fact that she doubted him preys on her mind. Still, how he's able to carry her like this at his age is beyond her. They stop from time to time so that he can rest and catch his breath and they pass the water bottle between them, each taking only a sip, and eat an energy bar and she looks at him admiringly as she chews. Another man would have let her walk back, as difficult and painful as that would have been, but not Arthur. She watches him gaze thoughtfully at the clouds as he chews. "Penny for your thoughts," she says softly.

"We should hike the Appalachian Trail." He looks at her. "We always talked about it."

She looks at him tenderly and smiles and puts her hand on his shoulder and brushes the hair at the back of his neck with her fingertips. There's that impish grin again.

"You'd have to get back in shape first," he teases.

"Yes, I would. I need to." Can she forgive him? Should she?

"C'mon, let's get going."

They sit by the fire sipping brandy after dinner and Arthur has been very quiet and pensive since they returned to camp. She hasn't wanted to ask what's on his mind. She has the feeling it's better to let him think his thoughts and share with her whatever it is he wants to when he feels ready. She watches the light from the fire play on his face.

"You're right," he says without looking up. "So was Landis."

"About?"

"Getting old. I'm not handling it well."

She's not sure what to say and sips her brandy and gazes at him as he stares at the fire.

"She left me a note…said I wasn't as virile as when she first met me."

It's a hurtful thing to say to any man and especially Arthur. Well, he seemed virile enough when she was riding on his back all afternoon. His body felt like a machine that refused to stop, that was determined to keep going no matter what. Is that what his insisting on carrying her back to camp was all about, proving to himself and to her that he's still the man he used to be? What if it were? If that's what he had to do to rekindle his spirit, then good for him for caring enough about himself and her to do it. "Arthur, come sit by me. I'm sure it's the injury and the thin air, but I can't get warm."

He moves to her side and puts his arm around her shoulders and she puts her arm around his waist and leans against him. She holds out her cup and he refills it and they sit sipping their brandies and watching the flames dance wildly, like spirits, happy to be alive for an instant and celebrating.

CHAPTER 16

Coach Futrelle stands on the sideline holding her clipboard at her side. She looks at the backs and goalie. "Ready?" The girls glance at each other and nod. They've faced Valley View's offense a number of times this season and held them scoreless in every game except one. They're confident they can do the same in this game. Coach looks at the forwards and midfielders. "Ready?" Like the backs and goalie, they glance at each other and nod. Coach looks at Kim and nods toward Valley View's bench. "She's gotten better."

Kim knows she's referring to the center fullback who wears her dark brown hair in braids and is surprisingly quick for her height and solid build. She has gotten better, although not good enough to thwart her scoring attempts. She's also one of the three girls who called her a boy earlier in the season and Kim suspects they're the ones who sent her the hurtful messages.

"Watch her."

Kim nods and stands and trots onto the field with her teammates for the kick-off.

It's a predictable game. Valley View makes a determined effort, but at the beginning of the second half they're down by three goals to one, Kim having scored two of her team's. The only remarkable thing about the game so far is the number of red cards, two and both shown to Valley View players for flagrantly fouling her. The first foul was a kick to her stomach by one of the three girls that left her doubled up on the field with the wind knocked out of her. The second was a vicious kick to her leg by another of the three that left her on her back and bleeding. They had to carry her to the sideline to get the wound cleaned and bandaged. Coach told her to sit out the second half but she protested and Coach finally relented. She was determined not to give the girls the satisfaction of keeping her on the bench and now she's playing through the pain.

With under three minutes left in the game her team is up by four goals and heading upfield on offense and she sees Valley View's center fullback, the only one of the three girls who hasn't fouled her yet, positioning herself in anticipation of their meeting in front of the goal.

Kim picks up speed and sees Brandy pushing the ball down her side of the field with the right fullback and midfielder harrying her. Brandy's having more difficulty than usual with this midfielder and Kim's despairing of the play developing as planned when suddenly Brandy unleashes a kick that sends the ball arcing across the field to Manju, their left forward, who's racing up her side of the field with her long black ponytail flying. Manju knocks the ball down off her chest and positions it in front of her and feeds it to Kim in the middle of the field with a well-aimed push pass. Kim taps it farther right, setting up for a kick and looks up and sees the center fullback directly in front of her and closing fast. There's that look again, the same look she saw on the faces of the other two girls who fouled her. It isn't competitive. It's mean, vicious.

She pushes the ball farther to the right and cuts back to the left in an attempt to throw the center fullback off balance and almost does, but she sees the girl has gotten better and is able to steady herself and recover quickly and now the girl's running right behind her with Valley View's right fullback closing in on her. In another instant she'll be trapped between the two girls.

She sees the goalie coming toward her with her arms spread wide, exposing the right side of the goal. She's put the ball in the net from this distance and in exactly this situation countless times before and could score this goal with her eyes closed. She draws back her right leg to kick and feels the blow to her crotch and everything goes white.

She writhes on her back and bites her lip and tries not to cry but the pain between her legs is excruciating and tears stream down her cheeks. Coach Futrelle and Valley View's coach lift her up and help her to the sideline with her teammates gathered around her. She spends the little time remaining in the game sitting on the bench on an ice pack with another between her legs pressed against her crotch. She stares at the girl with the braids, who was also red carded and is sitting on her team's bench chatting with the other two girls on either side of her.

The referee whistles the end of the game and Kim's teammates meet in the middle of the field to celebrate their win and join hands and hug, but she stays where she is and doesn't take her eyes off the girl with the braids and her two friends. She watches them stand and begin gathering their things and stuffing them into their sports bags and she stands slowly and gingerly and begins doing the same with difficulty. The first two fouls were bad, but the last one, that was too much and she has to do something about it. She'll probably be suspended for the next few games, maybe for the rest of the season and maybe lose her chance to win the MVP title. She doesn't care. She has to.

She waddles toward the parking lot and spots her grandmother waiting by her car. She sees the look of concern on Nana Eileen's face. Her grandmother just arrived to pick her up and can see she's hurt but has no idea what happened. She drops her sports bag next to the car and looks over her shoulder at the girl with the braids and sees her putting her sports bag into the back of her mother's SUV. The girl's mother is talking with the mother of the second girl who fouled her, who's putting her sports bag into the back of her mother's station wagon.

"Be right back, Nana," Kim says and waddles toward the girl with the braids, keeping her eyes on the back of the girl's head. When she's right behind her she plants her feet and clenches her right fist as tightly as she can. "Hey," she says. The girl turns and Kim sees the surprise and fear in her eyes and before the girl can get her hands up punches her as hard as she can in the face and watches her bounce off the back of the SUV and fall to the ground. "Oh, my God!" she hears the girl's mother scream but keeps her eyes on the girl, waiting to see if she's going to get up and do anything about it. She doesn't think so and sees the girl's just going to lie there whimpering and cowering with her arms covering her head. She sees the girl's mother kneel beside her and glances at the other girl and her mother to see if they're going to do anything but they just stand there staring at her hatefully. She looks back down at the girl and sees her wiping tears from her eyes as her mother inspects her bruised cheek and speaks consolingly to her as if she were a baby, which, as far as Kim's concerned, she is, a big one.

She turns and waddles toward her grandmother's car. She's aware of the pain in her right hand now. It seems to be lessening the pain in her crotch area somewhat but she knows it's just focusing her mind on a different pain and that she'll feel even worse before long because two parts of her body will be hurting badly. "Butch lez!" she hears the girl's friend yell and then the girl's mother scream, "You little bitch! I've got your jersey number! You're in big trouble!" Yeah, that's who she is, a "butch lez," a "little bitch."

She sits on the toilet with the bathroom door closed inspecting herself. Her right hand is swollen around the knuckles and aches. Her crotch area is purplish and the inside of both thighs are covered with reddish blotches. She slowly and painfully spreads her swollen labia and sees that her hymen is torn. From what she knows about it she thinks it will probably heal, not that it matters. It was bound to break sometime. She contracts her stomach muscles to try to get the flow of pee started but it's painful. Everything in the middle of her body aches. Finally the pee begins flowing in a trickle and that's even more painful. She bends forward and closes her eyes tightly and clenches her teeth and grimaces as the flow increases.

She sits next to Nana Eileen at the dinner table. She told her grandmother on the ride home what happened. Nana Eileen listened and nodded and said she understood why she did what she did, that it was an awful thing for the girl to have done to her. She can always share things with her grandmother without fear of being criticized or judged. She loves Nana Eileen more than anything and is happy she's there for her, which she always is.

She glances at her dad. She's also always happy when her family's together like this but knows he's here because it's "family talk" time and the talk will be about her. When everyone's done eating her mom asks her to share with them what happened at the game and she does, beginning with Cyd posting the photos from Fashion Island on her Facebook page and receiving the hurtful messages she's sure the three girls who fouled her sent her. Her dad leans forward and puts his elbows on the table and rests his chin on his clasped hands and listens with a concerned expression and when she describes the part about punching the girl who kicked her in the crotch she sees him raise his eyebrows and he looks like he's trying to keep from smiling.

"How well do you know Cyd?" Art asks.

"Pretty well."

"Mom's says she gave you a book about girls who like each other more than as friends."

Kim glances at her mom and sees her looking a little guilty, even though there's no reason for her to be. She's her mom and she knew she'd tell her dad about the book. She looks back at her dad. "Yeah."

"Why do you think she did?"

"She thought I'd enjoy it."

"Did you?"

"Yeah, it's a good story."

"How do you feel about her?"

Kim was wondering when someone was finally going to ask her this and it deserves an honest answer. "She's a good friend."

"Anything more?"

Kim feels Nana Eileen's encouraging pat on her back, letting her know that however she answers her family loves her. "Honestly, I don't know." Her dad nods and her mom sighs.

"Tell us about her," Art says. "What's she like?"

Kim thinks of all the things she could say about Cyd, that she's uncertain about her sexual identity, that Cyd finds in her someone she can talk with about it, that it's made her think about her own sexual identity and that she feels they're exploring things together and that just thinking about it is exciting, that she enjoys Cyd's interest in her, that Cyd's the first person, girl or boy, who's felt that way about her and it makes her feel special. She could tell them these things but knows the real reason her dad asked the question. "If you're asking if she's gay I don't know. I haven't asked her. What difference would it make anyway?"

Eileen rubs Kim's back soothingly and looks at Art. "Not all girls are interested in boys at their age. I wasn't."

Trey could tell there was a lot going through Kim's mind that she didn't share with them as she was thinking about how to answer the question, which is fine. It's her business. This new friend of hers intrigues him. Ever since Cyd came into Kim's life she's really begun questioning things and trying to figure herself out. She seems to have a better idea now than she did before she met Cyd. He'd be surprised if Cyd's gay. He agrees with his grandmother. Kim and Cyd are probably just the first important people in each other's lives and they've formed a close friendship and special relationship. He looks at his dad and mom. They're concerned about Kim, but they're not trying to suffocate her. They have her well-being in mind and are trying to guide her through a confusing period in her life. He wishes Emily were here to see how a family is supposed to work, helping each other, not hurting.

Art slowly rubs the scar on his cheek with a fingertip. "We love you, honey. We're just concerned about you."

"Don't worry about me," Kim says firmly. "I can take care of myself."

Art can see it in her narrowed eyes and the set of her jaw and glances at her swollen right hand and smiles. No doubt about it, better than he can take care of himself.

"How are you feeling, dear?" Eileen asks.

The throbbing has stopped and the pain has subsided to a dull ache. "Okay."

Eileen smiles proudly at her and looks at Art. "She's just like Gramma Eloise."

Kim watches as her Facebook page loads and sees Cyd's online, as she hoped, and almost immediately a message from her appears:

> been w8ting 4 u. how r u?
>
> hurt bad...fouled 3x by the girls who sent the messages. all red cards. kicked in the crotch. really painful.

She waits for Cyd's reply and after what seems a long time it appears:

> sorry.... my bad 4 friending them. :-(

She's reluctant to ask Cyd the question, but types it and stares at it and hesitates, then sends it:

my parents r worried ur gay. r u?

She waits nervously and wishes she could somehow reach out and grab the question and take it back. Cyd's reply finally appears:

would it change things between us?

no.

idk.... don't think so.

like boys?

idk.... boys don't see me. i'm invisible.

know the feeling. y do u want 2 hpd with me?

seems like a lot of fun! they sure had a good time! :-)

She thinks of the story and how similar but different Sarah and Jenny turned out to be. They had a long talk on the rock about themselves. Sarah said she'd been attracted to girls for as long as she could remember and had never been interested in boys and still wasn't. She said she was pretty sure she was lesbian. Jenny, on the other hand, said she'd always been interested in boys and still was. It's just that boys didn't seem at all interested in her. Jenny said she never dreamed she could feel toward another girl the way she did toward Sarah or that she could do the things she'd done with Sarah. She still didn't understand where the feelings came from or how she could have done what she did. She said she might never understand it, but it didn't matter to her. "Feelings are feelings." Jenny said, "and you can't help the way you feel." Sarah said that maybe Jenny was bisexual and Jenny agreed that maybe she was and she'd see. They told each other they were special friends who enjoyed giving each other pleasure and they enjoyed themselves at the pond for the rest of the summer. They promised each other that if Jenny lost interest in the sexual aspect of their relationship when she became involved with boys they'd always remain friends.

It was a nice ending, but Sarah and Jenny are characters in a story. She and Cyd are real people and real life isn't always so simple. The confusing thing to her and the question that remains in her mind is what's the difference between being a girl like Sarah and a girl like Jenny? They both had strong feelings for each other and enjoyed what they did equally as much. Is there a line between the two? She thinks there is, but it's fuzzy. She thinks she and Cyd are like Jenny and is curious what Cyd thinks:

think we're like jenny?

Cyd's reply appears almost immediately:

yeah.

So, now there's only one more thing she's been wondering about. To her it's the most important question and she types it and stares at it on the screen a few moments before sending it:

just dance or more?

She pictures Cyd sitting there, staring at the question on her screen as she considers her answer. Cyd doesn't seem to be in a hurry to answer this one and the thought occurs to her that maybe what Cyd's had in mind all along is the hopping around topless part and not the lying on the rock pleasing each other part. She doesn't think so, but maybe and what a shame that would be. She sees Cyd's reply finally appear and smiles:

more! :-)

me 2.

when can u come?

Not until she's healed and the bruises are gone, that's for sure:

a few weeks.

will ur parents let u?

She knows they will, despite their concern. They're not trying to run her life. They're just looking out for her and helping her to make good decisions about her life. That's why she loves them:

yeah. ;-)

~

Art eyes the navigation screen as he drives slowly along the street a couple of blocks up the hill from Pacific Coast Highway in Laguna Beach and pulls to the curb in front of Cyd's house. It looks like most of the others on the street, cozy and well-kept with bougainvilleas climbing up lattices on the front of the house and a small front yard bordered by neatly trimmed shrubs and three vibrant red flame trees. Cyd's mom is giving one of the trees a soak with the hose. June spoke with her on the phone and said her name is Audrey. She's attractive with auburn hair pulled back in a ponytail. She's wearing a black exercise bra and skintight black exercise shorts and he marvels at her muscle tone. She's obviously into fitness. She smiles and waves and calls to Cyd in the house and turns off the water and puts down the hose. He and Kim get out of the truck and Audrey walks over and holds the gate open.

"Hi!" she says, holding out a hand. "Audrey. Nice to meet you."

"Art. Nice to meet you too."

Audrey smiles down at Kim. "Nice to finally meet you! I've heard so much about you!"

"Same here," Kim says.

Art sees Cyd over Audrey's shoulder walking toward them from the house. She looks like a younger version of her mom and moves the same way, like an athlete, the same way Kim does. "Hi, Cyd," he says. "Nice to meet you."

"Same here," Cyd says and picks up Kim's overnight bag. "C'mon," she says and leads Kim toward the house.

"Stay for a beer?" Audrey asks.

"Sure."

She picks at the label on her bottle. "I'm a personal trainer. Always been into fitness. I was a Marine. Cyd's dad was too. That's how we met. We divorced when Cyd was four. He moved back to Oklahoma City where he's from. I'm from Maine, way up in the toes." She looks around at the sunny day. "I decided to stay here in paradise. No more winters for me."

"Cyd see him often?"

Audrey shakes her head. "He turned out to be a real asshole. He remarried and his wife could care less about Cyd. She resents her."

"You know about this Facebook business?"

"Sure. I know about everything that goes on in Cyd's life. We don't hide anything from each other. She learned early on that if we were going to make it, we had to be able to trust each other and be completely open and honest with each other about everything."

"So you know some girls think she's gay."

Audrey guffaws. "Cyd's about as gay as I am, not that I think there's anything wrong with being gay. You either are or aren't. I just happen not to be."

"So what do you think's going on?"

She sips her beer and places the bottle on the table and stares at it. "What do I think's going on…? I think Cyd's at that stage where she's trying to figure out who she is. I suspect it's the same with Kim. I think it's great they found each other." She looks at him. "Don't you?"

"Yeah," he says but knows Audrey knows he's not really sure how he feels about their friendship. "What's the plan?"

"The girls will do whatever they like, hang and have fun. I'm going out this evening." She sees his look of suriprise and concern. "Cyd spends a lot of time alone. She's very responsible. They have plenty of games and movies." She stares at the label on the bottle and picks at it and glances at him. "I won't be out late."

Art studies her as he turns things over in his mind. He knows he feels about Kim the way all father's do about young daughters. He wishes he could shield her from the harsh reality of life while knowing that the only way for her to become her own person is to encounter it and deal with it on her own. He smiles and shakes his head. Shield her? Most of the harsh reality she's had to deal with so far has been his doing. Who is he to be worrying about Kim? In a way, she's more mature and better able to take care of herself than he is. His mom's right. Kim's tough, just like his grandmother.

"We'll drop her off around five tomorrow. That okay?"

"That's fine," he says and stands to leave and smiles down at her. "Have fun this evening."

She smiles up at him. "Thanks. I will. Nice talking with you."

"Same here." he says and waves and walks off wanting to feel he's left Kim in good hands but still a little uneasy about the situation.

Kim presses the palms of her hands against Cyd's waterbed and feels it give way to her touch. Is it a mattress or a container? She shifts her weight and feels a gentle swaying motion beneath her. It feels a little like being in a boat. What must it be like to sleep on this thing? Well, she'll find out soon enough. She looks at Cyd, sitting cross-legged facing her on the bed. "How'd you get your own waterbed?"

"It was my parents'. I got it after my dad left. My mom never liked it."

Kim's spent so much time imagining what Cyd's room looks like and now here she is and it feels a little weird because it kind of looks like what she imagined but different and it's the different part that makes it seem strange. There are posters on the wall, one of the famous photo of Brandi Chastain on her knees on the field at the Rose Bowl baring her bra in triumph after the U.S. beat China to win the 1999 FIFA Women's World Cup. There's another of the team and one of the Dixie Chicks. There are a few photos stuck in the frame of the mirror on the wall, two of Cyd and her mom and one of her and she guesses her dad. There's a Marines pennant hanging above the mirror and a teddy bear wearing a Marines tee shirt in a miniature rocking chair by the dresser. There's the chair Cyd sits in when they're messaging and there's her laptop on the desk. The room looks much like her own, not at all girly. "I only just got my own bedroom again. My brother and I had to share one for a while."

"It must have been hard not having any privacy."

Kim shrugs. "You get used to it." She's about to say you can get used to anything but catches herself. It's not true. She never got used to living at Walt's. She put up with it just like her mom put up with her dad until she couldn't take it anymore and kicked him out.

"I didn't want my own bedroom," Cyd says. "I had a hard time sleeping alone when my mom and dad divorced. Every night I'd get out of bed and climb into bed with her, but she'd bring me back and tell me I had to learn to sleep by myself in my own bed."

Kim finds this fact very interesting. It's the first time Cyd's revealed anything about herself to suggest she isn't the strong confident person she experienced at Fashion Island. She climbs off the waterbed and walks to the desk and puts her hands on the back of the chair. "So, this is where you sit when we talk. It'll be different now that I've seen it. I'll know exactly how you look." She pulls back the chair. "Let me see you sitting here."

Cyd climbs off the waterbed and walks to the desk and sits.

Kim takes her phone from her bag and positions herself to take a picture of Cyd in profile sitting at the desk. She holds up the phone and frames the shot. "Pretend we're messaging."

"I'll send you one," Cyd says and begins typing.

Kim takes the picture and glances at the pennant again. "Your dad was in the Marines, huh?"

"Both my parents. That's how they met."

"Your mom's in great shape."

"She's a personal trainer." Cyd sends the message.

"What'd you write?"

"You'll see when you read it. Let's see the pic."

Kim stands beside her and holds out the phone so they can both see it.

Cyd makes a face. "I look awful."

"You look great!"

"I don't think so."

"Let's take one of us." Kim crouches so that her face is next to Cyd's and presses her cheek against Cyd's. She can tell Cyd's uncomfortable and doesn't press harder. It's so unlike when Cyd took the photos of them at Fashion Island and couldn't press hard enough. She takes the picture and they look at it. They're both smiling, but Cyd's smile looks forced to Kim.

Cyd makes a face again. "Ugh."

"You okay?" Kim asks as she puts the phone in her bag.

"Yeah."

"So what's the plan?"

"Walk into town, hang at the beach."

"Great. Let's go."

"Headed into town?" Audrey asks as the girls enter the kitchen.

"Yeah," Cyd says.

"Be back around five-thirty for dinner."

"Okay."

"If you see Angie and Phyllis, say hi!" Audrey calls to her.

"I will!"

Kim admires the view of the Pacific as they walk in silence down the hill toward Pacific Coast Highway. "Who're they?" she finally asks.

"My mom's friends. They own a gallery in town. They're really nice. They're from New 'Yawk' and sell 'awt' and drink 'cawfee.' They're fun. You'll like them. Mom's trying to help Angie lose weight. She feels bad about taking her money, though, because Angie hates working out. They spend most of the time chatting. Phyllis is really thin and isn't into working out at all. She doesn't care if Angie has some pounds on. She keeps telling her she's happy with her the way she is, but it doesn't make any difference."

They sit on the side of the boardwalk with their bare feet in the sand eating ice cream and checking out the crowded beach. There are people everywhere, sitting and lying on blankets on the sand, walking along the shoreline, standing waist-deep in the surf, playing volleyball. The boardwalk is filled with people too, who've been drawn to the water they way people everywhere are. They stand, some alone, others with a partner, others in small groups, gazing out at the ocean and taking pictures.

"Is it always like this?" Kim asks.

"On weekends. It's even crazier in the summer. Things start getting back to normal after Labor Day."

Kim puts a spoonful of mocha chip ice cream in her mouth and squints as she watches a pelican in the bright hazy sunlight diving for fish. Time and again the big white bird circles slowly about thirty feet above the surface of the water, it's head cocked slightly, eyeing its prey, and then tucks in its wings and drops bill-first into the water with a splash and bobs for a moment on the surface and then pulls its head back and flaps its wings and flies off jerking its head as it swallows its catch. She's impressed by the pelican's persistence and success rate. She wonders if all pelicans are as good at catching fish as that one. They can't be. Some must be better at it that others, just as some people are better at things than others, the way she and Cyd are better soccer players than most of the other girls in the league and she's better than Cyd. She watches the pelican dive again. "How'd you find out about the book?" she asks and sees by the way Cyd's shifting that she's uncomfortable with the question.

"A friend gave it to me."

"Who?" Kim watches the pelican flap its wings and take off swallowing another fish and waits for Cyd's answer.

"Allie," she finally says.

"How'd you meet her?"

Cyd stares at the horizon. "We were in pre-school and elementary school together, until her dad started making enough money to send her to private school. She told me once what he did, something to do with computers."

"She's pretty. I bet she's nice?"

Cyd nods.

"Why'd she give you the book?"

"I asked her the same thing I asked you, if she thought she could like another girl more than just as a friend. The next time we saw each other she gave me the book. That was last summer, just before she began private school."

Cyd seems finished with the story but Kim knows there has to be more to it. "And?"

Cyd shrugs. "I haven't seen her since then or heard from her."

"Try to get in touch with her?"

Cyd nods.

Kim watches the pelican fly off slowly flapping its wings, content for now with its stomach full of fish. "So, she thought you were gay and it freaked her out?"

"I guess so."

"Think she read the book?"

Cyd shrugs. "Dunno."

"If she didn't, she should've," Kim says. "Maybe she would've understood." Poor Cyd. Being dumped that way had to hurt. She clearly has a lot on her mind but doesn't seem to want to talk about it. It's like she's drawn a curtain between them.

Cyd stands and tosses her cup and spoon and napkin in the trash. "C'mon, let's visit the gallery."

They walk along Forest Avenue and check out the artwork in the windows of the galleries. Kim sees they're filled with seascapes and landscapes and most are painted in the same impressionistic style using the same pallet of bright colors. She recognizes from what she remembers of her trips to Laguna Beach with her dad and what she's seen of the surroundings that most of the paintings are scenes from around here, although some of the galleries display art and merchandise that has nothing to do with the place. One gallery has portraits painted on black velvet in the window, another a single large painting of a cabin in the woods at twilight that looks like an illustration from a children's book, another colorful swirling glass objects and another jewelry made of gold and silver and semi-precious stones. An aquamarine necklace catches her eye. She's struck by its sparkling, deep blue color.

"This is it," she hears Cyd say as they arrive at a gallery with a white sculpture in the window of a woman's naked body from the waist to the knees. She reads the sign over the entrance, "Sensual Expressions", and follows Cyd inside and sees a stocky woman with a broad face and strong features and black hair just like Edna Mode's, the designer to the Supers in *The Incredibles,* one of her favorite films. The woman is standing by a desk chatting with two plainly dressed women. She's even wearing the same black horn rimmed glasses as Edna and no makeup and a black tee shirt and black jeans. Kim hears the New "Yawk" accent and knows she has to be Angie.

Looking around she sees the gallery is filled with small and large sculptures, some done in stone of various colors, others in metal and all of women's naked bodies or parts of them, mostly torsos with arms, although there's one larger piece done in marble that shows a woman from the neck down holding out her arms and it seems that the woman is either about to take someone happily in her arms or has sadly just let someone go and Kim's impressed that the sculptor could make the same pose express opposite emotions.

"These are my favorites," she hears Cyd say and turns and sees her standing by a series of three small stone sculptures showing the interaction of two women using their torsos and arms. She walks to Cyd's side and studies them one after the other and can see the scene unfolding vividly in her mind's eye. A woman stands alone waiting for her lover, her hands placed delicately on her own breasts, touching herself in anticipation of her lover's touch. Her lover comes up behind her and puts her arms around her and slides her hands beneath the woman's and the woman leans back and turns her head to the side and her lover nuzzles her neck. The woman turns to face her lover and they embrace. It makes her wonder if she and Cyd will do the Himba Pond Dance. Given Cyd's mood, she has her doubts. She hears Angie's booming voice behind her. "I keep tellin' Cyd I'd be happy to give 'em to her!" She turns and sees Angie smiling down at her and her smile reminds her of the Cheshire cat's.

"All she has to do is come up with ten grand! Hi, I'm Angie. You must be Kim."

"Yeah, nice to meet you." Angie has such a strong physical presence and forceful personality. She could easily be intimidating but she isn't at all. Kim notices the three silver studs in the crescent of her right ear.

"We've heard a lot about you."

"Mom says hi."

Angie glances at Cyd. "Your mom's workin' me to death. To think I'm payin' her good money to do it! I oughta have my head examined!"

"Where's Phyllis?" Cyd asks.

"She'll be right back. She went to get cawfee."

Kim sees a slender woman enter the shop with a cup of coffee in each hand. Her salt-and-pepper hair is short and she's wearing sunglasses and a loose-fitting dark blue tee shirt dress. She has to be Phyllis and she doesn't walk, she glides gracefully. Phyllis arrives at Angie's side and hands her one of the cups and puts her sunglasses on her head and Kim's struck by the color of her eyes, the same aquamarine as the necklace in the window. Phyllis' face is narrower than Angie's and her features more delicate and Kim sees she also doesn't wear makeup. She notices the same three silver studs in the crescent of Phyllis' right ear and that she and Angie are wearing matching silver wedding bands. Phyllis smiles at her and Kim sees her smile is different from Angie's, very sweet and showing no teeth. "Hi. I'm Phyllis."

Unlike Angie, Phyllis is soft-spoken and has her New "Yawk" accent under much better control. "Kim. Nice to meet you."

"We've heard so much about you," Phyllis says.

Angie removes the lid from her cup and blows on the coffee. "Cyd tells us you're a great soccer player. I played lacrosse. I wasn't great, but I was pretty good, especially on defense." She looks Kim up and down. "Bet you'd make a good attack wing."

"First time in Laguna Beach?" Phyllis asks.

"I've been here a couple of times," Kim says, "surfing with my dad." She sees Angie's eyebrows go up.

"Surfer, huh?"

"Yeah, I love it."

"I keep tellin' myself I gotta try it," Angie says. "Looks like good exercise." She glances at Phyllis. "All that paddlin', ya know?"

Kim sees Phyllis roll her eyes and looks from her to Angie. There's been so much talk and concern lately about whether Cyd's gay and her parents have approached the subject so delicately and been so careful in choosing their words and gone out of their way not to seem judgmental, but she knows the way they really feel about it, that they hope she isn't and she realizes she doesn't know a thing about it or what it's like being gay and here are two women who are and who seem perfectly normal and happy. "Can I ask you something?"

Angie smiles. "Sweetheart, you can ask me anything you like."

"What's it like?"

Angie narrows her eyes a bit. "What? Being gay?"

Kim nods.

"Natural."

"Have you always been?"

"Yeah."

"And you knew all along?"

"Yeah. Well, not so much knew as felt. It's something you feel first and come to understand later, same as being straight."

"Ever been interested in boys?"

"Naw." Angie nods toward Phyllis. "She was once."

Phyllis smiles dreamily. "Seth Greenwald, when we were in sixth grade. He was gentle and quiet and very talented. He was clearly gay, although he didn't self-identify as gay then."

"What happened?" Kim asks.

"We'd go for walks in the evening. We'd find an out of the way spot in the park and sit on the grass and cuddle and kiss. It was all very innocent. I think what attracted us to each other was our both feeling different from the others. We were kindred spirits. We stayed friends through high school and then went off to college and lost touch. I did hear he finally came out."

Angie looks at Kim and narrows her eyes a bit. "Wondering if you are?"

Kim shrugs. "Just trying to understand."

"Good," Angie says, nodding.

"Does liking another girl more than as a friend mean your gay?" Kim asks and notices Cyd shifting nervously out of the corners of her eyes.

Angie glances at Cyd and looks at Kim. "Not necessarily. Sexual orientation's not black and white, you know?"

"Far from it," Phyllis says. "Straight people have same-sex encounters and gays have heterosexual encounters. Some people start off straight and become gay and others gay and become straight. Some people are attracted to both sexes and others aren't attracted to either. It's all over the map."

Angie looks at the girls. "Well, whatever you do, don't stress about it."

"How long have you been married?" Kim asks.

Phyllis smiles. "Since 2000 when Vermont legalized same-sex marriage." She looks at Angie. "It'll be legal here soon too," she says confidently.

Angie guffaws. "Don't hold your breath."

Phyllis wraps her arm around Angies' and snuggles against her. "You'll see. Sooner than you think."

Angie smiles at the girls. "She an eternal optimist. That's what I love about her."

Kim and Cyd walk along Forest Avenue back toward PCH and Kim keeps her eye out for that jewelry shop and stops and looks again at the aquamarine necklace and, yeah, Phyllis' eyes are exactly the same beautiful, sparkling deep blue. "They're really nice," she says.

"Yeah," Cyd says.

They're halfway back to Cyd's house and that's all they've said to each other and it's clear to Kim that Cyd's even more upset now about whatever it is that's bothering her. "I hope I didn't embarrass you, talking about being gay with them." She takes a few more steps before she realizes Cyd has stopped and turns and sees her standing there, looking at her anxiously. "You okay? What's wrong?"

Cyd searches her eyes a moment and looks down at the sidewalk. "Nothing. Let's go."

Kim's read all the *Harry Potter* books and enjoyed them, although she's not fanatical about them the way some kids are. She's seen all the movies too, but when Cyd suggested watching *Harry Potter and the Philosopher's Stone* she said sure. She's been uneasy ever since the incident walking home and hasn't wanted to say or do anything that might upset Cyd more than she already is. The most interesting thing so far about watching the movie is what happens when their hands brush against each other now and then when they reach into the bowl of popcorn between them for another handful. Cyd doesn't seem at all interested in holding hands.

It's also interesting how her understanding of Cyd has changed since she arrived. Cyd was the one who started it all, who took her hand at Fashion Island and was happy holding it and gave her the book. She seemed so confident when they were with her friends, but being here alone together she doesn't seem at all confident. She seems really unsure of herself and whatever it is that's bothering her she's either unable or unwilling to talk about it.

They munch their way to the bottom of the bowl of popcorn and sit back with their arms crossed staring at the screen. The movie's almost over when Cyd's mom arrives home and Kim can tell from her experience with her dad when she enters the living room that she's drunk, not as drunk as he used to get sometimes but close.

"Hi, girls. Have fun?"

Kim hears her slurred speech and glances at Cyd to see her reaction. There's none. Cyd doesn't even look at her mom.

"Yeah," Cyd says.

"See you in the mornin'." Audrey says, "Sleep tight."

Kim watches her walk unsteadily toward her bedroom and calls after her, "G'night!" She looks at Cyd, who's still staring at the screen. Now she's really confused. Why did Cyd invite her? What is she doing here? It doesn't make any sense. She wishes Cyd had never given her the book. Reading it filled her head with all sorts of ideas and she was really looking forward to their finally being together to see what would happen, but nothing good has and she's not even sure Cyd's happy she's here. Finally the movie ends and she looks at Cyd who's still staring at the screen as the credits roll. The flickering light on Cyd's face gives her an idea. "Do you have a flashlight?"

Cyd looks at her, puzzled. "Yeah. Why?"

"Get it."

"Why?"

"You'll see," Kim says, "Just get it." She jumps up and walks quickly to Cyd's bedroom and fishes the flashlight out of her overnight bag and waits for Cyd in her tee shirt and underpants in the middle of the floor with the bedroom lights off and her flashlight on, holding it pointing up under her chin so the light plays on her face. She sees Cyd arrive at the doorway holding a flashlight, but she stops and peers at her, looking even more puzzled now.

"What're you doing?" Cyd asks.

"Let's do the Himba Pond Dance," Kim says and sees Cyd make a face.

"We'll make too much noise."

"We won't make any noise. I'll show you." Kim watches Cyd slowly enter the room and shut the door and switch on her flashlight. The beam jitters wildly around the room as she works her way out of her shorts and finally comes to rest under her chin. Cyd's expression reminds her of the face of that ghostly, horrified-looking person on the bridge in that painting *The Scream.* Kim begins moving her body and mouthing the words to the Himba Pond Dance song and Cyd reluctantly mimics her. They circle each other a few times but Kim sees Cyd's really uncomfortable and slows and so does Cyd and they stop and stand facing each other, Cyd looking more troubled and confused than ever. "Not up for it, huh?" Kim asks.

"I guess not."

"What's wrong?"

"I dunno."

"C'mon," Kim says, "let's get in bed." She switches off her flashlight and stashes it in her bag and climbs onto the waterbed and settles in under the covers on her side and watches Cyd, who's still standing in the middle of the room holding her flashlight at her side with the beam pointed toward the floor. Finally Cyd switches it off and Kim hears a clunk as Cyd puts the flashlight on the nightstand and feels the bed sway and hears water sloshing as she climbs on and slides in under the covers and lies on her side facing her, keeping some distance between them. There's enough light coming from outside for Kim to see Cyd's eyes and she watches Cyd watching her like a frightened animal. Cyd can't seem to get comfortable and moves her legs this way and that and it reminds her of the time the girls called her a boy and she lay in bed thinking about it and couldn't get comfortable until she got into Trey's bed and he held her. "Hey," she whispers and holds out a hand to Cyd, "c'mere." She watches Cyd stare at her hand and is beginning to think she's not going to take it when her hand comes slowly out of from under the covers and does. She gives Cyd's hand a squeeze and her arm a gentle tug and Cyd comes wriggling toward her and stops when their faces are inches apart. "I thought we were friends." Kim says.

"We are," Cyd says and looks down.

"Could've fooled me." Kim watches Cyd move her palm slowly back and forth on the bedspread and finally sees her looks up at her.

"Why's it so easy for you?" Cyd asks.

"What?"

"Talking about things, like with Angie and Phyllis?"

Kim shrugs. "I dunno. We're like that in my family."

"I'm worried about my mom."

Kim knows why, but also that it's important that Cyd tell her. "Why?"

"She goes out every night and comes home like that. It's gotten worse lately. It seems weird for someone who's so into fitness to drink so much."

"Where's she go?"

Cyd shrugs. "Some bar."

"Does she have a boyfriend?"

Cyd shakes her head. "I asked her and she said she doesn't, but would like to meet someone."

Kim knows Cyd probably knows this already but that it's worth saying anyway. "She's lonely." She sees Cyd search her eyes a moment and then look down and nod.

"I wish I could do something to help her," Cyd says.

Yeah, it's tough. How many times has Kim wished she could do something to help her parents, to somehow make them forget all the bad things that have happened between them? The reality is there's nothing she can do, other than love them and be there for them and especially her dad, who needs all the love he can get. She puts her forehead against Cyd's and an arm around her waist and draws her to her. "You are helping her."

"How?"

"She can count on you. She knows you're there for her. That's all you can do."

"I guess."

Kim strokes Cyd's cheek with her fingertips and puts her lips gently on hers and waits to see what her response will be. After a long moment she feels Cyd press her lips and body against hers and she presses back. It's a sweet lingering kiss, like Sarah and Jenny's first kiss when they discovered they had feelings for each other. They pull back their heads and lay them on their pillows and gaze at each other's eyes until Cyd can't keep hers open any longer. Kim's tired too but forces herself to stay awake until she sees Cyd's asleep and when she does, closes her eyes and imagines the two of them alone in a boat in the middle of the ocean. All they have in the world is each other. The sun feels warm on their skin and pelicans circle overhead watching over them. Where they're headed is anyone's guess and it doesn't matter. They'll just let the current take them wherever it will and enjoy getting there together.

Audrey stands in the bedroom doorway in her bathrobe sipping her coffee and gazing at the girls, still sleeping and curled up under the covers facing each other. It's a sweet scene. She's happy Cyd has a friend like Kim in her life. Kim seems so grounded and sure of herself and Cyd's had a lot on her mind lately, which she hasn't been able to get her to talk about. She hopes Cyd confided in Kim. She's let the girls sleep but it's getting late. "Rise and shine!" she says and sees first Kim and then Cyd stir. Kim lifts her head and peers at her and yawns and then Cyd does the same. "Up 'n at 'em! Breakfast's ready!" she says and heads back to the kitchen.

Kim yawns again and rubs her eyes. "This bed is amazing. I dreamed I was a mermaid." "I dreamed I was drowning," she hears Cyd say and can tell she isn't joking.

Kim gazes at the hills going slowly by and smiles. Even though the Himba Pond Dance was a complete bust things turned out better than she could have hoped and she's glad she came. She learned a lot about Cyd, about her world and what's going on in it. It's good that Cyd has Angie and Phyllis in her life. They can help her a lot. What she should do is talk with her mom, just open up and share her concern about her drinking. It won't be easy. She knows that from her own experience with her dad. But she hopes she'll try. She looks at Cyd on the other side of the backseat gazing out the window at the Pacific and slides her upturned hand along the seat toward her. "Hey," she says softly and sees Cyd look at her and then down at her hand and smile and wrap hers around it and they both squeeze and hold hands the rest of the way home.

Audrey pulls into the driveway and Kim gets her overnight bag from the trunk and she and Cyd hug. "Thanks for inviting me," Kim says. "I had a great time. My turn next." "Hi!" she hears her mom say and sees her wave at Cyd's mom and walk over to her. Kim steps back and takes Cyd's hands and looks in her eyes. "Talk to your mom. Tell her you're worried about her drinking." She can see Cyd doesn't think she can. "You can do it. My dad had the same problem."

"Did you talk with him about it?"

"No."

"Then what makes you think I can?"

Kim squeezes her hands. "Try."

Cyd sighs and nods.

June walks over to the girls and smiles at Cyd. "Nice to finally meet you!"

"Same here," Cyd says.

Kim sees Cyd's mom standing with her phone in her hand staring down at the screen checking messages and walks quickly over to her. "Thanks for having me."

Audrey looks up and smiles. "Anytime, Kim."

Kim glances over her shoulder at her mom and Cyd and looks back at Cyd's mom and motions her closer.

Audrey steps forward and bends down slightly and Kim brings her mouth close to her ear. "She's worried about your drinking," she hears Kim whisper and feels a jolt and straightens up and stares at Cyd. How stupid is she that it took Kim to point out the obvious to her. Is she that far gone? She glances at Kim and sees her looking at her phone and looks down and sees that what she's really looking at is the way her hand is shaking. She feels weak and wants to cry. "Thanks, Kim," she says.

Kim yawns and closes her book and puts it on the nightstand and is about to turn off the light when she remembers the message Cyd sent her when she was taking her picture sitting at the desk and now she's really curious about what she wrote and climbs out of bed and turns on the computer and opens her email and finds Cyd's message waiting for her:

> scared 2 death of losing u as a friend!!! :-o

She smiles and shakes her head. She's struck again by how badly she misread Cyd, based on her first impression of her, and how much more she likes her now, having gotten to know her better. She clicks on the link and goes to her Facebook page and a new message from Cyd appears:

> thanx 4 coming. sorry i wasn't much fun. :-(
>
> had a great time. nice meeting ur mom & angie and phyllis.
>
> did u say something 2 my mom?
>
> about?
>
> her drinking.

She doesn't want to lie to Cyd, but also doesn't want to be seen as meddling or give her the impression she thinks she can't handle things on her own. There's also the possibility that Cyd's mom told her what she said. All she wants to do is help Cyd and it'd be a shame if she ends up offending her, which she seems very close to doing at the moment. It's a tricky situation, one she's never been in and she types and sends the only thing that comes to mind:

> y?
>
> talked on the way home. said she knows she's drinking 2 much and will try 2 stop.

ur there 4 her. that means a lot 2 her.

yeah. i guess. we'll c.

talk with angie & phyllis. they can help.

i will.

can't wait 2 c u again.

same here. thanx 4 being my friend!

same here. g'night. xoxoxo

xoxoxo!!! :-)

She smiles and shuts down the computer and turns off the light and climbs into bed and lies there thinking about Cyd and all the other people in her life and the fact that everyone, herself included, seems to be struggling in their own way with something, everyone except Nana Eileen, who seems to be the only one who's happy and content with her life. It doesn't seem to matter if you're young or old. There's always something and she wonders if it ever ends. She has the feeling it never does. It's sad and wearying to think so, but that seems to be the way life is. You just have to deal with it.

She remembers the way Cyd's mom's hand was shaking, just like her dad's used to. It seems a long time ago now and she thinks of everything that's happened to her dad and where he is now and knows that if Cyd's mom is going to change her life it isn't going to be easy and it won't be without Cyd's help.

CHAPTER 17

Magda rides beside Kaitlin as they follow Michael on their mountain bikes on his run on the road near the cottage in Berchtesgaden. She was attracted to him the moment she met him. She liked everything about him: his looks, his body – what great shape he's in! – his intelligence, his thoughtfulness and the way he listens carefully to what she has to say. She's happy for Kaitlin, but when she looks at Michael she can't help thinking about Kaitlin's text message from Carmel.

She hasn't mentioned the party to them yet. The right moment hasn't presented itself. Maybe this evening when they relax on the porch. Are they into that sort of thing? She doubts they've experienced anything like the parties. Despite the fact that Kaitlin has discovered she enjoys anal sex, she's shy and reserved. Michael seems like he'd be more open to the idea. It will be interesting to see how they react to her description of them. They'll probably have a hard time seeing past the sex to what the parties are really all about: freedom, shedding your ego.

The Nazis had it all wrong. They thought they could unite the German people and create a master race with one mind and one purpose by making them believe they were superior to all other people, but they failed miserably because they weren't interested in freedom, they were interested in enslaving people with their ideology of hatred and exclusionism and adoration of the Fuehrer. Brigitte and Keir weren't aware of it at the time and maybe she wasn't, either, not consciously, but thinking about it she realized the idea of the parties sprang from her abhorrence of the Nazi period in German history and her desire to do her part, however small, to prevent anything like that from ever happening again. The parties are as much a political statement as any anti-Nazi demonstration, although it's probably the last thing the people who attend them would suspect. No matter. She knows it and that's enough. All people are welcome, people of all ethnicity and skin color and sexual orientation and the parties serve as living proof that people can move beyond themselves, beyond their inhibitions, even if only for one night and with the help of a drug. Her hope is that one day, people will be able to act that way naturally, although she doubts that day will ever arrive.

"Magda!" she hears Kaitlin cry in alarm and glances at her and sees her swerving to get out of her way and struggling to stay on her bike. She's been so lost in thought and intent on following Michael with her eyes fixed on his back that as he drifted over to the left so did she and nearly ran into Kaitlin. "Sorry!"

The three of them sit on the porch after dinner sipping their beers. Magda tries not to stare at Michael, but each time she looks away it isn't long before she's looking at him again. "So, are you excited?" she asks him.

"About flying?"

"Yes!"

Michael nods and smiles. "Yeah, I'm really looking forward to it."

"You'll love it! We'll all be flying together. A friend is loaning me his three-seater." She looks out at the clear evening sky and the sprinkling of shimmering stars with more appearing as the darkness deepens and then at Michael. "It's beautiful, isn't it?" She sees him nod and smile again. "Just as I remember it," she hears Kaitlin say. She looks at her and smiles. "It's so good to have you both here," she says and looks back at Michael. "And to finally meet you. Be right back." She springs out of her chair and walks quickly into the house.

Kaitlin looks at Michael and sees him raise his eyebrows and she smiles and shrugs. She described Magda as being like a force of nature and he's beginning to get the picture.

Magda returns carrying a tray with a bottle of schnapps and three small glasses and a large hookah on it. "We have the house to ourselves, so we do as we please."

Kaitlin puts a hand to her mouth and stares wide-eyed at the ornate hookah with its curled tentacle-like stems. "Oh, my God! Look at that thing! Where'd you get it?"

Magda sets the tray on the table and sits on the edge of her seat. "Morocco. Magnificent, isn't it? A stem for everyone." She picks up the fourth. "This one's the 'missing man.'" She waves a hand over the tray. "So, schnapps and hash. You smoke, right?"

Kaitlin shifts nervously and glances at Michael. "Yeah, pot, every now and then, not a lot."

"Ever smoked hash?" Magda asks.

Kaitlin shakes her head and glances at Michael again and sees him shake his too.

"Hard to find in the States," he says.

"Not here," Magda says. "It's great! You'll enjoy it!" She unscrews the cap on the schnapps bottle and fills the glasses. "Wild berry schnapps, my favorite with black hash." She puts down the bottle and hands them each a glass and picks up hers and holds it out. *"Prost!"* she says and watches them lean forward and hold out their glasses to hers and clink.

"Prost!" they say.

She watches them toss back their schnapps and chase it down with a sip of beer. Good. She does the same and hands them each a stem. She takes the lighter from the table and places a stem between her lips and holds the flame over the bowl and draws until the ball of hash glows bright orange. She raises her eyebrows and nods at them and watches them place their stems between their lips, Kaitlin hesitantly and glancing at Michael, and draw and sees the orange glow reflected in their faces.

Good. Kaitlin and Michael slowly sit back and she does the same, holding the smoke deep in her lungs and feeling her head expanding and the world falling away beneath her. She looks through slited eyes at them and sees them leaning back in their chairs with their eyes closed. It's pure high-grade stuff she gets from an Afghani friend whose family back home produces it with loving care and for which she pays top price. The high is smooth and makes her feel weightless and judging from the looks of it, it's having the same affect on them.

She refills the glasses with schnapps and they toss it back — well, she and Michael do but Kaitlin sips hers tentatively — and chase it down with beer and she puts the stem between her lips again and watches them do the same and holds the flame over the bowl and draws and watches their faces glow orange again as they draw on theirs, Michael deeply and Kaitlin shallowly and they settle back in their chairs again.

"Let me tell you about the party you're invited to," Magda says and studies their faces as she describes it to them. Michael listens with fascination while Kaitlin stares at her wide-eyed and glances at Michael to see what he thinks of the idea and doesn't look happy about the fact that he seems intrigued by it. "You're not obligated to come. We can do something else or you can have the evening to yourselves. Whatever you please."

Kaitlin tucks her legs under her and crosses her arms. "I've never done Ecstasy." She looks at Michael. "Have you?"

"Yeah, once."

"You did?" she asks, surprised. "When?"

"Skiing at Mammoth. I met these two women and we ended up at their place."

"And?"

He glances at Magda and looks at Kaitlin and smiles and shrugs. "We fucked our brains out."

What else hasn't she heard about? Things feel like they're spinning out of control and this latest revelation has her feeling lost and helpless.

"This stuff isn't important, Katie."

She raises her eyebrows. "It isn't?" She looks at Magda and tries not to let it show that she finds her patient and understanding expression condescending but she's not sure she's managing it. She can't even feel her face, let alone control it.

"We're no different than animals where sex is concerned," Magda says.

Kaitlin doesn't like the sound of that but can't help admitting it's the way she felt that evening in the park with Manfred. All she could think about was having wild animal sex with him. It's strange. She hadn't associated being here at the house with her time with Manfred until this moment, but Magda's comment has brought it to mind and she remembers the three of them sitting here just as they are now, Manfred where Michael is, and then she and Manfred retiring for the night and sleeping in the bed where she and Michael are sleeping and she feels like a complete hypocrite. "I dunno," she says, "sex is important to me. I guess I'm just not into sharing."

Magda smiles and refills the glasses with schnapps. "Don't confuse sex with love," she says and waves them forward for another round.

Kaitlin stays where she is and watches Michael go readily and he and Magda clink their glasses and say, *"Prost!"* She watches them toss back their schnapps and put their empty glasses on the table and sip their beers. She's already plenty high and has had more than enough to drink and when Magda leans forward and takes her stem and lights the bowl of hash and draws deeply and raises her eyebrows and nods at them to do the same, she watches Michael take his but passes. She feels far away as he and Magda sit back, smiling with their eyes closed. They remind her of synchronized swimmers, whereas she feels like — what did Magda call it? — "the missing man."

Michael and Magda seem to be moving off together in another direction, leaving her behind and the thought crosses her mind to get up and go to bed, but when she tries to move she finds she can't. She looks at Michael for help but his head is back and his eyes are closed and he's smiling blissfully. She looks at Magda and sees her looking at her suggestively with hooded eyes. For the first time she sees the similarity between Magda and Manfred and why she hasn't seen it before is beyond her. Magda's toying with her the same way Manfred did, but for a different reason. She's felt it since they arrived by the way Magda hasn't been able to keep her eyes off Michael. She knows what Magda wants and that she's using her to get it.

She remembers telling Beatrice about Magda on the plane and how Beatrice listened patiently and nodded understandingly and said her experience with Manfred was a valuable lesson and made her promise not to allow herself to be used again, the way a mother makes her foolish daughter promise not to get knocked up by some uncaring guy she's become infatuated with. She promised Beatrice she wouldn't but isn't doing a very good job of keeping her promise.

"I had my first sexual encounter in your bedroom," Magda says.

Kaitlin glances at Michael and sees his eyes are wide open now and that he's looking at Magda with keen interest. She's disappointed to see him reacting like a typical man and watches him put his hands behind his head and his feet up on the table and cross his legs, getting ready to hear what she's sure he's hoping will be a graphic account, which it undoubtedly will be knowing Magda.

"It was summer and my brother had two friends visiting. The three of them were sleeping outside in a tent."

"How old were you?" Michael asks.

"Eleven. My parents were talking about my aunt at dinner. At the time she was suffering from migraines and experiencing temporary blindness and I wondered what it must be like to be blind and I remembered there was an eyeshade in the travel kit I kept from one of our trips to the States and I said I was going to wear it for a day. My brother and his friends bet me I couldn't do it, which only made me more determined, so I went and got it and put it on and felt my way back to the table and into my chair. Everyone knew how stubborn I was and my father said they'd be sorry they'd bet me. I was wearing it in bed that night. It was late. Everyone had gone to bed. I was sleepy, but not asleep and I heard someone come into the room, walking on tiptoes, trying not to make any noise. My impulse was to take off the eyeshade and see who it was, but then I thought it would be just like my brother or one of his friends to do something like this, just to win the bet, so I didn't. I just lay there listening and waiting to see what would happen. Nothing did for a few moments and then I felt the covers being pulled down and a hand on my breast and one between my legs and whoever it was began fondling and stroking me and it felt good. No one had ever touched me before. And then I felt a hand on my hand and whoever it was guided my hand to a surprisingly hard and warm penis. I'd seen my brother's, of course, and my father's, but never like that. I'd only seen erections in pictures and porn videos and I'd never touched a penis. He moved my hand back and forth until I got the idea and then let my hand go and we stayed like that, stroking each other until I felt him jerking and the air filled with a smell that reminded me of a stable and he stopped stroking me and tip-toed out of the room. I remember lying there afterward thinking about what had happened and how pleasurable and exciting the experience had been, especially since I didn't know who it was and that got me thinking. I realized it really didn't matter who it was. It could have been one of my brother's friends or my brother, even my father, and the experience would have been just as pleasurable and exciting." She can see Kaitlin's shocked and appalled.

Kaitlin looks at Michael. "I think I'll turn in." She manages to slowly uncurls herself and stands unsteadily and he stands and wraps an arm around her waist and leads her to the bedroom. She sits on the bed and begins pulling off her clothes.

"You all right?" Michael asks.

"Yeah. I just need to pee and brush my teeth and go to bed. I'll be okay."

"You sure?"

"Yeah. Go sit with Magda. It's rude to leave her there. I'm fine." Who is she kidding? She's not at all fine and sits on the toilet with her head in her hands and her feet planted wide, peeing and trying to make the bathroom stop spinning. She wipes herself and flushes the toilet and stands unsteadily and looks at herself in the mirror. She looks as bad as she feels. She squeezes a gob of toothpaste onto her toothbrush and hunches over the sink and brushes her teeth and glances up at her reflection and sees toothpaste foaming at the corners of her mouth. She looks like a rabid animal. Well, she is an animal, as Magda reminded her. It was animal desire that drove her into Manfred's arms.

She curls up under the covers and closes her eyes. Her head's still spinning but at least her bladder's empty and her mouth tastes of spearmint and she feels a little less woozy. Her body feels like it's floating and dipping and turning. It reminds her of the Tilt-A-Whirl ride at the fair. She's exhausted and wants to sleep but she's still too high and the jumble of thoughts going round and round in her head like clothes in a dryer is keeping her awake.

The murmur of Michael's and Magda's voices coming from the porch reminds her of when she was a little girl sitting in the back seat of the car, listening to the murmur of her parent's voices. She was aware of how little she knew about anything and was in awe of her parents, who seemed to know everything. She feels the same way now about Michael and Magda where sex and drugs are concerned. Magda's obviously into both in a big way.

These parties of hers sound debauched and their sole purpose, as Magda said, is to get high and have sex. She knows Magda embraces the unconventional and considers the narrow strictures of socially acceptable thinking and behavior to be loathsome and stifling. She figured she and her like-minded free-spirited friends were into some wild stuff, so why was she surprised by her description of the parties and react the way she did? The same goes for her story about what happened in the bedroom. Is she that much of a prude?

She's finding out more about Michael all the time; having anal sex with that woman at the Westin, doing Ecstasy and having sex with those women at Mammoth. What else doesn't she know about? It took a lot of courage for her to demand that they have anal sex. She felt proud of herself for having stepped way outside of her comfort zone. It seemed like quite an achievement, but now it just seems like the desperate act of an uptight woman who wanted to prove to her more experienced man that she isn't boring in bed. Who is she kidding? She's not in the same league as those two.

She's reminded of the first time she was on ice skates. Her dad was by her side and each time she'd take a tentative step and lose her balance and stumble and fall, he'd pick her up and brush her off and send her off again. How long will Michael keep doing it? He's extremely patient, but he's not her dad. Sooner or later she'll exhaust even his patience.

She listens to the murmur of voices and feels herself drifting off and now she's seated behind Michael and Magda in a glider and the three of them are aloft. The glider banks steeply and she looks through the canopy straight down at the ground far below. She knows the canopy is about to open and notices she's not strapped into her seat and wonders whether she'll fall to the ground or begin flying. It's strange that she feels so calm about the situation.

Magda gazes at Michael as they draw on their stems. The orange glow from the bowl makes his expression look devilish and while he's behaving like a perfect gentleman, there's no mistaking the desire she sees in his slightly hooded eyes. She knows her description of the party and her story about her first sexual encounter turned him on. How could they not have? He's a man. She's thinking about what sex with him would be like now more than ever and knows that if she wanted to she could have him right here on the porch. She isn't going to, though. Now's not the time.

She wonders what it must be like to feel the way Kaitlin does about sex. She never has. Sex and ego — Will people ever be able to separate the two? She and Brigitte and Keir can. She knows that Michael can too. As for Kaitlin, she knows she doesn't want to attend the party and given her reaction to the story, she'll see whether they're even still friends in the morning. She sits back and watches Michael do the same. "I know I'm extreme," she says, "I've always been. It's not something I can do anything about, the way a leopard can't change its spots."

"Ever been in love?" he asks.

"No. I don't trust it."

"Ever been hurt?"

"No. I won't let that happen."

"Why?"

"Germany was in love once, with a plain-looking, insecure delusional housepainter from Austria who fancied himself an artist. They adored him and trusted him and followed him like a flock of sheep. He led them to Armageddon and Germany lost. Tell me again why I should want to love anyone."

"That was different."

"Was it? I see the way couples manipulate each other. It's a power struggle. I won't play that game."

He grins. "You don't know what you're missing."

"Aiyee! What romantic nonsense!"

"Look," he says, "I know you feel strongly about what happened to your country, but your passion for freedom and these parties of yours don't seem to square. It seems a bit hypocritical."

The word hits her like a punch in the stomach and she tries not to let her anger show. "Hypocritical?" She can hear it in her voice, though, as well as defensiveness and hurt. She glares at him, not knowing what to say.

"Seems like you're on your own little power trip, feeding people a drug to make them feel free." He shrugs. "Reminds me of Huxley."

She hates being at a disadvantage and still doesn't know what to say. A brilliant blue and white streak of light flashing in the nighttime sky catches her eye, the debris trail of a meteor disintegrating as it enters the atmosphere. The light disappears as quickly as it appeared but the afterimage lingers in her eyes. Maybe it's the pilot in her, but she always thinks the same thing when she sees a shooting star, that it's a bad sign, that the firmament has cracked and the sky begun falling and maybe she'll fall out of the sky too, like a meteor, only she won't burn up before she hits the ground. It's the one superstitious belief she allows herself. "Forgive me for being a poor hostess. I'll say good night." She stands and walks toward the house. "Sweet dreams," she hears him say.

Kaitlin wakes with a throbbing headache and hears Michael's light snoring. She opens her eyes and lifts her head groggily from the pillow and looks over her shoulder at him lying on his back with his mouth slightly open. How late did the two of them stay up? More important, what did they get up to? She hears sizzling and smells frying meat and coffee. She shuffles into the kitchen, squinting in the bright sunlight and holding her robe wrapped tightly around her and sees Magda standing at the stove with her back to her. "Mornin'," she says, yawning and scratching her head.

Magda turns, tongs in hand, and smiles. "Good morning! Did you sleep well? How are you feeling?"

"Like I was hit in the head with a sledgehammer. Other than that, fine." Kaitlin shuffles over to the counter and leans back against it as Magda takes a mug from the cabinet and fills it with coffee and hands it to her. "Thanks." She looks at the bacon, ham and sausage grilling on the stove. "Wow! That's a lot of meat."

Magda grins. "A real German breakfast. It's barbaric, but we Germans are barbarians at heart. We made life miserable for those civilized Romans."

Kaitlin sips her coffee and watches Magda turn the meat. "I'm sorry I bailed last night. How much longer did you stay up?"

"An hour or so." Magda grins at her impishly. "Don't worry. We just talked."

Kaitlin knows she's teasing, but also that she wants Michael and feels she can have him anytime she wants and that he'd come willingly. Would he? Magda's still looking at her with that impish grin, waiting for her response to the tease. She nods toward the meat. "Careful you don't burn it."

The tow plane pulls the glider slowly toward thirty-five hundred feet and Kaitlin gazes out the canopy at the clear sky above and watches the ground below fall away. She and Michael sit side by side behind Magda, holding hands and listening to her in their headsets talking in German with the tow plane pilot. "Almost there," they hear her say and look at each other and grin. What a spectacular day and what an amazing feeling it is to be aloft together. Soon the tow plane will be gone and the only sound they'll hear will be the wind rushing past the canopy as they soar above Wasserkruppe.

"Here we go," they hear her say and see the tow cable release from the nose of the glider and disappear above them as the tow plane banks away. Kaitlin squeezes Michael's hand and they lean toward each other and kiss. They listen to the sound of the tow plane receding but she thinks she hears the sound of another plane approaching and searches the sky on her side of the glider. There sure are a lot of tow planes and gliders in the air today. They hear Magda speaking in German in their headsets again and the concern in her voice is unmistakable. They glance at each other anxiously and search the sky around them. No plane in sight but the sound of one approaching is growing louder. Magda banks the glider steeply, pressing them against each other and Kaitlin sees the wheels of a tow plane come into view slightly above them to the right and on a path to pass over them very closely.

"Shit!" they hear Magda shout in their headsets followed by a string of what can only be German curses and they hear a "thunk" and Kaitlin sees a tow cable sheer off a good-size piece of the outer wing on her side of the glider and watches it fall away and the tow cable disappear from view above them. The glider shudders and lurches violently and she can't help screaming. She looks at Michael and knows he's thinking the same thing, that they're going to die, but he's looking at her calmly, even though he's almost directly beneath her now and she sees him mouth, "I love you." She glances down at his hand and sees she's gripping it so tightly that her fingernails are cutting into his flesh and drawing blood.

She closes her eyes tightly as the glider banks steeper and dives almost straight down for what seems a very long time. She tries to convince herself that when the glider hits the ground nose-first she'll be dead before she knows it, but it's not a comforting thought and it doesn't diminish her terror in the least. Finally she feels the nose come up a bit and then a bit more and opens her eyes and looks at Magda's back. She can tell by the way her shoulders are moving that she's fighting hard to counteract the damage to the wing and get the glider flying level. If they get out of this, they'll have her to thank for their lives.

"It's okay!" they hear Magda say, trying to contain her anger. "I'm going to kill that idiot!" They look at each other. There really isn't anything funny about the situation and the last thing they should do is laugh but they can't help themselves, as people who realize they've escaped death can't.

The three of them stand on the tarmac, heads together and hugging. Magda steps back and looks at them. "An unfortunate incident. I'm sorry it happened. I hope it doesn't put you off flying."

Kaitlin hugs her again. "Thank you. You're amazing."

Magda hugs her back, her eyes fixed on Michael's.

The waiter places Kaitlin's breakfast of coffee and a croissant on the table in front of her and she studies his hands. His fingers are long and slender and his fingernails manicured. No wedding band. Is he straight, gay, divorced, a widower? Does he have children? She looks up at him. He's handsome, in his fifties maybe with a dark complexion and long face and glistening black hair combed straight back and a receding hairline that looks like an M. She's interested in him the way she's interested in everything this morning, like she's seeing it all for the first time. *"Danke,"* she says and the waiter nods in what looks to her like the modern day equivalent of a formal bow.

"Bitte," he says.

She watches him walk away, erect with his shoulders back, then looks at Michael and watches him gather egg and sausage on his fork. She sips her coffee and breaks off a piece of her croissant and butters it and takes a bite. She's heard about life-altering experiences but never experienced one until that moment when she thought they were going to die and screamed. She'll never forget the look of calm on Michael's face in her moment of terror. Her appreciation of his being in her life now is immeasurable. How does she feel? The word "selfless" comes to mind, all mind and spirit and no body, which, she imagines, is the way all people who know they should be dead must feel. She understands Michael's attitude about sex now. Love is love and sex is sex and the two don't necessarily have anything to do with each other. She waits until he stops chewing and swallows. "Waddaya think?"

He looks at her and shrugs. "We don't have to go."

She watches him take a sip of coffee and begin gathering more egg and sausage on his fork. "She'd understand, right?"

He looks at her and nods.

So what if he had anal sex with that woman at the Westin or a threesome at Mammoth? Who knows what else he's done that he hasn't told her about? It doesn't matter. It's not important. All that matters and is important is that he's here with her now and still loves her despite her foolishness with Manfred. She's no longer afraid of losing Michael. In fact, she no longer feels she has anything to lose. In a way, she lost everything in that moment of screaming terror and everything she now has feels like a gift. It's a joy just sitting here with him watching him eat his breakfast.

As for Magda's interest in him, she knows it's purely sexual. The woman is all appetite. So what if they went to the party and Magda and Michael had sex? It wouldn't mean anything. No, that's not right. It would mean everything. She'd no longer feel indebted to Magda for saving their lives. "On the other hand, it's not every day you get invited to an orgy."

He puts his fork on the side of his plate and picks up his cup and looks at her and grins. "True."

Magda's ring tone chimes and Kaitlin picks up her phone and puts it to her ear keeping her eyes on Michael's. "Good morning! Having breakfast at the hotel. Yes, we're coming. Okay, send it to me. Great. I will. See you this evening." She puts down the phone and leans back. "So, that's that then."

He narrows his eyes. "Said the spider to the fly."

The phone chimes again and she checks the message and sees it's Brigitte's address.

They're still laughing about the incident in the hotel room as the taxi turns onto Brigitte's tree-lined street and slows to a stop at the curb. They were freshening up after a day of sight-seeing and Kaitlin was standing in her tee shirt and shorts and sneakers staring down at the clothes in her open suitcase, trying to decide what to wear for the evening when Michael came out of the bathroom and she looked at him and saw his puzzled expression and it dawned on her how ridiculous it was to worry about what to wear and they fell together laughing on the bed.

She gets out and waits on the sidewalk as Michael pays the driver. She looks up Brigitte's house, or what she can see of it behind the high brick wall surrounding the property, a pitched roof with four gabled windows in front and a central chimney and chimneys on the sides. Nice digs. She calls Magda. "We're here. Okay." The taxi pulls away and Michael arrives at her side and looks up at the house.

"Business is good," he says.

She shrugs. "Or daddy has money."

They stroll hand in hand to the front gate and stand in the pool of light from the lamps on the ivy-covered posts flanking it, waiting for Magda to arrive and escort them in. Michael gives her hand a squeeze.

"Ready for this?"

She glances at him nervously. "Yeah, ready as I'll ever be." A moment later the gate opens and there's Magda in a white terrycloth bathrobe and white bath slippers with a big smile on her face.

"Aiyee! I can't believe you're really here!" Magda says and gives them each a hug and kiss on the cheek and turns and heads up the path toward the house.

They look at each other and know they're thinking the same thing as they follow her: neither can they.

They take in the interior of the house as they make their way toward the backyard. It has the feel of a country cottage but on a grand scale. The furnishings are sumptuous, a profusion of dark woods and leather, but the walls are covered with modern art and here and there they see gleaming chrome sculptures. The old and new harmonize well. Brigitte obviously has good taste and a good eye. They see swirling mist in the lighted backyard through the open French doors as they cross the living room and then people sitting in the pool around the sides.

They follow Magda to the pool and Kaitlin recognizes Brigitte with her impossibly platinum hair and eyebrows and sees she's sitting between two handsome young men who look to be in their mid-twenties. She assumes the man sitting near Brigitte is Kier and sees he's sitting between an attractive young woman with bright red hair and a handsome young man with a glistening shaved head. The young man and woman look to be around the same age as Brigitte's playmates.

They follow Magda around to the other side of the pool, discreetly checking out people as they do. Everyone's limbs are intertwined and most people are fondling and stroking each another. One woman is bouncing on a man's lap with her head back and her eyes closed and her mouth wide open. Another woman is kneeling in front of a man with her face in his lap. He's sitting on the side of the pool with his legs spread wide and his hands on the back of her bobbing head and he also has his head back and eyes closed and mouth wide open.

Magda nods toward the cabana and puts a finger to her lips to remind them there's no talking allowed. She lets her robe fall to the ground and steps out of her slippers and they watch her lower herself into the pool and glance at each other when they see the tattoo on the small of her back, a black swastika in a red circle with a red bar through it. Behind her on the side of the pool is a silver tray with champagne on ice and fluted glasses and a large bowl filled with what look to be chocolate covered strawberries and a small bowl containing a handful of tiny blue pills. They glance at each other again and walk to the cabana. Michael holds back the flap for Kaitlin and they step inside and as soon as he lets the flap fall back she turns to him and laughs nervously. "Okay, why does this seem ridiculous?"

"It's like being on a porn set."

"Yeah, that must be it. Oh, my God!" She covers her face with her hands and spreads her fingers just enough to peek at him. "I don't know if I can go through with this."

"We can leave."

She closes her eyes and straightens up and takes a deep breath and blows it out and looks him in the eyes. "No."

He smiles and chucks her under the chin and kisses the tip of her nose. "Listen, whatever happens, it's just sex."

She nods. "I know."

They walk to the pool, Kaitlin feeling very self-conscious about her nakedness, and lower themselves into it on either side of Magda, who smiles at them and stands and turns to fill the glasses with champagne. Kaitlin looks to her left and sees an older woman, maybe in her late fifties, and beside her a man around the same age and beside him a young woman. She looks to her right and leans forward and sees an attractive young black couple on the other side of Michael.

Magda hands Kaitlin a glass and a blue pill and the same to Michael and settles into the pool with hers. She holds out her glass and puts her pill in her mouth and watches them do the same and they clink and wash the pills down with champagne. She smiles and gives first Kaitlin and then Michael a kiss on the lips and settles back against the side of the pool and closes her eyes and smiles.

Magda looks very pleased with herself to Kaitlin and she's sure she's happily anticipating finally getting what she wants. She's also sure that Magda thinks the fact that they're here is Michael's doing and that he probably had to twist her arm to get her to come. She can't blame her if she does. She's given her every reason to believe she's afraid of her own shadow emotionally.

She looks around the pool at the people, all with variations of the same ecstatic expression on their faces and having sex of one sort or another. It strikes her as funny that what she's enjoying most about the party so far is having a good soak in the heated pool. They did a lot of walking today and she can feel her feet tingling and the muscles in her legs relaxing.

She looks across the pool at Brigitte and sees her smiling serenely with her eyes closed as the two young men flanking her fondle her breasts with one hand while presumably attending to her underwater with the other. It's the same with Keir, except the young man and woman flanking him are leaning across him and kissing. It's just like watching porn, except it's really happening and she's in it. The closest she's come to anything like this was getting stoned with her girlfriends on those hot, humid summer evenings in Schuylkill Haven and skinny-dipping in the above-ground pool in Jill's backyard. It seems laughable in comparison.

Her limbs feel like there dissolving and she's pleasantly elevated now and it occurs to her that she's been watching Brigitte and Keir for some time, in fact, that she's lost track of time and she looks to her right and sees the back of Magda's head bobbing up and down in Michael's lap. She looks at him and sees him looking back. He smiles and reaches out his hand and she takes it and smiles and they gaze at each other. What's happening between him and Magda doesn't bother her at all. It's just what she knew would happen and she isn't surprised that Magda didn't waste any time. All that matters is the look in Michael's eyes, which tells her everything she needs to know.

She feels a hand on her left thigh and sees the older woman gazing at her and that the older man beside her is now standing behind the young woman, who's bent over and holding onto the side of the pool, her eyes closed and mouth open and breasts swaying as he pumps. She notices the older man and the woman beside her are wearing wedding bands and assumes they're married and there's her husband banging a young chick right beside her. What's with these people? Well, she shouldn't criticize. After all, she's sure she'll be watching Michael doing the same thing to Magda before long.

The older woman is looking at her almost pleadingly now. Kaitlin smiles at her and the woman smiles back and she feels the woman take her hand and guide it to between her legs. She's surprised to find the woman is shaved. She's shaved a few times and it's always struck her as a lot of bother and for what? She strokes the woman and watches her husband as she does. He's standing in front of the young woman now, who's squatting down facing him with her hands on his butt and her head back and eyes closed and mouth wide open. The man is stroking his cock vigorously and Kaitlin expects to see him come on the young woman's face, just like in porn videos, but instead a stream of piss comes arcing out of him and she watches the young woman bathe happily in it, smiling as she turns her face from side to side. She's never understood the appeal of that sort of thing and, orgy or no orgy, it doesn't seem right to pee in the pool, but no one else seems to notice, let alone care.

She feels the woman pushing harder against her fingers as she strokes her and sees her eyes are closed now and her lips slightly parted and that she seems to be concentrating on visualizing someone or something. If she were inside the woman's head what would she see? It could be anyone and anything or nothing at all. She and Michael webchat when she's traveling and sometimes masturbate together to feel physically close and when they do, she masturbates just as she always has, with her eyes closed and imagining herself lying on her back naked in a meadow filled with beautiful wildflowers. It's the only way she can get herself off.

She sees the woman's mouth open wider and feels her hips begin bucking and she strokes her until the woman comes and relaxes. The woman opens her eyes and looks at her gratefully and smiles. It occurs to Kaitlin that she's just had her first same-sex experience and also that it seemed perfectly natural. She knows it's the drug but never would have thought it possible under any circumstances.

She feels a hand on her right thigh and sees Magda leaning toward her with a chocolate covered strawberry between her lips. She leans forward and wraps her lips around her half of the strawberry and she and Magda bite into it and gaze at each other's eyes as they chew. Magda brings her lips to hers and she feels her fondling her breasts and she fondles Magda's. They put their tongues in each other's mouth and Kaitlin feels Magda pressing her lips and body harder against hers and now Magda's stroking her between the legs and she has to admit it feels good and knows Michael is enjoying watching them. Magda puts an arm around her waist and lifts her up and guides her to the side of the pool and she sits on it. She watches Magda kneel in front of her and spread her legs and bring her mouth to her clit and the feeling of her kissing and licking and sucking it is fantastic. She looks at Michael and sees he's really enjoying watching this. She nods toward Magda and he stands and positions himself behind her.

So, this is it. This is where the debt gets paid. She pictures drawing a line on a page and writing a big fat zero below it. She watches Magda reach back and guide Michael into her where she's wanted him ever since the text from Carmel. Michael begins pumping slowly and Kaitlin watches his body move with that same steady pace and mechanical motion it does when he's running. She gazes down at Magda. She has the feeling Magda doesn't really need the drug to be doing what she's doing, that's she's completely uninhibited and the drug only heightens her pleasure. She's sure this is the last time this threesome business is going to happen, although, as far as Ecstasy goes, it would be nice to do it again with Michael, just the two of them, thank you.

It's strange to think that having Magda between them like this would bring them closer together, but it has, she knows it has. She can feel it. She looks down at her and sees she's lost in being fucked in the ass by Michael. He's doing an impressive job and she knows it will only make Magda want him more, but she knows Michael. Magda should enjoy it while it lasts because this is all she's going to get.

"*Nicht, bitte,*" Kaitlin says holding her hand over her coffee cup. The waiter nods and and walks to the next table with the coffee pot and she looks at Michael. "It's not helping."

He looks at her sympathetically and cuts into his Eggs Benedict. "Kind of like being hit by a truck, huh?" He grins. "It was fun, though."

"Yeah, it was, in a crazy sort of way." They were still high when they returned to the hotel and she had the opportunity to experience Michael's performance under the influence of the drug. It was marvelous and he was much gentler with her than he was with Magda and she wonders what kind of shape Magda's behind is in this morning. Magda's ring tone chimes and she picks up her phone and puts it to her ear keeping her eyes on Michael's. "Hi. Okay. Recovering." Not surprisingly, Magda sounds chipper. "Having a bite to eat, or trying to. Yeah, sure." She holds the phone out to him. "It's for you, 'Marathon Man.'"

He raises his eyebrows and takes it and puts it to his ear. "Hey! Okay." He looks at Kaitlin. "She does? Yeah, okay, see you soon." He hands her the phone. "She wants to see me."

"Big surprise." She looks up Magda's address and hands him the phone. "Go. I'll take a walk. Maybe it'll help."

"Aiyee! Good to see you!" Magda says and waves Michael into the apartment. "Thanks for coming!"

He looks around. "How are you? Get some sleep?"

"I slept late at Brigitte's, as I always do. Coffee?"

"I'm coffeed out."

"Beer?"

"Yeah, that sounds good." He follows her to the kitchen and watches her take two bottles from the fridge and open them.

"Glass?"

"This is fine." He takes the bottle and clinks hers. *"Prost."*

"Prost." She takes a sip. "So, what did you think?"

"It was wild."

"Did Kaitlin enjoy herself?"

He nods. "Yeah, she did. She's struggling today. The drug kicked the shit out of her."

Magda chuckles. "I can imagine."

He leans against the counter and crosses his arms. "So, what's up?"

She shrugs. "I wanted to see you. That's all."

"Here I am."

"I haven't forgotten our conversation that night on the porch. You said some things.... Well, you seem to understand me pretty well." She moves closer. "It's true what you said, in a way. I can be manipulative and controlling...." She moves still closer. "Selfish and possessive...." She places her hand on his forearm. "When I want something, I want it."

He cocks his head. "Seems you're used to getting what you want. I think maybe you're a little bit spoiled." He expects to see a flash of anger but instead she pouts and fingers a button on his shirt.

"Don't say that. You know I don't take criticism well."

The hurt "little girl" voice matches the pout perfectly. Both seem surprisingly out of character for her and he never would have expected them.

"Anyway, I want you."

"I thought you were Kaitlin's friend?"

"I am, but you're here."

"Because she told me to come."

"You see? She knows I want you and doesn't want to stand in the way."

"She told me to come because she loves me and trusts me."

Magda presses herself against him and looks up at him with doe eyes. "Maybe I love you too."

There's the hurt "little girl" voice again. "You want me, Magda. You don't love me." It's followed predictably by the pout.

"Why do you say that? It's not fair. I do love you. You can be all the things I admit I am and still love someone, can't you?"

Who's to say you can't. All he knows is that he doesn't believe her and it doesn't matter even if she does love him. "I'm not denying I'm attracted to you, but what happened last night was a one-time thing. I love Katie."

She steps back and glares at him. "All this talk about love! I'm sick of it!" She unbuttons the waistband of her jeans and unzips them and pulls her jeans and underpants down around her ankles and turns and puts her hands on the island in the center of the kitchen and spreads her legs and looks back at him over her shoulder. "Fuck me! Wherever you please! Do it! I know you want to!"

"Magda...."

"Do it!" She sees he's not going to. "Okay." She turns and kneels in front of him and reaches for his belt buckle. "I'll give you pleasure." She tries to unbuckle his belt but he grabs her wrists and she's frantic now. "You can come wherever you want!"

"Magda...."

"What's wrong with you! I told you I love you!"

"Magda, please."

She clings to the waistband of his jeans. "Do you want to humiliate me? Is that it? Okay! Do it! However you want!"

He pulls away and lets her wrists free. "I'm leaving."

"Oh, no! You can't go! You can't leave me like this!"

He walks toward the door. "Michael," he hears her cry, "don't go!" He opens the door and turns and sees her struggling to crawl toward him, hobbled by her jeans and underpants, reaching out to him and looking desperate. He steps out of the apartment and shuts the door. "Michael!" he hears her cry as he walks down the hall.

He finds Kaitlin lying propped up on the bed with her arms crossed and the remote in her hand staring blankly at the TV screen. "Hey," he says.

"Hey."

He tosses the room key on the table and removes his jacket and tosses it on the chair and sits on the side of the bed with his back to her.

She points the remote at the screen and turns it off. "Didn't go well, huh?"

He stares down at his hands. "What a nightmare."

"So, what happened?"

He shrugs. "She said she loves me."

"Huh, maybe she does. Why wouldn't she?"

He looks at her over his shoulder and frowns. "She doesn't love me. You know that."

Whatever went on at Magda's she can see that Michael's been shaken by the experience and thrown by Magda's saying she loves him. It's curious, but she finds his confusion about the situation endearing and for the first time in their relationship truly feels like his partner and that he needs her compassion and understanding. "Who's to say?" she says. "Anyway, as far as I'm concerned it doesn't change anything. We're still friends, if she wants to be." She sees his expression of disbelief. "What?"

"She tries to steal your man and you still want to be her friend?"

She shrugs. "I can't blame her for trying and good for her for giving it her best shot." She pictures that big fat zero below the line. It's all that matters.

CHAPTER 18

Henry squints as he steps into the bright sunlight and puts on his sunglasses. Everyone at some time or another must wonder what this moment would feel like and what their reaction to it would be, but few people actually experience it. He has and now he knows. It feels like a sunny March day in Southern California, just past eleven in the morning on a Tuesday with the rest of the day off to do with as he pleases and he'd like to get some writing done, as he usually does on his days off, but knows he won't today.

He sees three white pelicans in the distance flying in formation, birds he rarely sees just six miles to the east in Irvine but that are common here by the coast in Newport Beach. It seems significant that there are three of them, three being such a symbolic number in religion, in particular representing the Trinity. He's not religious but he is feeling spiritual. He watches them as he steps off the curb and walks toward his car in the parking lot. The sound of screeching tires and a blaring car horn stops him and he turns and looks at the driver, a woman around his age, maybe older. Perhaps she's a client of one of the plastic surgeons here. She's looking at him with a furious expression and cursing him, undoubtedly for his stupidity and she has every right to, although she doesn't know the half of it.

He has no one to blame but himself. He should have gotten himself to the doctor when he had that episode of blood in his urine two years ago, knowing that it's a symptom of pancreatic cancer, but he read online that it could also be the result of a urinary infection of some kind or a temporary blockage and when it cleared up a few days later decided it was probably one of the two. He's lived with the abdominal and back pain and occasional feelings of nausea for months now and it was only when he lately began noticing his darkened urine and the slight yellow tint to his eyes that he finally decided to get examined. He doesn't really know why he's been so irresponsible about his health. Does he have a death wish? He's always wondered whether his smoking and drinking are the result of one. He doesn't thinks so but it's a moot point now.

He's always liked Doctor Summers, a big, smiling affable man with a well-trimmed beard and a taste for medical garb with flair. His palm print shirt seemed perfectly suited to the good doctor's relaxed approach to discussing his medical condition and prognosis. Doctor Summers very tactfully didn't chide him for not having presented himself sooner. He's had other doctors who would have.

What to listen to? He scrolls down the list of music files on the screen in the car. It's a long and varied list and as he watches the names of the performers and composers go by — AC/DC, Beethoven, B-52s, Cheap Trick, Copeland — nothing seems appropriate until, far down the list, he sees The Paul Butterfield

Blues Band and selects *In My Own Dream.* Perfect. He listens and remembers the first time he heard the song. It was 1968 when the record was first released. He'd just arrived in Boston and hadn't yet met Anise or Claire. All that was still to come and thinking about it now, this song, so soulful with its plaintive chorus, "To satisfy what I thought I'd be, I kept on living in my own dreams," was a prologue to the story that was about to unfold and Gene Dinwiddie's eerily sinuous and explosive sax solo — Well, hearing it now still makes his skin tingle. He wishes he could cry like that sax but won't. He's never been a crier. It's neither a good thing nor a bad thing. It just is.

Donald Barthelme's short story "Nothing: A Preliminary Account" comes to mind, a feverish and hurried attempt to list everything that nothing is not. It would at a time like this. He remembers the day at BU when Barthelme gave them the assignment to write about nothing. It was an intriguing idea and he's sure he came up with something, although he can't remember what now. It was undoubtedly crap. When they reconvened the next week and everyone had read aloud what they'd written, Barthelme, looking every bit the first mate of a whaling ship with his longish hair and bushy beard and tired eyes, picked up his sheets of paper and read them his short story. Like the student of philosophy Barthelme was he managed to weave Heidegger and Sartre and Beckett and Shakespeare together with damselfish and ninnyhammers and tongue depressors and all manner of other "not nothings" in an intellectual arabesque that left his audience speechless and staring awe-struck at him, which, he remembers thinking at the time, was precisely the effect Barthelme was after. So, long overdue kudos.

He didn't give him any at the time. In fact, he was resentful of Barthelme's talent and the ease with which he seemed to have produced the piece and was even more resentful when it appeared in the next issue of *The New Yorker*. He suspected Barthelme had written it before giving them the assignment and knew that it was going to be published. He didn't know and didn't ask him. It's not important now. Barthelme's dead and all that remains of importance is his closing thought that in trying to list everything that nothing is not, "How joyous the notion that, try as we may, we cannot do other than fail and fail absolutely and that the task will remain always before us, like a meaning for our lives. Hurry. Quickly. Nothing is not a nail."

Joanne knows the meal is delicious but isn't enjoying it and can barely taste the food. It's a veal dish Henry loves to prepare and does well in honor of his ancestors on his mother's father's side who came from the Piemonte region of Italy and ended up in Perugia, "due to circumstances" as his grandfather would say mysteriously whenever he told the story, suggesting some dark secret. Henry said he has it in mind to do some research and try to find out what's at the bottom of it but hasn't gotten around to it. She didn't give it much thought at the time but the way he's looked at her ever since she arrived, smiling at her tenderly and a little sadly, she has the feeling he never will.

She places her fork on the side of her plate and picks up her wine glass and takes a sip and peers at him over the rim of the glass. She's been waiting to hear about his follow up appointment with his doctor this morning but he hasn't said a word about it. She knows about the episode of blood in his urine a couple of years ago and that he hasn't been feeling all that well for some time. She hates to be judgmental but it was foolish of him not to have seen his doctor about it then, especially at his age. She can't wait any longer and puts down her glass and sits back and crosses her arms and raises her eyebrows. "So?"

"Pancreatic cancer."

She suddenly feels like she's looking at him through the small window in a diving helmet and can tell by his expression there's worse news to come.

"It's spread."

"Spread" – She's always associated that word with pleasant things, like butter and jam on toast and peanut butter and jelly on bread and lying on her back and welcoming him between her legs and into her arms, but now it fills her with dread and she despises it. "What's the prognosis?"

He sighs and sits back and crosses his arms. "Six months, maybe eight. I'm okay with it."

She thought she was ready for worse news but can't believe she's hearing this. "With chemo?"

He shakes his head. "It would only prolong the inevitable. I'm not going that route. I want to enjoy the time I have left as best I can."

She picks up her wine glass, still with plenty of wine in it, and throws it as hard as she can against the wall behind him. It's good to see him flinch and look over his shoulder at the stain, concerned about the damage to the wall and carpet. It means he's still alive. She looks at the splatter of wine on the wall and watches the rivulets begin running down. The pattern reminds her of a Mother of Thousands sending out shoots, spreading life and death. She doesn't want to think anymore. She wants to pick up her knife and carve her skull open and pull out her brain and throw it as hard as she can against the wall too and watch him flinch again and look over his shoulder at the gray stain.

She loves him but could strangle him for having been so irresponsible about his health. She shakes her head and laughs nervously at the irony of this thought. Irresponsible? Who is she to think that? She buries her face in her hands. She just wants to stop thinking. "Hey," she hears him say. She feels him wrap his arms around her shoulders and she wraps hers around his waist and presses her face against his stomach and feels her body trembling. What's the point of being brave? It's not going to change anything.

He helps her up and leads her to the couch and they sit, not knowing what to say and not wanting to say anything, just holding each other and staring out the sliding glass doors at the darkening sky. "Have you told your sons?" she finally asks.

He shakes his head.

"You're coming to live with me."

He looks at her and nods. Yes, they should live together now.

"You're leaving Brooks Brothers. You need to finish the novel."

He nods. Yes, he does. He's let the story unfold slowly according to its own logic and has lately arrived at a place where he can see it finally coming together. It's a good thing to leave behind, a story informed by everything he's learned in life and left behind with the expectation that no one will read it and the hope that if anyone does it will ring true.

"We're getting married. I need to be able to make medical decisions for you."

He nods. Yes, of course, that's important.

"We're having a child."

He's puzzled. He always uses a condom, as she insists he does. Still, it's possible. "Are you pregnant?"

"No, but I will be soon."

He's about to ask if she's sure she wants to be left having to raise a child alone but thinks better of it. It would be insulting and undoubtedly infuriate her. He smiles. "Good. We can make love properly now."

Joanne studies Gene's and Frank's faces as they read the copies of the documents Henry's had prepared. Gene is named the executor of Henry's estate and he and Frank the sole beneficiaries. She'll have medical power of attorney, which is all she's concerned about.

They're both handsome in their own ways and younger than she. At thirty-six she's three years older than Gene and six years older than Frank. She's seen pictures of them when they were younger and of Claire and Gene looks even more like his dad now and Frank looks like his mom. Having observed Frank, she can animate Claire in her mind's eye, see her sitting upright in her chair the way he does, walking almost flat-footed, bobbing up and down slightly with very little shoulder or hip rotation the way he does, unlike Gene and Henry, who slouch in their chairs and saunter and seem to be taking their time even when hurrying.

The only people at the ceremony will be herself and Henry, his sons, her parents and Karen Whalen, the Methodist minister who'll marry them. Joanne was raised a Presbyterian and Henry a Catholic, although they both left the church long ago, but she thought it would be nice out of respect for her parents to have the marriage sanctioned by the church and Henry agreed. She knew he'd like Karen, who was recommended by her friend Kate at Bloomingdale's. Karen married Kate and her husband Matt, another couple with an age difference, although in their case Kate's the older of the two.

She sips her wine. She can see so much of Henry in Gene's posture and facial expressions and mannerisms and speech, the little comments and observations he makes, often offbeat and tinged with irony. It's uncanny how like Henry's hands Gene's are and how they both handle things and gesture in the same way. Gene is relaxed and open, but Frank is reserved, quieter and more watchful. As different as they are she can tell they've both been affected by their experience with their parents and she wouldn't be surprised to hear that neither of them is in a relationship. She senses they're both a bit wary of her, which is understandable, given the age difference between her and their dad and the fact that they've only just met. She hasn't told them she's HIV positive and doesn't intend to. As she told Henry, there's no reason for them to know.

Henry picks up his glass of beer and sits back and looks at Gene and Frank. "Any questions?"

She sees them glance at each other and then look at their dad. Frank shakes his head but Gene cocks his slightly and looks at her.

"Why aren't you listed as a beneficiary?"

"Your dad wanted me to be. I want you two to be the sole beneficiaries." She can't read his expression but can see he's turning things over in his mind. She watches him stand and pick up his beer and walk toward the door to the backyard. She knows he's off to have a smoke and think. She watches him step outside and slowly close the door behind him. She wants to follow him but gives him five or so minutes.

She finds him standing by the fence smoking and looking up at the sky and is struck by how similar his stance is to Henry's, a hip cocked and a foot out to the side and an arm around his waist. "May I?" she asks and makes a V with her fingers. She watches his hands as he takes a cigarette out of the pack and places it between her fingers and holds the lighter up to it. She slowly inhales and blows out the smoke and they stand side by side looking up at the night sky through the trees. "How are you with all this?" she finally asks.

"It's weird. He looks so healthy." He wishes he hadn't said that and glances at her.

She smiles reassuringly. "It's okay."

He looks back up at the night sky. "How did you two meet, anyway?"

"Brooks Brothers. I wanted to order a suit for my dad as a birthday present. My dad's one of his customers. He always enjoys talking with your dad."

"Yeah, Dad's a real student of people. He loves meeting them and listening to their stories. God knows how many he's heard. He's traveled all over the world and met a lot of people."

"People fascinate him," she says. "I think himself most of all. He's writing a novel."

Gene glances at her. "He's writing again, huh? That's good." He's about to say he hopes he finishes it and catches himself.

"How's Frank doing?"

"Okay. We haven't really had time to talk. He's still a little freaked out, but that's Frank."

"Yeah, I can see that. Your dad said your mom was pretty upset when he told her."

Gene draws on his cigarette and slowly blows out the smoke. "It's good they divorced. In the end all they did was make each other miserable. I remember the day they sat me and Frank down in the living room and told us they planned to divorce and Dad asked us if we had any questions, just as he did now. Frank didn't, but I asked what took them so long. I'd been wondering. They managed to develop a good friendship after they divorced. It's only natural she'd take the news hard."

It's remarkable how talking with Gene feels so much like talking with Henry and it's interesting that when Gene and Henry talk, Gene listens respectfully to what his dad has to say and defers to him, but standing next to him and listening to him now he's different, more himself, more confident.

Gene looks at her. "I'm there for you. I want you to know that."

"Thanks, that means a lot to me."

Gene glances at Frank and sees him still staring at their dad, as he has been throughout the ceremony in the backyard, his eyes a bit glazed. He knows Frank's still processing, trying to get his head around everything. Frank's always kept his emotions close to his chest. They've always been able to talk, though, which is good. They had a couple of beers when they returned to the hotel yesterday evening and he managed to get out of him that he's conflicted, which he obviously is, sad that their dad is dying and happy that he has Joanne in his life to care for him in the time he has remaining, but still resentful of the mess he made of his marriage to their mom and what it did to them. Pretty much the way he feels himself, although not so much the resentment toward their dad. He was older and understood it for what it was, two people who probably shouldn't have been together in the first place struggling to get free of each other.

He looks back at his dad. He can only imagine what it must be like for him, knowing that he only has a short time left to live. If his doctor's right he won't live to see the baby born. He seems to be taking it in stride, though, and he sure seems happy with Joanne. Who wouldn't be? She's attractive and intelligent and decisive, a solid partner. He'd like to have someone like her in his life. As it is he's at that point in his relationship with Carol where he knows it's over and it's only a matter of time before they go their separate ways. She'll probably head back to Boston or to Denver to be near her sister.

He's only had several relationships since he left home for college and they've all lasted about the same amount of time, three or four years, and they've all ended the same way, sort of fizzling out. He took the only piece of advice about marriage his dad shared with him and Frank to heart and he knew his dad was speaking from experience: if you have any reservations about marrying someone don't. They both know their dad doesn't regret having married their mom and that he was happy that the marriage produced the two of them. He was just being clear-eyed about the subject and they appreciated it. Having seen what their parents went through, it's understandable that he and Frank are cautious about relationships, but he knows they took their dad's advice too much to heart and are always looking for reasons to have reservations where none really exists.

Karen smiles at the newlyweds and looks at Henry. "You may kiss the bride," she says and watches them turn toward each other and smile and embrace and kiss. She looks at Joanne's parents and Gene and Frank and sees happiness tinged with sadness in their faces and perhaps a bit more sadness in the sons', which is understandable. Joanne's parents' eyes are on their daughter and it's interesting that Gene's have been too, while Frank's eyes are riveted on his dad's back as they have been throughout the ceremony. Joanne and Henry finish their kiss and look at her and she smiles and takes their hands in hers. "Congratulations. I wish you both every happiness."

Joanne stands beside Henry, listening to him and her dad talk about their love of John McPhee's writing, in particular his short story "Josie's Well." She feels her mom's hand on her arm and looks at her and sees her looking at her stomach.

"How are you feeling?" Mildred asks.

"Fine. Bloated, a little nauseous, tired."

"And the baby?"

"Doing fine." She sees the familiar look of concern on her mom's face. Her mom's perfectly aware that transmission of the disease at birth with a C-section is virtually impossible. She just can't help being a mom. Joanne gives her a nudge. "Stop worrying."

"I'll take care of the scar," Bryan says.

"I'm fine with the scar, Dad. I don't need any retouching." She feels Henry give her waist a squeeze.

"No, you don't," he says.

She feels his hand on the small of her back, massaging her gently. She tries to put the thought of how much she's going to miss his touch out of her mind and sighs and rests her chin on his shoulder. She doesn't want to get morose. Not today. She wants to concentrate on enjoying this moment and the next and as many moments as there are left. There'll be time enough to mourn.

Karen's amused that Gene and Frank are surprised to hear she plays basketball with the women at the women's correctional facility in San Bernardino, as if they can't picture her on a basketball court. Why should they be surprised? She's at least a head taller than both men and even more so than Frank. Well, she is pretty laid-back off the court. "Some of them are good," she says, "really good. This one woman TJ could have played pro ball, she's got that much natural talent, but there's too much street in her. She plays dirty and it keeps tripping her up. It's easy to outsmart a player like that. I keep telling her to use her head more and play smarter, but she is who she is. People don't change that easily."

Gene sees Karen's looking at Frank but he has the feeling she's reading his mind. His phone rings and he takes it out and sees it's Carol. "Excuse me," he says and steps away.

Karen glances at him. Gene seems to be dealing with things pretty well, as well as can be expected anyway. She's not so sure about Frank here. He's quiet and hard to read and she can see there's a lot going on behind those watchful eyes. "How're you with all this?"

Frank shrugs. "Okay."

She glances at Henry and sees him standing with his arm around Joanne's waist, holding her close, and looks back at Frank. "He's happy. That's the important thing."

Frank stares at his dad. "He sure wasn't like that with our mom. I'm sure they were happy in the beginning. By the time I came along things were bad. I don't think he was ever like that, though."

"Hold it against him?"

Frank glances at her and looks back at his dad. "I guess…a bit. It's only natural. I love him, but he sure made my mom's life a living hell."

"I'm sure his life wasn't a bed of roses, either. Maybe they just weren't right for each other."

He knows she's probably right, but that doesn't alter the fact. Anyway, he's not so much resentful of his dad's happiness as he is the distrust of relationships he unknowingly instilled in him. He saw firsthand how hurtful they can be. He learned to maintain enough emotional distance from women to avoid any of that and, as a result, is close to no one. He'd like to be, but each time he senses a woman wanting to get close to him he retreats to a safe distance until she gives up trying. He's not happy about it, but he doesn't seem able to do anything about it and he's pretty much resigned to never being close to anyone. It's sad, but there it is. He looks at Karen and sees she's been studying him as he's been staring at his dad. He has the feeling she's able to read him the way she reads this woman TJ on the court. He squints his right eye slightly, as he does whenever he's about to say something he considers even remotely revealing. "I'd like to see you play sometime. I bet you're fun to watch."

She grins. "I have my moments."

Gene stares blankly at the sky. He doesn't know why the news that Carol's been fired by the new executive chef at the country club where she's been working should come as a surprise. Every situation he's been in since deciding to pursue a career as a chef has turned into a nightmare and the only reason he's still in the business is inertia. He feels sorry for Carol, and guilty. They became romantically involved shortly after he arrived at the trendy gastro pub on Capitol Hill where he still works as a sous chef. She was handling banquets and felt uneasy about being co-workers and since his chances of moving up were much better than hers, she decided to work elsewhere. He didn't think it was right that she should leave and objected but she stood firm. The last he heard she and the executive chef were getting along fine. "But you were doing a great job. You were basically running the show until he arrived."

"Yeah, well, apparently we weren't on the same page. I dunno, Gene. I've had it with Seattle and I've had it with living in a shack in the woods and I've had it with not having the same days off and hardly ever seeing each other. I've just had it."

He's not surprised to hear this. She's been voicing her unhappiness about their situation for some time now and he can hear in her voice that getting fired is the last straw. "What're you going to do?"

"I dunno. I think I'll visit my sister and check out Denver. I've got the time now. Why not?"

He glances at his dad and Joanne standing together with their arms around each other's waist. "Seems like a good idea. Beth would love to see you. I hear Denver's a nice town."

"You sound like you want me to go."

"Isn't that what you said you wanted?"

"I said I thought I'd visit my sister."

Here they go again, nibbling at the edges. He's been here before in his relationships and he knows from experience that if he lets it, which he has in the past, this phase will go on for a year or more. He looks at his dad. A year from now he'll be dead but he's going to die happy. Where will he be in a year if he does what he usually does in this situation? Right where he is now. He doesn't like Seattle or living in their cramped quarters in Lakewood any more than she does, although, honestly, he doesn't mind the fact that their schedules don't allow them to spend much time together. Looking at his dad and thinking about his situation, he realizes he hasn't really valued time, that he's been taking it for granted and wasting it in relationships that end up going nowhere, for the most part because he's unsure if he wants them to go anywhere.

He's known Carol three years now. She's a nice person. He wouldn't have become involved with her if she weren't. But when he asks himself who she is in his life and how he feels about her and is honest with himself, she's a friend, someone who makes him feel less lonely living in a city where he knows only the people at the restaurant and doesn't have time to meet anyone else. The place is different and the person is different but it's another convenient relationship and it's an all too familiar pattern. Does he really want to continue this way? He sees his dad laughing and gesturing and holding the woman he loves close by his side. What's that expression his dad's so fond of? "Better alone than in bad company?" They'll both be better off if it ends. "I think it's time we went our separate ways, Carol." He waits for her response and when it comes isn't surprised.

"So, that's it? I spend three years of my life with you and leave my job so you have a crack at becoming *chef de cuisine* and all you have to say is you think it's time we break up? You're an asshole."

He hears the call terminate and looks at the screen:

Call Ended
00:04:57

In all the time he's been with her it occurs to him that the last four minutes and fifty-seven seconds have been the most important and valuable. He has been an asshole. Thinking that he could outrun himself by moving across the country to a new city and starting out fresh was an assholish idea to begin with. He hadn't changed and wasn't ready to change, but what's happened to his dad has given him a new appreciation of time and he's determined not to waste any more of his life hiding out in relationships. If he's ever in one again it'll be because he wants to be and he'll be present and engaged in it and work hard to make it succeed. As for being a chef, he's had it with *sous-vide.* He loves to prepare simple delicious meals and can cook for himself whenever he wants. It's time to stop punishing himself and put his chemistry degree to better use.

Kaitlin watches Henry collect Michael's paperwork as she waits for Michael to change out of his outfit in the dressing room. They're very pleased with how well things turned out, as Henry had assured them they would. Michael looks great in his outfit. At Henry's suggestion they decided on a tuxedo. He said that every man should have his own tux and that when you do, you find all sorts of reasons to wear it. That's been his experience anyway. It will compliment perfectly the white silk dress she's decided on. They also went with his suggestion about the piquet bib-front tuxedo shirt, which he said is a nice change of pace from the traditional pleated tux shirt and he's right. She couldn't be happier. "Thanks for all your help, Henry. You've been great."

"Michael's order is my last," he says and anticipates her surprise.

"You're leaving?"

"Yes, to finish a novel."

"That's wonderful! What's it about?"

He shrugs. "Life."

"You must hear a lot of stories."

"I do." He wishes he knew more about theirs. He's spent a few hours in total with them but he remembers the dynamic between Kaitlin and Michael when they first met. She was quiet and all eyes and seemed to have a lot on her mind and Michael was relaxed and easy-going and did all the talking and seemed like he was being very patient with her. Something's happened between them because they've arrived at a different place now. They seem much more comfortable with each other, more like partners who understand each other and work well together knowing they can trust and rely on each other. They've developed their own non-verbal language, which they use to communicate how they feel about things. She'll place her hand on Michael's arm and gently stroke it when she's considering something and he'll massage the small of her back or the back of her neck as he listens to her. It's openly intimate and nice to see. He's been admiring Kaitlin's necklace ever since they arrived. "That's a beautiful necklace."

"Thank you. A friend made it." His mention of the necklace and thinking of Magda brings the Berlin trip to mind, in particular the fact that it ended her habit of fingering the pendant nervously.

He leans forward. "It's a glider, isn't it?"

"Yes! How did you know?"

"I'm familiar with the medal." He studies the pendant and remembers the conversation he had with the Director at the lightweight container glass manufacturing company near Hannover. They were in the Director's office on a coffee break Henry could ill afford to take from videotaping operations in the plant for a product video he was producing for a computer company, but the Director had graciously invited him to join him and he knew he had to accept, European business culture being the way it was then. He and the Director sat in comfortable wing chairs with a silver coffee pot and two white porcelain cups and saucers on a silver salver on the table between them. It was very civilized. He noticed the glider pin on the Director's lapel as the secretary was pouring their coffee and asked him about it. The Director told him he belonged to a glider club and that his father flew gliders and was recruited into the Luftwaffe, at which point he stood and walked to his desk and opened a draw and returned with his father's Glider Pilot Badge of the German Air Force and handed it to him. "He was proud to be a glider pilot," the Director said, implying that was all his father was proud of about his service in the Luftwaffe.

"My friend flies them," Kaitlin says. "Her grandfather flew them."

Henry sits back. "Never flown in a glider. Have you?"

She nods and smiles. "It was an amazing experience." She wants to say terrifying and life-altering too and knows he would enjoy the story but leaves it at that. She's sure he's heard more than enough stories.

"I bet it was," he says and adds "flying in a glider" to the growing mental list of things he knows he'll never experience.

She studies his face. He seems lost in gazing at the pendant. It obviously has significance to him and she feels the urge to give it to him. She knows Magda wouldn't mind. After all, she did the same thing. "Do you think your wife would like it?"

He looks at her, surprised by the suggestion. "I couldn't take it."

"My friend will make me another." She unfastens the chain and takes it from around her neck and holds it out to him. "A belated wedding present."

He hesitates.

"Please! I insist!"

He smiles and leans forward and reaches out his hand and watches the necklace slither from her hand into his like a living thing and come to rest curled up in his palm. He closes his hand around it and feels its coolness against his skin. "Thank you. She'll love it."

Michael comes from the dressing room and hangs his outfit on the rack next to the desk. He sits next to Kaitlin and puts his hand on the back of her neck and gently massages it.

"Henry's leaving Brooks Brothers," she says. "You're his last customer."

Michael raises his eyebrows and looks at him. "I'm honored. Why're you leaving?"

"He's writing a novel," she says.

"I'm not surprised. Can we get a copy?"

Henry nods. "I have your email."

"Great!" Michael says and realizes Kaitlin's necklace is missing and looks at her. "Where's your necklace?"

"I gave it to Henry as a wedding present for his wife."

Henry shrugs. "She wouldn't take no for an answer."

Michael looks at her and smiles. "She's getting to be like that."

"So, all set with the wedding plans?" Henry asks.

Kaitlin nods. "Pretty much."

"It'll be a great day." He takes a mental snapshot of them as they are now, sitting across the desk from him with so much having passed between them as a couple and their journey together through life really only just begun. He's played his small part in it and now it's over. Chances are he'll be dead by their wedding day. If they think of him it will be just as he is now and if they think of him when Michael wears his tux afterward it will be the same, always the same. They'll be looking at the light of a long gone distant star, just as Joanne said. Mortality is no longer just a word to him. It's a heaviness he feels in his bones now. "I wish you both every happiness. It's been a pleasure." He stands and takes Michael's suit and shirt from the rack. "I'll get these in a garment bag for you."

"Don't forget about that copy of the novel," Michael says.

"I won't," Henry says and looks at Kaitlin and winks. "Have a ball and hoist one for me."

"We will."

Michael drapes the garment bag over the back of a chair at their outside table. "Be right back," he says and heads inside the restaurant.

Kaitlin takes her phone out of her bag. It seems the right time to call Magda, having just given the necklace to Henry. They haven't spoken since Berlin. She's been meaning to call her but has been putting it off. She feels the same way now she did then about what happened, but she's unsure how Magda feels about it and whether she still considers her a friend. She stares at her fingernails and listens to the rings. "Ciao! How are you?" she hears Magda say cheerily and feels relieved. "Fine! I've been meaning to call you!"

"Same here! Aiyee! One thing leads to another!"

"So, I'm calling to remind you about the wedding. It's October 30th in Hawaii. Are you still planning to come?"

"Yes! I wouldn't miss it! May I bring a guest?"

"Of course! Who?"

"Gretchen. You haven't met her."

Gretchen? She didn't think anything about Magda would surprise her and she doesn't know why this does. She doesn't have to ask if Gretchen is just a good friend. She can hear in Magda's voice that she's much more than that. "I look forward to meeting her. I'll send you the hotel info and stuff."

"Great."

"Listen, I gave the necklace to someone."

"You did? To whom?"

She knew Magda wouldn't be upset, just surprised and curious. "A man named Henry at Brooks Brothers. He helped us with Michael's outfit for the wedding."

"Brooks Brothers! My father loves Brooks Brothers! I remember we visited the store in Manhattan, on Madison Avenue I think it was. He was in heaven! So, why did you give it to him?"

"The way he was admiring it. He's been very nice and helpful. He married recently. I gave it to him as a present for his wife."

"You see? It has a life of its own and wants to keep moving. Who knows what will become of it? I'll make you another, not a copy, something else, as a wedding present."

"Has the swastika piece sold yet?"

"Yes! A wealthy businessman from Buenos Aires bought it, just as I predicted. My guess is he's either a closet neo-Nazi or a collector of Nazi memorabilia. Maybe he didn't know what he was looking at and just bought it as a pretty trinket for his wife or mistress. Who knows? Trying to maintain my balance between art and politics – It's like walking a tightrope. I'm always afraid of falling."

"Yeah. I can understand that. It's a delicate business."

"So, are you excited?"

"Honestly, no. I mean, I'm looking forward to it, celebrating with family and friends, but it seems more for their benefit than ours. Know what I mean?"

"I think so. I think a lot of brides feel that way. All that planning! It must be exhausting!"

"There's that, but it just seems like a formality to me. That's all it is anyway, making things legal. I won't feel any closer to Michael after we're married than I do now. I don't think it's possible to feel any closer to him. A lot changed for me on that trip. I have you to thank for that." She didn't want to bring up what happened or refer to it in any way, but it slipped out and now she wouldn't be surprised if Magda cuts the call short. She listens to the awkward silence and is beginning to think she should break it.

"I wish I could be as understanding as you," Magda finally says. "Well, I learned a thing or two about myself when you were here. I have you both to thank for that and especially that man of yours. He's really something."

"Yes, he is. You sound happy."

"I am! It's wonderful! It's Gretchen! We complement each other perfectly."

"Give her my best and tell her I'm looking forward to meeting her."

"I will. Give my best to 'Marathon Man.'"

She hears someone giggling in the background. It must be Gretchen and Magda's obviously told her about Michael's performance. "I will. Bye." She stares at the screen. What must the perfect complement to Magda be like? She can only imagine.

CHAPTER 19

June takes a bite of jam-covered toast and chews slowly as she watches Eileen at the kitchen counter pour hot water into her cup for tea. Eileen was out again last night "with friends", which is all she says lately when she goes out for the evening. June doesn't press her for details. She's happy Eileen's getting out more often and seems to be having a good time, whatever she's doing and with whomever she's doing it with. June doesn't think it's with Roland. Eileen hasn't mentioned him in a while. She seems different this morning, though. She definitely has something on her mind. June watches her bring her cup and plate of toast to the table and set them down and pull back the chair and sit, her thoughts clearly elsewhere. "Have fun last night, Mom?"

"I did, thanks."

"Dinner?"

Eileen nods.

"With?"

"Friends." Eileen lifts her cup with both hands and blows on her tea and takes a careful sip and places the cup back on the saucer. She picks up a piece of toast and begins spreading jam on it, studying her handiwork like a bricklayer. "How are things with you and Art?"

June glances down at her wedding band. It just seemed right to begin wearing it again when she left Walt's. Putting it on felt like putting a period at the end of the last sentence in an awful chapter in her life. How are things with her and Art…? "Okay, same as usual. Kind of in limbo."

Eileen raises her eyebrows but keeps her eyes on the piece of toast. "It's been that way for some time. Do you two have any plans?"

June shrugs and looks down at her coffee. "Art wants to get back together. You know that."

Eileen nods.

"I'm not sure what I want. We've been through a lot, Mom. I know he's trying to turn his life around. He's doing a pretty good job of it. I'll give him that. But some wounds take a long time to heal. I don't have to tell you."

Eileen nods again. "Well, it would be wonderful for the children if you two got back together."

June knows her mother-in-law well enough to know there's something going on in that head of hers. "Is there something you want to talk about?"

"No, no, I was just wondering."

Right, just wondering. Well, whatever it is she'll hear about it soon enough.

She takes her bagged sandwich and drink from Maria, a petite Latina with sparkling brown eyes and a bright smile and her favorite counter person at the cafe where she buys lunch at work. She knows from their brief chats that Maria's boyfriend Arturo didn't want to get engaged until he was earning enough to support them and send remittances home to his family in Guatemala and now there's an engagement ring on her finger. "Soon?" June asks hopefully.

Maria nods excitedly.

"I'm so happy for you!" June says and remembers the day Art put the engagement ring on her finger. The world seemed full of possibilities and the future looked bright and thinking about how things have changed saddens her.

She walks outside and sits at one of the tables and takes her sandwich from the bag and unwraps it and looks around at the people at the other tables, most of them employees dressed in black, as she is. She wasn't able to give Trey a good answer when he asked why people in retail wear black and now she wonders why herself. As if working in retail isn't depressing enough. It's like they're all in mourning for the lives they wish they were living.

She feels old and tired of the same routine. All she does is work and her days off are spent catching up on things she hasn't had time to do. She takes a bite of her sandwich and chews slowly as she looks around at the other employees eating their lunches. There has to be more to life than this.

She notices a pair of crows standing side by side on the curb beneath the hedges. One crow, the male she assumes, is pecking at the back of his mate's neck, lifting up the feathers like he's grooming her. The female seems to like it or doesn't seem to mind and stands staring straight ahead as the male pecks at her.

Maybe it's that her fortieth birthday is only two years away. She's always told herself that age doesn't matter, but maybe she's just been fooling herself. It seems she was just a kid and then a teenager and then engaged and married and then a mother of two and soon she'll be forty and feels joyless and weighed down by responsibility and if almost forty years have passed this quickly she can see that she'll be eighty before she knows it and can't imagine spending the next forty years feeling this way.

She notices the male crow's pecking is becoming more insistent. He's forcing the female's head down and draping his outstretched wing over her back and it's clear now that he's going to mount her. She feels a little embarrassed for the crows and glances around to see if anyone else is watching them. Apparently she's the only one. With a flap of his wings the male crow hops on the female's back and she spreads her wings against the curb to steady herself as he enters her and begins jerking violently. Not much difference between birds and people. You just do what comes naturally, which for female crows means letting your mate peck your neck and groom your feathers and push your head down and finally hop on your back and have his way with you. Not much difference at all.

"They're certainly enjoying themselves," she hears a man with what she recognizes to be an Iranian accent say and looks up to see him standing there holding a bag and drink and looking at the crows with raised eyebrows. He looks at her and smiles.

"Crowded today," he says. "Mind if I join you?"

She smiles and pulls her things a little closer to make room for him. "No, not at all." He looks to be around fifty and is handsome with an olive complexion and dark brown eyes and black hair. He's impeccably dressed in a black suit and white shirt with French cuffs and silver and black and blue plaid tie and matching silver pocket square. He's obviously an employee at one of the high-end stores and reminds her of Henry and she guesses he also sells men's suits. He takes a sandwich out of his bag and unwraps it.

"Where do you work?" he asks.

"Macy's."

"Ah! I work at Bloomingdale's. So, we're family. Sharam," he says and bows his head slightly.

"June, nice to meet you. Which department?"

"Men's Suits." He glances at her wedding band. "Does your husband buy his suits at Macy's?"

"He doesn't wear suits. He bought an outfit recently at Brooks Brothers. I bought my son clothes for cotillion there too. Pricey, but worth it."

"Did Henry assist you?"

"Yes! You know him?"

"Of course. He's the best. He's leaving in a month or so."

"Oh, I didn't know! Is he retiring? He doesn't seem that old."

"He's writing a novel. Says he's going to devote his time to finishing it. He married recently. I haven't met his wife. She's much younger. I told him, 'Good for you! She'll keep you young!'"

June glances at Sharam's wedding band. "Does your wife work in retail?"

He finishes chewing and sips his drink. "She did. She died several years ago. Cervical cancer."

"Oh, I'm so sorry."

He shrugs. "She's gone but not gone. We're like birds that mate for life." He nods toward the crows, now standing side by side again on the curb. "Maybe like those two. She will always be the love of my life. Just thinking about her comforts and encourages and inspires me."

"That's so...sweet...really," June says. Now she feels guilty for having allowed herself to wallow in self-pity. She knows Art loves her and that despite everything she still loves him and that it would be better for the four of them if they were back together, but while he's been trying to win her back, she's been passive and non-committal and feeling sorry for herself. Is she experiencing a mid-life crisis? Well, whatever it is she's going through, some mate she is. It's a wonder Art's still trying. "I'm sorry," she says, "your name again?"

"Sharam."

"Yes, forgive me, it's a beautiful name. It was nice meeting you." She stuffs the sandwich wrapper and napkin into her lunch bag. "And thank you for telling me about your wife."

He nods. "Nice meeting you too. It was a pleasure."

June steps out onto the patio with her phone in hand and squints in the bright sunlight and looks around at the buds on the trees that are just beginning to open. "April," she remembers her sister saying, "from the Latin *aperire,* 'to open.'" Named for her birth month, as they both were, April studied up on hers when she was a kid and learned that she and Buddha share the same birthday, April 8th. "That's about all we have in common," April said. "I've got more in common with a pit bull than Buddha." She's the one who said it and she knew what she was talking about. April learned that her birthstone was the diamond and joked, "Yeah, we'll see how many of those I get." None as far as June knows. April insisted that Jack not buy her an engagement ring saying it was a waste of money, which, strictly speaking, it is. That's April.

June sits at the table and calls her and puts the phone to her ear. "Hey, how are you?" she hears April ask. "Fine. Happy Birthday, Buddha!"

April guffaws. "Yeah, right. What's the weather like there? Tell me it's beautiful."

"It's beautiful. The buds are opening on the trees."

"You'd never know it's spring here. There's still three feet of snow on the ground."

"No one held a gun to your head."

"I'm not complaining. It suits me fine. I just got off the phone with Mom and Dad. Haven't spoken with them in a while. We had a nice chat."

"Neither have I. I've been meaning to call them. How are they?"

"Okay. Dad's working on Grady's boat now. He spends enough time on it he should get paid for it. Mom's Mom. She's got a million things going on. Said she's put on some weight so she and Janice have started going for long walks every day."

"That's good. How's Jack?"

"Fine. He's working on the snowmobile. He may get an article about the trip published in *Outside.*"

"Wow! That would be great! Tell him I'll keep my fingers crossed."

"I will. How are the kids? I'm not sure I'd recognize them now."

"Doing well. Growing up. You remember how it is."

"Brother, do I ever. What's up with asshole?"

June sighs, not surprised but saddened to hear that April's animosity toward Art is as strong as ever. "We see each other now and then. We have dinner with the kids, sometimes just the two of us." She isn't surprised by April's silence, either. She knows what her sister wants to say is that she thinks she's a fool for having anything to do with him but doesn't want to and is trying to think of something else to say but having a hard time. June spares her and breaks the silence. "He wants to get back together, Sis. He's been doing a pretty good job turning his life around. He's getting his teacher certification. He had a lot of issues with his father to deal with and maybe he didn't do such a good job of dealing with them. Nobody's perfect."

"Issues with his father — What a pile of horseshit. Well, you do as you please. He wouldn't get a second chance with me."

"Jesus. What if everybody were like you?"

"The world would be a better place. Believe me."

"Listen, April, I might not agree with you but you're my sister and I love you. I need to know that if Art and I get back together you're not going to let it come between us. I don't want you out of my life. Your Trey and Kim's aunt, for God's sake." June listens, waiting for April's answer. She knows just what her sister looks like on the other end of the call, scowling, her eyes fixed on something, her lips pressed so tightly together that the blood has drained out of them.

"Yeah," April finally says, "don't worry. I'm there for you."

"Thanks. It means a lot to me."

"Good hearing from you, Sis. Thanks for the call."

"Enjoy the rest of the day, Buddha. Talk with you soon." June puts the phone on the table and looks at the opening buds on the trees. It's the time of rebirth and renewal and it's ironic that she's been defending Art while she's been reluctant to give him a second chance. Sure, they see each other, but she's kept her distance emotionally and through it all he's been patient and understanding, careful not to pressure her, letting her take her sweet time making up her mind about what she wants to do. Not many men would have worked as hard as Art has to win back a woman's love and not many men would have put up with such an undecided and unenthusiastic woman, not for long anyway. Can she be happy with Art again? Can she make him happy? Is it possible she's forgotten how?

She finds Henry sitting at the desk in Men's Suits working on someone's order and looking dapper, as usual. "Hi, Henry."

He looks up and smiles. "June! What a pleasant surprise!" He stands and walks around the desk and gives her hug. "It's great to see you," he says and motions her toward a chair and sits facing her. "How've you been?"

"Fine, and you?"

"Fine. How's the family?"

"Everyone's doing well. I met your friend Sharam recently at lunch."

"Ah! A charming guy. We worked together once."

"He is. He said you're leaving Brooks Brothers."

"Yes, at the end of the month. I'm just finishing up a few customers' orders and then — *finito.*"

"He said you're writing a novel."

"I am."

"That's wonderful! What's it about? I know some writers don't like to talk about their work."

He shrugs. "Life."

"I can't wait to read it.

He takes a notepad from the desk and a pen from his pocket and hands them to her. "Give me your email address." He studies June's face as she writes. She looks weary. "Still with Walt?"

She shakes her head. "A lot's changed since we last saw each other."

He notices she's wearing her wedding band. "You and Art back together?" he asks hopefully.

She shakes her head and hands the notepad and pen back to him. "That hasn't changed."

He keeps his eyes on hers as he tears off the top sheet and folds it and puts it in his shirt pocket with his pen and tosses the notepad on the desk. He can see she's struggling with her feelings for Art.

"So," she says, "Sharam mentioned you married! That's wonderful! Congratulations!"

"Thank you."

"Who's the lucky lady?"

"Her name is Joanne. She's an analyst at PACBOND. She's younger."

"Sharam mentioned that. She must be really something."

He nods. "She is."

"How'd you two meet?"

He hesitates and considers which version of the story to tell her. He could easily tell her the one without Art in it. He knows the way Art feels about her and that he wants her back, but he has the feeling they're still going round in circles and that it's because of her uncertainty about her feelings for him and what she wants. Perhaps the thing to do is precisely what his instinct is telling him not to. "Art introduced us." He watches her eyes widen.

"Art?"

He nods. "They met when he was doing construction work on her house. They saw each other for a while, more as friends than anything. Not long after she stopped in to have a suit made for her dad for his birthday and, well, the rest, as they say, is history."

She leans forward slightly and looks at him intently. "What's she like?"

"Attractive, brunette, light brown eyes, intelligent, witty...." He sees this isn't doing anything for her. "The first thing I noticed about her was her fingers and toes."

June nods slowly and leans closer. "What about them?"

"They're long and slender, very sexy."

She can see in his eyes he's completely in love with her. Art looked that way once, when he told her the first thing he noticed about her was the sweep of her neck and collarbones and shoulders. For her it was the veins in his forearms. She remembers thinking she was a freak for being fascinated by them. What type of person finds the veins in someone's forearms fascinating? A vampire! They seemed alive under his skin and she couldn't stop looking at them and stroking them. She would have been perfectly happy at the time doing that forever. She looks at Henry and smiles. "I'm so happy for you both."

He leans forward and takes her hands in his. "I know it's none of my business, June, but I hope things work out."

She suddenly feels like crying and catches her breath and glances around. She doesn't want to cry here, although she knows Henry wouldn't mind. She looks in his eyes. "Have you ever been loved by someone and felt that person's love was the best thing that ever happened to you and that loving that person back was the best thing for you to do but were afraid to do it?"

He smiles and nods and squeezes her hands. "June, it's the story of my life."

The food is advertised as "authentic Irish cuisine" and maybe it was hundreds of years ago when June's ancestors were living in peat houses and boiling everything to death on an open fire. It was Art's idea to try this restaurant and she was game, but as soon as the plates were put in front of them piled high with mousy-colored meat and over-cooked potatoes she suspected they were in for a bad meal and one mouthful confirmed it. The food is almost tasteless. Art usually has no problem cleaning his plate but even he's given up and has turned his attention to enjoying his beer, which she now knows is the real business of the place. She listens as he tells her about his latest read, *The Hidden Reality,* and while the possibility of other universes existing alongside ours seems plausible, she can't quite get her head around it and finally has had enough of hearing about all this airy mathematical conjecture and puts her fork on the side of her plate, maybe a little too loudly, and sits back and crosses her arms. "What're we doing?" she asks.

"Whaddya mean?"

The waitress arrives and eyes June's plate. "Everything okay?"

"Fine," she says, keeping her eyes on Art's.

"Just not hungry?"

She shakes her head.

"All done?"

She nods.

"Can I wrap it up for you?"

"No thanks."

The waitress takes her plate and glances at her empty glass. "Another?"

"Please."

The waitress glaces at Art's almost empty glass and looks at him and sees him nods and walks away.

"What's up?" he asks, a bit puzzled by her question and concerned, given the way she sounded and now looks, that what he's about to hear is that she's decided they should stop seeing each other like this.

"I went to see Henry."

He smiles. "How's he doing?"

"He's leaving Brooks Brothers. He's writing a book."

"I'm not surprised. I bet it'll be good."

"He told me about Joanne." She waits to see what his reaction will be but there isn't much of one, just curiosity, like she told him she's decided to change her hair color.

"What about her?"

"That you two were dating and that they're married."

He smiles again and sits back in his chair. "Yeah, we were for a while. I'll be damned."

"Why didn't you tell me about her?"

"You were with Walt."

Okay, fair enough. "What's she like? Describe her to me."

"She's an analyst at PACBOND. Very sharp."

"Notice anything about her?"

"Such as?"

"I dunno, anything? Her fingers, her toes?"

"She has ten of each," he says, puzzled by her mention of them.

She's about to ask if they had sex but thinks better of it. What difference does it make? She can tell by what Art said and the way he said it that Joanne was just a friend. It's fascinating to her that the same person who Art considered a friend could so captivate Henry. How does that happen and do we have any control over it? She doesn't think so. It's the same with her and Art. She knew from the moment she met him that her feelings for him were different and she knows it was the same for him and despite everything that's happened between them that feeling of specialness, of being meant for each other is still there. The bond has been tested time and again and strained to the breaking point but it's still in tact. Could she ever feel this way about another man? It's possible, the way multiple universes are possible. She gives them better odds.

They're silent on the drive home, feeling there's too much to say and uncertain where to begin. Art pulls into the driveway and June watches him move to open his door to get out and walk around and open hers as he always does when he drops her off, but she places her hand on his forearm to stop him and he turns and she sees him searching her eyes in the darkness as she searches his.

So, here they are. They've been stuck, unable to move forward because of her doubt and indecision and now it's up to her to decide what happens next. She asks herself one last time what she truly wants and the answer is as it always has been lately, to have the man she loves back in her life and to have him love her and to love him as she once did. Will they be able to? She's not sure. Anyway, she hopes so and that's better than where they are now. She smiles and sees him smile. "Stay," she says.

Eileen looks up from the newspaper at June and Art as they enter the kitchen, June in her bathrobe and Art in the same sport shirt and slacks she saw yesterday evening when he picked up June. "Well, this is a pleasant surprise!"

"Mornin'," June says and takes two mugs from the cabinet.

"I thought I heard a man in the house last night," Eileen says.

Art smiles and sits across from her. "Was my snoring that loud?"

"Your snoring was fine," June says and fills the mugs with coffee.

"How was the restaurant?"

"Awful food." June says and places a mug in front of Art and sits next to him.

"Good beer, though," Art says.

Eileen studies their faces as they sip their coffee. She can see things have changed. It's there in their eyes. She can hear it in their voices. They're easier with each other now. Well, no time like the present. "I have a little confession to make. I haven't been going out with friends." She looks at Art. "Your father and I have been seeing each other."

Art and June look at each other and stare at her wide-eyed.

"He wants to give it another try."

"And?" Art asks.

"I want to. He's a different man now. He can thank Landis for that. It was all finally too much for him. He's much calmer now, more settled, more at peace with himself. I want to say he's more like the man I first met but he's never really been the way his is now."

June reaches across the table and puts her hand on Eileen's. "That's great news, Mom. I'm happy for you both."

"Thank you, dear. I wanted to tell you, but...." Eileen looks at Art and back at June and smiles. "It wasn't the right time. Anyway...." She looks around at the kitchen and back at Art. "There's this house."

"It's a lousy time to put it on the market, Mom."

"I'm not thinking of selling it. Your father and I don't need all this room. His condo is all we need. It's nice and cozy. We want you to live here with your family." She looks from Art to June and back at Art. "It's about time, don't you think? You owe it to yourselves and the kids." She watches him look at June and June at him. She knows just how they feel, afraid of letting each other down again but hopeful they've learned how not to and wanting to try. June looks forgiving and Art grateful and their eyes are filled with love.

June puts her hand on Art's forearm and looks at Eileen and nods. "Yeah, Mom, we do."

CHAPTER 20

Kim eyes the people coming and going at the Forever 21 entrance to South Coast Plaza. "Luck doesn't have anything to do with it," she says. "You've gotten better and most of your teammates have too. That's why you've done so well."

Cyd puts another spoonful of Cherry Vanilla ice cream in her mouth and savors it thoughtfully. "I guess. We're not as good as you guys, that's for sure."

"Anything can happen. You know that." Kim digs her spoon into her Chocolate Chip Cookie Dough.

"If we end up playing each other," Cyd says, "I want you to win."

Kim looks at her and narrows her eyes. "Waddya mean?"

Cyd shrugs. "I want you to win and be MVP. That's all."

"If we end up playing each other you have to defend against me the best you can."

Cyd looks at her and back at the people and shrugs.

"Promise me!"

Cyd shrugs again.

"You owe it to me and your team!"

Cyd looks at her. "You're my best friend. It's important to me."

"Well, it's important to me that I earn it. It won't mean anything if I don't, so promise me!"

Cyd shrugs and looks away again. "Sure."

Kim puts another spoonful of ice cream in her mouth and wonders at the fact that at mid-season the possibility of their teams playing each other for the league championship seemed remote, but now it seems almost inevitable. Cyd's team only has to beat Oak Canyon, a team they've done well against all season, and her team only has to beat Vista Mar, who they've dominated. She'll have to keep working on Cyd about this. It won't do to have her walk through the championship game and hand her a win and the MVP title. "Do you think she's pretty?" she hears Cyd ask and is surprised by the question, mainly because it's the first time she's ever heard Cyd use the word "pretty." She sees her looking at a girl around their age walking quickly toward the plaza entrance. The girl has shoulder-length blonde hair and looks to Kim like a walking advertisement for Victoria's Secret, a store she's always considered silly with its bowed and frilly bras and panties and "PINK" printed on everything. "I guess," she says. "Why?"

Cyd shrugs, gazing at the girl. "I dunno. I don't feel very pretty."

There's the word again. Kim looks at Cyd's hair. The first thing she noticed when Cyd arrived was that she's wearing it longer now and kind of styled. It looks nice. She studies Cyd's profile, her gently sloping forehead and wing-like eyebrow and straight, slightly upturned nose and full lips and sharp chin and long neck and strong shoulders and shapely arms. She's always thought Cyd's pretty, although she's never told her. Cyd didn't seem to care about her looks but she sure seems to now. "I think you're pretty."

Cyd looks at her skeptically. "You do?"

"Yeah."

"Well, I don't feel pretty," she says and looks away again.

Kim scrapes up the last of her ice cream and puts it in her mouth and sucks on the spoon and puts it in her cup. "So what's with looking pretty all of a sudden?" she asks and Cyd shrugs.

They stroll toward Macy's and check out the window displays and pass by Victoria's Secret and Kim's suddenly aware that Cyd's no longer beside her and turns to see her standing by the window staring at something. She walks back and sees it's a white lace-trim panty with a pink and black leopard skin pattern and matching bra. She glances at Cyd, who seems hypnotized by it."C'mon," she says and takes Cyd's hand and leads her toward the entrance. "Let's check it out."

She never thought she'd ever actually set foot in this store. From outside it looks like a dark cave aglow with lurid red light and that's just how it is inside. She's surrounded by all manner of underwear and the entire idea of the place just seems silly to her. Underwear's underwear, what's the big deal? It sure seems to be to the women and girls browsing in the store, though. They stand in front of the displays and admire the bras and panties like they're works of art in a museum and the group of teenage girls gathered around a table heaped with thongs are positively giddy as they pick up this one and that and hold them against themselves and wiggle and giggle. She looks at

Cyd and Cyd still has that same expression on her face, like she's hypnotized.

They wander through the store looking at the items on display and Kim stops a passing salesperson, an attractive young woman wearing a pink top and pink and white striped short shorts. "Where's that leopard skin set you have in the window?"

"Sure. Over here."

The young woman turns and Kim sees "LOVE PINK" printed in purple across her butt and they follow her. What's so special about pink and who came up with this pink for girls and blue for boys business anyway? She just doesn't get it.

"Here you go," the young woman says and points to a row of the sets hanging on a rack. She looks at Kim and raises her eyebrows. "For you?"

Kim nods toward Cyd. "My friend."

The young woman eyes Cyd and takes one of the sets off the rack and holds it out to her. "Try this. It should be your size."

Cyd takes it and looks at Kim. "Try something on with me."

"I don't need any underwear."

"C'mon, just for fun."

The young woman smiles and eyes Kim and walks away and returns holding a sporty gray cotton set with purple accents and holds it out to her. "Try this. I think it'll look nice on you."

Kim takes it and looks at it and has to admit that it is more the type of thing she'd choose if she were going to buy something, which she isn't.

The young woman nods toward the dressing rooms. "Over there."

They close the door and begin undressing, putting their clothes in separate piles on the bench. Kim glances at Cyd as they do. She can see that while her own body still looks boyish, Cyd's is much more developed. She actually has breasts and curvy hips and a nice butt. They put on their sets and stand side by side checking themselves and each other out in the mirror. "I look like a boy in girl's underwear," Kim says and sees Cyd frown at her.

"You don't. You look pretty."

There's that word again and Kim watches Cyd stand behind her and bring her face next to hers and thrills at the feel of Cyd's hands on her shoulders.

"You should wear your hair longer," Cyd says, pressing her cheek against Kim's and gazing at her in the mirror.

"Think so?" How she wishes Cyd would do more with those hands.

"Yeah. I think you have really pretty eyes."

There's that word again and she's beginning to really like the sound of it. "Think so? I think yours are pretty too." She looks at her own flat chest in the mirror and then at Cyd's breasts and admires the cleavage the bra she's wearing has created. "I wish I had boobs like yours."

You will," Cyd says. "Anyway, it's not how big they are that matters."

This sounds promising. "Whaddya mean?"

"It's how sensitive they are. Remember Jenny's?"

She does and thinking about Jenny's breasts and what Sarah did with them makes her nipples hard and she feels a tingling sensation between her legs. She sees her nipples poking against the thin fabric of her bra and sees Cyd's looking at them too and grinning.

"I bet yours are really sensitive too," Cyd says.

They are, very, as she well knows from touching herself and the prospect of Cyd touching them is dizzying. She wants Cyd to more than anything and thinks she's going to but isn't sure and helps her along. "I dunno…let's see…," she says and watches Cyd's hands move to her breasts and feels them touching her and then gently fondling her. Cyd begins brushing her nipples with a finger and Kim gazes at her eyes in the mirror and it feels amazing and she doesn't want her to stop, ever.

"Well?" Cyd asks.

"Yeah…they are…very…." Kim says. The tingling sensation between her legs is increasing and it occurs to her that she's wearing a panty she's planning to hand back to the young woman and won't be able to if they're wet. She sees Cyd looking at her crotch now.

"I bet you're really sensitive down there too."

As amazing as Cyd's touching her breasts and nipples feels, the thought of her actually touching her down there transports Kim to a place she's only been in her fantasies. She's never wanted anything more than to feel Cyd's hand between her legs. "I dunno…let's see…," she says softly and watches Cyd's hand move down her body and slide beneath the waistband of her panty and feels it arrive between her legs. She spreads them wider and leans back against Cyd, just like the women in that sculpture did against her lover. She reaches back and places her hands on that nice butt of Cyd's and pulls her closer. She gazes at Cyd's eyes in the mirror as she slowly strokes her and now Cyd moves her hand inside her bra and Kim thrills at the feel of Cyd's hand against her skin as she fondles her breast and rolls her nipple between her thumb and forefinger.

She closes her eyes and remembers lying in bed touching herself and imagining how it would feel if Cyd were doing the touching. She knew it would feel good, but what she imagined was nothing compared with the way she feels now. "Hmm...," she hears Cyd purr in her ear, "feel good?" "Yeah...great...." She feels Cyd press her cheek harder against hers and opens her eyes slightly and sees Cyd gazing at her in the mirror with that sweet smile, which only adds to her pleasure. No one's ever looked at her the way Cyd is now and it seems to her by Cyd's dreamy expression and the way she's touching her that Cyd's enjoying giving her pleasure as much as she's enjoying receiving it.

She closes her eyes again. "Do you climax?" she hears Cyd whisper and the question sends a thrill so strong through her body that it takes her breath away. "Almost...I get close...not yet...." She feels Cyd place a finger lightly on her clit and a finger on either side of it and begin stroking her. "Maybe you just need a little help," she hears Cyd whisper and knows she's grinning by the sound of her voice. She feels Cyd pressing a little harder on her clit as she strokes it, slowly at first, then a little faster and faster still, increasing the pressure as she does. She squirms and begins breathing faster and shallower as the sensation she feels between her legs surpasses what's she's felt before. It's deeper and more intense and she feels it filling up her body and taking control of it. Cyd presses even harder and begins stroking her faster and she begins trembling and her legs begin shaking and she's standing on tiptoes now and can barely keep her feet on the floor as she thrusts against Cyd's fingers. It doesn't seem possible that the pleasure she's experiencing could intensify, but it does and she opens her mouth and squeezes her eyes shut as tightly as she can. She wants to make noise as she climaxes, feeling the pleasure explode between her legs, but bites her lip and forces herself not to.

She feels Cyd's arms around her waist now, holding her tightly and Cyd's keeping her cheek pressed against hers and she takes a deep breath and blows out slowly, then another and another and finally opens her eyes and sees Cyd smiling sweetly at her. She looks at her own face in the mirror and sees that her cheeks and neck are rosy pink. Maybe that's what "LOVE PINK" means. Well, she and Cyd have their own secret now. She gazes at Cyd's eyes and remembers wondering if there's a line between feeling the way Sarah and Jenny did about each other and being lesbian and she knows now there is, especially having met Angie and Phyllis, that the two things have a lot in common but are different. "Thanks," she whispers.

"That's what friends are for," Cyd says and kisses her on the cheek.

Kim watches sadly as Cyd unwraps her arms from around her waist and moves to her side and begins studying herself in the mirror again, turning her body this way and that. "You look great in that," she says encouragingly.

"Think so?" Cyd asks uncertainly.

"Yeah. You should buy it."

Cyd glances at the price tag. "Huh. Maybe I will. What about you?"

"I told you. I don't need any underwear." Kim watches Cyd look herself up and down and sees she's still uncertain.

"I dunno...," Cyd says. "What's the point? No one's gonna see it anyway."

The idea comes to Kim and she grins. It happens like that sometimes. It just comes to her. She doesn't know how or why or from where, but it does and she knows just what to do. "Buy it," she says, sounding just like her mom when her decision is final. She steps out of the panty and, sure enough, there's a wet spot on the crotch.

The young woman looks at Cyd and raises her eyebrows. "How'd it work out?"

Cyd holds out the bra and panty. "I'll take these."

The young woman nods and takes them and looks at Kim.

"All set with underwear," Kim says and hands her the bra and panty and is relieved that the young woman doesn't inspect them.

They follow her to the front counter and Kim watches Cyd pay for her things and take the Victoria's Secret bag and they walk down the corridor toward Macy's to meet her mom. Dressed as Cyd is in a loose-fitting blue plaid shirt and baggy gray shorts and black and white check Van's slip ons, she doesn't look like the type of girl who'd be carrying a Victoria's Secret shopping bag. Kim notices Cyd glancing down at the bag, like even she can't believe she's carrying it, but she walks differently now, swaying her hips slightly. "My brother saw the photo of us at Fashion Island," Kim says. "He thinks you're pretty."

Cyd looks at her and makes a face. "He does?" This is surprising news. She thinks she looks awful in that photo. "He's fifteen, right?"

Kim nods.

"What's he like?"

"Okay. He can be a pain."

"What does he look like?"

"My dad."

Cyd tries to imagine a young version of Kim's dad and can kind of see it.

"He acts like him too. Actually he's more like my grandfather."

"How?"

"He can be snarky sometimes. Don't get me wrong. Trey's nice. You'll meet him later."

June's at the counter putting a customer's purchases in a bag and sees Kim and Cyd walking toward her. She notices the Victoria's Secret bag in Cyd's hand, which surprises her. She knows how silly Kim thinks the whole idea of the store is and isn't Cyd a little young to be buying racy underwear? Kids are growing up too fast these days. She has to stop thinking "old." Every generation feels that way about kids. She hands the customer her bag and thanks her. "Hi, guys," she says as the girls arrive at the counter. She looks at Cyd's Victoria's Secret bag and raises her eyebrows. "Victoria's Secret, huh? Whadja buy?" She sees Cyd blush.

"A bra and panty."

June grins and leans on the counter and clasps her hands. "Let's see."

Cyd puts the bag on the counter and takes them out and holds them up.

"Wow!" June says and looks from the leopard skin panty and bra to Cyd and sees her blush deepening. Why would a shy self-conscious kid like Cyd choose these? Well, now that she's looking at her, Cyd has filled out since she last saw her. Girls' bodies change quickly at this age. It occurs to her that she wasn't much older than Cyd when she bought her first bra and panty set, which she thought looked racy at the time but was actually pretty tame as things go these days. She bought them for the same reason Cyd probably did. She wanted to look and feel sexy, even though she was the only person who saw her in them when she looked at herself in her bedroom mirror and the only person who knew she was wearing them at school. It made going to school exciting and she remembers fantasizing that she would faint in the hall and people would unbutton her clothes so that she could breathe and her secret would be revealed and all the boys and male teachers would ogle her. It was silly but fun and she suspects Cyd's in the same place now. It's all the result of biology, arriving at fertility, getting ready for childbearing. It's always been this way and always will be, but that's no reason not to have fun with it. She should buy something sexy to spring on Art. It's been a long time since she's done that, too long. She doesn't want him to feel like he's living with a sexless lump. She grins at Cyd. "I bet you look great in them."

"She does!" Kim says.

June looks at her. "Try anything on, honey?" She'd be surprised if Kim did and isn't surprised to see her make a face.

"I don't look good in that stuff."

"She does!" Cyd says, "She looked really pretty!"

June raises her eyebrows. She is surprised but realizes she shouldn't be. It was only a matter of time before someone arrived in Kim's life to awaken her interest in looking and feeling feminine and it seems that someone is Cyd. Cyd might be just entering young womanhood and Kim just leaving girlhood and the two might feel like they're on different planets, but there's not much difference between them and they'll both be in the same place soon enough. She smiles at them. "C'mon, let's get out of here."

Kim stares blankly at the TV, not really watching the movie, and reviews how her plan has unfolded so far. Trey arrived home late in the afternoon and she introduced him to Cyd and watched Cyd carefully to see what her reaction to meeting him would be and just as she knew Cyd would, she blushed and looked at him like a puppy ready to follow him around. He disappeared into his room and he and Cyd didn't see each other again until dinner and she saw Cyd stealing glances at him with that same puppy dog look on her face. She saw Trey finally notice and begin looking at Cyd with more interest. Her parents won't be home until around midnight so they have the house to themselves and plenty of time but now they're wasting it watching this stupid movie and she's impatient to advance the action. "Is it just me," she asks, "or is this movie lame?"

Cyd looks nervously at Kim and then Trey and back at Kim. She's the guest and wants them to know she's fine with whatever they want to do. "It's okay."

"It sucks." Trey says.

"Let's play Scrabble," Kim says.

Trey looks at her uncertainly and sees she's keeping her eyes on the TV. He glances at Cyd. He and Kim have developed their own style of Scrabble, stream-of-consciousness, commenting on every word and its connection to other words using the nuances of language they've learned well from their parents and especially their dad. Cyd seems kind of shy and not very talkative. He's not sure she's up to it. "You sure?" he asks Kim.

"Yeah," she says not taking her eyes off the TV.

"I like Scrabble," Cyd says.

Kim springs to her feet and walks quickly to her room and returns with the game and a pen and piece of paper and sits down on the living room floor and opens up the box and takes out the board and makes three columns on the paper and writes her and Cyd's and Trey's names at the top of each column as Trey and Cyd sit around the board. They each take a rack and pick a tile from the bag and hold it up. Kim sees Cyd's is a blank and grins. "You first."

Cyd picks seven tiles from the bag and arranges them on her rack and Kim and Trey do the same. "How do you guys play?" she asks.

Kim keeps her eyes on her tiles. "No holds barred, anything goes, slang, abbreviations, foreign words, whatever." She knows playing Scrabble is a good idea. She just doesn't know how good yet. It all depends on whether Cyd can play the game the way she and Trey do. She knows Cyd's going to need help and encouragement and she's ready to give her all she can. She watches Cyd impatiently out of the corners of her eyes as she considers what word to lay down first. She sees Cyd finally pick up a tile and place an **S** on the star in the middle of the board and spell **STROKE**. Excellent! She knows Trey will comment on this and every other word, as they always do, but this time she's going to try her best to keep her mouth shut and let Trey and, hopefully, Cyd do the talking. This word has a lot of possibilities and she's eager to see what he has to say about it.

"You mean like a heart attack?" he asks.

"I was thinking of swimming," Cyd says and takes new tiles from the bag and places them on her rack.

Kim frowns slightly. That was disappointing. Cyd needs to push herself and Trey needs to stop messing around and play the way they usually do. She writes down Cyd's score. "Or someone stroking you," she says and doesn't have to look at either of them to know they both got the message. Now the only question in her mind is how interested in Cyd Trey is. She watches him place an **S** over the **E** in **STROKE** and spell **SEXY**. She grins. Yes! "Good one," she says and sees Cyd staring down at the word and picking at the skin of her thigh.

Cyd studies her letters and sees the **Y** in **SEXY** and spells **BODY**.

Trey grins. "Stroke sexy body. That's good."

Cyd sees now what their style of play is like, very suggestive, and that this game is going to be as much about sex as they can make it. She's uneasy about it but will make an effort to play along. She's the guest. She studies her tiles and sees the **S** in **STROKE** and spells **SMILE** and is relieved that it seems harmless.

Trey glances at Cyd and nods. "Good." He studies his letters and the board and sees the **E** in **SMILE**. "Check this out," he says and spells **ECSTATIC**, emptying his tray and grinning at Cyd.

Kim and Cyd look at each other with raised eyebrows and then at Trey. "Wow!" they say.

Trey tallies up his word score as he fishes in the bag for new tiles. "Twenty-four. Even better than 'sexy.'"

Kim writes down his score and is happy to see that he and Cyd have a thing going on now. He's focused on her and she's focused on him and they're making frequent eye contact.

She studies her letters and the board and sees the second **T** in **ECSTATIC** and spells **TITS**.

Trey eyes the word thoughfully for a moment. "Is the person with the sexy body whose tits are being stroked smiling ecstatically or the person stroking them?"

Cyd picks at the skin on her thigh. "Why not both of them?"

Kim keeps her eyes on her tiles. "Definitely the person being stroked."

Trey looks at her and smirks. "How would you know?"

Kim glances at Cyd. "I told you he could be a snarky."

Cyd looks from Kim to Trey and down at her tiles. She likes the way they tease each other. Kim is her best friend, but there isn't that type of chemistry between them. It would be nice to have someone like Trey in her life. She concentrates on her letters — the two **V**s are troubling — and studies the board and sees the **S** in **TITS** and there it is, kind of sex ed, but a great word and she spells **VULVAS** and looks up at them proudly.

Trey stares down at the word. "Excellent! So, we're on to anatomy." He studies his letters and the board. "What can we do with anatomy…? Ah!" He sees the **R** in **STROKE** and spells **GRAB**.

Kim frowns and writes down his score. "We don't like being grabbed. We like being stroked." She glances at Cyd and sees her staring down at Trey's word and picking at the skin of her thigh again. She'd love to tell Cyd that Trey's definitely a stroker. She eyes her letters and studies the board and sees the **C** at the end of **ECSTATIC** and winces. "Okay, sorry about this. I know it's ugly, but it's all I've got." She spells **CUNT** and writes down her score and fishes in the bag for new tiles.

Cyd stares down at the word. The only person she's ever heard use that word is her mom once when she was talking on the phone with her dad. Her mom was kind of drunk and called her dad's wife that. She looked it up in the dictionary and read that one of its meanings is a woman men think is bitchy or mean, but she's not thinking of that meaning now. She's thinking of its vulgar slang anatomical meaning and glances at Trey and knows by the way he's looking at her that he is too and that he knows she is. She feels herself blush and looks down at her tiles. She does wish she had someone like Trey in her life. Someone to have the kind of fun with only a girl and boy can together. "Hey, pokey puppy," she hears him say and looks up to see him grinning at her. She looks at him pleadingly as if to say she might be slow but she's new to this game and trying her best so just bear with her. She looks at the board and sees the open **S** of **SEXY** and spells **SLY**. She looks at Trey and watches him as he studies the word. He looks up at her and smiles and lays down an **H** and spells **HORNY** using the **Y** of her **SLY**. The word's always struck her as crude but she can't help smiling.

Kim's feeling better about things now. She's been eyeing the **L** of **SMILE** and spells **PILL**. She fishes in the bag for a tile and looks at Cyd. "You?"

Cyd shakes her head. Her mom's been suggesting she should begin taking birth control since she's at that age when girls become sexually active, but there's no reason to. It's like she's invisible to boys. Trey's the first boy who's looked at her this way and seems interested in her and while it makes her feel uncomfortable, it also feels nice. She studies her letters and the board and sees she's got nothing for letters and searches for something, anything to play and notices the **M** of **SMILE** and looks at her letters again and sees a word and spells **ROOM**. She pictures a nice cozy one with just herself and Trey in it.

Trey doesn't see any play and mixes up his letters to see if something will pop out at him and notices the free **R** of **ROOM** and glances at his letters again and spells **WRAPPER**, a nice word score but seemingly off track. He looks at Cyd and sees her gazing at the word.

She says the word to herself. It reminds her of the sound of a buzz saw and she imagines Trey using it to cut away all the concern and worry about her mom's drinking from her life. She pictures the two of them in that nice cozy room again, now with their arms wrapped around each other.

Kim's at a loss but keeps glancing from her letters to **WRAPPER**, dangling there enticingly. She has the feeling she can do something with it but can't see what until it occurs to her that she can spell **HOOTERS** using the **E** and her blank tile for the **S** and lays it down.

"Breasts or the place?" Trey asks.

"Breasts," Kim says.

Cyd looks at Trey. "Is it true you have to have big boobs to work there?"

"Dunno," he says. "I think the outfits make them look big."

Kim glances at Cyd's breasts and remembers how great they and her cleavage looked in that bra and fishes in the bag for more tiles. "You don't need any help."

Cyd feels herself blush again. "My boobs aren't that big."

Kim grins. "Big enough." She looks at Trey. "We tried on underwear at Victoria's Secret today. Cyd looked great in hers."

Trey stares wide-eyed at his sister. "You were in Victoria's Secret?"

Kim shrugs. "Yeah. So what?"

"She looked really pretty!" Cyd says. "You should have bought that set."

Trey grins at Cyd. "Buy something?"

She nods and feels her blush deepening.

Kim keeps her eyes down. "Bra and panty set, leopard skin, really sexy."

Cyd knows by the way Trey's looking at her that he's imagining her in it. It's embarrassing but also exciting. She feels he can see her body right through her clothes and her skin is tingling all over. She studies her letters and the board and places an **I** above the first **O** in **HOOTERS**, just to get her move over with. She waits for Trey's reaction and he looks at her and raises his eyebrows.

"The nymph or the moon?"

"Does it matter?"

He grins and narrows his eyes. "Choose."

Cyd shrugs. "The nymph I guess." She's studying Western Civilization this year and enjoying learning about Greet mythology. She was fascinated by the story of Io, the nymph Zeus fell in love with and turned into a cow to hide her from his jealous wife Hera who made Io wander all over the world being stung by a fly until she went mad. The story struck her as fantastic and crazy and yet somehow very human.

"Good," Trey says and smiles.

Kim keeps her eyes down. "I hope you take better care of her."

He glances at Kim and looks at Cyd and sees her looking at him like she hopes so too. He studies his tiles and the board and adds an **N** under Cyd's **IO**.

Kim and Cyd look at the word and then Trey. "What's that?" they ask.

"An atom or electron with an electrical charge. The name comes from the Greek word for 'going.'"

Cyd isn't surprised to hear it's the Greeks again. "We haven't studied that stuff yet."

"Don't worry," Trey says with a smirk, "you will."

There's so much Cyd feels she doesn't know. She's been more mindful of that fact lately and it's made her passionate about learning. She's been perfectly content spending time alone in her room reading a book or article online. Her love of Greek mythology led her to study Roman mythology and she's spent hours reading about it, alone. She glances at Trey. She knows he enjoys reading and learning too. She can tell. How nice it would be to read and study together in that nice cozy room.

Kim glances from Cyd to Trey and looks back down at her tiles. Things couldn't be going better. She eyes her letters and the word **HORNY** and adds **F** and **U** to the **R**. "I like the way 'fur' sounds…soft…smooth…nice to touch."

Cyd spells **MUFF** using the **F** in **FUR** and looks up to see Trey looking at her with his eyebrows raised again. She fishes in the bag for more tiles. She knows the other meaning of the word but that's not what she was thinking. "You know, the furry thing you put your hands in to keep them warm?"

Trey grins. "Right."

Bingo! Kim can barely contain herself.

Trey spells **JAM** using the **M** in **MUFF**.

Kim glances at him and frowns. "We don't like being jammed, either." She glances at Cyd and sees her blushing again. She's never seen anyone blush as easily or as much as Cyd. It seems all Trey has to do now is look at her.

The bag is empty and they're running low on tiles. Kim spells **JAW** using the **J** in **JAM**. Cyd spells **DEW** using the **W** in **JAW**. Trey spells **ADZE** using the **D** in **DEW** and explains that it's a tool for cutting wood. Kim spells **IDEA** using the **A** in **ADZE** and Cyd places a **Q** under the **I** in **IDEA** and is thankful to be able to spell even that. Coming up with words is getting to be impossible.

Trey studies the board wanting to get rid of the rest of his tiles and end the game but can't see how until he notices the **A** in **WRAPPER** and spells **NADA** using a blank tile for the **D**. He holds up his rack and smiles triumphantly.

Kim tallies up their scores while Trey and Cyd gather up tiles and put things back in the box. She notices them reaching for the same tiles and their hands touching too many times for it to be accidentally. Good. "I got a hundred, Cyd got a hundred and four and Trey got a hundred and forty-six."

Cyd looks admiringly at Trey. "I knew you'd win. You know so many words."

"I read a lot."

"Show Trey what you bought," Kim says, doodling on the score sheet. "I'm sure he'd love to see it."

Cyd looks at him uncertainly. "You would?"

Trey smiles. "Sure. Let's see it."

"Okay," she says and begins getting up.

"With you in it," Kim says without looking up.

Cyd freezes.

Kim looks up at her and shrugs. "What's the big deal? It's like wearing a bikini at the beach."

Cyd glances at Trey and looks back at Kim. "I dunno...."

Kim knew this moment would arrive. It's the most important one and for her plan to succeed she has to coax Cyd past it. She's confident she can and fixes her eyes on Cyd's. "What's the point of buying it if no one's gonna see it?"

Cyd looks to Trey for the final words of encouragement.

He raises his eyebrows and shrugs. "She's right."

Cyd stands and looks down at them. "Okay. Where? Here?"

Kim keeps her eyes on her doodling. "In the bedroom. You get into it and we'll be in."

"Okay," Cyd says and turns and walks quickly toward the bedroom.

Kim drops her pen on the paper and looks at Trey. "See ya."

"Going somewhere?"

"For a walk." She stands and looks down at him. "She wants to feel pretty."

"She is pretty."

"You know that and I know that. Have fun, Zeus," she says and turns and walks toward the kitchen.

He picks up the paper and studies Kim's doodle. That's what he though he saw her drawing, a curvy female torso clad in skimpy spotted underwear.

He finds Cyd in the leopard skin bra and panty standing sideways in front of the vanity mirror, looking away from him at her reflection. Her pose reminds him of those of young virgins and nymphs he's seen depicted in Classical paintings. She's holding her hands up in front of her chest with her fingers loosely intertwined and one foot behind the other with the heel up and the leg bent slightly forward at the knee. He can easily imagine her hair decorated with a wreath of braided flowers and songbirds hovering above her head. He catches her eye in the mirror and she quickly turns to face him and covers her breasts and crotch area with her arms and hands as best she can. She leans to the side and looks behind him.

"Where's Kim?"

"She went for a walk," he says and sees she's puzzled. "She'll be back." He smiles and walks toward her and stands in front of her. "Let's see your outfit." He holds out his hand and she reaches out slowly and takes it, keeping her other hand over her crotch, and lets him move her arm out to the side. He holds out his other hand and she reaches out slowly and takes it and lets him move that one out to the side. He looks her up and down and grins. "You look great." He can see in her eyes that she wants to believe him but her hope is quickly replaced by doubt and she looks down at the floor.

"You're just saying that."

"No, I mean it. You look like an Amazon."

She's read about the Amazons, the nation of women warriors, in her study of Greek mythology. She remembers the picture of the bronze statue of a helmeted Amazonian queen stringing her bow, preparing for battle. The woman looks strong and brave and confident but she's sure she doesn't look anything like that to Trey and all she feels is awkward and nervous and uncomfortable. He lets go of her hands and she brings her arms slowly to her sides. She thinks she knows what happens next but has no idea what to do and waits to see what he does. He moves closer and puts a finger under her chin and raises her head so that she has to look at his eyes and does and then his lips and his eyes again.

"Ever been kissed?"

She shakes her head and looks down again.

"Wanna be?"

She shrugs and shifts nervously.

"It doesn't hurt."

She looks at him and frowns as if to say she might be inexperienced but she's not stupid. He moves closer and slowly puts his arms around her waist and brings his face closer to hers and she looks back and forth form his eyes to his lips and feels his lips pressing against hers and sees his eyes close.

He isn't surprised that she isn't responding yet, that she's just standing there with her hands at her sides letting him kiss her. He figures she's trying to decide how she feels about it and what she wants to do next and finally he feels her place her hands lightly on his back and press her lips lightly against his, then a little harder and he opens his eyes just enough to see that hers are closed now and he can tell she's beginning to relax and enjoy herself. He moves her toward the bed.

The only other person who's held her this way, really held her is her mom when she was little. When her dad held her it always felt like he was about to drop her, which is what he did in the end, moving away like that. It's not a great feeling knowing your dad doesn't care enough about you to come see you or have you come visit him. Even when he calls on her birthday he sounds inconvenienced, like he can't wait to get off the phone. It isn't her fault things didn't work out between him and her mom but he sure treats her like it is. Is it any wonder she's steered clear of boys? What if they were all like her dad? She's felt safer with girls. She could trust girls, well, except for Allie. Allie didn't understand her at all.

She's wondered what it would be like to be touched by a boy. They seem so rough about everything but not Trey. His touch is gentle. He's touching her the way you touch something fragile, really carefully so you don't break it. It feels nice. She wondered about French kissing too. The idea of having someone's tongue in her mouth always seemed gross to her and she thought she wouldn't like it but does. It feels nice. It's like they're continuing the conversation they were having when they were playing Scrabble, only in a different way now, with their tongues.

She feels his hand moving slowly down her stomach and her body thrills in anticpation of where it's headed. The only question in her mind is whether he's going to put it inside her panty and if she should let him. It seems silly not to. She wants him to and knows it will feel great and parts her legs slightly. She feels his hand slip beneath the waistband and begin gently stroking her between her legs and she squirms and shudders and holds him tighter and kisses him harder.

She moves her hand down his back and across his butt and around to his thigh and slides it slowly toward his crotch and feels him parting his legs as she places her hand on the hard lump in his shorts and gives it a squeeze. Should she put her hand inside his pants? She knows he wants her to. It seems silly not to with him touching her way the he is, giving her so much pleasure. Shouldn't she please him? She slips her hand beneath the waistband of his shorts and boxer and wraps it around his surprisingly firm and warm cock and feels him arch his back and she begins slowly stroking it.

She loves the way he brushes the wispy hair on her mound as he rubs her clit, every so often twirling it and giving it a gentle tug. It feels special, like something he only does with her. It's nice to think so anyway. She knows he's done a lot more than this with girls. She can tell by the way he caresses her breasts gently and squeezes and rolls her nipples and kisses her collarbone and neck while he strokes her that he's had plenty of experience.

She wondered what this moment would feel like, just as she knows Kim did, someone else touching her and making her come. She thought it would be Kim doing the touching and she didn't think it would be a boy, but here's Trey and she couldn't be happier. His touch feels amazing. The way her body feels, vibrating, makes her think of the tuning forks in the music room at school when she strikes them. She can hear the humming sound her body is making and wonders if he can too. She can feel how wet she is now between her legs. Does he think it's gross? He sure doesn't seem to. If fact, he seems to really like the fact that she is. She feels herself verging on orgasm and can tell by the movement of his body and his panting that he is to and they do together and she feels her hand covered with his come. They rest a few moments and she opens her eyes and looks at his and blushes, embarrassed now that she made him come in his pants. "I'm sorry," she says.

He smiles. "Promise me something."

She nods.

"Don't ever apologize for making me come."

She smiles and feels her blush deepening and nods again and he kisses her. She hears Kim return and draws her head back and looks at him sweetly and sadly. "We should stop," she whispers.

"We don't have to. Kim won't come in."

"We should." She gives him one more lingering kiss and reluctantly takes her hand from inside his pants and feels him take his from between her legs and a part of her with it. "Do you really think I look pretty in that picture?" she asks and sees he has no idea what she's talking about.

Kim sits on the bench sucking on an orange half and looks down the sideline past the table with the two trophies on it, one for league champion and the other for league MVP, at Cyd who's sitting on her team's bench hunched over with her head down and forearms resting on her thighs. It's been a hard fought match so far and she realizes now that there wasn't any need to ask Cyd again when they were chatting online yesterday evening to promise to play her best today. With the first half over and her team down by a goal she knows now why Cyd's team surged during the last half of the season. Cyd's a much better player. Her athleticism has really improved. She's stronger and faster, more powerful and more confident. She's able to anticipate her moves in a way she wasn't before.

It's been awhile since the two of them faced each other but she saw it immediately when Cyd defended successfully against her first field goal attempt, kicking the ball away before she could strike it. She's been able to score only once, her team's only goal so far and all she needed to set a new record for goals scored in a season, but Cyd almost kicked the ball away that time too and it just cleared the fingertips of the goalie's outstretched hand when she leapt to block it.

She looks down at the orange rind in her hand and lets it drop to the ground and watches it roll over and come to rest empty-side-up and feels something new. For the first time since taking up the sport she doubts her own abilities. She's always felt confident in her ball handling and goal scoring. She's always wanted the ball and been aggressive when she's gotten it and fearless in her attack, but now she's not so sure and thinks that one goal she scored was really just luck or, worse, that Cyd could have blocked it and was just doing her a favor letting her score so she'd set the record.

She walks onto the field with her teammates for the start of the second half and Cyd walks over to her.

"What's up with you?" Cyd asks.

"I dunno…nothing's working."

"I'm not gonna give it to you. Play!" Cyd says and turns and walks to her position.

The score is stalled at 2 to 1 with Kim's team down a goal as the second half drags on. Her team's backs and goalie are doing a good job defending against Cyd's team's best striker and Cyd is continuing to do a good job defending against her and she senses a subtle shift in the mood of her teammates. They're not looking to her to get open or feeding her the ball when she is, as they usually do. They're looking to Manju and she's getting the ball now, although she's not having any more success scoring. This can't end this way, it just can't and she's trying hard to resist the feeling that she's powerless to do anything about it.

With five minutes left in the game she and her teammates begin heading upfield on offense and she has the ball and sees Cyd positioning herself to defend against her. She glances to her right at Manju who's running abreast of her along the sideline and nods toward the far corner and Manju nods back. She used to have a lot of confidence in this play, feeding the ball to a player in the corner who kicks it back to her in the center of the field in front of the goal, but now it seems like a long shot. It's worth a try, though. They've got nothing to lose or, rather, everything. Cyd reads the play and shouts to her left fullback and midfielder and points toward the corner. When Kim's about ten yards from Cyd she lofts the ball toward the corner and sees Manju there to receive it. Manju knocks it down off her chest and sidesteps her defender and kicks the ball into the center of the field and Kim tries her best to get to it but her moves aren't working and Cyd keeps forcing her away from the ball. She's relieved to see Brandy beat her defender to the ball and feed it back to Manju who's outrunning her defender away from the goal toward the ball. Manju reaches it and turns quickly catching her defender and the goalie offquard and immediately kicks it toward the narrow undefended part of the left side of the goal. The ball rolls just out of reach of the diving goalie's hands into the net. Okay, at least the score's tied. They still have a shot.

Kim's about to head downfield and notices Manju lying on her back holding her ankle, her face contorted with pain. No one tried to tackle her, so she must have sprained it when she turned quickly. They gather around her and Coach kneels beside her and inspects her ankle. She helps Manju up and Kim and her teammates watch the two of them walk slowly to the sideline, Manju hopping on one leg. Not good. Kim sees Dara, Manju's sub, stand and walk onto the field. Dara's good but not as good as Manju. Kim has no feel now for how this game will end, another unpleasant new feeling.

With under a minute remaining she and her teammates head upfield on offense again and she has the ball and sees Cyd in the distance moving toward her to defend and the goalie coming out of the goal behind her. She glances to her left and sees Brandy's defender all over her and to her right and sees Dara's defender all over her and she can't think of anything to do except go straight at Cyd and see what happens. Cyd's moving toward her quickly now, blocking any shot at the goal. Kim tries a stutter-step to the left to throw Cyd off balance but Cyd stays with her and kicks the ball away to the right. That's it. That was their one chance and she blew it.

She glances to her right and sees Dara get to the ball first and without hesitating kick it like a placekicker, sending it in a high arc toward the goal and all the players stop and stand watching the ball's flight. Kim sees the goalie has come too far out of the goal and is backpedaling furiously to try to get under it. The goalie raises her arms and spreads her fingers wide but loses her balance and falls backward and the ball lands just beyond her head in front of the goal and bounces up into the top of the net.

The players on both teams look at each other, stunned and amazed and no one more so than Dara who, Kim sees, is staring at her wide-eyed with her hands over her mouth, unable to believe what just happened and looking like she's unsure whether to rejoice or cry. Kim feels the same way and walks over to her and puts an arm around Dara's shoulders. They're joined by their teammates on the field and from the bench and they all gather around in a circle with their arms around each other's shoulders and as Kim looks at the faces she sees they're all happy and relieved and also unable to believe what just happened. They'll never know if Dara's kick was sheer luck or inspired skill. It's the type of miraculous thing they'll remember and tell people about the rest of their lives and each of them will tell her own version of the story and they'll all in their own way be true.

The players and parents gather in a semicircle in front of the trophy table and applaud when the brief presentation ceremony ends and Coach places the championship trophy back on the table and Kim the MVP trophy next to it and Cyd walks up to her, grinning with her arms stretched wide and they hug and Kim hears Cyd say, "I knew you'd do it." They step back and Kim looks her in the eyes. "It was luck."

Cyd shakes her head. "No such thing. Remember?"

Kim stares at her. Cyd's the better player now and they both know it. She made her play her heart out for the same reason she did what she did in the dressing room at Victoria's Secret: true friendship. There are friends, and then there are friends like Cyd. She remembers how afraid Cyd was of losing her as a friend, but now she's the one who's afraid of losing Cyd as a friend, afraid that Cyd's outgrowing her, moving beyond her and will leave her behind waiting to see what happens next in her life and the idea of her not being there to share it with when it does is awful. She wants to tell Cyd how she feels but for the first time in her life can't think of anything to say.

"So, MVP," Cyd says, "any plans for the summer?"

Kim shakes her head.

"Let's spend it together, a month at my place and a month at yours. Waddya think?"

Kim feels her eyes filling with tears. "I think it sounds great," she says and puts her arms around Cyd's waist and presses her cheek against hers and sniffs.

Cyd gives her a hug. "You okay?"

"Yeah," Kim says, smiling and hugging her back, "fantastic."

CHAPTER 21

Kaitlin sips her champagne and smiles contentedly as she looks up at the flood lit pink façade of the Royal Hawaiian and at the semi-circle of flaming tiki torches stuck in the sand and around at the faces of the family and friends who've traveled far to be with her and Michael to celebrate.

The wedding ceremony was nice, simple and brief, presided over by Karen Whalen, the minister her friend Kate at Bloomingdale's recommended. They'd been planning on using a local minister but she called Karen on the off chance and was surprised and happy to hear that she and her boyfriend were planning a trip to Hawaii anyway and that she'd be happy to accommodate them. It wasn't until they met at the hotel to discuss the ceremony that she learned Karen's boyfriend is Henry's son Frank and that she married Henry and Joanne. Small world. She's glad she called Karen. She's been great and she and Frank make a cute couple, Karen being so much taller.

It's so sad about Henry. They were shocked when Frank told them the real reason he left Brooks Brothers was because he had terminal cancer and not very much longer to live. They never would have suspected. He looked fine. Frank said Joanne took very good care of him and that he passed peacefully and never really experienced any pain. He said his dad managed to finish the novel and that Joanne will send them a copy. He said she wants to let some time pass before reading it. That's understandable. Frank said Joanne's due soon and that it's a girl, which his dad was very happy about. His dad said he always wanted a daughter.

She looks at her mom, standing with Karen and Frank and her dad and Debby. Her mom is trying her best to be sociable but she's still as prickly as ever. She can tell by her mom's body language and the way she looks at her dad that she still hasn't forgiven him and reminds herself she has to have that conversation with him sometime, maybe while they're here.

She sees Beatrice and her husband Arnold, a charming man, chatting with Magda and Gretchen. She can't imagine Beatrice not being here. She was so instrumental in helping her make her way through her emotional minefield and spending time with her mom again has made her appreciate all the more having Beatrice in her life. She's not surprised that Beatrice and Magda have hit it off so well. They're kindred spirits, both in their own ways no-nonsense hard-nosed types. She smiles as she tries to imagine what Beatrice would be like high on Ecstasy in Brigitte's pool.

What a piece of work Magda is, though. She never knows what to expect from her. They were waiting for Magda and Gretchen to join them for breakfast in the hotel restaurant the morning after they arrived from Berlin. Their first impression of the two of them when they entered the restaurant was how complementary their appearances were, Magda with her dark hair and brown eyes and Gretchen with her blonde hair and blue eyes and it wasn't until they were almost to the table that she noticed the white gold filigree chocker collar around Gretchen's neck and the thin chain connecting it to Magda's belt. She wasn't going to comment about it and she knew Michael wasn't, either, but Magda asked how they liked it and they said they thought it was a marvelous piece of work and Magda looked at Gretchen, who was gazing adoringly at her, and said she made it as a present for Gretchen "so she can't stray." Keeping Gretchen on a chain struck her as antithetical to everything Magda said she believed and she knew it did Michael too. They were surprised to hear Magda say it was Gretchen's idea and she understood then what Magda had meant by "perfectly." That curious detail aside they're like any other happy couple.

She looks around at the rest of the guests, pleased to see everyone enjoying themselves, and gives the arm of Michael's shirt a gentle tug and he glances at her and she nods toward the beach and puts her arm in his and they walk toward the shore and the dark Pacific.

"Howya doin'?" he asks.

"Okay. Just want a moment alone."

"Everyone seems to be having a good time."

She nods and looks at the rows of advancing waves and listens to the sound of the surf, growing louder as they near the shore. They stand with an arm around each other's waist in the wet sand and look out toward the horizon. "So, here we are," she says, "off on our great adventure." She feels him give her a squeeze and squeezes him back. She looks at him, handsome in his outfit, and raises her glass. "Here's to Henry."

"To Henry," he says, raising his.

She sips her champagne and looks in his eyes. "Whatever happens next, I want you to know I love you and I'll always love you."

"Sounds ominous."

"I'm just thinking that I'm bound to stumble and fall."

He shrugs and looks out at the horizon. "So am I. So what? We're not perfect. The important thing is to help each other up when we do and keep going and take it one day at a time."

She tickles him in the side and grins. "'Marathon Man.'"

"'The secret of life is enjoying the passage of time.'"

She's heard that before. She knows she has. It's a song lyric, but she can't remember the song. She puts her arms around his waist and feels his around hers and they gaze out at the darkness. She thinks of where she and Michael are now at this moment in their lives and everything they have to look forward to in the future, having children, raising them, sending them off to college or wherever it is they'll go, seeing them married, having grandchildren, caring for each other in old age until one of them loses the other. It's too much and too long a span of time to imagine and trying leaves her feeling overwhelmed. She reminds herself she's always been a sprinter and doubts her ability to stay the course over the long haul. She knows he's right, though. Life really is like a marathon and the thing to do is just take it one day at a time and try to enjoy it. She doesn't want to disappoint him or herself. She'll try her best and with his help she'll make it. She tightens her arms around him and feels his tighten around her.

She sits on the side of the bed wrapped in the hotel's luxurious white terrycloth bathrobe, which she's decided to have added to the bill and take home, listening to Michael brush his teeth and fingering the ribbon on the gift box containing Magda's wedding present. She knows it's a necklace but that's all she knows and she's been curious to see what Magda made for her ever since she handed it to her. Now's as good a time as any. She unties the bow and undoes the wrapping paper and sets them aside on the bed and removes the lid and looks at the necklace. The pendant is heart-shaped and golden-brown and shaded slightly darker vertically in the middle and at its center are rosy, radiating puckered grooves. Is it her imagination? She laughs and covers her mouth with her hand and shakes her head. Michael comes out of the bathroom and she holds the box out to him. He looks down at the necklace and raises his eyebrow. "So it's not just me?" she asks. They laugh and she takes the necklace out of the box and fastens it around her neck and models it for him. He looks from the pendant to her eyes and sits on the side of the bed next to her and puts his arms around her waist and kisses the nape of her neck and undoes her robe. "The secret of life is enjoying the passage of time." She remembers! James Taylor! That song that sounds like a nursery rhyme! How does it go? "There ain't nothin' to it, any fool can do it." She lies back on the bed and gazes up at Michael. There's hope for her yet.

Karen walks hand in hand with Frank on the wet sand along the shore in the early morning with Diamond Head wreathed in clouds in the distance. The day they first met seems a long time ago, although it was only a matter of months. If someone had told her then that they'd be here now she would have had a hard time believing it.

They're such an unlikely pair. She suspects it's a matter of opposites attracting. Those old saws are so for a reason. There's the height difference, of course, but beyond that she's so open and welcoming and he's so guarded and wary of people. Her first impression of him was that he was handsome and intelligent and articulate, although he listened more than he spoke and used as few words as possible, but what really got her was the way he looked at her, squinting his right eye a little like an artist studying a potential subject, sizing her up and considering her worthiness. She found herself wanting to come out and ask him, "Am I? Just tell me!"

Even though they exchanged email addresses that day she doubted she'd hear from him again and thought that if she did, it would be to unburden himself about the loss of his dad. She was surprised and happy when his first email arrived. It was brief and he made no mention of his dad and simply told her how much he'd enjoyed meeting her and that he hoped they'd see each other again sometime and so began their correspondence.

As time went by they became easier with each other and began opening up. He said that even though they'd only spent the one afternoon together and that his impression of her was that she was relaxed and easy-going, he sensed there was another side to her personality, a wilder side that she kept under tight wraps. She thought a long time about how to respond and finally decided to just be honest and said she felt there was, but that the opportunity hadn't arisen to give it expression. He asked if she thought that being a minister and physically imposing affected the way people perceived her. She said she did, that men found her intimidating because of her height and kept their distance while women sometimes came on to her, assuming she was gay. She realized in answering his questions that precisely because of her experiences with men and women she'd gone out of her way to try not to draw attention to herself and now here was Frank coming at her like a freight train and she began trying to think of herself more as a woman and less as a minister. She found it telling that she actually had to try, but it felt good and exciting.

He shared with her that he developed the quality of stealthiness early on. He knew how to be within earshot of his parents without their knowledge. He learned a lot eavesdropping on their conversations, that his dad was seeing other women, that he was spending money on drugs that should have been going to his and Gene's college fund or the IRS, that he was having an affair with his Italian teacher. Despite which, he loved his dad. He was a good father, if a lousy husband.

His parents' experience as a couple put him off relationships. He didn't trust them. No matter how rosy things seemed at the outset, they all seemed destined to end badly. He said he heard about his friends' relationships all the time and no one seemed truly happy and most people seemed miserable. "What's the point?" he asked and as soon as she read the question she knew it was the most important one he'd ever ask her and she thought a long time about her answer. When she finally sat down to respond she'd considered the question from every conceivable angle and when she stopped typing and reread her answer it seemed a jumble of psychology and philosophy and religion and romance and she deleted the entire thing and typed, "Let's go to Hawaii," and sent it off.

She'd only been to Hawaii once before, during spring break her freshman year in college. Her memory of it was of a week spent drinking with her friends in the bars in Waikiki. She remembers one late night walk along the beach with a guy from one of the bars. They were both drunk and he wanted to fuck on the beach, which she didn't want to do and kept pushing him away but he wouldn't take no for an answer and she ended up smacking him so hard he fell face down in the sand and she walked off and left him there moaning. Still, she remembered how beautiful the place looked and had always wanted to return someday. It seemed like a nice place for the two of them to experience together and when she read his reply, "Sure. Never been there. Always wanted to see it. When?" she felt relieved and happy and hopeful in a way she never had before.

She was excited about the trip, but when she began preparing for it and opened her closet her clothes looked tired and old and she thought of Henry and decided to visit Brooks Brothers and see what they had to offer. She'd never shopped there and was pleasantly surprised by what she found and bought a few outfits. Frank complimented her on the one she's wearing, a red, white and blue tattersall button down shirt and khaki above the knee shorts with pleats and cuffs. She's carrying the woven sandals so they don't get soaked and enjoying the feel of the cool wet sand between her toes and the surf washing over her feet and ankles. She bought the slinky black cocktail dress and black low heel pumps, so she wouldn't tower over him, at Nordstrom and wore it their first evening out. She was delighted when Frank said, "You're the best thing that ever happened to that dress. They should pay you to wear it." She'd never been complimented like that and never dressed to please a man before but that hooked her on doing so for Frank.

The fun came when they returned to their hotel room. Frank was in the bathroom and she was getting out of her dress and he came into the room wrapped in the hotel bathrobe and sat on the bed with his legs crossed and watched her. She'd undressed in front of men a few times before, when she was in college, but always hastily and the objective was to get her clothes off and herself under the covers as quickly as possible. She'd always been self-conscious about her body as well as her height but not this time. She was eager to see Frank's reaction to the lingerie she was wearing. She'd never bought that type of stuff before and did on a whim at Victoria's Secret when she left Brooks Brothers. When she tried on the red hiphugger panty and matching demi bra in the dressing room and looked at herself in the mirror she was amazed by her cleavage and the way her legs seemed to go on forever.

She took her sweet time getting out of her dress and hanging it up in the closet and placing her shoes neatly beneath it. It felt delightfully naughty. She wanted him to get a good look at her and when she turned she saw him looking at her waist with an amused expression. She looked down saw she'd overlooked removing the tag from the panty and felt like a complete fool, but he smiled and held out his hand and she climbed on the bed and took it and felt relieved when he pulled her to him and wrapped his arms around her and she was damned if he was going to feel like he'd spent the night with a minister.

When they finally lay tangled together in the sheets, sweaty and laughing, he looked at her and said, "You're an animal." It reminded her of the porn movie she and her best friend Spring watched on a sleepover when Spring's parents were out for the evening. The man in the scene said the same thing to the women after her impressive display of deepthroating. She was pleased that Frank seemed so satisfied and happy and above all calm. She has the feeling he hasn't experienced a lot of calm in his life. "You bring it out in me," she told him and meant it.

She looks out at the ocean and glances down at the top of Frank's head and smiles as she remembers the incident in Waikiki when they were walking around the day they arrived. It seems funny now, but it scared the bejeezus out of her at the time. She worried about the height difference more and more in the weeks leading up to the trip. She comes from a long line of tall people and thought she'd never stop growing but topped out at six-five. She took to slouching when she began getting interested in boys to minimize the height difference and her mom would scold her about it. "Don't slouch! Stand up straight!" her mom would say and she would, until she was out of sight of her mom. She was slouching as they set out on their walk in Waikiki and she heard Frank say, "Don't slouch! Stand up straight!" sounding eerily like her mom. She felt a jolt run through her body and stood up straight and looked at him and saw him grinning at her. "You look sexy when you do," he said and she hasn't slouched since. "I dunno what to think," she hears him say. He's still working through their conversation about Gene and Joanne and how they correspond regularly now. "It's good to have someone to talk with," she says gently, "share things with. Isn't it?"

He glances at her. "Yeah. There's just something about it."

"Would it be wrong if they ended up together?"

He shrugs. "I dunno. I guess not."

"Stranger things have happened. I married a couple that learned by accident before they married they were mother and son. They didn't tell me and she came to me afterward to ask for forgiveness, not for marrying, but for not having told me."

He looks at her and squints his right eye slightly. "I bet you did."

She nods. "Everyone deserves forgiveness."

"This isn't anything like that."

"No. It isn't." She doesn't know where Joanne and Gene are in their relationship but she does know love makes anything possible.

He looks at the waves rolling in and breaking on the shore and stops and takes the envelope out of his pocket. This is as good a place as any. He unfolds the envelope and opens it and sprinkles some of the ashes on the water and closes and refolds it and puts it back in his pocket, saving the rest to sprinkle on some other distant shore his travels in the world might take him to, as his dad requested and he promised he'd do. They stand looking down at the ashes dispersing on the surface of the water and he looks out at the horizon and up at the sky. "Think there's more than this?"

She sighs and puts her arms around his waist and rests her chin on his shoulder. "Let's not talk shop."

He looks in her eyes and sees a woman who's happy just being here with him and wants only to love and be loved. What the hell difference does it make if she believes in an afterlife or what he thinks about Gene and Joanne or anything else for that matter? What's important is that he's here with her and she's the first woman he feels truly comfortable being with and whose motives he doesn't want to second-guess and maybe it's time to leave well enough alone and just trust that their feelings for each other are true. He feels he should say something, apologize for being an idiot or tell her he loves her, but words don't seem right at the moment and he sees her gazing at him and smiling sweetly, waiting to be kissed and he feels grateful to be the one she's waiting for and puts his arms around her waist and kisses her and it's a kiss intended to leave no doubt in her mind about his feelings and he knows by the way she's kissing him back and moving with him as they sway that he's found his partner in life and to hell with the rest of it.

Joanne stands in the dark in the solarium by the window, a glass of white wine in her hand, gazing at the full moon or what she can see of it through the trees. It looks so big and seems so close, like a searchlight trained on her. It's rising quickly and will soon be above the trees staring down at her with that familiar worried expression. She reminds herself that it's not rising. She's dipping. She's always thought of the moon as rising, just as she does the sun, and always will and the fact that the Man on the Moon's expression is a random arrangement of impact craters doesn't change what she sees when she looks at it and never will.

She fingers the pendant of Kaitlin's necklace nervously. Henry was amazed when she unwrapped and opened the gift box and removed the necklace and looked at it and said she recognized it and told him the story. His eyes sparkled and he smiled as he listened and when she was finished he just nodded. She happened to be wearing it the afternoon he died and he said he wondered if we aren't all like that necklace, moving from life to life, as Hindus believe. That was just before she administered what would be the final dose of morphine, larger than usual, at his request. Well, now he knows.

She feels the baby kicking and puts her hand on her belly and rubs it, hoping to calm her. The C-section is two days away and she's so ready to give birth. She's been in a state of chronic exhaustion for the last month. Her body's swollen and her joints ache and everything, even standing here looking at the moon, is an effort. She's been good about not drinking but doesn't feel at all guilty about enjoying her glass of wine and it's helping her to relax, which she's having a hard time doing this evening.

She wasn't surprised when she received an email from Gene after the funeral asking how she and the baby were doing. It struck her as thoughtful and the type of thing the older son would do in the situation. She emailed him back with the mundane details and asked how things were going with him. Days went by without hearing from him, which struck her as curious, but she didn't give it much thought.

When his next email arrived and she opened it and saw that it was a lengthy response to her simple inquiry she was surprised and intrigued. She read about his relationship with Carol and everything that led up to it and what he thought he'd learned about himself and his voice and honesty and self-deprecating humor seemed very familiar, eerily so. It was like hearing from Henry, but different. When she finished reading she sat back and considered what she'd read. He believed he'd arrive at a place where he could be a good partner in a relationship. That was the gist of it and there wasn't a hint of an overture.

At first she thought the best thing to do would be not to respond, but the more she thought about it that seemed ridiculous. Here he'd sent her a lengthy soul-baring email and she'd have nothing to say about it? No, that wouldn't do. She let the days go by and thought about it and finally decided to respond in kind and sat down and wrote an email describing everything that led up to her meeting his dad, including the fact that she was HIV positive and how she'd been infected, and how knowing his dad had changed her, made her stop thinking and acting like an animated corpse and gave her the desire to become engaged in life again. She sent it off holding her breath.

She walked through work the rest of the week and wandered around the house in the evenings and all she thought about was when his response would arrive and what it would be. When it finally did it was brief. The subject was, "So...," and the message was, "We're sort of in the same place." She stared at the "sort of" a long time. It struck her as very deliberate and she wouldn't be surprised if his deliberation over whether or not to keep it in was the reason he'd taken so long to send it off. She could see the way his mind worked, like Henry's, but different. At that point she felt she knew everything she needed to know about Gene without having to ask or him having to tell her. She knew he had feelings for her and that it didn't matter to him that she was his dad's widow and about to give birth to his child. The question was what to do about her feelings for him? That's when she decided to read Henry's novel.

She'd been putting it off until after the baby was born, why she didn't really know, but it felt like the time had come. Opening his laptop and turning it on felt just as she knew it would, like opening a crypt and summoning him back from the dead. She stared at the screen as the document loaded and finally the first page appeared and she wasn't surprised by the title: *The Italian Lesson.* "Life," that's all he ever said about it with a shrug and, of course, it would be about his and his most important relationship, the one that finally woke him up. What surprised her was the dedication: For Joanne. Follow your heart. Did he know? Did he foresee it somehow? She wouldn't be surprised. In any event, she felt she had his approval and encouragement to bring her emotions to the surface and try to sort them out. All she knew was that she had feelings for Gene and didn't want to be alone. What she planned to do about it she didn't know.

They continued their correspondence and it became obvious that he was in the same place she was and also that he didn't want to be the first to share his feelings anymore than she did. She knew it wasn't because of shyness on his part and assumed it was because of propriety, as was the case with her.

Then came his email a week ago saying he'd like to be there when the baby is born. She knew it wasn't because he felt responsible to be but thanked him for the offer and said it was very thoughtful and told him he didn't have to come. He said he knew he didn't have to, that he wanted to and that's all she needed to hear. She told him to come and how she wanted him to arrive, not to call from the airport, to take a cab and let himself in. It's the only way she'll find out the one remaining thing she feels she needs to know about him.

So, here she is, gazing at what little she can still see of the moon, sipping her wine and waiting. She hears the front door open and feels her skin tingling and closes her eyes. She listens as he enters and puts his suitcase down in the hall and closes the front door. She listens to his footsteps coming through the living room and the kitchen and stop at the entrance to the solarium.

She imagines him looking at her, a shadowy figure standing here in the dark. What must he be thinking? Is this really what he wants? Is he ready for it? She listens as he walks toward her and stops behind her and anticipates the feel of his hands on her shoulders. She knows that's where he'll touch her first. Henry's touch was wonderful, if ephemeral. He touched her the way you touch something delicate. She's hoping Gene's touch is different, as talking with him has been different.

She feels his hands on her shoulders. Maybe she's just imagining it but it feels like the touch of a man who's found something he's been searching for and now that he's found it is determined not to let it go.

She leans back against him and sees Henry's face in her mind's eye gazing at her in that way of his, as if admiring her spirit, her soul, that beautifully perfect part of her that's immune to all the disease and heartache in this imperfect world. She feels the baby kicking again and reaches up and takes Gene's hands and places them on her belly. She feels his arms tighten around her and his hands slowly rubbing her and sees Henry smile and close his eyes and she opens hers.

She didn't cry when Henry died or when she learned she was HIV positive. She hasn't cried since she was a kid but now she feels her eyes filling with tears and the tears streaming down her cheeks and when there are no more tears to shed she sighs and stares out at the darkness. It's a bittersweet moment. She has the feeling everything in her life that's led up to it and especially her time with Henry has been prologue to the story that's about to unfold. She's ready to begin it now, to give birth and be a mother and move on together with Gene and turns to face him.

Made in the USA
Charleston, SC
30 October 2013